A Game of Scandal

KATHRYN SMITH

A Game of Scandal

AVON BOOKS
An Imprint of HarperCollinsPublishers

This is a work of fiction. Names, characters, places, and incidents are products of the author's imagination or are used fictitiously and are not to be construed as real. Any resemblance to actual events, locales, organizations, or persons, living or dead, is entirely coincidental.

AVON BOOKS
An Imprint of HarperCollins*Publishers*
10 East 53rd Street
New York, New York 10022-5299

Copyright © 2002 by Kathryn Smith
ISBN: 0-7394-2658-3

For Lynda

For carting your little sister around
when you went swimming with your friends.
For letting me sit between you and David on the couch.
For letting me kick you off the couch.
And for always making me feel like someone special.
I'm still not as special as you.

Chapter 1

London
Spring, 1818

*T*en years.

A decade had passed since she'd left him. One hundred and twenty months.

Over the years, there had been times when he hadn't thought of her. The period he'd spent in Nova Scotia had been one of those. Being in a strange place had given him more to see, more things to concentrate on, other than how much he still missed her.

Now that he was back in London amongst the familiar, with the anniversary of her betrayal upon him, the memory of her flooded his mind like water fills a cup. It had been ten years since he'd lost the woman he loved, and the heart she had unknowingly taken with her.

Oh, yes. It was also the anniversary of his father's death, but that gave him far less pain than it once had. Far less than the loss of his heart, because he'd let his heart go in order to clean up the mess his father had left behind.

Standing at one of the many windows that lined the wall of his study, Gabriel Warren, Earl of Angelwood, braced his forearm against the polished oak frame and leaned forward until the sill bit into his thigh and his forehead brushed his wrist. The eyes that stared back at him in the glass reflected not only the grayness of the day, but the cold bleakness of his mood as well.

He was lonely. In Halifax, there had been scores of people willing to keep him entertained with a story or two over a pint of ale. There was always a dance or a tavern to visit, always someone to welcome you into their home and feed you until you were close to bursting. Of course, he hadn't been an earl in Halifax. He'd simply been Garnet's partner—a businessman of some importance.

Now that he was home, he was back in his own sphere. He didn't mind reverting to the familiar—at times being an "ordinary man" had been rather trying—but he missed the company of his friends. Julian had yet to return from the Continent and Brave, a new father, was happy to stay as far away from London as he could with his wife and son. Gabriel had missed the birth of his honorary nephew, and that bothered him as well.

As was his habit, he searched the street beyond with a keen eye, hoping that this day would be different, and that *she* would suddenly appear on his doorstep with an explanation as to where she had disappeared to eighty-seven thousand, six hundred hours ago because he still wanted to know.

He still *needed* to know.

With a disgusted snort, Gabriel withdrew from the window. Not even a week back in London, and already he was falling into old habits again.

Pathetic.

He would need to find something to throw himself into. Something that would put an end to this obsession. Perhaps it was time to continue his fight against gambling in England.

A knock sounded on the door. Uncharitable and angry at himself, Gabriel barked, "What is it?"

The door opened, revealing Robinson, Gabriel's butler. The man looked more like a laborer than a servant, with his thick neck and massive shoulders, but he possessed the most piercing set of pale blue eyes Gabriel had ever encountered—and the driest wit. His family had been with the Angelwood earls for generations. He was the only servant Gabriel employed who treated him more like a man than a master. One of the side effects of having grown up together, Gabriel supposed. It made the butler too familiar, but Gabriel really didn't mind.

"Lord Underwood is here, my lord. He says it is a matter of great importance," Robinson informed him gruffly, meeting his gaze with a flat stare that said he didn't think it could possibly be *that* important.

Blaine Foster, Viscount Underwood, had been a friend of Gabriel's for years. He had also been a friend of Phillip, Gabriel's father. Blaine had helped him pick up the pieces after his father's death—not an enviable task.

Sighing, he rubbed the back of his neck with one hand. The muscles there were tight, making his head ache with the tension. He was in no mood for company, but Blaine wouldn't have told Robinson it was important if it weren't.

"Give me a minute," Gabriel instructed, wincing as his fingers found a particularly tender spot at the base of his skull. "Then send him in."

Robinson gave a sharp nod. "As you wish." And with a bow as clipped as his tone, the butler backed out of the room and shut the door with a gentle click.

Dropping his arm to his side, Gabriel crossed the wine-and-gold carpet to the heavy mahogany table on which several crystal decanters sat, dark and tempting with their promise of respite. Lifting one by its cool, thick neck, he pulled the stopper and poured a generous measure of scotch into a glass.

He had to pull himself together before Blaine came in, and

that meant pushing *her* out of his thoughts—or at least as far from his thoughts as he could push her. She never went away completely. He'd long ago accepted the fact that she probably never would.

He emptied the glass in one gut-burning gulp and poured himself another. The thought of her wasn't enough to make him want to get thoroughly foxed anymore—it hadn't been for years—but the liquor would rinse away the sour taste her memory left in his mouth.

Ten years ago, Lilith Mallory had walked out of his life without so much as a whisper. She'd left the country shortly after his father had shucked off his mortal coil, just days after she and Gabriel had celebrated their impending engagement by making love for the first time. Her father had refused to tell Gabriel where she'd gone, but that hadn't stopped the twenty-one-year-old earl from turning the world upside down looking for her—after he'd recovered from the shock of his father's death. He never found her, nor did she ever try to contact him.

It was as though she had simply dropped off the edge of the world.

And like the love-struck fool he was, he never got over her. She'd been the first woman he ever loved—emotionally and physically—and that kind of loss and betrayal was not something a heart easily recovered from.

If it ever recovered at all.

He was obsessed. He knew it. He understood it. Sometimes he even took comfort in it. The memory of Lilith and her desertion was the one constant in his life. And even though it hurt like hell to think of her, his heart still lurched whenever he saw a woman with flame-red hair.

"Am I intruding?"

"Blaine!" A wide grin split across Gabriel's face as his old friend stepped into the study. He was across the room in three long strides, clapping the smaller man warmly on the shoulders as he drew him into the center of the room. Gabriel had always looked up to Blaine, the only friend of his father's who'd ever paid attention to him.

"It's good to have you home, Gabe," Blaine commented fondly as he seated himself in one of the thickly padded, gold-and-beige patterned armchairs in front of Gabriel's desk.

Gabriel smiled. "It's good to be back. Can I get you a drink?"

A few moments later, when both of their glasses had been filled, Gabriel leaned against the edge of the desk and studied his companion carefully. Not as old as Gabriel's father would have been, yet much older than Gabriel, Blaine had been friend to both men. There was no reason for Blaine to be uneasy in his presence, but he had a tenseness about him, a stiffness to his movements and expression. The hair that a year ago had been as dark as Gabe's own was now peppered with silver, and Blaine's usually bright green eyes were dull and tired.

"What is it?" Gabriel kept his tone casual despite his concern.

Blaine laughed—a brittle sound—and took a deep swallow of scotch. "I'm sorry to come to you with my paltry problems, especially since you've just returned, but I did not know who else to speak to—who else I could trust."

Blaine was well liked and well respected by almost every member of the *ton*. The fact that he felt Gabriel was the only one he could turn to did more than warm the cockles of Gabriel's heart. It scared the hell out of him.

"Has something happened to Victoria?"

Blaine shook his head. "No. My wife is fine. It's Frederick."

Frederick was Blaine's oldest son and heir. Gabriel hadn't seen the boy in some time. He must be in his early twenties now.

Gabriel sipped his drink. "What about Frederick?"

Blaine frowned into his glass. "He's gotten himself into some trouble."

"Trouble?"

"He's always out with his friends, drinking, racing horses, chasing women."

Gabriel grinned. "Sounds like a normal lad to me."

Blaine raised his head. Gabriel was taken aback by his friend's worried gaze. "He's been gambling."

Gabriel's blood chilled at the mere sound of the word. Gaming and the campaign against it had been one of his pet projects for years. Unfortunately, it was the favorite pastime of much of the *ton*, and getting Parliament to pass any laws against it had been virtually impossible. He knew from personal experience just how dangerous gaming could be, particularly if one developed an addiction, as his father had done.

He would hate to see Frederick lose himself in the same fashion.

"Tell me what's happened." *Now.*

Taking another swallow of scotch, Blaine leaned back in his chair. "I can only repeat the story he told me, not that I doubt my son's honesty for a moment."

Gabriel didn't bother to remind his friend that a son would lie about almost anything to avoid his father's wrath, not when they were discussing something so serious. Fortunes had been lost over a game of cards. Women traded their virtue for their vowels. Families were often destroyed simply because some fool had wagered everything on a card or a roll of the dice.

"A fortnight ago, Frederick was out with some of his friends. They went to a club on King Street for supper and ended up sitting down to a game of cards. One of the other boys then suggested they try their luck in the back rooms."

Gabriel stiffened. It wasn't unusual for gentlemen's clubs to have tables for cards or other games of chance, but dice and wheel games were prohibited in gaming hells and were often played in back rooms such as Blaine described. These rooms were also where gentlemen interested in serious play might find a high-stakes game.

"And did Frederick go?" Gabriel asked, his tone carefully neutral.

Blaine shook his head. "No." Again he laughed bitterly. "Although perhaps he wouldn't have gotten into trouble if he'd stayed with his friends."

Finishing the last of his scotch, Gabriel set the empty glass aside and folded his arms across his chest. "Don't get cryptic on me now, Blaine. Not if you expect me to help." There was no censure or gruffness in his tone, just gentle encouragement.

With a sigh, the older man nodded. "I appreciate your friendship, Gabe. Frederick sat down to a game of faro. I don't imagine you've ever played it?"

Gabriel shook his head. He'd gambled only once in his life. Long before his father's death, he and his friends, Brave and Julian, had gotten into a card game. Luckily none of them developed much of a taste for it and quit after losing a few guineas.

"I am familiar with the rules, however." If he remembered correctly, faro was a simple game in which the player bet against the house as to what card the dealer would turn up, winning if his guess was correct.

"Frederick says he was having an exceedingly good run of luck," Blaine continued, and Gabriel didn't doubt it. The people who ended up in the most trouble were the people who believed their run of luck would hold.

"Then his luck turned?"

Blaine nodded, staring into his glass again. "He made a large wager, more than he could afford, confident that he would win."

Gabriel's smile was a mixture of bitterness and sympathy for his friend. "But he lost."

"Yes."

He sighed, knowing what came next. "And you had to pay his debt."

Lifting his head, the older man met Gabriel's gaze with the

angry look of a concerned father. "He says the dealer cheated."

Gabriel frowned. That wasn't the kind of charge to be made lightly. "Is he certain?"

Blaine's expression tightened. "I trust my son, Gabriel."

Holding up his hands, Gabriel shook his head. "I'm not accusing Frederick of lying, but that's a serious charge to make. He actually saw the dealer fleece him?"

A light flush crept up the other man's cheeks. "Not exactly, but he says there was definitely something odd about his behavior." He leaned forward. "Gabe, will you help me?"

Gabriel didn't hesitate. After all Blaine had done for him after his father's death, Gabriel would do anything he asked. "Certainly. What do you need?"

"I want to make certain this doesn't happen to anyone else. I want you to help me prove the house cheated. I want it shut down."

Something about the brightness of his friend's gaze made Gabriel uneasy. "How?"

Blaine set his glass on the desk. "Go to the club—"

"Go to the club!" Jerking upright, Gabriel stomped halfway across the room before turning. "Are you mad? I cannot go to a club! It would make me look like a hypocrite."

The older man rose to his feet, coming toward Gabriel with a pleading expression that a friend would be hard-hearted not to be moved by. But this was one time Gabriel couldn't help. Not when it went against his principles.

"Gabe, please. Someone has to stop them, and I promised Frederick I wouldn't get involved."

"You're a good father, Blaine," Gabriel replied lamely, on the verge of incredulous laughter.

"Then you'll go?" The older man's expression was hopeful. "You'll help us?"

For Christ's sake! His own father had been a pathetic gamester; everyone knew his reputation. The stories about him were endless. Did Blaine have any idea of what he was asking?

He must, because he had seen what gaming had done to

Gabe's father, and he didn't want the same thing to happen to his own son.

Weakening, Gabriel sighed as he met his friend's gaze. "What are people going to say when they see the Angelic Earl in a gaming establishment?"

"Angelic Earl" was what the Corinthians and the dandies called him behind his back. It was meant as an insult, as though Gabriel were denying his very blood by refusing to gamble, whore and drink himself brainless. They thought him laughable for not wanting to squander his fortune and what youth he had left on their sordid diversions.

"Think of how much good it will do your cause if you can go into the House of Lords with proof that one of their clubs is cheating them."

It was the only thing he could have said to convince him, and Blaine knew it. The *ton* was fiercely protective of their vices until one turned on them. If Gabriel could prove that a club was swindling them, he could plant the seed of doubt in their minds. Perhaps they'd begin to wonder if *all* their clubs weren't cheating them. At the very least, he could then use their paranoia to convince them that gambling was a danger to society and that those who perpetrated it had to be stopped . . .

Or they might laugh him right out of the House. But if he could prove it, if he could get enough support behind him, he just might have a chance at keeping the promise he'd made his father.

His head full of exactly what a coup this could be, Gabriel turned to Blaine with a cool, calculating smile. "What's this place called?"

The other man's sigh of relief was audible. He seized one of Gabriel's hands and shook it profusely. "Mallory's. It's called Mallory's."

Gabriel froze, his heart snapping against his ribs. "Mallory's?"

Blaine nodded, his brow puckering slightly. "Yes. Do you know it?"

Shaking his head, not in response, but to clear it of the insane longing the sound of that name instilled in him. "No. I do not."

"No," Blaine replied with a slight chuckle, "why would you? Even if you had been in the country when it opened a year ago, you still would never have stepped inside such a scandalous place."

Scandalous? Even such bastions of society as White's and Brooke's invited gaming. Hell, White's even had its famous betting book. From what Blaine had told him, this Mallory's was just another gentlemen's social club. Why was it so different? The question continued to plague him for the rest of Blaine's visit, through the discussion of how Gabriel would handle the investigation, through his assurances that Frederick would never know, and through Blaine's heartfelt thanks.

Curiosity got the better of the earl as his friend prepared to leave. "What's so scandalous about this place?"

Blaine looked around, as though what he was about to say was so terrible, he didn't want anyone else to hear.

"It's run by a woman."

A woman? A woman named Mallory?

Blood roared in Gabriel's ears as icy pinpricks danced in his veins. He gave himself a brisk mental shake. It was just a coincidence. That was all. It couldn't be her.

The Lilith he knew would never do something as ludicrous as own a gaming club.

Ludicrous.

Lowering the newspaper to her lap, Lilith Mallory laughed as she spoke. "People don't actually pay money to read this, do they?"

Her companion, Mary, looked up from her sewing. She was sitting by one of the windows to take advantage of the last vestiges of daylight. Dressed in her usual shades of beige and cream, Mary matched the decor of the parlor to perfection, although Lilith knew without a doubt that it was merely a coincidence. Mary never wore anything but beige and cream. In fact, "the less color the better" seemed to be the older woman's motto.

"What is it you're reading?" Mary asked, slipping her needle through the shift she was mending. "The Reverend Sweet's column?"

"Indeed," Lilith replied dryly.

Mary smiled, her wide lips curving in a way that made her well-lived-in features soft and almost delicate. "Then yes, people do pay good money to read it."

Rolling her eyes, Lilith shook her head. A pin bit into her scalp as she did so, causing her to wince. Damn things. Eleven years of wearing her hair up and her scalp still hadn't gotten used to the pulling and poking.

"If people are willing to purchase drivel like this, then I believe we're in the wrong business, my friend." Snapping the paper back into rigidity, Lilith resumed her reading.

"They say you're nobody unless the reverend rips you to shreds in one of his articles." Mary's voice was filled with wonder. "I've heard that some ladies of the *ton* have started using his column as the basis for their guest lists this season."

The idea of any member of the *ton* doing anything so pretentious didn't surprise Lilith one bit. After all, her mother would have been silly enough to do such a thing.

"Prepare yourself, then, Mary," Lilith replied as her gaze landed upon a particularly laughable paragraph in the good reverend's Sweet Rewards column. "I expect the invitations to start rolling in."

"*What?*"

In the space of time it took Lilith to lower the paper, Mary had crossed the gold-and-ivory carpet and flounced onto the sofa beside her.

"He's written about Mallory's?"

Lilith shot her friend an amused glance. For a woman who claimed to have had her fill of the opposite sex, Mary certainly seemed to have a keen interest in the Reverend Geoffrey Sweet. "Not precisely. He wrote about me."

Laughing in what could only be described as maniacal glee, Mary snatched the paper out of Lilith's hands. "Let me see!"

Lilith merely smiled at the other woman's exuberance. There was a time when she'd believed Mary had lost her joy for good. When she first met Mary, her husband had dragged her into the center of the street and was holding some kind of barbaric divorce ritual.

He'd been trying to auction her off to the highest bidder. She was no good to him anymore, having failed to produce any sons, and anyone who wanted her could have her for the right price. It was a wife auction, and apparently it was nothing new to the lower orders. Their ideas of what made a marriage were a bit different from those of the aristocracy—from those of the church, in some cases—and their idea of divorce was no different.

Outraged, and having some idea of how it felt to be cast aside like a piece of useless baggage, Lilith had paid the man's price. Her manservant Latimer had posed as the interested husband-to-be. It was one of the best things she had ever done, for not only had she purchased the older woman's freedom, she had found a friend in the process—something she hadn't had in a long time.

There was only one secret between them, and that was Mary's real last name. She never divulged it to Lilith. Instead, she called herself Mary Smith. No one would ever come searching for Mary Smith, she said, just in case her husband changed his mind.

And Lilith, who had spent much of the past ten years hoping for someone to find her, couldn't understand her friend's need for anonymity.

Not bad. She'd managed to go half a day before thinking of Gabriel Warren.

"Here it is! I found it!" Mary's velvety brown eyes widened with delight. "Listen to this."

Lilith had already read some of what Mr. Sweet had to say

about her, but if it made Mary happy to repeat it, then she was willing to listen. It might help keep the painful memories of Gabriel and his betrayal at bay.

For a little while.

" 'One of the most disturbing and dangerous evils to ever descend upon our society is that of gaming,' " Mary began, her voice taking on, with mock severity, the tone of a preacher before his flock.

" 'Even more disturbing than man leading his fellow man down this path of licentiousness is the knowledge that the gates of Hell are guarded by one whose very sex dictates that she be man's helpmate, not his Judas. It is because of this that I strongly urge you, dear readers, to resist the pull of a certain club owned by a certain flame-haired female, whose very name betrays her true nature.' What does he mean, your name betrays your true nature?"

Lilith arched a brow. That Sweet even mentioned the origin of her name showed his knowledge of other cultures. In Hebrew lore, Lilith was a mythical she-demon. Not even her mother, who simply liked the odd name, had been aware of the symbolism she bestowed upon her only daughter. If she had, Lilith would have ended up with a much sweeter, much more *English* name.

"In some cultures, Lilith is the name of the original fallen woman," she replied. "Older even than Eve. The original wife of Adam, Lilith was cast out of Eden when she refused to lie beneath her husband."

Mary's eyes widened.

Chuckling, Lilith continued. "Some revere her as a goddess, others revile her as a demoness. Obviously the reverend falls into the latter category. What else does he say?"

" 'It is my duty as God's advocate to warn you that once you are inside those portals of debauchery, L.M.'s lure is as tempting and as ripe as the very fruit Eve offered up to Adam.' "

"Sounds as though the reverend has an unnatural interest

in my portals," Lilith remarked, rising from the sofa. "Honestly, could he have made me sound any more wanton? 'Tempting and ripe' indeed."

Mary smiled, deepening the lines around her eyes. "I wager we will have a full house tonight, thanks to his column."

Hands on her hips, Lilith turned, the forest-green silk of her skirts rustling as she did so. A thought occurred to her. A sly, naughty thought that brought a self-satisfied curve to her lips.

"Mary, I want you to send a letter of thanks to the good reverend."

The older woman gaped at her. "You can't be serious!"

Smiling, Lilith sashayed across the carpet to the large oak desk where she conducted all her club business. She unlocked the top drawer and reached inside, pulling out twenty pounds' worth of counters.

"Enclose these with the letter. Tell him how much I appreciate the notoriety his column has given Mallory's. Tell him . . ." She paused. How to best unsettle the pious, pen-wielding clergyman?

"Tell him that if he ever wants to be led into temptation, he has only to ask."

Cackling, Mary tossed the newspaper onto the cushion beside her and stood. "Lilith, you're shameless!"

The word wasn't meant as an insult, but still, it did smart a bit. Her smile tightening, Lilith shrugged. "I have a reputation to uphold."

A reputation as scandalous as her namesake's. A reputation she'd done nothing to earn except give herself to the man—the *boy*—she had loved. Ten years ago, Gabriel Warren had taken much more than her virtue. He'd taken her ability to show her face in society without being whispered about. He'd taken away all the balls and parties and invitations that a girl of her age and rank should have enjoyed. He'd taken away all her friends. He'd taken her heart and her pride.

But perhaps he'd done her a favor. After all, living with her aunt Imogen had provided much more in the way of adventure than anything London could have afforded her. She'd enjoyed more freedom, more independence, than any of her acquaintances at home. She met exciting people, made new friends. Yet all she had wanted was for Gabriel to come find her.

He never did.

"I need to get to work," she said, jarring herself out of the past and back into the present. "I must inspect the club before it opens. Bring me that letter when you've finished. I wish to read it before we send it to Reverend Sweet."

Mary looked surprised. "You're actually serious about sending it?"

This time Lilith's smile was more natural. "My dear Mary, have you ever known me *not* to be serious?"

The club was already bustling with activity when Lilith appeared downstairs for the evening. As was her habit, she paused in the corridor separating the club from her private entrance and checked her appearance in the large, gilded mirror there.

As usual, Luisa, her maid, had worked miracles. Lilith's unruly hair was pinned on top of her head in a sleek, sophisticated style. A faint dusting of powder took the shine from her nose and cheeks, and a subtle blending of carmine on her cheeks and lips gave her a natural-looking glow. Topaz drops hung from her ears, brushing her jaw when she moved her head. A matching necklace glittered around her throat.

Smoothing the skirts of her amber silk gown, Lilith was satisfied that she could not look any better. No society matron could find any fault with her appearance—and there would be such women in the club that night. There always were. Mallory's was the one social club in London that was open to both gentlemen and ladies. There were separate gaming, dining and retiring rooms for both sexes, as well as areas where men and women could socialize with each other if they wished.

At first Lilith had hesitated to open her doors to women,

fearing it would prove a hindrance rather than a help. She couldn't have been more wrong. Society ladies were even more bored with their husbands than their husbands were with them, and they flocked to Mallory's to gamble, socialize and flirt with gentlemen who Lilith knew were *not* their husbands.

In fact, catering to both sexes had opened up a wealth of possibilities to Lilith, for it was from the women that she heard the best gossip, who was having an affair with whom, who was on the verge of social ruin. And from the men she learned who was in danger of losing a fortune and who was cheating on his wife.

Lilith couldn't have planned it any better. While the people who frequented her club often held her in the same estimation as dirt, they paid to be there, whether by subscription, drinking her liquor or losing heavily at her tables. What they didn't realize was that they were in a position to pay a far heavier price, for Lilith knew things—things that many people would want to keep private. And Lilith wasn't above using that information to her advantage if the need was there.

After all, it wasn't as though any of them had stood by her ten years ago.

She strode down the corridor, past the paintings and delicate plaster scrollwork that lined the pale blue walls. The blue-and-gold carpet with its fleur-de-lis pattern silenced her footsteps, so that the only sounds in the hall were the rustling of her skirts and the low rumble of conversation coming from the male side of the club.

The rumble grew louder as she entered the main hall. Here the carpet gave way to polished stone. Warm beige tiles, inlaid with dark blue and gold, formed diamond patterns throughout the paler stone. Fluted columns in the same shades of blue and sand supported the ceiling in each of the four corners.

The centerpiece of the hall was a large statue of Venus emerging from her oyster shell. A glass dome above bathed the statue in a flush of sunshine during the day and frosted it with moonlight at night. The Italian sculptor who created the statue claimed to have based her face and figure on Lilith herself, but Lilith couldn't see any real resemblance, except for the fact that the goddess was a tad on the voluptuous side.

"Good evening, Mr. Dunlop," she said to a handsome gentleman admiring the Venus.

"Good evening to you, my dear Lady Lilith," the Scotsman replied with a bright twinkle in his blue eyes. "I was just noticing that this attractive young lady looks an awful lot like you."

Mr. Dunlop was a young, wealthy merchant who'd made his fortune in textiles. He had more money and charm than some of England's most affluent families, but nowhere near the arrogance.

Lilith smiled at his flirtatious tone. "Do you think so?"

"Aye. And a bonny lass she is, too." He grinned. "Are you on your way into the club?"

"I am."

"Then perhaps you'd give me the honor of joining me at one of the tables. A woman as lovely as yourself can only bring good fortune."

Inclining her head in a slight nod, Lilith accepted the arm that was offered. "I'd be delighted, Mr. Dunlop."

It was fortunate that Lilith liked the textile merchant, otherwise she would have had to think of an excuse not to join him. It wasn't good business to refuse someone of his wealth with such a lust for gaming. Mr. Dunlop won at her tables just as often as he lost, but he spent an enormous amount of blunt entertaining friends, buying them all the food and liquor they could possibly want. Lilith had made a lot of money off Mr. Dunlop and his acquaintances in the past year, and she'd feed him grapes and fan him with a palm leaf if that was required to keep him coming back.

Mr. Dunlop was one of the few men who flirted with her but never took it any further. He was charming and he made her laugh. And he reminded her very much of another black-haired, charming scoundrel who used to make her laugh all the time. The comparison shouldn't have worked in Mr. Dunlop's favor, but it did.

"There is something I feel I should tell you, Lady Lilith," Mr. Dunlop began as the footmen opened the doors of the club for them.

"I thought we agreed that you'd call me Lilith." Nodding to the footmen, Lilith kept her gaze centered on the opulent, richly masculine room before her. Not every table was in use, but the majority were. Many gentlemen were in the dining room or the smoking room, or even in the private parlors in the rear. By the time midnight rolled around, all the gaming tables would be filled and the level of conversation would make speaking in a normal tone difficult.

"Only if you call me Stephen."

Just inside the doors, near a potted palm, Lilith stopped and turned to face her companion with a sincere smile. "All right. What is it you wanted to tell me, Stephen?"

He smiled, a multitude of laugh lines fanning out around his eyes. "I think you should know that a strange gentleman is here tonight, asking about you—and the club."

Lilith quirked a brow. "Gentleman? Is he handsome?" Her light tone belied the thumping in her chest. Was it Bronson or one of his men? And if so, what mischief was he up to?

"Not so handsome as myself," Mr. Dunlop replied in his thick brogue, "but he cuts quite a figure. Big man with black hair and pale eyes."

This time when Lilith's heart leapt, it jumped straight into her throat. Was it true? Earlier she'd heard a woman in a shop mention that the Earl of Angelwood was back in London. Would he dare show his face in her club? Had he finally come for her?

Well, he was too damn late.

She was getting ahead of herself. There was no evidence that this mystery man was Gabriel. Lots of men had black hair and pale eyes—Samuel Bronson for one. Bronson was also a large man, and while Gabe was certainly tall, he'd never been what someone might call big. But then, he'd been a mere one-and-twenty the last time she saw him.

Dear Lord. What if it was him?

"Lilith?"

Glancing up, Lilith caught Mr. Dunlop's concerned gaze. "Are you quite all right?"

"Yes. I'm fine, Stephen, thank you." She smiled, even though she feared her face might crack. "Do you know where this gentleman is now?"

Mr. Dunlop shook his head. "I told him to speak to Latimer."

Latimer was the club manager and just one set of Lilith's eyes and ears at Mallory's. He knew everyone of importance in London and if he didn't, he made sure he found out. He could tell her the identity of this nosy visitor. And if it was Bronson, Latimer would have already asked him to leave. Latimer didn't take kindly to Lilith's rival poking around her club. He didn't trust Bronson, and neither did Lilith, especially not since he'd become more forceful in his offers to buy Mallory's. There had been several acts of vandalism toward Lilith and her club lately, and she believed Bronson was responsible for them.

Lilith sweetened her smile. "I wonder, would you think me so terribly awful if I left you to your own devices this evening? I should very much like to find out who this gentleman is and what he wants."

Mr. Dunlop grinned crookedly. "If anyone can find out what a man wants, it's you, Lilith. Off with you, then. I know what it's like to be married to one's business. Come find me later if you wish."

With a grateful smile and a squeeze of his arm, Lilith set off through the crowd. Most of the men were dressed in evening attire, making it difficult for her to single out just one. Nevertheless, she sorted through them, looking for a man of good height and size with black hair. She found none.

Where was he?

Her heart heavier and her stomach uneasier than she

cared to admit, Lilith drifted toward the far side of the club, where the French doors were open to allow the evening breeze to cool the room. She didn't want to concede, not even to herself, that she had been hoping to see Gabriel. She was so tired of not knowing what had happened. Even if he hadn't loved her as she had loved him, she just wanted to know the truth.

And she wanted to knock his bloody teeth down his throat.

She murmured phrases of encouragement as she walked past the tables. Most of the men didn't care about her reputation, although they certainly wouldn't speak to her in mixed company. They smiled and raised their glasses. Some made thinly veiled sexual overtures, but wisely kept from going too far. The last man to proposition her had been barred from the club indefinitely, and no one else was willing to risk such punishment. Lilith's pride didn't take offense that none of them thought she was worth the risk. Their reluctance to upset her showed her just how much power she actually had over them. It was a very exhilarating thought.

She was laughing at a joke the Duke of Wellington told her when she spotted a very tall, very powerfully built man with thick, collar-length black hair step out onto the balcony. Her entire body froze at the sight of him. She couldn't see his face, just the breadth of his shoulders in his evening attire. His jacket and trousers were an exquisite cut, the fit and fabric belying the wearer's wealth. There was no doubt in Lilith's mind that even if this wasn't Gabriel—and really, this man was much too big to be the boy she remembered—he was indeed the man she was looking for.

Intent upon her quarry, she chased after him, ignoring those who tried to snare her attention as she passed. She lost sight of him as he moved farther away, and she quickened her pace.

Plunging into the dark balcony, she shivered as the cool night air embraced her. It was only April and the evenings were still a little chilly, especially after the hard rain they'd had earlier. Still, she did not turn back.

She stood there for a moment, in a puddle of light cast through the open doors. Then, as her eyes grew more accustomed to the darkness, she moved cautiously away from the sanctuary of her club. All her life she'd been taught that there was safety in light and numbers. Out here, in the night, she was vulnerable. Vulnerable to one man who was either friend or foe.

But there was no one there. Lord Braxton and Lord Somerville stood smoking cheroots just beyond the French doors, but they were so deep in conversation that Lilith didn't ask them if they'd seen her mysterious gentleman. They probably hadn't even noticed her.

The balcony extended to her right, into almost complete blackness at the far end, where it met with one of the rooms she often used as an office. The curtains there were drawn to keep anyone from knowing whether the room was occupied or not. Recently the club had suffered a minor break-in—also believed to be Bronson's doing—and Lilith didn't want to give any thieves an open invitation by leaving her office wide open.

She moved past some potted plants, past a table and chairs where gentlemen could sit and have a quiet drink. She was almost to the end of the balcony and still no sign of her prey. But he was there. He had to be.

Her breathing harsh in her ears, she reached the far end of the balustrade. Nothing was there but darkness. Frowning, she turned and glanced behind her. She could see Lords Somerville and Braxton still chattering away, but no one else.

Where was he? He couldn't have just vanished into thin air.

Bringing her gaze around again, Lilith fought the strangled gasp that rose in her throat. The door to the office was open.

The bastard was inside, and she had a good idea what he was up to.

She'd had enough of this. If Bronson thought he could intimidate her so easily, he had another think coming. This time she was going to catch his henchman and exact a little revenge of her own against Bronson and Hazards, his club.

Slowly, silently, Lilith tiptoed toward the door. She'd have to use the element of surprise and then scream vehemently in the hope that Somerville and Braxton would come to her assistance. At least they would be able to stop the thief if he tried to escape past them. If he ran into the club, Latimer and some of the staff would be able to stop him.

Lilith didn't want to think what might happen if he decided to attack her.

Her fingers trembling as they touched the cool glass, Lilith held her breath and gave the door a gentle push.

It flew open with so much force and speed that it knocked her off-balance. She didn't even have time to scream before two strong hands gripped her shoulders and steadied her. She looked up.

And she still didn't scream, but she wanted to. Because the man holding her was staring at her with eyes so pale and clear she could see her own reflection, and because he was indeed a thief.

Ten years ago, he had stolen her heart.

Chapter 2

Gabriel was prepared for the slap. In fact, he welcomed it. The sting and the ringing in his ears forced him to recover most of the breath he'd lost at the sight of her.

Damn, but the years had been good to her. Under the glow of the wall lamps, Lilith was a study in the multitude of colors among crimson, ivory and gold, and every shade of her threatened to take his breath again. She was even more beautiful than he remembered, despite the garish cosmetics she'd used to make her lips and cheeks red and her eyes dark. The body beneath that gauzy amber gown was softer and fuller. The generous curves of her breasts and hips only reinforced the fact that she had become a woman.

A woman whose club might have cheated Frederick Foster.

He rubbed his cheek where her hand had struck it. There would be a mark. Good. Come morning, he would need a reminder that this had actually happened, that she was truly real. "Hello, Lil."

She stared at him, her eyebrows perfect inverted V's over wide, stormy eyes. Her Cupid's-bow lips parted as though she was seeing something she hadn't expected to see.

How long had she thought to hide from him? She had to have known he would come eventually. He'd been back in England only a short time, but she must have realized that once he learned she was here, she would have to face him.

Or maybe she thought he wouldn't. After all, her father had made it perfectly clear that a man—a *boy*—like Gabriel, with his scandalous parents and a fortune dwindled by both, would never be the proper match for *his* daughter, even if he had ruined her.

The reminder of how she'd slipped out of his life and never once looked back blackened any tender feeling this reunion might have brought. The spot where she slapped him throbbed as his jaw tightened.

"Nothing to say?" Gabriel arched a brow, his tone mocking. "I expected at least a hello. How long has it been—eight, nine years?"

"Ten," she replied, her teeth clenched, her expression murderous.

So she did remember. Good.

"What are you doing here, Lord Angelwood?"

He tried to ignore the stab of pain in his chest at her use of his title. "Why, Lady Lilith, has no one warned you about me?"

Bracing her hands on those ripe hips, Lilith stared him down with a gaze so cold a chill crept down his spine. "It's a little late for that, don't you think? No one needs to warn me, my lord. I know full well what you're capable of."

Her voice had deepened over the years, but it was still as crisp and biting as a schoolmaster's switch. And it still made Gabe want to kiss her and caress her until it became nothing more than a husky whisper.

"Capable of?" He took a step toward her and wasn't surprised when she didn't retreat. Their torsos almost touching, Gabriel leaned toward her, smiling as her body stiffened.

"My dear Lily," he murmured against the velvety shell of

her ear. "It's been ten years. You have absolutely no idea just what I'm capable of."

She shivered, but made no move to escape him. A thrill coursed through Gabriel's body. The scent of her, oranges and cloves, filled his senses. It suited her, ripe and succulent with just a touch of bite overlaying a warm sensuality. Did she remember that night when it had been impossible to determine where one of them began and the other ended? When he'd been so deep inside her, so much in love, that they'd been the same person?

Driven by something much more powerful than any sense or reason, Gabriel ran the tip of his tongue along the ridge of her ear. Closing his eyes, he breathed her deep within himself, letting her fill him, mind and soul.

Her fingers wrapped around his forearm like a vise. Whether it was to stop him or steady herself, he didn't know.

"You still taste the same," he whispered, lifting his head.

The gaze that met his was as hard and cold as granite, but her cheeks and throat were high with color and her nostrils flared slightly.

She released his arm, pushing at him as she did so. "You take liberties, my lord."

The throaty timbre of her voice struck Gabriel square in the chest. She wasn't immune to him.

"Liberties?" Was his smile as twisted as it felt? "There was a time when you begged me to taste you. Have you forgotten?"

Christ, what was wrong with him? He was so hot and hard for her, it felt more like torture than any kind of liberty. He wanted her. He wanted to punish her, forgive her, and most of all he wanted to know that he hadn't been the only one in love a decade ago.

He wanted to know why she had left him.

Her mouth tightened. "I wish I could forget."

Her remark was meant as an insult, but Gabriel couldn't help but laugh. She hadn't been able to forget him, either. If the memory of him caused her one-tenth the pain that the thought of her caused him, he would be happy.

She backed away from him then, as though she realized she'd given too much away and needed to put some distance between them.

"I asked you what you were doing here."

Gabriel shrugged. His body felt her withdrawal too keenly for comfort. "I came to see you."

Now it was her turn to laugh. A big, booming sound that made his heart heavy with a bittersweet sorrow. It was good to hear her laugh, but she didn't believe him. Of course he wasn't being one hundred percent truthful, but the fact that she doubted his word indicated just how little she thought of him now.

He moved to the desk behind him and sat on the polished oak surface. This entire office, from its burgundy carpets to its dark paneling, had a masculine feel, yet from what he'd learned earlier from several acquaintances, this was Lilith's office.

Which showed just how little her patrons knew her. This might be the office Lilith used during club hours, but he was certain she had a private office somewhere else in the building. An office that reflected her personality more than this one. That was where he would find any evidence to prove her establishment wasn't as honest as it should be.

And if the evidence were there, he would indeed uncover it. He wouldn't stop until he did.

She was staring at him, her head tilted to one side as though she was contemplating a particularly fascinating riddle. It was nice—even if he didn't trust it—to have her look at him that way, without coldness in her gaze.

He watched as she crossed a small expanse of the wine-and-brown carpet and seated herself in one of the chairs facing the desk. Facing him. Another sign that this wasn't really her office. She would have placed herself behind the desk, where she would have the most power. She crossed her legs, giving him a tantalizing peek at one ankle. Her posture was lazy, like a sun-drunk feline.

"You seemed surprised that no one had 'warned' me about

you," she said, a little of the crispness gone from her tone. "Why did you come here, Gabe?"

Oh, she was good! She hadn't forgotten how to manipulate him, either. The languid posture, the glimpse of stocking, the softness of her voice as she spoke his name—it was all designed to get what she wanted out of him.

And he wanted to give it to her. Wanted to throw himself at her feet and tell her how wretched his life had been without her. Wanted to tell her about his promise to Blaine; wanted to beg her to say it wasn't true, that she was still his Lily and couldn't possibly have changed that much.

But she had changed. She ran a gaming club and she painted her face. She was cold and cynical and much more world-weary than the girl he'd known. She'd ceased to be his Lily the night she left him, and Gabriel knew better than to trust her a second time.

"I came here to see what you'd become, Lil."

Those big eyes of hers narrowed. "And congratulate yourself?"

Congratulate himself? What the hell was she talking about? "I don't think either of us has done anything worthy of congratulations, do you?"

She flushed at that, a dull red creeping up from the low neckline of her gown, over the plump swell of her breasts, to the crest of her forehead.

"It seems that I am about to become your enemy," he told her, folding his arms across his chest. His jacket pulled uncomfortably through the shoulders.

She smiled humorlessly. "I figured that out a long time ago, my lord."

Back to that again, were they? "Then you know about my plans?"

"I know a great many things about you, my lord, but the way your mind works isn't one of them," she replied, the schoolmarm tone slipping back into her voice. "Perhaps you should enlighten me before I decide to have you removed from the premises."

She wouldn't hesitate to humiliate him in such a way; Gabriel could see it in her eyes.

"I'm surprised that no one has taken the pleasure of informing you of the cause I took up after my father's death."

The pallor that swept over her face was enough to tell him just how deeply his father's death had touched her. She'd liked his father. The odd times their families had socialized, the late earl always wanted Lilith to be his partner in a game of whist. Gamblers, both of them. His father would have been proud of how wealthy Lilith had become. Would she be as proud of him if she knew just how much his addiction had cost both him and his son?

"What cause?" Her voice was tight.

A perverse part of Gabriel couldn't wait for her reaction. "The outlawing of gambling in England."

Laughter was not the reaction he had anticipated. It wasn't the full-blown chortle of earlier, but rather a quiet, disbelieving chuckle, like a mother might give when a child announces he plans to be king one day.

Her laughter faded when she saw the expression on his face. "You're serious?"

Gabriel nodded, his jaw aching with the effort to keep it shut.

Now she looked almost sorry for him. "They will never agree to it."

"Why not?"

She chuckled. She seemed to enjoy laughing at him. "Because ninety percent of the men you want to convince are some of my best customers. They will never agree to something that will negatively affect their own lives."

"You think so?" His tone was challenging.

Her smile was arrogant. "I know so."

Never had he wanted so badly to put someone in her place. "And what about that ten percent who have drastically depleted or lost fortunes at establishments such as yours? What about the people who have had loved ones take their own lives over gaming debts?" His voice rose with emotion.

"What about people who have been ruined because they're driven to gamble?"

Lilith's cocky demeanor was still in place, but Gabriel could see the uncertainty in her eyes. "They are not my concern."

"No?" He slipped off the desk and closed the distance between them. Bracing each hand on the chair arms, he made her a prisoner with his body. "They should be. They are the ones in my corner."

She met his stare unflinchingly, silently telling him just what she thought he could do with his corner and his ten percent.

"You of all people should know what a small, close-knit group the *ton* is, Lil. The House of Lords is even smaller and has the fortune—or misfortune, depending on how you look at it—of being all male. Sooner or later, someone in your ninety percent will be affected by gaming, whether he takes a big loss himself or sees a friend, brother or son do the same. Perhaps one or two wives will take a tumble as well."

"You're talking nonsense," she snapped, but he'd broken though her composure, he could see. "What you are talking about would take years."

"Would it? I don't think so." He lowered his head so that their breaths mingled. "I think it could happen fairly quickly with the right person pushing it along, reminding them. And when they look for someone other than themselves to blame, they're going to turn to you—the outsider, the *woman*—to shoulder the responsibility of tempting them to their ruin."

She glared at him, her anger so obvious he almost drew back from it. "I could make a fine example out of you, Lilith. I could make you a ruiner of men. After all, look at what you did to me."

She bolted from the chair, pushing him aside with a strength that was both surprising and encouraging. She was not a woman who would give up without a fight. She had her convictions. He hoped honesty was one of them.

"The only thing I ever did to you was love you more than

you deserved," she informed him hotly. "I don't know what you hoped to gain by coming here tonight, Gabriel, but if your intention was to bully me into closing down my club, you are going to be sorely disappointed."

His lips twisted. "You've only disappointed me once, Lil. I haven't decided whether or not I'm going to let you do it again."

She inhaled deeply. The action pushed the lush expanse of her bosom upward, pulling the golden fabric of her gown taut against the impressive swells. She was fairly trembling in rage. The sight of it shouldn't please him as much as it did, but he'd spent the past ten years being so angry with her that it was good to know he could still get to her so easily.

"You must realize that your very presence in my club is a detriment to your argument, Lord Angelwood."

And he rather liked the way she wasn't sure of what to call him. She skipped back and forth between his name and his title so much, he wondered if she was aware that she was doing it.

"Not at all," he responded cheerfully. "I'm merely adhering to the adage 'Know thine enemy.' How can I fight what I don't know?"

He closed the distance between them, taking advantage of her stony silence. Wrapping one hand around the warm curve of her neck, he pulled her flush against him, ignoring her cry of outrage.

"And I think we both agree, Lil, that you and I know each other *intimately.*"

His lips descended upon hers, silencing her protests with a need that shook him to the soles of his feet. He hadn't meant to kiss her, but he couldn't help it. After so many years of missing her, of remembering just how sweet she'd tasted, he'd had no choice but to put his mouth to hers. His tongue traced the bow of her lips, slid over the smooth surface of her teeth. She tasted of cream and nutmeg, sweet and spicy and as warm as pudding.

She didn't encourage him by mating her tongue with his. But neither did she try to stop him. It was as though she was waiting . . . waiting for him to make the decision for her.

Reluctantly, he withdrew his hand from her neck and brought it up to cup her cheek. He brought his other hand up to do the same. He had held her like this the first time he'd kissed her, because he was afraid she'd turn away or tell him to stop.

The sound she made this time was very much like a sob, and Gabe's heart shattered at the sweetness of it. She hadn't forgotten, no more than he had. And when he deepened the kiss he felt her arms come up between them, so that her fingers clutched the lapels of his jacket, just as they had with that first kiss.

Something was happening and if he didn't stop it soon, they'd end up on the floor and he wouldn't be able to fulfill his promise to Blaine, let alone to his father.

But part of him knew it would be worth it just to feel Lilith wrapped around him again.

But it was she who pulled away first. With her lips red and wet, she clung to his jacket and stared at him with an expression that was a mix of happiness and horror.

"Enemy," she whispered.

Ice water in the face couldn't have been more effective. Gabriel dropped his hands. She released him as he drew away.

"Are you going to leave?" She asked the question as if she already knew the answer.

He wanted to. Right then, Gabriel wanted nothing more than to get as far away from her as possible so he could clear his head.

"No," he replied, watching the surprise flicker across her features. "I still haven't seen everything I came to see."

"Well, you are not going to see anything skulking about in my private office."

He didn't have a response to that, so he didn't even bother to try.

Smoothing a hand over her already impeccable hair-style, Lilith moved to the desk. She withdrew a key from her cleavage—God, how he envied that key!—and inserted it in one of the drawers.

When the drawer was locked again, she came back around and held out her hand to him. There were gaming markers in her palm. About a hundred pounds' worth.

"Here," she said, lifting her hand. "The only way to find out what kind of establishment I run is to play."

Her generosity was astounding and Gabriel couldn't help but wonder what she hoped to achieve.

"No, thank you. I don't play. The last gamble I took was with you."

It was the wrong thing to say. The strange truce brought about by their kiss was ruined by his careless remark.

Lilith's fingers tightened around the markers. Her knuckles whitened as she made a fist. Did she plan to plant a facer on him? He still hadn't recovered from that slap.

"Well, we both know which one of us lost that one, my lord. Care to settle the score?"

"Lost?" he echoed, not bothering to pretend he had mis-understood. "I seem to remember it being offered willingly."

She flushed again, but not so deeply this time. Twin crim-son splotches blossomed on the ivory smoothness of her cheeks. She'd always had skin like porcelain, and that foolish powder she wore only made it paler.

"There are worse things for a woman to lose than her virtue, Lord Angelwood," came the frosty reply. "Her pride and reputation, to name but two. If she's particularly foolish, then she loses her heart as well."

"I lost, too, Lily," he told her, his voice little more than a whisper. "What about that?"

He watched her throat as she swallowed. Was she going to cry? He didn't know what he'd do if she cried.

"What do you know of loss?" Her fist cleaved the air be-tween them as she brought it down. "Which one of us ended up a social outcast? Which one of us can't show our face in public without having people whisper and sneer as she walks by? You still have your friends. Where are mine?"

The emotional force of her outburst leveled Gabriel. He opened his mouth to respond, to say something, anything that might ease the anguish in her gaze, but she cut him off.

"If you believe yourself to be the injured party in our affair, you are greatly mistaken. You seem to be living the life you were supposed to, while mine has taken a turn no one could ever have predicted." Her eyes glittered with wetness as she hugged herself. "Tell me, Gabriel, which one of us do you think has the most regrets?"

Gabriel swallowed hard against the lump in his throat. He couldn't do this. Not anymore. Not tonight.

"I have many regrets, Lilith. Loving you wasn't one of them."

He didn't wait to hear her reply. As soon as the damnable words left his mouth, he turned on his heel and swept out of the office through the main door. To hell with poking around the club trying to gather information. He had to get out of there. Blaine would simply have to wait.

His enemy knew him all too well.

What did he mean, he didn't regret loving her?

It had been two days since Lilith had found Gabriel in her office and she had yet to put the meeting—or that kiss—out of her mind.

More important, what had he been doing snooping around *her* club—*her* office? He'd been looking for something, but what? Thank God she kept all the club records in her private office upstairs.

Whatever his motives, he hadn't come solely to see her. Lilith knew that for certain.

She also had no doubt that he would have made love to her if she hadn't stopped him. She'd been tempted to let him do just that. When he held her as he had all those years ago, it was as though they were back there again, and for a moment she let herself believe she was seventeen and that he loved her. But then sanity returned, and thank heavens for it. She would have despised herself for being so weak. After ten years of little intimate contact with men, it would be disgusting to realize that Gabriel was the only one who could persuade her beyond reason with only a kiss.

She was sitting at the desk in the same office where that kiss had taken place. From time to time her gaze drifted to the spot where they'd stood, or to the chair she'd been in when he hovered above her. More often than she liked, her attention went to where he had sat on the desk. She didn't even have to close her eyes to envision how the fabric of his trousers pulled across the heavy muscle of his thighs, or how his jacket strained at the shoulders.

He was taller than she remembered, and bigger. So much bigger. How did a nobleman get that big? Only hard work and physical activity led to a body like that. And if Gabriel had to resort to physical labor for some reason, she wanted to know why. She wanted to know all his secrets. If he truly was out to get her as he had intimated, she would need every weapon at her disposal to fight back. That was why she had given every one of her contacts the task of finding out whatever they could about the Earl of Angelwood.

Such as why he was so set against gambling. His father had loved a good game of chance, and rumor had it that the old earl had been shot in a duel over gaming debts. Lilith wasn't so certain she believed that story. It was hard to imagine anyone shooting someone as lovable as Gabriel's father; besides, no one had ever admitted to being the one to pull the trigger. In fact, not even the gossips knew for certain who his opponent had been.

Was that why Gabriel hated gaming so? Because his father had been supposedly killed over a debt?

Even if she believed the rumors about the late earl's death, Gabriel's battle against gaming seemed a rather gigantic task for a young man to undertake. A task that could never be realized. Of course, Gabriel wouldn't see it that way. He always believed that anything was possible if one worked hard enough.

Hadn't he courted her in much the same way? Flirting and being charming and doing everything he could to worm his way inside her heart and bed before tossing her aside.

Yesterday she'd discovered that many of her patrons had thought it a great joke not to tell her of Gabriel's campaign against gambling. Her informants around town advised her that those who actually believed he had a leg to stand on thought it smashing fun to sit back and speculate as to what would happen when Lilith and Gabriel met again. Others simply didn't see him as a threat. Normally Lilith wouldn't, either, but she knew him well enough to understand that he wouldn't give up easily.

At least she had had the small victory of watching him depart the club immediately after he left her. She'd unsettled him enough that he couldn't continue with his original plan.

He'd unsettled her enough that she didn't even want to get out of bed the next morning.

Aunt Imogen would have teased her for being such a coward. Men were nothing to be afraid of, as far as she'd been concerned. A woman only had to find a man's weakness and she could control him as easily as a trained poodle. *And a man doesn't need to be walked every day*, she'd concluded.

Lilith smiled at the memory. She missed Aunt Imogen. The old woman had taught her to stand on her own two feet, to not care what people said or thought. The only person Lilith had to answer to and for was herself. She was never to forget that.

Aunt Imogen had left her an independent, rich woman. So what if she didn't have a reputation? Not a good one, anyway. She was free of society's dictates. She could do whatever she wanted. Live wherever she wanted. Love whomever she wanted.

How unfortunate that Lilith's heart had seen fit to love only one man.

A knock at the door thankfully put a halt to the direction

of her thoughts. Lilith didn't want to think of Gabriel any-more. Not for a little while at least.

"Come in!"

It was Mary, carrying a tea tray and the day's paper. "You've been locked up in here all morning. I thought you might enjoy a nice cuppa."

Oh, yes, tea would be divine. "You're a savior, Mary. Will you join me?"

They sat on the sofa. The burgundy upholstery was well padded and the extra cushions provided even more comfort. It was a good thing she hadn't discovered that when Gabriel was there, for she might not have regained her senses.

Enough. She was *not* going to think of Gabriel, not when she had to think of some way to replace the shipment of co-gnac that was supposed to arrive yesterday. It had been de-stroyed by vandals between the docks and the club.

Were they still vandals when you knew whom they worked for? There was no doubt in Lilith's mind that the men were in Bronson's employ. Far from intimidating her, the rival club owner was quickly becoming a nuisance. If she allowed these little attacks of his to continue, they could spiral out of control.

"Any good news this morning?" Lilith asked, lifting the cup of hot, fragrant tea to her lips. It was heaven.

Mary hesitated for the briefest moment before handing her the paper. "I'm not sure how good it is, but I think you'll be interested in what's on page seven."

Intrigued by the older woman's apprehensive expression, Lilith opened the paper to page seven. It took her only a few seconds to find the article Mary meant.

It was the society page.

Lately, this writer heard that a certain heavenly earl was seen socializing at one of the city's most opulent of social clubs. This would not be such a delicious occurrence were it not for the fact that this lord has made it his mission to abolish gaming in our fair city, and that the owner of said establishment is a lady with whom Lord A once had an intimate acquaintance. Anyone care to make a wager as to whether or not the lady will persuade Lord A to give up his quest?

She'd told him his visit to her club wouldn't go unnoticed. She should feel happy about the fact that society was questioning his motives, but all she felt was tired.

Lilith fought to keep her expression blank as she tossed the paper aside. "You'd think they'd have something better to prattle about than a decade-old scandal."

Mary's gaze held no censure, but her tone showed she was hurt. "You didn't tell me Lord Angelwood came here."

"I didn't tell anyone." What good would telling have done? It wouldn't change anything, wouldn't have made seeing him any easier.

Mary's warm fingers clasped the cold hand that lay on the brocade between them. "Are you all right?"

Lilith squeezed the woman's hand before withdrawing her own. Mary's friendship was one of the most treasured of her life, but she didn't want to get emotional. She'd given Gabriel enough tears.

Setting her saucer in her lap, she lifted her cup with both hands, warming them. Smiling self-consciously, she fixed her attention on a tea leaf stuck to the rim. "For years I've imagined what my reunion with him would be like. On good days he tells me he suffered a life-threatening illness, or was abducted by pirates on his way to find me. He begs for my forgiveness. Whether or not he gets it depends on my mood."

"And on bad days?"

Lilith twisted her head to meet Mary's frank gaze. "On bad days he tells me I wasn't worth coming after."

She wasn't certain what she expected her friend's reaction to be, but she was relieved when all Mary did was nod.

Taking a sip of her tea, Lilith puckered her brow. "In all my daydreams he never challenged my being the injured party."

Mary spooned more sugar into her cup. "But he did when you saw him?"

Lilith nodded, still frowning. "Mary, he spoke as though *he* was the one who had been betrayed, as though I owed him."

I could make a fine example out of you, Lilith. I could make you a ruiner of men. After all, look what you did to me.

Mary raised her cup. "Interesting. He didn't explain himself?"

Shaking her head, Lilith placed her cup and saucer on the table. "He acted as though I should know." How could that be?

The night of her mother's ball, she and Gabriel had sneaked away for some privacy. She took him to her chamber, where, trembling and eager they had shared their bodies and pledged their love. They hadn't been caught until much later, when Lilith's mother and a friend came to see if Lilith was indisposed—she'd been gone so long. They found them at the mirror, Gabriel helping Lilith repair her hair. Both were fully dressed, and the bed had been straightened, but one look at them was enough to ascertain what had been going on. A particularly nasty moment later, her mother said she could smell Lilith's wickedness the minute she walked into the room. Many years passed before Lilith realized what she'd meant.

The next day, the entire *ton* knew of the scandal. No one came to call. Her friends sent her notes back unanswered. Invitations ceased to arrive and still Gabriel didn't come. Two days after that, her father decided to dispatch her to Italy.

She sent Gabriel a letter telling him what was going on. When he didn't reply immediately, she attributed his silence to the death of his father—a tragedy that tore at Lilith's heart because she wasn't allowed to leave the house to share her grief with Gabe and his mother. But when no reply arrived at all, she began to wonder if perhaps he had been using her.

Two days later, she set sail and Gabriel still hadn't come. She wrote to him from Aunt Imogen's villa, letting him know where she was. Never once did she receive a reply.

So just where did he get the idea that she was the one to blame? And more important, how far would he take this vendetta against her?

Most of Mallory's was aboveboard, but the back rooms were used for private gaming and Lilith knew that sometimes that gaming included illegal dice games. If Gabriel happened upon one of them, he could make life very difficult for her indeed. And if he started poisoning her customers against her . . .

She was just going to have to stop him. But how could she fight him when women weren't allowed to argue in the House of Lords? Gabriel could say whatever he wanted to about her there, yet she could never defend herself.

Or could she?

"Mary, will you have a boy go round to Lord Somerville's? Have him tell the earl I need—no, *wish*—to see him at his earliest convenience. And also, have someone send for Mr. Francis."

Mary's nose wrinkled at the mention of Lilith's loyal but somewhat questionable business associate. "What need do you have of *that* man? Either of them, for that matter."

Lilith poured herself another cup of tea. "Mr. Francis is going to find out exactly what the Earl of Angelwood has been up to these past ten years. Help me know my enemy, so to speak."

"And the earl?"

Learning back against the sofa cushions, Lilith smiled smugly. "Lord Somerville is going to help me keep my ninety percent."

"What you are doing is blackmail."

Bracing her forearms on the desk, Lilith smiled at the red-faced man sitting across from her. "That's a nasty word, Lord Somerville. What I'm doing is looking out for what is best for each of us."

Lord Somerville didn't look very impressed. In fact, he looked very much like a spaniel Lilith's mother once had. A good dog. Not too quick on the uptake, though.

"I have no intention of telling Lady Somerville about your . . . *sessions* with Lady Wyndham. Do you think Lord Angelwood can make the same promise?"

Somerville shrugged his narrow shoulders. Every man seemed to have narrow shoulders now that Lilith had Gabriel's to compare them to.

"Angelwood's always seemed like the honorable sort. At least he was before he left for the Colonies. Can't see how he would have changed."

Lilith arched a knowing brow. "So honorable that he didn't even make a declaration of marriage to the young girl he ruined?"

It was a cheap shot—at both herself and Gabriel—but it was worth it if it made Lord Somerville question Gabriel's integrity. From what Lilith had gleaned, Gabriel was held up as something of a paragon by most members of the *ton*.

"Allow me to make this easier for you, my lord." If she made it any easier, she'd be doing it herself. "As far as I'm concerned, you and Lady Wyndham do nothing more daring in my private parlors than indulge in a friendly game of whist."

Somerville's telltale blush made that theory even more ludicrous than it sounded.

"But Lord Angelwood doesn't even want you to do that. He doesn't want gaming of any kind, so if you and Lady Wyndham can't play whist here, where are you going to play it? If Lord Angelwood succeeds in outlawing gaming, you will have a hard time finding any place, let alone an establishment such as Mallory's, that allows both gentlemen and ladies to come and go without suspicion."

Lord Somerville understood her now. She could see it dawning in his puppylike eyes. The whole conversation left a bad taste in Lilith's mouth. She wasn't above using blackmail when necessary to achieve her ends, but it was an unsavory business. At least Somerville stood to lose if Gabriel succeeded in ruining her for a second time. She'd meant it when she said he and Lady Wyndham would have a hard time finding another place to meet, and while she despised the act of adultery, two consenting adults could do whatever they wanted in her back rooms, provided she didn't have to know about it.

No doubt they had their reasons. Perhaps they were in love. If they were, Lilith felt sorry for the pair of them. Love didn't mean anything once a man's body parts became involved. Hadn't she learned that lesson well enough herself?

"So," Lilith piped up when Somerville remained silent, "do we have an agreement?"

The earl nodded eagerly and Lilith realized just how young he was. Too young to be unhappy in his marriage and diddling with another woman. Would she and Gabriel have ended up the same way if they had married? Would he have tired of her so soon?

"Good." Smiling, she withdrew several sheets of paper from a desk drawer. "I've taken the liberty of writing your speech. Shall we go through it together?"

Again Somerville nodded. "Are you certain you won't tell anyone about Hen—Lady Wyndham and myself?"

Lilith's smile deepened, became almost coy as she noticed his cheeks redden slightly and his gaze turn embarrassed.

"Lord Somerville, I assure you that I am the very soul of discretion."

Grinning happily now, the young earl took the papers from her and began reading. Lilith almost sighed aloud in relief.

If Gabriel Warren thought he was going to ruin her so easily a second time, he was in for a big surprise.

Chapter 3

Where the hell had Somerville come from?

And more important, how had he managed it?

His jaw tight, Gabriel followed the younger man as he left the Court of Requests, one of the old chambers where the House of Lords met. Somerville was going to meet someone, which Gabriel determined from the way the earl glanced around to make certain he wasn't being followed.

That Somerville didn't see him only proved Gabriel right about the man's lack of intelligence. Somerville was a good man and friendly to a fault, but he hadn't the intelligence or the wit to write the speech he'd just given in front of the House.

Gabriel's cause had made more than one peer shake his bewigged head and roll his eyes, but they always allowed Gabriel to have his say. Some even agreed with many of his points—especially when he mentioned the number of peers who had been ruined by gambling in recent years. When he finally sat down, Gabriel felt as though he had finally gained some ground. Then Somerville stood.

His firm conviction that gambling shouldn't be outlawed had roused the mood of the room to a fevered pitch. He talked of God-given rights, liberty and a better future. Hogwash, all of it, but if Somerville had suggested they try to overthrow the throne, half the men in that chamber would have been behind him.

Gabriel knew only one person who had that much passion to write such a speech. A person who stood to lose everything if he succeeded in having gambling outlawed.

Lilith.

He'd heard her voice in that speech almost as though she had been standing there, saying the words instead of Somerville. If anyone else noticed Somerville's sudden gift for oratory, he was too caught up in the words to realize they'd been placed in the young lord's mouth by someone else. But Gabriel knew. And he'd wager—yes, wager—his last ten quid that Lilith had written that speech.

He knew she'd try to find a way to fight him. He just hadn't expected her to act quickly and effectively. Her words had made his own speech seem dull and spiritless, despite all the truth and facts it contained. Still, he knew several members had begun to see things his way. He would not lose their support, especially not to a woman who might have made her fortune by cozening other people out of their money.

His suspicions were confirmed as he followed Somerville out into the street. The fair-haired man opened his umbrella against the rain and headed straight to a black-laquered carriage fronted by four chestnut horses. It didn't bear Somerville's crest and it was too fancy to be a hack. As the door opened, Gabriel caught a glimpse of familiar red hair beneath a flamboyant, flower-laden hat.

Fastening his greatcoat around him to ward off the damp, he shoved his beaver hat down on his skull and folded his arms across his chest. Standing there under the arch, barely sheltered from the rain, he must have looked ridiculous, but he didn't care. He was going to wait until Somerville exited her carriage and then he was going to have a chat with Lady Lilith Mallory.

Ten minutes later, he was still waiting.

By God, if Somerville stayed in there with her much longer, Gabriel was going to haul him out by the throat.

Just when he thought such force might be necessary—when he imagined one too many things that might be going on inside the carriage—the door opened again and Somerville leapt out.

Gathering his resolve, Gabriel grimly set out toward the street. He didn't even make it three steps before Lilith took matters into her own hands.

"Gabriel, darling!"

Nothing like attracting attention. Every passerby, every lord exiting the House behind him, stopped to appreciate the sight of Lilith leaning out of her carriage. Wearing a gold-colored pelisse and a hat with huge gold and rose cabbage roses pinned to the front of the upturned brim, she was a vision of radiance in the otherwise gray and dismal street.

"Do come join me!" she cried, a seductive smile on her full lips.

"She wouldn't have to ask me twice," a gentleman behind Gabriel remarked. Gabriel didn't turn to see who it was. He was too busy trying to plan just how he was going to kill her. Strangulation sounded good.

Her smug expression faltered somewhat as he stomped toward her. But she leaned back and allowed him to step into the carriage. She didn't even protest when he shut the door.

Not smart, Lil. I could have your skirts up around your ears before you even thought to scream.

Would she scream for him to stop or to continue?

It was the anger that made him so randy for her. It had to be. He'd had more sexual thoughts in the past three days than he'd had in the past three years. He hadn't been a monk since losing her, but finding her again certainly made him feel as though he had.

"What are you up to, Lilith?"

She pouted. It didn't look right on her. "Now, Gabriel, there's no need to be so cross."

He scowled at the lush, carmine curve of her lower lip. She was wearing cosmetics again.

"You look like a harlot." *Angelwood, you are a bastard.*

Lilith blinked, and for a second the cool, sophisticated veneer she presented disappeared. What was left was the vulnerable young girl he'd fallen in love with. It was like a punch in the gut.

The mask slipped back into place as she ran a gloved palm along his thigh. "Haven't you heard, Gabriel? *I am* a harlot. You made me one."

Checkmate.

He caught her hand in his, lifting it from his leg. For a split second he was tempted to settle that hot little palm against his crotch. She pulled her fingers away before he could decide.

"Is that the hold you have over Somerville? You're having an affair with him?" A bitter taste settled in his mouth.

Leaning back against the squabs, Lilith lifted the window blind long enough to peer out at the rain and then dropped it again. She didn't bother to smile when she turned her attention back to him.

"Not that it's any of your business, but no, Lord Somerville is not my lover. He did offer once, but that was quite some time ago. Is that what you wanted to hear?"

By God, he should have hauled the little cur out of the carriage by the throat.

"So he's arguing your case in Parliament to ingratiate himself into your bed, is that it?" Why were they even having this discussion? Whom Lilith shared her bed with was none of his concern.

But the fact that it wasn't him chafed like an overstarched cravat.

"No," she replied as though she agreed that he was a complete idiot. "Lord Somerville helps me because he does not want to see me lose my club. Now, let's change the subject, shall we?"

Gabriel shrugged. Anything as long as he didn't have to think about her in bed with someone else.

"I'd like to invite you to be my guest at dinner tonight."

He couldn't have heard her correctly. "I beg your pardon?"

She tried again, slowly this time. "I said, I would like you to join me for dinner."

The sight of those full lips accentuating every word caused the beast between his legs to raise its head. Literally.

He was dubious at best. "For dinner? At your club?"

She nodded.

"What the devil for?"

She didn't look so certain of herself now. "Because I think we have much to discuss."

It was his turn to be in control. Stretching his legs out before him, Gabriel linked his fingers across his abdomen. "Such as?"

Lilith scowled as he made himself comfortable. "Such as, how does a man of your social position come to have the body of a laborer?"

Gabriel's breath caught at the question, but he kept his expression guarded. "Why, Lilith, have you been studying my body?"

She didn't even blush—even as her gaze dropped to his groin, a groin that tightened further under scrutiny. Damn her.

"That's a bit hypocritical coming from a man who had his tongue in my mouth two nights ago, don't you think?"

Warmth crept up his cheeks, but it wasn't embarrassment that caused it. "You've always had a fine mouth."

That got a reaction from her. Her frustration with him was almost tangible. Inhaling a deep breath through her nose, Lilith met his gaze with barely concealed impatience. "Will you come to dinner or not?"

If he pushed her any further, she might rescind the invitation, and despite the fact that they didn't agree when it came to gambling or which one of them had been in the wrong ten years ago, Gabriel wanted to spend the evening with her. Even if it meant walking into a trap.

Besides, it might allow him to do a little snooping. Perhaps if he repeated that possibility long enough, his heart would cease its frenzied pounding.

"I would be honored to join you for dinner."

She smiled, her relief obvious. "Good. Shall we say eight o'clock?"

"I shall be there." Rising, he opened the carriage door and stepped out into the wet afternoon. "Oh—and, Lilith?" He stuck his head back inside.

"Yes?"

"If you dare wear any of that ridiculous face paint, I'll leave."

"This won't do. Give me the other one."

Clifford, Gabriel's saintly valet, rolled his dark eyes heavenward and handed his employer the coat of dark blue superfine. Again.

"I think this one looks better," Gabriel remarked, shrugging into the coat. He tugged at the cuffs. "What do you think?"

"An excellent choice, my lord." The valet's tone was completely devoid of inflection.

Gabriel scowled at his reflection in the mirror. The reflection scowled back. "I don't know. Maybe I should go with the claret."

Clifford cleared his throat as Gabriel began to remove the coat—for the third time. "I don't mean to be impertinent, my lord, but it is half past seven."

Damn! He was going to be late, and all because of his vanity. It wasn't that he wanted to impress Lilith. He just didn't care to leave the house not looking his best.

Yes. That was it.

"Are you certain this one is the best?"

Clifford nodded sagely. "I am, my lord. The lady will not be able to resist you."

Gabriel snorted. His valet knew clothes, but he knew absolutely nothing about women if he thought a well-knotted cravat and the right coat could persuade a woman like Lilith to let him have his way with her.

Regardless, there wasn't time to change again. As it was, he ran the risk of being late if traffic was the least bit thick. He lived in Mayfair, and practically every coach on its way out of that section of town would be heading in the same direction as his—toward St. James's Street and King Street, toward the clubs, Lilith's being one of them.

She hadn't placed Mallory's on St. James's, next to such male bastions as White's and Brook's. Instead, she'd boldly positioned it on King Street, just a short walk from Almack's, a place that wouldn't even let a woman like her in the door. They'd danced their first waltz at Almack's.

Gabriel checked his appearance one last time. He hadn't been this nervous since he'd made love to Lilith all those years ago. He didn't fool himself into thinking that was what she had planned for him tonight. If Lilith did set out to seduce him, love would have very little to do with it. And thanks to his mother's countless affairs, Gabriel knew that that kind of emptiness was not something he wanted.

He didn't bother to entertain the idea that Lilith might still harbor feelings for him. But she was no more immune physically to him than he was to her, and that was something Gabriel might be able to use to his advantage if he kept his wits about him.

"Did you get the flowers?" He made for the door.

Clifford followed. "Yes, my lord. They're waiting for you downstairs."

As was Robinson with his coat, hat and gloves. The butler looked like a lowly rook on the chessboard marble floor, his demeanor so solemn, one might think Gabriel was going off to meet his executioner.

If only Robinson knew the truth, that just seeing Lilith

again—rising to the challenge she offered him—made Gabriel feel more alive than he had in years. He would enjoy going up against her because she would be as ruthless as he. He didn't want to destroy her, although he would be lying if he said there wasn't some part of him that wanted to hurt her as she had hurt him. Personal feelings aside, he couldn't forget that Frederick Foster claimed she had cheated him.

He couldn't forget his father and what gambling had cost him. What it had cost Gabriel himself.

"Have a good evening, my lord," the butler said in his usual gruff tones.

Gabriel smiled. "I sincerely doubt it, Robinson, but thank you all the same."

As he left the house and jogged down the steps to where his carriage waited in the drive, Gabriel couldn't help but wonder if it would be possible for him to keep his personal feelings separate when it came to dealing with Lilith. When Blaine had come to him a week ago, he'd had no trouble accepting Frederick's side of the story, but that was before he'd discovered who the owner of Mallory's was. Perhaps Lilith didn't know that her employees were cheating. If that was the case, he owed it not only to Frederick, but to Lilith as well to uncover the truth.

What would happen to her if he succeeded in convincing Parliament to outlaw gambling? Oh, he knew she said it would never happen and some days he believed her, but he had his convictions and he would stick to them.

Would Lilith leave England again if he closed her club? The thought of losing her once more cut him deep inside. This was ridiculous. The only reason Lilith had any power over him was because he didn't know what had taken place. All they had to do was be honest with each other, and then there wouldn't be this tension between them. They would be able to get on with their lives and he would halt her operations and that would be the end of it.

Yes. The end of it. All he had to do was ask her what had gone wrong. Why she had left. He would have married her if she'd stayed, and then her reputation would have remained relatively unsullied. He'd wanted to marry her. He'd even had a ring. He still had it. She could have been his countess these past ten years rather than a . . . a . . .

An independent businesswoman with no one but herself to answer to? A wealthy, powerful woman who held the fortunes of those who snubbed her in the palm of her hand? Would her life have been so much better if they'd married?

Perhaps not, but his would have been.

They probably would have had a houseful of children by now. They would spend most of their time in the country and visiting friends, such as Brave and Rachel and their child. A child he had yet to see.

He couldn't bring himself to make the trip to Yorkshire. He was happy for his friend, but he couldn't be around all that love and the things he might never have. He *should* have those things. He wanted them badly enough.

And what really rankled him was the fact that every time he thought about being a father, it was Lilith he pictured as the woman bearing his children.

Staring out the window at the passing scenery, he tried to put that image out of his mind.

The traffic wasn't too thick, and before he knew it, they were rolling up in front of Mallory's.

Gabriel and his flowers were met at the door by a large, pleasant-looking fellow who introduced himself as Latimer, Lilith's butler, doorman and all-around man of affairs. He seemed friendly enough, but Gabriel had a sneaky suspicion that Latimer wouldn't hesitate to take his head clean off his shoulders if he thought Gabriel was a threat to Lilith.

He wasn't sure if the fact that the man was treating him as though he *wasn't* a threat bothered him or not.

He followed Latimer's lanky form through the sumptuous blue entrance hall, pausing for a moment to admire the statue of Venus in the center. Had Lilith posed for this? If she had, she'd posed nude.

Gabriel was filled with a sudden desire to break both of the sculptor's hands, even as his own fingers itched to touch the Venus's plump thigh.

They exited the hall via a door to the left. Down a quiet corridor to the end. Latimer turned the knob for him, bowed and left him with a gentle yet warning glance.

The door swung open, revealing a large, inviting parlor decorated in shades of cream, beige and gold.

Lilith stood in the center of the patterned carpet, breathtakingly beautiful in a gown of rich gold satin. Her only jewelry was the diamonds dangling from her ear lobes. Her hair looked almost crimson in the lamplight, piled up on her head so that one thick chunk waved heavily over one shoulder.

But it wasn't the sight of her hair that Gabriel found arousing, nor was it because the neckline of her gown displayed a generous amount of her shoulders and impressive bosom, although both certainly played a part in the stirring in his loins.

It was that she wore not even the barest touch of paint on her face. Her eyes, her smooth cheeks, her incredibly voluptuous pink lips were completely naked to his gaze.

She'd done as he'd asked. The knowledge was humbling—and so fiercely arousing that he found it difficult not to say to hell with dinner and have her instead.

"Hello, Gabriel," she purred in that honey-smooth voice of hers when he'd embarrassed himself by being stupidly silent. "Won't you come in?"

"Why do I get the feeling that once I come in, there's no turning back?"

Lilith's mouth was as dry as sawdust as Gabriel shut the door and prowled across the carpet toward her. His thick black hair waved back from the rugged cast of his features, and his eyes glittered like diamonds beneath his arched brows.

"Now, Gabriel, do I look that dangerous to you?" Thank God she sounded cockier than she felt.

"Yes," he replied, extending a bouquet of bright orange flowers toward her. "A woman as lovely as you is extremely dangerous to a man with no defenses."

She shouldn't let his flattery sway her, but she couldn't stop the tremor that raced up her spine as the deep, melodic timbre of his voice flowed over her. She couldn't even meet his gaze when she accepted the flowers, afraid that he would see just how deeply he affected her.

"Thank you." She cradled the blooms to her chest, her heart bursting as she realized what they were. "Lilies." Her voice was little more than a hoarse squeak in her own ears. Damn him! She would not cry. *She . . . would . . . not . . . cry.*

"I thought you might like them."

She looked at him. Really looked. And behind the composed mask she saw a glimmer of vulnerability in his eyes. Could it be that the bright, delicate flowers weren't meant to be a painful reminder of his nickname for her, but rather a pleasant one?

She wished she could bring herself to totally believe it. Hadn't he told her in so many words that he was going to do his best to suspend her club business? She wouldn't put it past him to try to soften her up this way. She'd do it to him.

"Thank you." And she meant it, regardless of his motives. The lilies were beautiful.

The table was set for their meal. A vase of roses sat in the middle of the Brussels lace, surrounded by china and silverware. Lilith removed the flowers from the vase and tossed them unceremoniously into the hearth. The small fire spat at the offering.

The smell of burned roses hanging in the air, Lilith filled the vase with the lilies.

"I hope those weren't from another admirer."

He meant it as a joke, she could tell from his tone, but there was an underlying note of seriousness in his voice. He seemed to harbor some kind of perverse interest in her romantic life. Did he think that just because she'd been foolish enough to make love with him at age seventeen, she hadn't learned to be more selective over the years? Her body was not something she shared freely. He should know that.

"I have no admirers." Her gaze locked with his. "Only gentlemen who think a woman like me should be thankful for their advances."

His face darkened, the murderous expression of a possessive man.

Oh, Gabe, you've no right. No right to me at all.

"If anyone has harmed you—"

Lilith silenced him with a wave of her hand. "No one has done anything. Do you think I've survived these past ten years on blind luck? I can take care of myself and anyone else who comes along, Gabriel. Of that you may have no doubt."

He nodded, a stiff jerk of his head. He was angry. Whether or not the emotion was directed toward her, she had no idea, although she rather liked the idea of him being jealous. After so many years of having no one to give a damn, it was a comforting feeling.

"Will you have some wine?" She lifted the bottle from the bucket, where it sat chilling. "It's one of those sweet German whites you always used to like."

His generous lower lip curved slightly. "It was you who always liked sweet wines, not me."

"But—" She looked from him to the bottle and back again. She couldn't have been wrong. "You told me you liked them."

Gabriel chuckled. Oh, how she had missed that sound! "I said that because you liked them. I would have said I liked walking on broken glass if I thought you liked that, too."

And he would have. Over the years, Lilith came to believe his devotion had been merely a clever ruse to get into her drawers, but now . . . Was it possible that he really had loved her as much as she'd loved him?

If that was true, then what had happened? What had she done . . . ?

Oh, no! None of that. She'd spent enough time crying and wondering if the blame was hers. She thought she'd put that firmly behind her. She was not the one to blame. She couldn't fight her parents, not without Gabriel beside her, and he'd been conveniently absent when they called her a whore, and when they'd put her on that boat to Italy.

"I still like them." The old resentment rising within her made her tone a little chillier than she'd intended.

His smile faltered a little. "Then I would love a glass."

It was all Lilith could do not to fling the bottle at him. How, when they were supposed to be enemies, could he just open up and make himself vulnerable like this?

Very easily. He obviously didn't mean a word he said. He was merely trying to wear her down and get the upper hand. Well, two could play at that.

She poured them each a glass, and plastering what she hoped was a seductive smile on her face, she put a little extra swing in her hips and carried both glasses to the sofa.

Glancing over her shoulder, she saw that he was still standing by the dining table. "Aren't you going to come sit with me?"

She didn't need to ask twice. Gabriel moved toward her with the natural grace of someone comfortable in his own skin. It was a predominantly male trait, most women being too occupied with not tripping over their hems, or wondering if their hair looked all right, to just relax.

He'd grown into a fine figure of a man. As a youth, he'd been mostly arms and legs and shoulders. And arrogant! Oh, he'd thought he was such a prize catch. Always teasing her with glimpses of his body, as though he expected the mere sight of him to drive her into a frenzy of desire. She had to admit that sometimes it had. At seventeen, she'd never seen anything finer than Gabriel Warren.

At seven-and-twenty, she still hadn't.

He took the glass of wine she offered and seated himself beside her on the sofa. Oh, dear. She hadn't expected him to sit so close. The sofa was too small for them to sit comfortably. Lilith's hips and Gabriel's shoulders put them a little closer than was proper. Close enough that Lilith could smell him—clean and spicy and that warm, sweet scent that was undeniably Gabe. Like pie, straight from the oven.

He turned to face her. "Why did you invite me here, Lil?"

She opened her mouth to speak, but he cut her off. "Be honest. Were you hoping to somehow change how I feel about gambling?"

"Yes," she admitted. "I was. Just as you were hoping to soften me up by bringing me flowers."

Gabriel shook his head, his expression grim. "I brought you flowers because I wanted to. You can't change my mind, Lil. No one can."

For some reason, his words hurt. It didn't matter that he said *no one* could change his mind. All that mattered was that he said *she* couldn't.

"Why?" she demanded, setting her glass on the table in front of them and rising to her feet. "Are you so determined to ruin me a second time?"

He stood as well, staring at her as if she were speaking a language he didn't understand. "Ruin you? You think I want to abolish gaming just to ruin you?"

"Abolishing gambling will ruin me, Gabriel. Mallory's is the only thing I have. It's the only thing that matters. You take it away from me and I am ruined."

Lilith could see in his eyes that he didn't like the responsibility of that. "I don't want to ruin you."

"You did it before."

"I didn't mean to."

"But you did."

"You left me."

Left him? He thought she left him?

"I didn't leave you!" She punctuated the retort with a jab in his chest. It hurt her finger. "You didn't come forth with an offer of marriage and my parents sent me away rather than deal with the scandal."

He rubbed his breast where she'd poked it. "My father had just died!"

Balling her hands into fists, Lilith stepped up so that their torsos barely touched. "You were supposed to be in love with me, Gabe, and you didn't even tell me your father had died. I had to read it in the papers." How that had hurt to find out that way.

Guilt softened his features. "I'm sorry. I know how much you cared about him."

Her throat constricting painfully, Lilith blinked back unwanted tears. She would not give him the pleasure of seeing her weaken. "He meant more to me than my own father, and I wasn't even allowed to attend his funeral."

She didn't bother to add that now she visited the late earl's grave once a week. It was none of his business.

Gabriel's hands settled on her shoulders. "I'm sorry."

She believed him. She just didn't know what he was sorry for. Maybe, like her, he was sorry for all of it.

Tears threatened again, blurring her vision, thickening her voice. "Sorry isn't quite good enough anymore. It's too late."

He pulled her closer, hauling her against him so quickly she had no chance to fight.

"It's never too late," he murmured and covered her lips with his own.

She could fight. His hands left her shoulders to cup her skull, leaving her arms and hands the perfect chance to pummel him and release all the anger and hurt inside her.

She didn't fight.

Firm and insistent, his lips moved against hers, parting them. So sweet. The taste of wine lingered on his tongue and Lilith matched his strokes with her own as her pounding heart threatened to burst right out of her breast.

Her hands slid up the solid warmth of his chest, the palms tickled by the dark blue wool of his coat. Her fingers itched to crawl inside—inside his waistcoat, inside his shirt—to touch the soft, dark hair that covered his chest. She used to tease him about having so much hair. As if she could have had any idea if he had an abnormal amount or not.

She clutched his lapels instead. If she touched him the way

she wanted to, she wouldn't be satisfied with stopping there. She wouldn't be satisfied until she had the entire magnificent length of him bared to her touch and taste. And if she made love to him, she would not be able to fight him when he tried to take her club away.

And making love to her wouldn't stop him from doing just that.

"Stop." She panted, pushing hard against his shoulders in order to get her head out of reach of his mouth. "We can't do this."

"Good God, woman," he muttered, holding her head still with one hand. "Don't you ever shut up?"

He lowered his head again. It would be so easy for her to let him kiss away all her doubts. Too easy. Had she learned nothing where he was concerned? He might not have intended to ruin her, but he had. And he'd never done anything to atone for it.

"I said, stop!" She shoved as hard as she could against him, then stumbled when he released her.

"How can you do this?" she demanded, pressing a palm to her thundering heart. "How can you kiss me as though the last ten years never happened?"

His smile was rueful. "Rather easily, I'm afraid."

"And do you find it just as easy to ruin me, my lord?"

He flinched at her icy tone. "Lilith, I told you. I never meant to ruin you."

"Maybe not then, but you certainly mean to now. Or am I to take from your actions that you have changed your mind about closing my club?"

Gabriel folded his arms across his chest, a defensive gesture that said more than any words ever could.

"I think you know the answer to that. Lilith, it's not just your club. I'm not out to close Mallory's alone."

"Is that supposed to make me feel better? To make me give up and watch you take away the one thing that means anything to me?" Oh, God, couldn't she say more than two words without wanting to burst into tears?

"You can't expect me to do that, Gabe. Not because of what happened between us. *Especially* not because of what happened between us."

"Lily—" He broke off on a sigh.

"This afternoon you called me a harlot and now you want to call me by a pet name? Which is it?"

He just stared at her, a muscle ticking in his jaw as only a man's could. He didn't understand that his actions weren't right simply because he thought they were. How could she expect him to? Gabriel had always been a black-or-white sort of person, and she had spent the past decade discovering all the varying shades of gray.

"Do you despise me that badly?" She choked on the last word and hated herself for it.

Gabriel's face darkened like a thunder cloud before a storm. "This isn't about you! This isn't even about us!"

He wanted to shout, did he?

"Then what is it? Tell me!"

It was a strange thing, watching all the fight drain out of a person. Gabriel's shoulders slumped and he suddenly looked very, very tired.

"I can't."

Lilith sneered at the apologetic tone. It was too much to expect honesty out of him. "Can't or won't?"

He ran a hand through his hair as he met her gaze. "Does it matter?"

"No. It doesn't." Turning her back to him, Lilith crossed the carpet with her spine as rigid as a post. She was cold inside, numb right down to her toes.

Yanking open the door, she turned back to him, ignoring his sorrowful expression. He should be sorry. By God, she'd make him sorrier.

"Thank you for coming this evening, Lord Angelwood, but I find I'm suddenly feeling a little under the weather. Please accept my apologies." How dignified she sounded. How frigidly polite. It was her mother's voice. It seemed to suit the moment.

He took a step toward her. "Lily—"

Her teeth ground together. "*Get out.*"

He didn't argue. He merely nodded and headed for the door. He paused on the threshold.

"We're not finished, Lilith. You'll have to see me again eventually."

She'd never hated him as much as she did at that moment.

"The next time I see you, Lord Angelwood, will be in Hell."

Chapter 4

She slammed the door in his face.

Angry, confused and in a state of arousal, Gabriel stared dumbly at the heavy oak door that stood between him and Lilith's rage.

He couldn't blame her for being angry. He'd kissed her as if he had the right—as if they were lovers and not adversaries. She'd asked why he was against her and he wouldn't—couldn't—tell her. She'd made herself vulnerable to him and he'd refused to do the same.

All he had to do was tell her about his father's inability to live life rather than wager on it. He only had to tell her about his father's death and all that had happened afterward—how he'd had to deal with his mother's histrionics, how the responsibility to refill the family coffers had fallen on him, how he'd rebuilt a fortune in secrecy so no one would learn the truth.

But he couldn't do that. Not only because he couldn't trust her not to use it against him, but because he didn't want her to know the truth. She had liked his parents. His mother and father had been very friendly, charming people despite their irresponsibilities and careless natures. It was bad enough that she knew about his mother's affairs and his father's gaming. She didn't need to know the rest.

He'd wanted his father to have more dignity in death than he had in life. He had wanted to keep scandal as far away from the family as possible. His mother had seemed to realize how important this was as well. She never had another affair after the death of his father. In fact, she'd gone into mourning for him and stayed that way until her own death three years later.

He wouldn't be one-and-twenty again for all the gold in the kingdom, not if he had to go through everything again. He'd been too young to handle himself properly. If only he could have known then what he knew now.

Like the fact that Lilith hadn't willingly left him as her father had intimated. He'd seen the truth in her eyes. That kind of hurt couldn't be fabricated; of that Gabriel was certain.

It all made sense to him now, as though a veil had been lifted. Back then he hadn't believed her father at first, but when he never heard from Lilith he began to suspect the old man had been right. Gabriel was so morose about his father's death, he'd found it easy to believe Lilith had abandoned him as well. Idiot.

She hadn't told him why she hadn't written. No matter. He'd get to the truth eventually.

With a sigh, Gabriel turned away from the door and started toward the intersecting corridor that led back to the club. He was startled when a woman practically flew out of the entrance to that same corridor. It was Lady Wyndham. Gabriel was friends with her husband. She didn't see him, or if she did, she didn't acknowledge him. She simply scurried across the carpet to a door at the opposite end of the hall where Gabriel stood.

Shaking his head as she closed the door behind her, Gabriel rounded the corner. The very idea of women being admitted into such a place seemed wrong, as strange and startling as it would be to see a woman at Oxford. Yet he could almost hear his mother's voice in the back of his head, insisting that women should be allowed the same rights as men, particularly if they were to fulfill their potential as humans.

His mother had been a student of Wollstonecraft when it suited her. She'd also played the part of a witless, helpless female with amazing proficiency when the need arose. And she had also practiced what she preached, indulging in her own addictions as freely as his father. Except in the case of his mother, her addiction had been men. *Younger* men.

"Watch out!" he cried, coming back to the present just in time to avoid a head-on collision with another gentleman.

The man's fair head came up, horror dawning across his features as he realized whom he had almost collided with.

"A-Angelwood."

"Somerville."

The shorter man shifted from one foot to the other. "You're the last person I expected to see here."

"Yes, I suppose so." Gabriel kept his tone as bland as his expression.

What was Somerville doing here? Was the earl on his way to see Lilith, not knowing that she'd made plans with him? Or had Lilith's invitation been part of a setup? Had she purposely dressed to entice him, only to have Somerville burst in at an inopportune moment and literally catch him with his pants around his ankles? Had Lilith plotted to blackmail him, only to have her plans ruined by her own anger?

Somerville managed a nervous smile. "No hard feelings about what happened at the House, eh? Politics and all that."

The politics Gabriel had no problem with. It was the "all that" that made him want to smash Somerville's head into the wainscoting until the wood splintered.

"No," he replied from between clenched teeth. "No hard feelings at all. Now, if you will excuse me?"

Was it his imagination or did Somerville actually sigh in relief?

"Yes, er, of course. Have a good evening, Angelwood."

Gabriel's lips twisted. "I intend to, thank you."

Somerville didn't move, forcing Gabriel to walk away first. Cursing silently, he strode toward the club entrance, as tempted to look back as Orpheus must have been. Finally, when he was certain Somerville was no longer watching, and he could stand the suspense no longer, Gabriel glanced around, certain of which direction the young earl had taken.

He scowled as Somerville turned right, not left. Surely he knew which parlor Lilith was in?

Quickly, quietly, Gabriel moved back down the corridor. Hugging the wall, he peered around the corner to see what Somerville was up to.

What was that old adage about Peeping Toms seeing things they didn't want to see? Or was that eavesdroppers?

Lady Wyndham opened the door for Somerville with such a sweet and loving smile that Gabriel felt guilty for witnessing it. If possible, Somerville's expression was even doughier.

They were in love. The realization hit Gabriel like a cricket ball to the head. They were both married to other people— good people—but they were in love with each other. That was what Somerville hadn't wanted him to see.

And that was how Lilith had managed to enlist the earl's assistance in her campaign against him.

That Lilith hadn't taken Somerville as her lover filled Gabriel with a happiness that shamed him. No, they weren't lovers, but their relationship had a far darker connotation.

Was she outright blackmailing Somerville, or had she tried to pretty it up as something else? And wouldn't a woman capable of blackmailing a man in love be just as capable of cheating a green boy out of his quarterly allowance?

Lilith had said that the only way to determine what kind of establishment she ran was to play. Gabriel wasn't prepared to take such drastic measures just yet, nor was he ready to judge her guilty. A little extortion didn't make her completely without morals. In fact, he had stooped to such tactics once or twice himself.

No, if he was going to uncover the truth, he had to talk to

the men who gambled at her tables. He would have to find them somewhere else, however. If he started asking questions here, she'd find out, and Lord only knew what kind of information she had on other members of the *ton*. She could quite possibly buy a lot of silence with what she knew.

Right. Off to White's, then.

Pivoting on his heel, Gabriel once again set off toward the exit. His determination grew with each stride.

The muffled crash of breaking glass sounded over his right shoulder.

Lilith. What had she thrown? A plate? A glass? Had she thrown it in anger or in anguish? Did it matter? He was to blame, regardless.

Gritting his teeth, Gabriel reached for the doorknob.

And this time, unlike Orpheus, he didn't look back.

"Angelwood! How the devil are you, man?"

Gabriel took the breath-stealing slap on the back with a cough and a grimace. "I was fine before you broke my spine, Wyndham." *By the way, Somerville's tupping your wife behind your back.*

His booming laugh reverberating throughout White's club, the viscount gestured to a nearby table. "Sit, man, sit! I haven't seen you in a long time. By God, you look good."

Sitting, Gabriel studied his friend as Wyndham—Wynnie to his close acquaintances—ordered a bottle of claret. He didn't understand. Wynnie was handsome enough—not as pretty as Byron, but his good-natured personality more than made up for that. He was affable, rich and a good deal of fun. Everyone liked Wynnie. So why was his wife having an affair? And why with someone so dishwater-dull as Somerville?

Wynnie, his cheeks ruddy from drink and laughter, brought his fist down on the table with enough force to shake it. "Damn my eyes, but it's wonderful to see you! Thought you'd never return from across that mud puddle. What the devil were you doing there anyway?"

If Gabriel told him he'd never believe it, not without much

more explaining than Gabriel was prepared to give.

"I was visiting an old friend." Not the complete truth, but not a lie, either. Over the years, he and Garnet had become friends as well as partners.

The waiter set a bottle and two glasses on the table, and Wynnie filled both goblets until the claret reached the rims.

Gabriel raised his brows and chuckled. "Are we back in school? I haven't seen a glass filled like that since we used to have contests."

Wynnie's grin grew as he raised his glass. "You mean we've stopped?"

As their glasses clinked together, sending two swallows' worth of wine splashing to the tabletop, Gabriel was tempted to ask his friend if he wouldn't have as much fun at home with his wife. Then he remembered—*again*—that Wynnie's wife wasn't home.

Carefully, Gabriel lifted the claret to his lips. He had no desire to spend the remainder of the night with a stain on his shirt. Wynnie, he noticed, was already sporting a rather large one on his waistcoat.

The wine flowed over his tongue, leaving behind a pleasant, heady aftertaste that made Gabe wish he had a cigar.

As if reading his thoughts, Wynnie produced two from his inside jacket pocket.

Gabriel grinned. "I should have known you'd come prepared."

"I usually do," the viscount replied jovially. "So, Gabe, you know I must ask you if the rumors about you and Lilith Mallory are true."

Gabriel's smile faltered. "What rumors?"

Wynnie appeared not to notice his friend's change in demeanor. "That you're the lucky man bedding her, that's what. I didn't give it much credit at first, knowing how you are about such things."

"How I am." Did he look as dumbfounded as he sounded?

"Mmm. Everyone knows you're nearly monkish—discreet as well. Lilith Mallory is the last woman I'd expect you to pursue, despite the fact that every man in town's been sniffing after her like she was a bitch in heat."

Gabriel didn't want to hear this. "Wynnie—"

Wyndham brushed him aside as though he hadn't heard him. "A little on the plump side for me, but you know what they say about soft cushions and all that. Then I remembered your past history and it suddenly made sense, seeing that you weren't going to be plowing a field you hadn't tilled before—"

"Stop!"

Wynnie gaped at his outburst, as did several other gentlemen seated nearby.

"I am *not* having an affair with Lady Lilith!" Gabriel informed him in a sharp whisper. "Don't you think that would make me a bit of a hypocrite, having a relationship with a gaming-club owner when I'm trying to abolish gambling?"

Wynnie boomed with laughter, attracting a few more curious stares. "You're not still going on about that foolishness, are you?"

For the first time that evening, Gabriel was beginning to sympathize with Lady Wyndham. Everything was a joke to Wynnie. It was what had made him so entertaining when they were younger.

Right now, it only served to make him extremely annoying.

"There is nothing between Lilith and me but the past," Gabriel informed him. "And the fact that she's trying to fight me on the gambling issue."

"You're not afraid of a woman, are you?"

That thunder-roll of a laugh was beginning to give Gabriel a headache. Wynnie was drunk and Gabriel was far too sober to deal with him.

"I'd be a fool not to be wary of someone who had such a vested interest in having me fail."

That remark made Wynnie laugh all the harder. Like a frustrated child, Gabriel kicked him under the table.

"Ow!" Scowling, the viscount rubbed his shin. "What the devil did you do that for?"

Flashing an apologetic smile, Gabriel shrugged. "Sorry, old man. Just getting comfortable."

Wynnie didn't look convinced.

"So," Gabriel began, seizing control of the conversation while he could, "have you ever played at Mallory's before?"

Forgetting his leg in favor of another drink of claret, Wynnie nodded. "Of course. Got the duty to m'title to spend the majority of my time here, but Mallory's is as fine a club as any, and Lilith employs the best chef in the city. Has the best liquor, too."

Gabriel didn't doubt that Lilith went all out. He'd seen the club for himself. It was top-notch as far as opulence and taste were concerned.

"And have you ever heard of anyone having any . . . *trouble* with the club?" *Very subtle, Angelwood.*

Wynnie's brow furrowed. It was a rare occurrence. Surely twice in one night should be some kind of record.

"What kind of trouble? There's been the odd fight, but that scary Latimer fellow puts an end to that fairly quickly."

Gabriel sipped his wine. It was finally down to a decent level in his glass. "What about cheating? Have you heard anything about that?"

"Oh, to be sure!"

Gabriel's heart leapt at his companion's affirmative answer. Was it excitement or disappointment that was the cause of this pounding?

Wynnie's usual grin was back in place. "A few months back, Pennington got caught pulling cards out of his sleeve while playing against Wynter. Latimer didn't have to toss Pennington out; Wynter took care of that. Terribly good thrashing."

"What about the house?" Gabriel pushed. "Has anyone ever suspected the club itself of cheating its patrons?"

Wynnie shook his head. "No. Haven't heard a thing, but from what I've seen, Mallory's takes extra precaution against such things. Fresh cards, inspected before every game. Latimer and a few others watch over everything. Clubs have to be careful. A rumor like that could ruin them."

Narrowing his eyes, the viscount stared at him. "Is that what you're after, Gabe? To ruin Lilith Mallory?"

Indignation, hot and sharp, exploded in Gabriel's chest. "I am not! Why does everyone assume I'm trying to ruin Lilith?"

Wynnie shrugged. "Not like you haven't done it before."

Gabriel's fingers tightened around his glass. After word of how he and Lilith were found by her mother had spread throughout the *ton*, Lilith's reputation hadn't been the only one tarnished. Instead of telling the truth about why he hadn't married Lilith, he'd allowed the lies to continue, rather than creating another scandal. No parent would let him anywhere near a daughter for the longest time after that. Not that it had mattered. The only woman he wanted was gone.

"I have no desire to ruin anyone, Wynnie," he replied on a tired sigh. "I think I'm done for the night. Can I give you a ride home?"

Wynnie shook his head, sending a lock of dark hair over his forehead. "I'm going to stay here for a bit." He grinned. "Henrietta's no doubt in bed by now anyway. She won't miss me if I'm out for a few more hours."

His smile strained, Gabriel rose to his feet. Henrietta was Lady Wyndham, the woman who no doubt was in bed, just as her husband thought. Only with another man. Of course her husband could stay out as long as he wanted.

"You're a lucky man, my friend."

The bleeding had finally stopped.

With a grimace that was partly from the sight of her own blood and partly due to self-disgust, Lilith gingerly peeled the rest of the handkerchief away from her hand.

It wasn't that much of a cut. More blood than anything else, but it would probably leave a scar. Stupid, stupid, stupid! What on earth had she been thinking?

She hadn't been thinking at all. After slamming the door

on Gabriel and his attempt to placate her, she'd been so overcome by rage and hurt that she'd picked up the nearest object and thrown it as hard as she could.

The crystal goblet had shattered easier than a young girl's romantic notions. Such notions, Lilith had recently discovered, were much more difficult to gather up and dispose of, but so were their wounds much harder to ascertain. She'd bled more over Gabriel the first time.

"Can I get you anything?" Mary asked. Dear, sweet, unflappable Mary.

"You had better bring me some hot water and clean bandages, if you would, please, Mary. Better bring some whiskey, too."

Mary nodded. "Yes, I've heard that strong spirits are good for cleaning wounds. I shall be right back."

Lilith watched her leave, not bothering to tell her that the whiskey was for her, not for her hand.

Lud, but she needed a drink! Something with bite so she'd stop whining over a man who didn't deserve it any more now than he had ten years ago.

Not once during all the times Lilith had imagined herself asking Gabriel why he hadn't come after her had he replied that he couldn't tell her. What was there not to tell?

Her father must have told him she'd left England willingly, but she couldn't imagine why. One would think that a father with a ruined daughter would be happy to see her married to the man who had ruined her, not living in exile in Italy.

Perhaps Fleetwood Mallory had been glad to be rid of his troublesome youngest child. It left him more energy to devote to his heir.

It was difficult to remain angry at her parents and her brother. She was glad they'd sent her away; otherwise she would have ended up at the bottom of the Channel with them when a freak storm blew up during a return trip from France.

Lilith hadn't felt their loss, couldn't even summon a tear

for the three of them together, let alone just one. How could she? You had to know a person—or at least have some degree of feeling for him or her—in order to mourn.

She eased her guilt by making herself believe that Gabriel had robbed her of her capacity to feel at all, but two years ago, when her aunt Imogen passed away, Lilith felt as though her entire world had fallen apart.

In a way it had. Aunt Im's death left her alone in the world, friendless. Her only companion was Luisa, her maid. The two of them decided to leave Venice—too many memories. They came to England, and Lilith faced the society that had shunned her, not on bended knee, but with her head held high. She determined to set them all on their ears, to make them come to her, and she'd succeeded.

So why wasn't it enough?

"I got the bandages and the whiskey," Mary announced, reentering the parlor. "Latimer insisted on sending glasses along, even though I told him the whiskey was for your hand."

Placing the tray on the table by the sofa, Mary cast a suspicious glance at her friend. "It *is* for your hand, isn't it?"

Lilith's lips curved into a weary smile. "Not exactly."

The older woman didn't so much as blink. "Good thing Latimer sent two glasses, then."

It was hard not to cry out as Mary cleaned the gash in her palm, but Lilith managed to do with the odd hiss. Afterward, her hand bound in fresh white linen, she leaned back in her chair with her glass of whiskey and sighed. She was exhausted.

Mary settled onto the sofa, eyeing the empty table. "So you didn't even make it to dinner."

"No," Lilith replied crisply, bristling a bit from the amusement in her friend's voice. "I tossed him out."

The older woman's eyes widened. "Do you want to talk about it?"

What was there to tell? Sipping her whiskey, Lilith shrugged. "He still plans to abolish every gaming establishment in England."

"So his mission isn't against you and you alone. That must give you some comfort."

"Indeed," Lilith drawled. "I asked him what had happened, Mary. He used his father's death as an excuse at first, but when I pressed, he said he couldn't tell me."

Mary frowned. "Couldn't?"

Lilith laughed. Lord, but she sounded like a bitter old crone! "Makes you wonder just what in the name of God stopped him, doesn't it?"

The older woman's expression was careful, her gaze gently assessing. "You think he didn't want you."

"Yes," Lilith admitted, tears prickling the backs of her eyes. "That's exactly what I think. What else is there?"

Mary's wide lips curved at the corners. "That perhaps Lord Angelwood has a secret he doesn't want you to discover."

Lilith snorted. "You've read too many novels."

"Don't be obtuse," Mary scolded, setting her barely touched whiskey on the table. "If he didn't care then—if he doesn't still care now—he'd tell you so. He hardly seems like the type to mince words."

We're not finished, Lilith. You'll have to see me again eventually.

"No." It was little more than a whisper. "He's not."

Mary's brown eyes sparkled. "But he hasn't told you that. Why?"

"Because he wants something."

The sparkle disappeared. "Aside from your intelligence when it comes to business, you are perhaps one of the slowest-witted females I've ever met."

Stupefied, Lilith stared at her companion. "I beg your pardon?"

"He obviously didn't tell you because he's afraid of your reaction!"

Now, this was just ridiculous. "Gabriel Warren, afraid of me? Preposterous!" The boy she'd known hadn't been afraid of anything, a trait that the man he'd grown into seemed to have retained.

"Then why not say, 'I changed my mind'? Or 'I got tired of your face, you stupid old cow'?"

The last was said with such vehemence, Lilith suspected that Mary's husband had said the very same thing to her.

"But whatever it was that happened, Lord Angelwood couldn't bring himself to tell you the truth, because he either didn't want to hurt you or felt ashamed."

Ashamed? Gabriel? What could he possibly be ashamed of where she was concerned? For heaven's sake, she'd been there when his mother ran her hand down the front of Lord Byron's trousers!

Of course, Lady Angelwood hadn't known she was watching. Gabriel's mother might have played fast and loose, but she hadn't been an exhibitionist.

Still, the idea that Gabriel might be hiding something was easier to accept than the suggestion that he harbored feelings for her. Their past was just a convenient way for him to manipulate her. Why else would he kiss—twice!—a woman he hadn't seen for ten years, if not to play upon her former stupidity?

"Mary, I believe you might be onto something."

The older woman smiled. "Who would have thought that after ten years the two of you would still love each other?"

Lilith shot her a dark look. "Right now, I have my doubts that Gabriel ever loved me, Mary, and I most certainly am *not* still in love with him."

"But—"

"What I meant," Lilith interrupted before her friend could say something to make her reconsider that last statement, "is that I believe you're correct in assuming Gabriel is hiding something. Why else would he have broken into the office that night?"

Why indeed. And why had he acted so seductive and possessive? If he was truly the jilted lover he claimed to be, shouldn't he have been angry? *She* had been angry. That she remained so lent a credence to Mary's theory she didn't want to consider.

No, Gabriel's sensual intimidation was all a ploy. He didn't want her. He wanted to *distract* her. And since her body had responded to him, he was obviously using that against her so she wouldn't discover what he was really up to.

"Perhaps he wanted to be alone with you."

Lilith's frown deepened at the hopeful tone. "I would think that you of all people would be more sensible. If your husband did such a thing, would you consider it so romantic?"

Mary's face drained of all color and immediately Lilith was ashamed of her callousness.

"Mary, I—"

"My husband," Mary said softly, jerking to her feet, "was a full-grown man, not a boy. And you can hardly compare his auctioning me off like a head of cattle to a young man who had more pressing things to take care of after his father's death than chase you halfway across the Continent."

Struck dumb, Lilith could only gape as her friend—her only friend—strode from the room with as much dignity as she could muster.

What an idiot she was! Selfish, stupid idiot! Did she think that just because her heart had been broken, her suffering was greater than anyone else's? People had suffered worse heartbreak than hers—and more than once, in some cases.

She had little to excuse herself save for the fact that society made it very difficult for a girl to stop loving. Young men had other pursuits, such as their titles and their horses, their gambling. Young women had only parties and other young women. The former was a venue in which every eligible young man was compared to the offending member of his sex. The latter provided little more than an endless stream of meaningless chatter that ultimately led to tearful discussions of that same heartbreaking swine.

And having been hurt by Gabriel, she had taken extra precautions to keep any other young man from getting that close to her again. After a while it became a habit. A few times she'd met someone who piqued her fancy, usually because he had a broad grin; and once, because he had unusually pale gray eyes. But the encounters never amounted to anything. Lilith made sure of that.

Was it any wonder that she never truly had got over him? She'd been letting his betrayal rule her life ever since it happened.

No more. This time she wouldn't sit back and let him have his way. She was going to fight him, and if he thought he would be up against the same naive girl she'd been a decade ago, he'd be sorely disappointed.

How many disappointments for him did that make now? It seemed as though she added a new one to the list every day.

Gabriel wasn't the only one capable of playing on the past to achieve his own goals.

A knock sounded on the door. Hoping it was Mary returning to allow her to apologize, Lilith called out for her to enter.

It wasn't Mary. It was Latimer.

The rangy servant wore a cautious expression as he stuck his head in around the door. No doubt he'd seen Mary's angry countenance and feared his employer's mood might be just as black.

"Mr. Francis is here to see you, my lady."

Francis? Odd time of night for him to be calling. Normally he came during the day, when the club was closed and there was little danger of anyone recognizing him.

"Send him in, please, Latimer."

A few moments later, Mr. Francis entered the room. A big man with a thick shock of silver hair and a closely trimmed beard, Francis had the ability to blend into all levels of society. For as an investigator, his appearance was definitely an asset. He could pass as an affluent country squire or a lowly laborer. In fact, Lilith wasn't completely convinced that the personality he portrayed with her wasn't just another disguise.

Tonight, Mr. Francis looked every bit the well-fed country lord.

"Lady Lilith," he began with a small bow. "I do hope you'll excuse the intrusion."

"It is of no consequence, Mr. Francis." She gestured for him to sit. "Have you news for me?"

Flipping out the tails of his black evening coat, the investigator seated himself on the sofa. "I'm not completely certain, but I thought I should come see you all the same."

It was best, Lilith had learned, not to appear too eager. "Go on."

"I was at White's this evening, trying to gather information on Lord Angelwood as you requested."

Lilith's heart skipped a beat. "What did you discover?"

Mr. Francis shook his head. "Other than what you already know, very little, I'm afraid."

She fought to keep her disappointment from showing. Nothing worth knowing ever came easily.

"I now have the exact dates of Angelwood's departure to Nova Scotia and his arrival back in London. I should be able to track down some of the men who sailed with him. Perhaps they'll have some interesting news for us regarding the purpose of the earl's sojourn."

Lilith nodded.

"Excellent. Now, what were you saying about this evening at White's?"

"Lord Angelwood appeared at the club while I was there. He was in the company of Lord Wyndham."

The loudmouth Gabriel and his friends called Wynnie. Lilith remembered him, a big, braying ass of a man who drank too much. Always very friendly when his wife wasn't present. Lilith didn't blame Lady Wyndham for preferring Lord Somerville. At least Somerville had enough sense to know when to keep his mouth shut.

"I didn't overhear the entirety of the conversation, as I was waylaid by other business"—Lilith raised a brow at that—"but I did hear Lord Angelwood ask Lord Wyndham if he'd heard any stories about Mallory's. He seemed particularly interested in whether or not anyone had ever been accused of cheating."

Cheating? He wanted to know about cheating? Of course. Men had their awful barbaric code of honor. If one caught another cheating, it often led to the challenge of a duel. Fortunately, cheating rarely happened at Lilith's tables. The hospitality of Mallory's was good enough that few wanted to risk being barred for life for cheating.

"What was Lord Wyndham's reply?"

Mr. Francis smiled. "He told the earl of your policies for dealing with such behavior, Lady Lilith."

It was clear that Gabriel wanted to find evidence to support his claim that Mallory's and all other gaming establishments were evil, by pointing out how many duels had been fought and lives lost over unfair play. Well, he was out of luck in that regard. No gentleman had ever challenged another in Mallory's.

But that aside, what a hypocrite Gabriel was! Talking about closing her club down and then heading off to White's! Did he plan to stop gambling at his precious all-male haven as well?

Knowing Gabriel, she thought that was exactly what he had planned. Foolish, idealistic idiot.

Lilith took a sip of her whiskey. She hadn't bothered to offer Mr. Francis one. This whole debacle with Gabriel was making her forget her manners. "And that was all you overheard?"

The investigator nodded. "That was it. A few minutes later, Lord Angelwood got up and left. I followed him, but he went straight home."

What, no mistress, no carousing until dawn with his cronies? Maybe there was no one for him to carouse with. Braven was married now, a father. And Wolfram was off on a tour of the Continent with his younger sister. The two of them had been Gabriel's best friends. How many stories had she endured about the three of them only because she loved the way he smiled when he spoke of Brave and Jules? He must be incredibly lonely without them around.

But what concern was that of hers? Lonely or not, he was snooping around, asking about her business—which was proof enough that he had no intention of giving up his foolish quest. If it weren't for the fact that he'd purposely targeted her club, Lilith could almost feel sorry for him.

What drove a man to fight such an impossible battle? What had made Gabriel so set against gaming? He certainly wasn't brought up to think it evil. His mother and father had been lifelong gamesters. And it had been the old earl who had taught Lilith to play picquet.

The old earl. The more Lilith thought about it, the more she thought Gabriel's father was the key. Gabriel had never seemed bothered by his father's gaming when they were younger, but perhaps something had happened to make him change his mind. Likely he blamed his parents' love of games of chance and other fast society pastimes for their deaths. Neither one of them had been very old when they died. Had his mother had an affair with a gambler? Had that been the last straw for the old earl? Perhaps he'd challenged the lover to a duel—could that be how Gabriel's father died? She couldn't remember ever hearing of the cause of death. Maybe the answer was there after all.

"I want you to find out whatever you can about the death of the former Earl Angelwood," Lilith told the investigator as her suspicions took hold in her head. "I have a feeling that if we uncover the truth about that we will have the reason for his son's conviction."

Mr. Francis nodded but didn't question her. "I will look into it."

"Oh!" she said as the thought suddenly occurred to her. "I don't suppose you've been able to ascertain whether or not Bronson was behind the recent acts of vandalism against my club?"

Mr. Francis shook his shaggy head. "Not yet, but I'm fairly

certain he was indeed the culprit, although I've been unable to get anyone to actually say it out loud. Have no fear. The men who work for Bronson aren't always the brightest. They'll brag eventually."

Lilith hoped so. A lost shipment of brandy or cigars here and there didn't cost her too much money, but if the attacks continued, the loss would soon add up.

"Thank you for coming by, Mr. Francis," she said, rising to her feet. "I trust I'll hear from you as soon as you've discovered anything about Bronson or the death of the previous Earl of Angelwood."

Mr. Francis also rose. "You may rest assured that I will report immediately after I learn anything, Lady Lilith."

Lilith smiled, well pleased with the way of things. "Excellent. Good evening to you."

After the investigator left, Lilith realized he hadn't even asked her what she'd done to her hand. He probably already knew, she thought with a chuckle.

Still cradling her whiskey glass, she crossed the parlor to the window to stare out at the darkness beyond.

It had begun in earnest, this game between her and Gabriel. Lines had been drawn, strategies set into motion. All that was left was to play it through and establish who was to be the victor and who the defeated one.

And whether or not there was a difference.

Chapter 5

"**L**ooking for someone?"

Turning from the spectacle of twirling dancers, fluttering fans and jewels glittering on nearly bare bosoms, Gabriel smiled. Yes, he was looking for someone. He was looking for Somerville. The only reason he had accepted Lady Wyndham's invitation was because he was hoping to talk to her lover.

"I just like to look," he replied. "Good evening, Blaine. Is Victoria with you?"

The older man nodded his head in the direction of a group of ladies across the room. "She's with Lady Sefton. Got to stay in good standing with the Marriage Mart patronesses, you know."

"Surely Frederick has a few good years left before he needs to go shopping for a wife?" Gabriel inquired.

Blaine chuckled. "I should hope so. The lad's barely twenty. Perhaps he'll take a page from your book and stay a bachelor as long as possible."

It was on the tip of Gabriel's tongue to inform his friend that he hadn't been much older than Frederick when he'd found the woman he wanted to spend the rest of his life with. Perhaps it was because of his mother. Perhaps it had simply been because he was young, but no one had ever once entertained the idea that he had actually wanted to marry Lilith. They all thought he'd ruined her because he was randy and she was willing.

Which was only part of the story.

They stood silent for a moment.

"Have you found anything incriminating against Mallory's yet?" Blaine finally asked.

Gabriel stared into his glass, centering his thoughts on the tiny bubbles swimming there before lifting his gaze to his friend.

"Nothing that puts me any closer to discovering the truth, no."

The older man frowned. "The truth? You know the truth. Frederick was cheated. All you need to do is prove it."

Spoken like a true father.

Inwardly sighing, Gabriel turned to fully face Blaine. "Why didn't you tell me that Lilith Mallory was the owner of the Mallory's club?"

Still frowning, Blaine shrugged. "What difference should that make?"

"Do you not remember what happened between Lilith Mallory and me, Blaine?"

The viscount's answering stare was as blank as a sheet of parchment.

Gabriel couldn't bring himself to come out and say it, not when it made him feel so guilty. "Ten years ago? A scandal? Remember?"

Blaine's eyes widened. "That was *her*?"

Gabriel nodded. He wasn't surprised that Blaine hadn't put the pieces together before now. He'd been in the country when the scandal broke, Victoria having recently been delivered of twins. He hadn't come to town until Gabriel wrote of his father's death, and by then Blaine had an entirely different scandal to face—and cover up—than Gabriel's own.

Rubbing the back of his neck, he exhaled a deep breath. "I've put you in a bit of a predicament, haven't I?"

That was certainly an understatement.

"A bit," Gabriel agreed with a slight smile. "You see why I'm in no hurry to reach a verdict."

Blaine's expression suddenly became very guarded. "Surely you don't doubt the validity of Frederick's claim?"

Would a young man lie to avoid his father's wrath and disappointment? He didn't have to think about that one. Perhaps Blaine should.

"I didn't say that."

Gabriel didn't like to think that Frederick had lied, especially not when that lie involved Lilith, but he had bent the truth once or twice himself when dealing with his own father. He didn't doubt for an instant that Frederick would rather lie than tell his father he'd squandered his allowance.

Blaine's gaze hardened. "Just what *are* you saying? That you would take the word of a woman who has built a fortune by robbing others of theirs over the word of a family friend simply because you once had an affair with her?"

"Don't." The word was spoken so softly, Gabriel was amazed Blaine even heard it, but he did.

"You still have feelings for her."

Gabriel turned away from the accusation, but it hung in the air between them like a blade. Staring at but not seeing the dancers, he took a deep swallow of champagne.

Most men would have thought better than to continue, but Blaine had known Gabriel too long to be intimidated by a scowl. Gabriel allowed it because Blaine had been so good to him after his father's death, but he wasn't a boy anymore and he didn't need someone questioning his motives.

"Are you certain your personal feelings have not clouded your judgment?"

Gabriel turned on him, a sudden burst of anger flaring his nostrils and tightening his jaw. "Are you?" he demanded.

The older man stared at him. Clearing his throat, he glanced around them. Sheepishly, Gabriel did so as well. Thank God no one was watching. The gossips would salivate all over themselves to determine what could cause the Earl of Angelwood and his father's dearest friend to argue in public.

"Gabe, be sensible." Blaine's voice was softer now, like a father's to a misbehaving child. Gabriel rolled his eyes.

"If you prove Lilith Mallory cheated my son, you'll have a solid argument to take to the House. But if you get involved with her again, your credibility is going to disappear faster than Prinny's waistline."

Blaine wasn't telling him anything he hadn't already thought of, but that didn't make it any easier to hear.

"I am not involved with Lilith."

"No?"

Gabriel downed the rest of the champagne and shoved the empty glass at a passing footman. He didn't look at his friend. "No."

He'd had enough. He wasn't going to discuss his relationship with Lilith—whatever kind of relationship it was—with anyone.

Blaine caught his arm as he tried to walk away.

"Unless you want me to give the gossips something to really talk about, Blaine, you will release me now."

He didn't have to ask twice.

"You have never spoken to me like that before," Blaine said, his expression stricken as his hand dropped to his side.

A stab of guilt pierced Gabe's chest. His tone was oddly detached. "You've never given me reason before. I'd prefer that you never do again."

Blaine's expression softened. "I am sorry to have offended you, my friend, but you know that you cannot argue for the abolishment of gaming in this country and be the lover of a woman who makes her living from it. Sooner or later, you will have to choose."

Folding his arms across his chest, Gabriel met the viscount's dark gaze. "I'm not her lover, Blaine, but if I were it wouldn't be any of your damn business. I promise you I will find out if—that's right, *if*—Lilith's club cheated Frederick."

"And *if* it did?"

Blaine had never taken such a haughty tone with him before. It filled him with both remorse and anger.

"Then I will confront Lilith and determine whether or not she knew about it, and if she did I will do something about it."

With a bitter laugh, Blaine shook his head. "You really think she'll admit to it?"

Gabriel's jaw tightened. "Do *you* really think that if a club made a habit of cheating, your son would be the only one to have noticed?"

He didn't bother to wait for Blaine's reply before turning on his heel and walking away.

Lady Wyndham's parties were always a huge crush and this one was no exception. Winding through the press of warm, perfumed bodies, Gabriel worked his way toward the balcony.

Blaine was right, of course. He shouldn't let his feelings for Lilith get in the way of his work. True, he wasn't quite certain just what his feelings for Lilith were, but they certainly weren't impartial. He didn't want to believe her capable of cheating any more than Blaine wanted to believe that Frederick might have lied.

Putting Lilith out of business because he'd managed to abolish gaming was one thing. Putting her out of business because he'd destroyed her reputation was quite another. As much as he'd never intended it, he had already ruined her once in the eyes of society. He wouldn't do that again unless it was absolutely necessary.

And to be honest, he wondered if he could do it even then.

"Angelwood." A sweet breath of cigar greeted him as he stepped out into the balmy night air. "Didn't expect to see you here tonight."

Just the man he was looking for. "Good evening, Somerville. I'm not surprised to see you at all."

Somerville stiffened, a thin trail of smoke drifting from his nostrils as he exhaled. "Oh?"

"Every hostess wants you and your lovely wife at their soirees," Gabriel replied, closing the distance between them. "You're a very popular couple."

The blond man grimaced. "So it would seem." He withdrew a silver case from his pocket and offered it to Gabriel. "Smoke?"

Gabriel accepted the offer. Once he'd lit his cigar, he leaned his hip against the balustrade and regarded Somerville thoughtfully. "Still, it's a little brazen to bring your wife to your lover's house, is it not?"

Somerville didn't miss a beat. "In London? It's all the fashion, my good man."

"Indeed," Gabriel agreed with a smile at the other man's wry tone. "Your private life is none of my business, Somerville—"

"You're right. It isn't." Somerville met his gaze evenly. "Any more than yours is mine. So why do I get the distinct impression that your next question is going to concern Lilith Mallory?"

That transparent, was he? Somerville had seen him at Lilith's club. And no doubt he'd seen him get into Lilith's carriage that day outside Parliament. He must have heard the rumors. He had to know there was something going on.

"I must tell you, however, that I don't like to talk about my friends. I'm not going to tell you anything she wouldn't want you to know."

Gabriel raised a brow at that. A moment of silence passed while he blew smoke rings at the sky. "Do you consider Lilith your friend, Somerville?"

There was no hesitation in the younger earl's reply. "I do. A few days ago, I wouldn't have been certain, but now . . ." He shrugged.

"So it was friendship that persuaded you to argue against me in the House and not blackmail?"

Somerville's jaw tightened. He didn't look so young when

he was angry. Gabriel smiled. He didn't want to like this man who was sleeping with his friend's wife, but he couldn't help but admire him. Gabriel was bigger, older, and his title had more wealth and power behind it. Still, Somerville wasn't about to be intimidated by him.

Blue eyes glanced around to make certain they were still alone. He wasn't as slow as Gabriel originally thought. "What could Miss Mallory possibly know about me that would be worthy of blackmail?"

Gabriel tapped ashes over the side of the balcony. "Did she threaten to expose your relationship with Lady Wyndham if you didn't argue for her?"

The younger man grinned, deep dimples appearing in each cheek. "No. At first I thought that was her intention, but it wasn't."

More smoke rings. "What was?"

"She told me you wanted to outlaw her club." Somerville's gaze was painfully open. "It would be more difficult for Hen and me to meet if Mallory's were to close its doors."

His mouth twisting bitterly, Gabriel inclined his head to one side. "And we wouldn't want you to have to put an end to your adultery, would we?"

Somerville dropped the stub of his cigar, crushing it beneath his heel. "Don't attempt to pass judgment, Angelwood. That's God's job, not yours."

"Do you love her?" Where the devil had *that* come from? Would love make being unfaithful all right? His mother had claimed to love his father, but that hadn't stopped her.

Somerville seemed as surprised by the question as Gabriel himself was. "Do you think I would risk Wyndham's wrath and injuring Lady Somerville if I didn't?"

Gabriel shrugged. "People have risked more and survived the loss."

The other man shot him a shrewd glance. "What did you risk?"

How had the conversation become turned in this direction? Gabriel couldn't remember. "I risked losing the woman I loved because of my pride. And then I lost her."

Somerville's smile was sympathetic. "Was your pride worth it?"

Inhaling deeply on the cigar, Gabriel realized he'd been asking himself that same question for the past decade.

"I thought so at the time, but my opinion has changed over the years." Laughing ruefully, he breathed out a lungful of smoke. He coughed.

His lips still curved in a faint smile, Somerville rubbed a hand through his hair. "Miss Mallory might have written the words I spoke in the House the other day, Angelwood, but the sentiment was all mine. I have a personal stake in seeing that club remain open, and if that means advocating gambling, I'll do it."

Nodding, Gabriel flicked his cigar over the railing, watching it fall to the stone walkway below. "I never thought the task before me would be a simple one, but thank you for your candor. You may rest assured that I will hold our conversation in the strictest of confidence."

"As will I."

There was a moment of understanding between them, the fledgling realization of respect and possibly friendship despite adversity.

Somerville chuckled and raked his fingers through his hair again. "I don't know about you, but I could use a drink."

Gabriel grinned. "So could I. Shall we go inside?"

They'd just entered the warmth of the ballroom when a commotion nearby caught their attention.

Lifting his head, Gabriel gazed toward the double doors, where the crowd was parting like the Red Sea before Moses. One by one, the guests stepped back, clearing a path that led from the ballroom entrance. A path, Gabriel noticed, that led straight to *him*.

"Good God," he whispered as a shocked murmur rose around him.

It was Lilith. Dressed in a daring gown of rich garnet velvet.

Her eyes were lined seductively with smudged black kohl, and her red lips were as curvaceous as the hips swaying beneath that sensuous fabric. Her burnished, heavy hair was piled artfully on top of her head, leaving the pale column of her throat bare and drawing the gaze inevitably to the creamy expanse of her shoulders, and lower to the high swell of her breasts above the gown's square neckline. She wore not one piece of jewelry. She didn't have to. Lilith shone all on her own.

How the hell had she gotten past the footmen?

Gabriel felt rather than saw the curious gazes that fell upon him as Lilith glided—no, *slithered*—toward him. He couldn't take his eyes off her. She was gaudy, she was glorious.

"Hello, my lord," she purred, stopping not even a foot away from him. "Care to dance?"

Could he see her heart hammering in her chest? It was thumping against her ribs so hard, Lilith was certain her fear was apparent to everyone present.

Bloody hyenas could probably *smell* it.

"How did you get in here, Lily?" Gabriel demanded as he swept her up into a waltz that tangled her feet and made her head spin.

"Lady Wyndham let me in," she replied, clinging to his thickly muscled shoulder in an effort to keep from stumbling. "Slow down, Gabe. This isn't a race."

He slowed his pace a bit, shorting his long strides to match her shorter legs. "What did you do? Remind her that without your club she and Somerville wouldn't be able to carry on their affair?"

He knew about Lord Somerville and Lady Wyndham?

"No. I told her I'd only stay long enough to speak to you."

He twirled her around. She'd forgotten what a good dancer he was. "And she believed you?" He said it as though he didn't believe it himself.

Trying to ignore how solid and warm he felt beneath the damp iciness of her palm, Lilith raised her gaze to his. There was no way he could feel the chill of her hand through both of their gloves, but Lilith had the strong sense that he was looking for a chink in her armor. Under the glow of a dozen chandeliers, his eyes shone like mirrors. Reflected back at her Lilith saw a woman with too much cosmetics and not enough dress. What a scandalous dress. What had she been thinking?

She'd dressed as they expected her to. Next time she'd wear white and shock them all.

"I told her she could have me tossed out if I didn't leave in ten minutes."

His smile mocked her. "That's not much time."

Right. It wasn't. Time to get down to business.

She forced a smile. "I came to see you, Gabe."

Another turn. His fingers tightened around hers. He was so warm. "I already assumed that, *Lil*."

He wasn't going to make this easy. She hadn't expected him to. There was so much left unsaid between them, so many complications. Wanting to trust, not wanting to trust. Anger. Desire. The need to be the winner.

As if her life needed any more complications. Mary still wasn't speaking to her and she had two men trying to put her out of business. Bronson wanted her gone because she was competition. Gabriel wanted her gone because he'd turned into Mr. Righteous Morality.

Well, she wasn't going anywhere. She planned to beat them both. Bronson was easy. She simply would give him a taste of his own medicine, show him she wasn't about to back down. Gabriel was going to be more difficult, but Lilith would triumph. The information Mr. Francis had given her that morning just might help her do it.

"Your ten minutes is ticking by," Gabriel informed her. "Did you come here to talk or merely to dance?"

Lifting her chin, Lilith stared into his eyes. His tone might be cool and civil, but his gaze wasn't. He wanted her. He was, after all, still a man, and a man didn't have to like a woman to want to bed her.

What was her excuse?

"I wanted to ask you for some business advice."

His brow puckered, drawing those black brows together. "What makes you think I would be a good person to ask about business?"

Now for the trump card. "I was considering investing in a business called Seraph Sails and Shipping. I thought you would be the perfect man to ask, given that you own half of it."

He faltered. Only for a second, but it caused him to miss a step and almost tread on her toes. Or maybe he had done it on purpose; she couldn't tell.

His expression darkened as his hold on her tightened. She winced as he squeezed her injured hand. As though sensing her pain, he relaxed his hold somewhat. Her hand still hurt, but she kept her head held high, eyes locked with the stormy gray of his.

"If you think to blackmail me, think again, madam," he growled from between clenched teeth. "I won't stand for it."

Lilith laughed. It was forced and it sounded as such, but it was still loud enough to draw a few curious glances.

"My dearest Gabe, why would I blackmail you? And for that matter, who the devil would care? To be sure, the *ton* might have a giggle over the Earl of Angelwood having indulged in trade, but it's hardly anything that would *ruin* you."

She allowed her gaze to drift carefully over his angry features. "You have secrets, don't you, Gabe? Things you don't want them"—she jerked her head toward the other dancers—"to know. Things you don't want *me* to know."

His eyes like ice, he stared at her. "What do you want?"

Oh, how he must hate her at that moment! And for a split second Lilith wondered if she was doing the right thing. She should just walk away from him, leave him in peace, let him fight his foolish losing battle and forget she had ever loved him.

"I want to know why you chose to make an example out of me."

His gaze dropped shamelessly to her chest before climbing back up to her face. Lilith willed herself not to blush. Better men than Gabriel Warren had admired her more openly.

"Perhaps I believe you'll make a worthy adversary," he replied. The low timbre of his voice brushed along the bare flesh of her shoulders, sending a shiver down her spine.

"There is that," Lilith taunted, drawing her shoulders back so that her chest was pushed forward, straining against the dark red velvet. "But I think there's a bit more to it. Care to hear what that is?"

His expression smoothed into one of cold composure. "Go ahead."

She moved closer, so that their bodies were much, much closer than what was proper. She could feel the heat of him against the exposed flesh of her throat and chest, even though he wore enough layers for both of them.

"I think you have more of an interest in me than that I own a gaming club."

He snorted. "You flatter yourself."

Lilith smiled. "Someone has to." Undaunted, she continued. "What is it, Gabriel? Why did you choose my club to show your face? Why this interest in Mallory's?"

He raised a brow. "You tell me."

Shaking her head, Lilith smiled again. He was stalling. She didn't have much time left before her ten minutes were up. She wouldn't allow him to lead her away from her goal.

"You want something from me."

His gaze never left hers, and Lilith could see the shutters close behind his eyes, as if he didn't want her to look too deep inside his soul. "I thought I got that ten years ago."

Her smile faltered at the quick stab of pain in her heart. "Somehow I have the feeling that what you're after now is much more valuable."

Surprise flickered in his eyes, followed by a brief flash of sorrow. It was the sorrow that shook her. He wasn't completely unfeeling toward her. It pained him to be near her. What he was after must be important indeed.

"What is it, Gabe?"

He shook his head. "I'm not going to discuss this with you now."

It was all she could do not to trod on his toes. "Yes, you are."

His expression hardened. "No, I'm not."

"You can't hide it from me forever. I'll find out the truth. Who knows? I just might uncover a few more secrets of yours along the way." The tightening of his jaw should have given her satisfaction, but it didn't.

"So do you want to tell me, or do I have to go digging?"

He stared at her. "I think your ten minutes are up."

Lilith's heart lurched. Not yet. She still had a few minutes left. "What is it, Gabe? You told me this retaliation wasn't personal, that it wasn't about us. So why are you after me and not someone else?"

"I told you, I'm not going to discuss it here."

Clenching her jaw in frustration, Lilith lifted her chin. "But you *will* tell me. Or I swear to God I'll dig up every skeleton you've got and lay them out for all of England to see. You try to ruin me again and I'll make you sorry for it."

His laughter mocked her. "How? You'll ruin me? I'd have an easier time making you respectable."

His words hurt and enraged her. Nostrils flaring with the effort to control her breathing, Lilith glared at him. She was practically shivering with fury. "If you want to play that way, my lord, I'm more than willing."

His lips twisted. "You always were."

Oh, that was it! The insufferable gall of this man! Who did he think he was? She hadn't been the only one willing. He'd been *more* than willing.

Lilith's chin went up another notch. She was desperate and didn't like herself very much at that moment. "If you won't tell me, I suppose I shall just have to occupy my time with discovering why you lowered yourself to the merchant class in the first place."

Gabriel's nostrils flared. "I will not let you blackmail me. You listen to me, Lilith—"

"No," she cut in. Lady Wyndham was working her way toward them. Lilith's time was almost up and she hadn't gotten him to confess yet.

She moved closer. They were touching now. He stiffened. "You will come to me tomorrow, Gabriel. And for the first time in your life, you are going to be honest with me, because I will find out if you are not and I will make you pay for it. I won't let you take away the only thing that matters to me. Not without a fight."

He stared at her. Lilith held his gaze, even though she was certain he was seeing things she didn't want him to.

"At one time you said that I was all that mattered."

"That was a long time ago." Slipping on a cool, seductive smile, Lilith added, "You are a very attractive man, Gabriel."

His look brightened with heat. He wasn't immune to her. It was disturbing, this tension between them. They didn't like each other. They didn't trust each other, yet they wanted each other.

Lilith's smile faded. "I won't deny that part of me still wants you." It was more of a confession than she'd intended to make. She wanted him—not just the boy he once was, but this determined man he'd become. "But I'm not going to let that distract me from doing what I have to."

He understood her. She could tell from his expression. He understood because he felt the same way.

"Good," she said with a bit more relief than she liked. "I expect to see you tomorrow for dinner." She stepped back, wanting to leave the ball before Lady Wyndham actually tossed her out. That would be just too embarrassing.

Gabriel held her fast. "This isn't a game, Lilith. If you fight me, you're going to lose."

"Life is a game, Gabe," she informed him evenly. "I decided a long time ago that if I'm going to get what I want I have to play to win."

They were locked in a battle of wills that neither was prepared to back down from.

"Lady Lilith." Lady Wyndham's voice broke the moment. "I'm afraid I must ask you to leave my home."

Gabriel didn't come to her rescue, not that Lilith had expected him to.

Still holding his gaze, she flashed a coy smile as she stepped out of his arms. "Come by the club when you have decided you want to play."

Then she turned and allowed Lady Wyndham to escort her across the floor. Whispers and snickers followed them. Lilith kept her chin up despite the trembling in her knees and met the accusatory stare of one elderly woman with a brazen wink—at the old gel's husband.

"Well?" Lady Wyndham demanded once the ballroom doors had closed behind them.

"I'm not sure," Lilith replied, her limbs shaking as she took her wrap from the waiting footman. "I think I reached him."

The tiny woman steered her down the corridor, away from the footmen. "Do you really think you can convince him to leave your club alone?"

She looked up at the hopeful tone in the other woman's voice. This evening's performance had been planned by Lilith, Lady Wyndham and Lord Somerville earlier that afternoon. The lovers had surprised Lilith by willingly offering to help her stop Gabriel from closing her club.

Lilith had no idea why they had made such an offer. Surely Lady Wyndham and Lord Somerville could arrange another meeting place if Mallory's didn't exist. Perhaps they'd come to think of the club as their special place. She and Gabriel had had a such a place at one time. And Lilith was now convinced that what Lady Wyndham and Lord Somerville shared was not just a common affair. They were in love. In love, and yet could never be together. What was left of the romantic girl she used to be felt for them.

"I do," she replied. "I do think I can convince him."

If there was one thing Lilith was certain of, it was her ability to taint. She might not be able to change Gabriel's mind completely, but she had no doubt that enough time in her presence would sully his own reputation, and he would have to give up his foolish quest.

The knowledge gave her little pleasure.

"Good," Lady Wyndham replied breathlessly. "I was beginning to worry that—well, you know."

Yes, Lilith knew. "Don't worry yourself. I'll take care of everything. Now, perhaps you should toss me out into the street before someone becomes suspicious."

Lady Wyndham appeared almost guilty when she said, "Hardly a fitting way to thank you for all you've done for us, is it? You've been so kind, and I repay you by pretending I despise you."

Lilith's smile was gentle. "I'm not that benevolent, Lady Wyndham. I have my own agenda to meet."

Lady Wyndham turned to face her. To the footman standing near the front door, it must have looked as if she were giving Lilith a serious setting-down, even though he couldn't hear her quiet tone.

"You can't hide your true nature from me, Miss Mallory. I've proof of your good heart."

Lilith smiled ruefully and turned to leave. She took only a few steps before replying over her shoulder, "Don't try to reform me, my dear lady. That's someone else's job."

Hours later, as Lilith prepared for bed, she wondered if she'd done the right thing. Running the stiff-bristled brush through the tangled waves of her hair, she paced the carpet in her nightgown and wrapper, replaying the evening in her mind.

Would Gabriel come the next day? Would he be honest with her and tell her what was going on? Or did he think she'd been bluffing about ruining him in return?

Indeed, he knew her well enough not to think that.

There were so many things she wanted to know that Mr. Francis hadn't been able to tell her. Such as, why had he gone into trade in the first place? He had intimated that there had been rumors of the old earl leaving debts, but no proof.

Was that why it meant so much to him to abolish gambling? And what lengths would he go to in order to see it happen? More important, what would she do if he succeeded? Mallory's wasn't just a club, it was her only tie to the society that shunned her—a society she still foolishly wanted to be a part of at times. It was also a substitute—albeit a poor one—for the husband and children she didn't have.

Or so Samuel Bronson had once insinuated. But regardless of how right he was about Lilith's wanting children, it was the husband she could do without.

Oh, why didn't Gabriel turn his attention toward Bronson? *He* was the kind of club owner that should be put out of business.

Perhaps she should plant a bug in Gabriel's ear about Bronson and the goings-on at his club, Hazards. Or maybe Bronson would try harder to put her out of business if it looked as though she was hiding behind a man.

She tossed the brush onto the dressing table with a loud sigh. She wished Mary were there to talk to, but that was yet another thing on her to-do list. Apologize to Mary. She'd almost gathered enough courage, but showing her face at Lady Wyndham's had depleted a good store of that.

"Frustrated?" came a familiar voice from behind her.

Stifling a scream, Lilith whirled around. "What the hell are you doing here?"

Gabriel slipped one long leg over the sill of her open window and thrust the rest of his large body into the room.

"You really should have better security," he told her as he stood. "Anyone could climb up here."

"Anyone who is half insane," Lilith retorted. Security was the reason she'd had the lower branches of the tree outside her window cut off. How Gabriel had made the climb, she had no idea—and she didn't want to know, either.

He grinned. He actually grinned! Had he completely forgotten their conversation already? He couldn't have. Either he really was insane—which Lilith doubted—or he was foxed.

Crossing the carpet so that they were face-to-face, Lilith

scowled as she caught a whiff of his breath. "Have you been drinking?"

The grin grew. He looked so young when he smiled. Lord, it hurt her just to look at him.

"Do you think I would have come here and climbed that tree if I'd been sober?"

She laughed at that. "No. How did you decide which room was mine?"

"It was the only one that still had candles burning."

Hardly a romantic sentiment. Was that truly what she'd expected? She'd as good as blackmailed him earlier.

Besides, she'd made it clear that she wasn't interested in romance. And she wasn't. Not at all.

"Why are you here, Gabe? Not to act out the balcony scene from *Romeo and Juliet*, I wager."

His gaze assessed her. "You wager a lot, don't you, Lil? Never did understand how you and my father could get so much enjoyment out of taking stupid risks."

What did his father have to do with anything? Before she could ask, he changed the subject.

"I'm here because you said something in the ballroom and I never was able to reply."

Raising a brow, Lilith schooled her features to hide her anxiety. Was he going to confess to her? Was he going to tell her why he had centered all his attention on her? A complex mess of hopes and suspicions ran through her head. Was she a threat? An easy target? Or did he find her as impossible to stay away from as she found him?

"What?"

His hand snaked out and caught her by the back of the head, his fingers tangling the hair she'd spent so much time brushing smooth. He hauled her closer, so that her breasts pressed hard against his chest.

Startled, and all too aware of him through the thin lawn of her gown and wrapper, Lilith could only stare as he brought his head closer to hers.

"I want you, too," he whispered and claimed her lips with his own.

Heart hammering, blood humming, Lilith let him kiss her. She even clamped her own hands to his skull so he couldn't pull away if he tried. The wound on her left palm smarted, but she didn't care. She opened her mouth to him, tasting the warm, lingering traces of brandy and cigar.

This was madness. It didn't make sense. It was wrong and yet nothing in the past ten years had felt so incredibly, so undeniably, *right*. Their lips moved together, insistent and almost frantic as their tongues teased and tasted. Every nerve in Lilith's body thrilled at the contact, even as a voice in her head shouted for her to stop. She couldn't stop. Wouldn't stop. And if he took her to bed, she knew she wouldn't have the strength or the inclination to stop him. She'd let him do whatever he wanted to.

And then the next day they'd go back to fighting each other, because deep down she knew that whatever this *thing* between them was, it really was separate from everything else. It was ten years of frustration and not knowing and pain. It had taken on a life of its own.

He broke the kiss, and something inside made her let him pull away, even though she didn't want him to go.

"I'm ready to play," he whispered, his damp mouth mere inches from her own.

Stunned, Lilith could only stand there and watch dumbly as he turned and slipped out the window. He cast one last, lingering look at her from his perch in the tree, his gaze traveling over every inch of her with an intensity that caused every pulse in her body to throb.

He disappeared. Rushing to the window, Lilith saw him drop to another branch with an agility that was so cocky it put her heart in her throat. She could barely make out his features in the darkness. He dropped again and she could see nothing but the white of his shirt far below.

"I'll be here tomorrow night for you to deal the first

hand," he called from the ground, and Lilith was too breath-lessly anxious to care if anyone else could hear.

A chuckle rose up on the warm breeze, caressing Lilith's cheek with a softness that left a trail of gooseflesh along her shoulders and made her breasts tighten in response.

"But, Lil, after that it's my turn."

Chapter 6

He shouldn't be enjoying this.

At first he'd assumed that Lilith would want a private meeting, in the broad light of day, to demand he explain himself. But Gabriel should have known that she'd surprise him.

She'd invited him to dinner—a very public dinner, where they would be in full view of her patrons. Clearly, she meant what she said about trying to ruin him.

Standing in the middle of the men-only side of Mallory's, Gabriel watched the goings-on around him with a barely veiled sense of anticipation. Lilith's challenge added an element of excitement to entering her club, as though his mere presence might be enough to put that angry flush on her skin and drive her to pursue her goal.

She threatened to destroy him, to uncover all his secrets, and even though he knew he couldn't allow her to do it, he half wished she would, just so he wouldn't have to worry about protecting them anymore.

But beyond all that, he enjoyed baiting her. He liked knowing he could still get passion out of her—even if it set them against each other as much as it brought them together.

He was very much in danger of putting himself in the same situation Blaine had warned him about, but he resolved to keep his feelings for Lilith separate from his investigation. At the same time, he refused to believe her capable of such underhandedness. He knew Lilith, maybe not so well now as he used to, but still . . .

And last night, when he'd been drunk and foolish enough to climb that tree outside her window, he'd seen a glimpse of his Lily underneath her cool facade. With her hair down and her face scrubbed clean, she'd looked like she had on other nights when he'd sneaked up to her window. And when she smiled, it was very easy for him to forget all that had passed between them and to pretend they were young again.

He wanted her. And the only things that kept him from trying to have her were guilt over his wanting, that he didn't trust her and that tongues were already beginning to wag about them. If he weren't careful, he'd ruin his own reputation. A reputation he'd worked hard to build over the past few years.

And yet here he was, willing to take that risk if he could prove Lilith innocent of cheating. Because if he was wrong, if the young woman he'd fallen in love with no longer existed in any form, then it would be his fault, because he had chosen to protect his family from scandal while Lilith became the center of one.

He really would have been the ruin of her.

"I didn't think you'd come."

That low, crisp voice sent a shiver down his spine. He turned to face her, unprepared for the jolt that hit him square in the gut at the sight of her. In a gown of dark green satin, with her vibrant hair in an elaborate classical style that left much of the thick mass flowing down her back, Lilith looked like a porcelain doll. A doll that any man would die to play with.

She'd even condescended to wear fewer cosmetics than usual. Her skin was a truer shade, and only her cheeks and lips held any trace of false color.

"I hear that a lot lately," he replied when he had found his voice. "Makes me wonder why the devil everyone's so surprised."

Hands clasped behind her back, she came toward him—close enough that he could smell the citrus warmth of her scent. A confident smile curved her lips. He kept his gaze locked on hers, despite the enticing thrust of her breasts.

"Perhaps we were all secretly hoping you would not appear."

Her teasing tone was contagious. "To what end?"

Stopping no more than a foot away from him, Lilith arched a brow. "Is it possible my lord does not realize that he often does his best to intimidate those around him?"

Gabriel choked on a laugh. "I most certainly do not!"

Lilith took another step closer, her smile beguiling. "You do, too. I must say your technique has drastically improved over the years."

Flirtation was not a skill Gabriel had ever bothered to perfect. His mother's behavior had given him a strong dislike of fluttering eyelashes and innuendo. Whenever he approached a woman he made his intentions clear, but with Lilith, he found himself simply enjoying playing the game. Perhaps because he was so determined to win.

"I've much improved in other areas as well," he informed her, eliminating the scant inches between them.

Her gaze was shrewd and cool. "Of that I have no doubt."

Gabriel grinned at the sharpness in her voice. "You've improved as well, Lil, like a fine wine."

She snorted at that. "Are you making reference to my age, my lord?"

"Stop that foolish 'my lord'-ing." He ran the pads of his fingers over the smooth flesh of her cheek. She jumped at the contact. "I was going to wax poetic about your heady potency, your full body, but perhaps you aren't the sort of woman to be wooed by such compliments."

Lilith laughed—nervously, he thought—and took a step back. "Why Gabriel, I almost believed you sincere for a moment."

It was then that he remembered her challenge—the game, as she'd called it. She thought he was toying with her. Perhaps he was, but that did not mean he was lying.

"I've said many things in the past that I haven't meant, Lil, but complimenting you has never been on that list."

Her smile was shaky at best. "You never were free with flattery. You're a rarity amongst your sex in that respect." She dropped her gaze to the floor.

Her softly spoken words washed over him, chilling him deep inside. Had no one in the past ten years treated her as she deserved to be treated? Surely wherever she had hidden from him, there had been someone who treated her like a lady. A sensual, incredible lady.

He'd like to tear that someone's arms off.

"Why didn't you write to me?" The question was a whisper in his own ears. "I would have brought you home."

Her face went as white as snow. Her eyes were unnaturally dark and bright against the paleness of her cheeks. "Don't you dare play this game with me. I wrote you more letters than I could count until I finally realized you had no intention of 'bringing me home.' I will not allow you to make it my fault."

She wrote to him? Impossible! He'd never received any letters from her at all. Nor had any of her family members responded when he wrote to them, except for her aunt Imogen in Venice. She had sent him a very nice letter, sympathetic and understanding, but nevertheless urging him to go on with his life and leave her niece alone.

"They never arrived."

Her stormy eyes narrowed and she took several faltering steps backward. "That's not possible. You're lying."

Gabriel followed her, stung by her accusation. "What purpose would that serve after all these years? If you did indeed write, then someone intercepted your letters."

Her sneer was mocking. "And just who would want to do something like that?"

"Who were you staying with?"

Hands on her full hips, she glared at him. "My aunt Imogen in Italy. She was the only one who would have me."

Her aunt Imogen. Bitterness rose in the back of his mouth, coating his tongue and throat. Imogen had told him to move on with his life. That she didn't know where Lilith was, and the whole time the old bitch had done her part to keep him from ever finding Lilith. Why?

"Could she have had reason to take your letters?" He kept his voice low and calm. Flying into a fit of fury would not do him any good. Lilith's tone indicated how much she thought of her aunt. If he told her the old woman had lied to them both, she would demand proof—if she didn't throw him out on his backside first—and he didn't know if he had proof at all.

Color crept back into Lilith's cheeks. "Why would she do something like that?" The hard edge of her voice was softened somewhat by the smallest tremor of doubt. She didn't want to think badly of her aunt, and he didn't blame her, not after the way her family had treated her. But she wasn't wholly set against believing him, either, which gave Gabriel more joy than he cared to admit.

"You would be better equipped to answer that than I," he replied.

Frowning, Lilith shook her head. "Aunt Imogen would never do anything to hurt me."

"She may not have seen it that way." He didn't feel half as diplomatic as he sounded. If Lilith's aunt had intercepted her letters and thereby kept them apart, Gabriel hoped the old cow was burning in her own little corner of Hell for it.

Lilith continued to frown, worrying her lower lip with her teeth as she did so.

"Let's have no more maudlin talk of the past, shall we?"

Gabriel suggested, his tone falsely bright. "It is enough for me to know that you wrote."

Her head snapped up, her eyes wide. "You believe me?"

Gabriel's lips curved. Did she sound so surprised because she found it much harder to believe him or because she was lying? Somehow he didn't think it was the latter.

"Of course. Why would you lie after all these years?"

Lilith only nodded, obviously distracted. He could almost see the thoughts playing out in her head. If he believed her, then perhaps she should believe him, but if she believed him that meant she would have to entertain the idea of her aunt lying, and that would be difficult for her to accept. Gabriel had no intention of helping her find the truth. The seed of doubt had been planted, and she would have to work the rest out for herself.

"Shall we go in to dinner?" he asked when she remained silent. He wanted her to think about things, not dwell on them.

"Yes," she replied, snapping out of her reverie and taking the arm he offered. "Let us go in."

They left the gentlemen's club and crossed the foyer to a door near the building's entrance. This was the dining room, where clients could dine before gaming.

Tonight, the room was filled almost to capacity.

Everyone stared as the two of them walked in. Some paused with forks halfway to their mouths, food spilling back onto their plates. Some waited until they'd passed to start whispering. Others didn't.

That sense of anticipation returned. He'd been wrong to underestimate her. This was what she wanted—to cast doubt on him in the eyes of society.

The thought that a mere association with her could cause so much damage angered him. How had it come to this? All she had ever done was give him her body. And he'd taken it. Why was she the pariah and he the goddamned Angelic Earl?

Their table was situated near a large potted palm, so that

while they were visible to the other patrons, they were also afforded a touch of seclusion.

"I trust this table is satisfactory?" she asked as he held her chair.

"Quite," he replied with a smile. Had she chosen this spot to put him on display, or because she didn't trust herself to be alone with him?

Lord knew he didn't trust himself alone with her.

The waiter came with a bottle of wine. Gabriel wasn't surprised to discover it was German white. Lilith never did like red wine. It gave her a headache.

They made polite small talk until the first course arrived. Two glasses of wine each and a plate of oysters later, the conversation started to stray into what could have been dangerous territory but wasn't. Probably, Gabriel thought, because both of them *wanted* to go there.

"I was sorry to hear about your parents," he told her as he emptied the wine bottle into both their glasses.

Her answering smile told him she was glad for the sentiment but that it hadn't been necessary.

"Were you? I must confess, the news had very little effect on me at all." She drained her glass and motioned to the waiter to bring another bottle.

Gabriel found her statement hard to believe. Lilith had never received her parents' forgiveness, nor they hers. Discovering you were all alone in the world was hard to accept. He knew, because he'd done it himself. Of course, she'd had her saintly aunt Imogen to look after her.

Her gaze jerked to his, startling in its intensity. "I was, however, very upset to hear about your father."

Oh, Lil, you'd be even more upset if you knew the truth.

"I'm sorry I didn't tell you myself." He meant it.

Again she smiled as though she wasn't quite sure whether to believe him or not. "It's all right. You had more pressing things to take care of than chasing me across the Continent."

The way she said it, the self-mocking tone, made Gabriel

frown. "There have been times over the past ten years when I've had my doubts about that."

The waiter brought the wine and more food. Lilith waved the young man away when he tried to fill her glass, taking the bottle from him and pouring the liquid herself.

"I think it's safe to say we've both had our share of regrets, Gabriel. There's nothing to be done about that now."

"I think we are doing something," he argued, holding up his glass for her to replenish it.

"Are we?" Leaning back in her chair in a very unladylike fashion, Lilith arched one angular brow. "Do you think I would regret ruining you, Gabriel? Will you regret closing my club?"

"Yes," he replied honestly.

Her other brow lifted. "Yes to which question?"

He drank from his glass. The wine was sweet yet tart, not unlike Lilith herself. "To both. I think you and I stand to suffer some very serious regrets if we're not careful, Lilith."

"Eat," she insisted grimly, changing the subject as she shoved his plate toward him. "It is getting cold."

They both ate, and drank. At first the food was like sawdust in Gabriel's mouth, but as time wore on, it began to taste better. And they began to talk again. Even when they were younger and argued, they couldn't stay silent with each other for long. There was something between them that made not communicating impossible. They had to talk to each other, even if it was about nothing. Anything was preferable to silence.

They talked about people they once knew, people Lilith hadn't seen in years. People who didn't speak to her now when she saw them on the street. Gabriel found himself trying to make their lives sound terrible, just to give Lilith some measure of satisfaction.

"Oh, Serena Abernathy," he said with a slightly unsteady wave of his hand. "She married some frog and got fat. Dreadful, really."

Across the table, Lilith laughed. Deep and throaty, the sound was music to his ears.

"Gabriel, are you certain you're not embellishing just a little bit?"

Shrugging, Gabriel grinned. He'd had too much wine and it was showing. But Lilith was tipsy, too, so what did it matter?

"Thank you," she murmured, her hand hovering over the empty dishes between them.

Gabriel seized her fingers, almost dragging his coat sleeve through the Devonshire cream in which they'd dipped their strawberries, out of his fear that she might withdraw before he could touch her.

Their gazes locked and Gabriel didn't care if others were watching.

"Would you care to come upstairs for a drink?"

Would he! Only it wasn't a drink he had in mind. Nor, he'd wager, was it what she had in mind. She expected him to tell her why he'd singled Mallory's out, and he was going to have to tell her.

As he followed her out of the dining room, he became increasingly aware of the stares and whispers behind them. Hadn't their entrance caused enough of a stir? Lilith, he noticed, seemed oblivious to it. Either she was a good actress, or this kind of thing happened to her more than Gabriel cared to know.

A few gentlemen and ladies milled about the main hall, commenting on the statue of Venus or their losses at the tables. There were just enough of them to make a good-sized audience, and Gabriel realized that she wasn't inviting him upstairs so they could talk in private; she had done it so whoever was standing in the foyer would see him follow her into the corridor leading to her private rooms. The news would be all over town come morning.

And strangely enough, he couldn't bring himself to care. Perhaps it was the wine. Perhaps he was just bloody tired of being an "angel." Regardless, he was going to allow Lilith this moment of satisfaction. He would have his own soon enough.

And just what would that satisfaction be? Closing her club? Taking away the one thing she claimed to care about? Maybe he'd get to come inside her as well. That would be satisfying, wouldn't it? He could hurt her again, and this time he wouldn't even have a good excuse for it, except for a promise to a dead man that he hadn't been asked to make.

Once they were upstairs, she led him to a room that wasn't her boudoir, but rather an office. Her private office.

If she was cheating customers, this was where the evidence would be.

"No," he protested, overcome by something very much like panic as he stood on the threshold. "If we're going to talk it's not going to be in an office. Where are your apartments?"

He didn't wait for her before he started down to the other end of the corridor, opening doors as he went. Having a drink in her office would make it easier for him to search it later, but he would feel dirty if he looked for evidence against her now, even though she was planning to use this night against him.

"Gabriel!" she called from behind him. He could hear the swishing of her skirts as she ran after him.

He was already in her bedroom when she caught up with him. The threads of reason were fraying at an alarming rate, and it took all his willpower—and his pride—not to throw himself on that big oak bed and beg Lilith to have her way with him.

"You wanted to know why I singled Mallory's—you—out," he blurted.

She halted not even halfway across the room. Something in his expression must have alarmed her, because she didn't look so certain now. He didn't blame her. Surrounded by her belongings, the air smelling faintly of her perfume, he was entirely overwhelmed. This had been a bad idea. A very bad idea. He wanted to go back to her office.

"So why did you?" she asked, her voice soft.

Gabriel ran a hand through his hair. There was no easy way to tell her. "I was told that a gentleman was cheated at one of your tables. I was asked to prove it."

Lilith's face was pale, so pale that the slight rouge on her cheeks seemed heavy and garish. To her credit, however, she remained steady on her feet. Most women—most men, even—would have swayed under such a charge.

"Prove it?" she echoed, her eyes wide as she stared at him. "You believe it?"

"I don't know what I believe," he replied honestly. "I know what I would like to believe."

"Who is it?"

Should he be impressed or alarmed by how calm she sounded? He shook his head. "I gave my word that I wouldn't reveal the person's identity."

Lilith's stormy eyes narrowed. "How do I know this person even exists?"

"Do you really think I would have come after you, after Mallory's, if he didn't?"

"I know what *I* would like to believe," she retorted, not missing a beat.

Touché.

Her stare bore into him as though she was trying to peer into the depths of his soul. Perhaps she could.

"You realize, by telling me this, you've given me the chance to hide any evidence that might prove me dishonest."

He nodded.

An expression of understanding softened her features. For better or for worse, she'd finally realized why he had told her. It wasn't because of her threats to ruin him, but because he wanted her to know that he couldn't believe her capable of such an act.

"None of my staff would cheat, either," she informed him.

"You don't know that."

"I trust them."

"I don't."

She nodded, as though this kind of thing happened every day. But where was her temper? The accusations? Why was it that they could calmly discuss something as serious as cheating, yet couldn't discuss what had happened ten years ago without hurting each other?

Lilith's gaze flickered to the floor and back to him again. "This could look very bad for Mallory's if it is true."

Gabriel nodded. "It could, yes." He paused. "I am going to determine the truth, Lil. With or without your cooperation. You know that." *And I have every intention of using what I find to my advantage.*

He didn't have to say that. She already knew. He could see it in her eyes.

An eternity passed before Lilith drew a deep breath. "You will want a list of my dealers, I suppose."

What? She was going to help him? "That would be a good place to start, yes."

Her mouth set decisively, Lilith gave her head a sharp nod. "I will allow you to conduct your inquiry. I will even give you my full cooperation, but under one condition."

He raised a brow. "And what would that be?"

"I want a full apology when you discover just how wrong you are."

Gabriel almost chuckled at that. Of course she would want to make him grovel. "Agreed."

"And I want your word that when you learn just how wrong you are, you'll find another club to persecute."

Basically, she was asking him to stay the hell out of her life. It was a promise Gabriel didn't know if he could keep.

"Agreed."

She swallowed. He watched her throat constrict. "Thank you."

How difficult had it been for her to utter those words? Probably about as difficult as it had been for him to promise in the first place.

But walking out of Lilith's life wasn't something he had to

worry about for a while. For the time being, he had her cooperation. He had *her*.

"Do you have plans for tomorrow evening?" he heard himself ask. Where the devil had that come from?

Lilith looked as surprised as he felt. "The same as any other evening, to be here. Why?"

"I was thinking about going to the theater."

She must have heard the uncertainty in his voice, because she smiled ever so slightly. "Are you trying to ask me if I'd like to join you?"

He nodded determinedly. "I am."

Her smile grew but remained hesitant. "Are you certain that is a good idea? People will talk."

Yes, they would. Did he care? Not really, no. Perhaps he should.

"Will you come?"

She hesitated, and for a moment Gabriel's heart ceased beating.

"Yes," she said finally. "I will come."

"Wear something suitable," he ordered gruffly; why, he had no idea. "And you are not to wear any of that awful face paint, either. I will personally wash your face if you do."

Rather than getting angry or defensive, which he expected, Lilith laughed, sending a ripple of relief coursing through him.

"Listen to you. You sound just like a husband. Why have you never married, Gabriel? You'd be so very good at all that stuffy propriety."

Was it his imagination, or did she sound just the tiniest bit hopeful? Trying vainly to ignore the pain in his chest, Gabriel closed the distance between them. "Because, my dear Lilith, you are the only woman I wanted to ask."

He met her gaping expression with a shaky grin. "Now, shall we go have that drink? And let's make it a long one. I don't want the gossips accusing me of finishing too quickly."

* * *

"I feel naked."

Standing in front of her cheval mirror, Lilith smoothed her damp palms over the cool russet silk of her skirts.

Luisa pooh-poohed her. "You look beautiful," the abigail assured her in rapid Italian. "Like the lady you were born to be."

Lilith didn't bother to tell the woman that that was exactly why she felt naked. Her scandalous gowns and cosmetics were her armor. Whenever she wore those clothes, she expected the barbs and the whispers. She fit the role society had thrust her into. In this dress—one that Gabriel would consider "suitable"—her face bare and her hair wound atop her head in an elaborate yet sophisticated coil, she felt like a young girl playing dress-up in her mother's clothing.

The gown was beautiful, purchased on a whim the last time Lilith had visited her modiste. She loved the color, loved the style, but she would look like a hypocrite wearing something so elegant in the club.

The square neckline was low, but not nearly as low as on some of the gowns Lilith owned. The only adornment was the darker-russet-and-gold embroidery at the sleeves and hem. For jewelry, she wore pearl drops at her ears and a simple pearl choker around her neck.

And, true to Gabriel's wishes, her face was bare. The color in her cheeks had been put there by the pinch of Luisa's strong fingers. And a good thing, too, because she'd be deathly pale without it.

She was nervous. It was ludicrous, but true nevertheless. She was nervous about being seen in public with Gabriel. Scared that she would forget herself and actually pretend that the evening was real, that she was a proper lady, and then someone would remind her in a truly brutal fashion that she wasn't.

And she didn't want Gabriel to hear the things they said about her. Oh, not that she had forgiven him for abandoning her. It would take more than a trip to the theater for that, but what happened in the past was between them, and if anyone was going to make Gabriel feel guilty, it would be her.

Or himself. Lilith had a strong suspicion that Gabriel's regrets almost equaled her own.

And what about this cheating nonsense? He'd certainly seemed sincere about the charge, and although Lilith was almost convinced he wouldn't have come anywhere near her if it weren't true, she couldn't help but distrust him just a little bit. After all, she'd spent the past decade thinking the worst of him.

But the charge couldn't be true. Her staff was too honest. Lilith made certain that she hired people with honor and integrity. At least she thought they had honor and integrity. Besides, wouldn't something like that show up in the books? Maybe not, if the dealer was really good. Not if he—or she—altered the numbers at the end of the night.

All of her employees were supposed to keep track of winnings and losses at their tables, and Lilith balanced the cash boxes at the end of every night. Surely she would have noticed . . .

Now Gabriel had her doubting her staff. How easily she wanted to believe everything he told her. It was disgusting. He was wrong. And she would prove it.

"I will fetch your wrap," Luisa said, in English this time. "I will be right back."

While the maid was gone, Lilith dabbed perfume behind her ears and in her décolletage. The scent of orange and cloves drifted upward, the familiar aroma calming her chafed nerves.

Would Gabriel approve of her appearance? It shouldn't matter, but it did. Just as his claim that he never got her letters mattered. She found it hard to believe that *all* her letters could have gone astray, but he'd sounded so sincere that the question of exactly what had happened to them had plagued her for the rest of the night. If it hadn't been for all the wine they'd drunk, she wouldn't have slept a wink. And as it was, the question was the first conscious thought she had upon waking.

Aunt Imogen always took care of the post. Was it possible that she'd simply neglected to mail her letters to Gabriel? It seemed too awful a crime to accuse of the woman who'd been like a mother to her, but if Gabriel was telling the truth, what else could have happened?

He had to be lying. That was the simple answer. He didn't want to hurt her with the truth, and so he was trying to pass the blame to a dead woman who couldn't defend herself. Or perhaps it was a ruse to distract Lilith so he could plot against her and her club. Aunt Imogen would never do such a thing, not when she had known how much Gabriel meant to her.

Enjoy your youth, Lilith. You will always be able to find a man, but the chance to find oneself is a luxury not often afforded to our sex. You will forget about your earl and someday be glad that you did. What girl is equipped to be a countess at seventeen? It would destroy your spirit, my dear. Trust me. I was young once myself, you know.

Those words, spoken so long ago, had been accompanied by the stroking of Lilith's hair as she lay sobbing on her bed. Sobbing over Gabriel and the fact that he hadn't written, that he hadn't answered her letters. What if . . . ?

"Here is your wrap," Luisa announced, reentering the room with a cashmere shawl in her hands. "Will you meet him here or downstairs?"

"I'll go downstairs," Lilith replied softly, shoving her mind back to the present as the maid draped the shawl over her arms. "I'll be in the office."

But there was already someone in the office when Lilith got there. It was Mary, and even though she felt awkward to see her friend, Lilith thought it was much more preferable than being alone with her thoughts.

"I'm sorry. I didn't know you were here."

Mary looked up from the papers spread across the desk. Her expression was guarded. "I'm working on the accounts.

Our brandy suppliers want more money if they have to deal with Bronson's threats."

Lilith nodded. "Give it to them. Any word as to how Bronson reacted to our retaliation?"

It hadn't been much of a retaliation. Lilith had arranged for two of Bronson's own shipments to be delayed, causing a minor wrinkle in the workings of his club. It wasn't an open act of aggression, but enough so that he knew Lilith wasn't about to let him intimidate her.

"Nothing yet." The older woman's gaze skimmed her from head to toe. "Are you going out?"

"Gabe—Lord Angelwood—is taking me to the theater."

Mary's smile was coy. "Is he, now? Well, that sounds like much more fun than accounts. I do have plans, however, to write a letter to Reverend Sweet later this evening."

Intrigued, Lilith crossed the carpet to the desk. "Did he accept the play tokens?"

The other woman laughed. "Are you joking? Of course he did not! He returned them with a rather scathing reply, insinuating that you were trying to corrupt him as surely as Eve corrupted Adam."

Lilith clapped her hands together and laughed. "How do you intend to answer?"

"I am simply going to tell him you were only having a bit of sport with him—no hard feelings and all that. You look lovely, by the way. Gabe—*Lord Angelwood*—is bound to be impressed."

Blushing under her friend's teasing smile, Lilith averted her gaze, then jerked it back again. "I am sorry for our . . . disagreement. I hope you can forgive me."

"Forgive you?" Mary flopped back into the chair with an expression of surprise. "My dear friend, I forgave you five minutes after it happened. 'Twas you who kept your distance."

It was? Lilith hadn't realized. She'd been too caught up in Bronson's machinations, *and* in Gabriel's, to see that she had been the one who'd perpetuated the strain.

"Then I am truly sorry for being such an idiot." Sinking into one of the chairs in front of the desk, Lilith sighed. "Oh, Mary, I fear I am beginning to lose sight of what's important."

"You will find your way," she assured her. "You always do."

Lilith's answering chuckle was bitter. "Do I? I think perhaps I've always found *a* way. I am not so certain it is always been the right one for me."

"It would appear that you and Lord Angelwood have been given a second chance."

She snorted. "I'm not so certain of that, either. Part of me thinks he's simply out to ruin me again."

"Because that's what you would like to do to him?"

Lilith shrugged. "I am not sure what I would like to do, that's the problem. There is a part of me that still wants revenge, yes, but the more time I spend with Gabriel, the more I realize that I do not hate him. I'm not sure I ever did. Does that make sense?"

Nodding, Mary smiled gently. "The people we love are those with the power to hurt us the most. Both you and Gabriel seem to have been hurt by the past, but I think you would rather forgive each other than continue to hurt."

"And what if he closes my club? How am I to forgive him for that?"

Mary tilted her head to one side. "Would you find it easier to forgive yourself for ruining his reputation in front of his peers? Will revenge make you happy?"

"I—" Lilith couldn't think. "I honestly do not know."

"No? What does your heart tell you it wants most? Mallory's or the man you love?"

Lilith's heart jumped into her throat. "I most certainly do not love Gabriel!" But she didn't sound convincing to herself, and probably even less so to Mary.

She couldn't still love him, could she? It was ludicrous. She was seven-and-twenty now, not seventeen. He was no longer a sweet, awkward young man. He was grown and had changed almost as much as she had.

But had they really changed that much? Whenever they were together and not at odds, it often seemed as though they hadn't changed at all.

A knock sounded on the door before Lilith could even try to answer her friend's question.

"Lord Angelwood is here, Lady Lilith," the footman announced when Lilith bade him enter.

"Thank you." Rising to her feet, she turned to Mary with a shaky smile. "Wish me luck."

"You don't need it, but I shall keep my fingers crossed if it makes you feel better."

It would. Toes wouldn't hurt, either.

As she left the office Lilith exhaled slowly, trying to fight the butterflies in her stomach. It was just the bloody theater!

Gabriel was waiting for her in the club foyer, as were a dozen curious onlookers. Lilith tried to ignore the appreciative and surprised stares that met her entrance.

"Lady Lilith, we shall all feel your absence this evening," Mr. Dunlop announced as she walked by. Then, softly: "You'll put them all in a state of shock."

Lilith flashed a grateful smile at the Scotsman. Gabriel looked less than pleased.

"Good evening, Lord Angelwood." Lud, but she sounded like a breathless simpleton! Yet how could she not when the man before her robbed her of all sense and reason? He was stern and foreboding, sensual and teasing, and even his frown made her want to smile.

"Lady Lilith." He said it like he meant it. "You are in exceedingly good looks tonight."

His gray eyes lit with a devilish glint and Lilith couldn't help but smile in response. "Thank you, my lord. I had an exceedingly good dresser."

His gaze never dropped from hers, but Lilith felt it caress her body as surely as if he raked it from the top of her head to her toes. "An enviable task indeed," he murmured.

Blushing like an idiot schoolgirl, she took the arm he offered and allowed him to escort her outside and into his waiting carriage.

"Will anyone be joining us tonight?" Lilith asked once the carriage was in motion. It was either talk or throw herself across the distance between them and molest him right then and there! For a respectable gentleman, he certainly made her want to live up to her reputation as a fallen woman.

Of course, he had been the one to fell her in the first place.

"You remember Braven, don't you? He and his wife have come down from Yorkshire and will be joining us."

Lilith remembered hearing about one of Gabriel's closest friends many times in their youth. She also knew that Lord Braven must have heard about her as well. Was that why Gabriel seemed to be avoiding her gaze? Or was it because he didn't want her to see that he hadn't wanted to be alone with her, as she had stupidly hoped?

"I did not know he was in town."

He cleared his throat. "They just arrived this morning."

Lilith had to smile. So that was it. She should probably be insulted, but she found it impossible.

"He had to come to town and make certain I didn't get my claws into you again, did he?"

Gabriel finally looked at her, a self-deprecating grin curving his lips. "More likely he wanted to see me get my comeuppance."

"Ah. The truest and best of friends, then."

His grin grew. "The very best."

Lilith toyed with the fringe on her shawl. "Then I look forward to meeting him and will do my best not to disappoint him or his bride."

"I don't think you could disappoint them if you tried, Lil."

She grinned, too—at the teasing note in his voice, the use of his pet name for her. This was one of those times when it felt as though the past ten years hadn't happened. But they had.

"Gabriel, will you do something for me?"

Something in her voice must have alerted him to the importance of what she was going to ask him, because his expression changed to one of concern.

"What?" he asked.

"If—*if*—you do discover that someone in my employ is guilty of cheating, will you tell me before you make it public knowledge? I should like to have a chance to take action of my own."

He watched her carefully for a moment, probably wondering if that action would have anything to do with interfering with his own plans. That wasn't what she intended at all. She only wanted to dismiss the guilty party—if there was one—and try to save as much face as she could before the news got out.

Gabriel nodded. "Yes. I'll let you know first."

"Thank you." Her words were sincere. Obviously he believed her motives for wanting to know, and that meant he still had some degree of trust where she was concerned, even if it was minuscule, just as some part of her trusted him to keep his word to her.

If it weren't for their differing views on gambling and his quest to prove her a cheat, Lilith could almost imagine there might be a chance of their picking up where they had left off. But there was too many issues between them, and even though both wanted to see new laws invoked, Gabriel wanted to take it to the extreme. Why?

She could ask, but she had the feeling he wasn't ready to tell her. She hadn't done anything worthy of his trust and he wouldn't willingly give her anything to use against him. Oh, she could say that she'd never do something so despicable as to use personal information to win this battle between them, but she would. Like a rat, if she was boxed into a corner, she would use everything at her disposal to fight her way out.

She'd become quite a piece of work.

"You're very quiet all of a sudden."

Gabriel's voice brought her back to the moment. She forced a smile. "Forgive me. I was merely woolgathering."

"You were doing more than that. Would you care to talk about it?"

This was not the time for him to be her friend—or anything else, for that matter. It would be all too easy for her to take him up on it.

"No."

He chuckled, the sound far too low and personal in the close confines of the carriage, especially since the dim lamplight softened his chiseled features and reminded her of the boy she'd loved.

"Thinking about me, were you?"

"Of course not!" she snapped and then cursed herself, for her peevish tone would only convince him he was right.

He laughed again. "I hope your thoughts of me are as good as the ones I sometimes have of you, Lil."

"You think of me?"

Gabriel's good humor seemed to vanish. "I cannot believe you have to ask."

"What kind of thoughts?" She had to ask, even though she wasn't entirely certain she wanted to know.

"Ah!" he cried, sounding for all the world as if he were choking. "Here we are."

The carriage rolled to a halt, and before Lilith could utter another word, Gabriel had the door open and was climbing out.

"I told Brave to meet us outside. I'll go find his carriage and come back for you. Wait here."

He closed the door, muffling the sounds of laughter and horses that filled the night air. Alone, Lilith felt his departure acutely. The space that had seemed so small with him in it was now cavernous.

He thought of her. Such secretive thoughts that he couldn't admit to them. Good. The knowledge put a smile in her heart even as her mind told her nothing could ever come of it.

The carriage door opened.

"That was fast," she remarked in a teasing voice. "Did you find your friend?"

The head that poked through the entrance wasn't Gabriel's.

In fact, the sight of it struck such fear and dread into Lilith's heart that all thought of Gabriel vanished.

"Bronson."

Her rival grinned, revealing teeth that looked more like they belonged to a wolf than to a man. "Good evening, Lady Lilith. Pretending to be quality tonight, are we?"

"I was born 'quality,' sir. I have no need to pretend."

The cold, sharp tone would have worked on any other person, but not on Bronson. He seemed amused by her rancor.

Bronson's pale eyes glittered. He would be a handsome man if he weren't so vile. "But you are not quality anymore, unless being some lord's whore makes it such these days." He dragged his glance along the length of her, leaving a trail of invisible slime on Lilith's flesh.

"I like you better with your lips painted and your tits pushed up."

Such vulgarity sounded strange coming from that face and that mouth. Because it was so odd, Lilith's reaction was all the more acute. Hot pinpricks of shame danced along her back, making her want to cover herself completely with the shawl.

She didn't. Bronson was just showing his roots. A man could crawl out of the gutter—he could even pretty himself up a bit—but a man like Bronson carried some of that stench with him for the rest of his life.

"And I like you better at a distance, Mr. Bronson. Now, if you will be so kind as to be on your way? I'm expecting Lord Angelwood to return at any moment."

Bronson's gaze narrowed. "Some of us club owners want to know just what your game is. Angelwood is determined to close us all up."

Lilith regarded him evenly, clenching her jaw to keep it from trembling. Bronson scared her. He was like a wild animal, cagey and unpredictable. And ultimately ruthless.

"Maybe so, but at least he hasn't resorted to theft and vandalism in his attempts to close my club."

Bronson's expression hardened. "If I'd known all it took to

get between your legs was a fancy waistcoat, I'd have visited my tailor."

Lilith laughed. Not the reaction Bronson had hoped for, given the darkening of his cheeks.

"If that was your goal, you chose the wrong way to go about it, Mr. Bronson. Getting into my bed takes more than a man like you could ever aspire to achieve. Now, please leave."

To her surprise, he actually pulled back. Only his head remained in view. Smiling in a manner that looked more like a snarl, he tipped his hat to her. "Enjoy the play, Miss Mallory. And make sure you have the earl see you safely home. This area's not safe for a woman, especially not one as pretty as you."

And then he was gone, leaving Lilith stiff with fear. Had Bronson just threatened her life? Oh, dear God, she never thought their rivalry would come to this!

She reached for the door, trying to bring it closed again, but it was wrenched out of her fingers with a force that made her cry out and dive into the farthest corner.

Had Bronson returned?

"Who the hell was that?"

It was Gabriel. Dear, sweet, strong Gabe. And he was scowling like a child whose favorite toy had just been taken away.

Accepting the hand he offered, she lifted her gaze to his as he helped her to the ground. Staring into the silvery concern—and yes, jealousy—in his eyes, Lilith plastered a false smile on her face.

"No one."

Chapter 7

"Tell me who he is."

Frowning, Lilith waved his arm off her chair. "Shhh."

Slumping back in his chair with a scowl of his own, Gabriel reluctantly turned his attention back to the play. He didn't even know what the damn thing was about. All of his energy had been focused on trying to find out the identity of the good-looking sod he'd seen Lilith talking to.

And what had he said that had scared Lilith enough for her to cower in a corner? Lilith did not scare easily. She was too hardheaded for that. So why did this man scare her? Had he tried to accost her? And if he had, why didn't Lilith tell him?

Perhaps she hadn't wanted him to make a scene. He had to admit he would have been sorely tempted to break the nose of any man who would dare insult Lilith in such a way. For that matter, so would Lilith. No, the threat the man offered hadn't been one so base as sex, or if it had been, there had been much more to it.

Much more.

Onstage, the lead actor was babbling something about the inconstancy of women. With the roar of jocularity going on in the pit below, it was hard to tell just what the fool was saying.

Christ, he hated the theater.

Lilith, on the other hand, gave every appearance of a woman having the time of her life. Perched on the edge of her chair, her palms curved around the balustrade, she watched the performers with all the rapture of a child given a box of sweets. What it was she found so fascinating, Gabriel had no idea, but she laughed and clapped and whispered with Rachel, Lady Braven, with an enthusiasm he found startling.

He was thankful for Brave and Rachel's presence, even though his friend had indeed come to London out of sheer nosiness. Last year, when Brave had married and was falling in love with his countess, Gabriel had used himself and Lilith as an example of how not to conduct a proper relationship. He'd also told his friend he never thought to see Lilith again. He couldn't blame Brave for wanting to witness the reunion for himself. He'd do the same thing.

And when Gabriel invited them to join him and Lilith at the theater, they'd been all too happy to oblige. It would be good for Lilith to be treated well by two members of the *ton*. It also prevented Gabriel from being alone with her. He behaved so out of character whenever she was near that he didn't trust himself not to draw the loge curtains and take her right there. Wouldn't the gossips have a time with that! The Angelic Earl screwing Lilith Mallory in the Drury Lane!

Damn hypocrites. As though any of them were much better. Lilith had been a young girl when their affair ruined her. Half the *ton* conducted affairs right underneath their spouses' noses. Yet somehow they were better than Lilith because they managed to keep their escapades from becoming too public.

Hadn't his mother been the same way? Her affairs were legendary among the *ton*. Her reputation, her secret "treatments" from disreputable physicians. Whether it was disease or pregnancies or even both that the physicians were "curing" his mother of, Gabriel didn't know. He didn't want to know.

He'd loved both of his parents, but even now he didn't understand them. It was a very difficult thing, wanting to be like them in some ways and so utterly ashamed of them in others. He didn't gamble because he didn't want to be compared to his father. He didn't bed every woman who glanced sideways at him because he didn't want people saying he'd inherited his mother's lusty appetites.

And yet here was Lilith, a scandalous woman with a gambler's heart, and Gabriel wanted her more than he'd ever wanted anything else. She made him want to take chances and throw caution to the wind.

As Lilith stared raptly at the stage below, Gabriel allowed himself the luxury of studying her. The deep russet color of her gown warmed her flesh to smooth ivory. The pearls around her neck glowed, lighting her bare skin. And her scent, that heady mix of orange and cloves, flooded his senses.

She made him feel one-and-twenty again. Wanting her, needing her—urges that were overpowering. The merest thought of her was enough to make his chest ache. What he wouldn't give for the chance to go back and change things.

Lilith must have felt the heat of his gaze upon her. She turned her head toward him, a curious expression on her face.

It took all the strength Gabriel could summon to smile. If he didn't, then she'd see the regret and longing on his face. He wasn't ready for her to know just how deep those feelings went. Not yet.

He held her gaze far longer than necessary, searching the wide, stormy depths of her eyes for some sign that he was not alone in this obsession. He saw nothing.

He looked away, focusing for a moment on where her hands gripped the railing—her gloves pulled tight across her knuckles—before settling it on the stage. And there his gaze, if not his attention, remained for the rest of the play.

When it was over, Gabriel watched surprise flicker over Lilith's features when Rachel invited her to tea the following afternoon. His liking for Brave's wife soared to new levels. Her willingness to thumb her nose at society and offer her friendship to Lilith meant more to Gabriel then he could ever explain.

"I trust I shall see you sometime tomorrow as well, Gabe," Brave murmured, coming to stand beside him.

Gabriel smiled. His friend's interest in his life was as amusing as it was heartwarming. He, Brave and Julian had always been there for each other, through the deaths of parents and siblings and other personal tragedies. No doubt Julian would move heaven and earth to get home to England if he knew about Lilith. For that reason, Gabriel chose not to inform him of the situation in his last letter.

"I would never turn down the chance to see your son."

"Excellent!" Brave replied with more jocularity than Gabriel was used to. "Why don't the two of you come together?"

Good God, Brave was trying to play matchmaker! Gabriel would have laughed out loud if he hadn't been shocked into silence.

He and Lilith could hardly refuse and so, neatly wrapped up in Brave and his wife's little trap, Gabriel bade them good night and escorted Lilith outside to the waiting carriage.

"They seem like very nice people," Lilith said once the carriage was in motion.

"They are. I couldn't ask for better friends. I believe you can count them as yours as well."

"Yes." Her voice held more than a trace of wonder. "They did seem to like me, didn't they?"

"Does that surprise you?" That it might surprised him. The unfortunate circumstances of her reputation aside, how could Lilith possibly be surprised that someone liked her?

Sitting back against the velvet squabs, she nodded, a self-conscious smile curving her lips. "Yes, it does. I'm not accustomed to being all that likable."

"Don't be foolish," he replied more harshly than he had intended. "Of course you're likable."

The look she shot him was one of thinly veiled amusement with just a hint of sadness. "I have one friend, Gabe. One."

When they were younger, Lilith had people competing for her attention wherever she went.

Leaning forward, Gabriel reached across the distance between them, seizing one of her hands. From their clasped fingers, he raised his gaze to hers.

"You have me." She did. As surely as he breathed, he belonged to her and she belonged to him.

She frowned and pulled her hand away as though his touch burned. "You're not my friend, Gabriel."

"What am I, then?" He wasn't sure he wanted to know.

"I'm not certain, but if you were my friend you wouldn't try to hurt me as you are."

Not again.

"Lily—"

"Are you coming into the club when we arrive?" Hands tucked under her arms, where he couldn't possibly reach them without forcing himself upon her, she stared out the window at the dimly lit street passing by.

Fine; let her change the subject if that was how she wanted to be. It saved him the trouble of having to lie or tell partial truths.

"I thought I might, yes."

She jerked her head in a stiff nod. "Understand that I shall have business to attend to when we get there. I won't be able to entertain you."

Something about the way she said the word "entertain" struck a chord within him. Did she think he saw her as some kind of joke?

"'Twas your idea to play this game, Lily. Not mine."

From her dark and narrow glance he felt rather than saw the full effect of her anger.

"So I should just sit back and let you ruin everything I've worked for? Give you the satisfaction of winning?" She snorted. "I do not think so."

Gabriel sighed. "Even though I told you why I've singled Mallory's out, you are still determined to make this about us, aren't you?"

Her lips twitched—a bitter mockery of a smile. "As determined as you are to insist that it is not."

Is that what he was doing? Using Blaine's request as some thinly veiled excuse to be near her, to punish her for breaking his heart all those years ago?

No. She was simply trying to make him doubt himself.

His tone was soft. "What is it that you want?"

She was staring out the window again. "I want my life back. I don't want to be an outsider in the world I was born into. Not anymore."

"And forcing you to give up your club will give me what I want—is that what you think?" His jaw was so tight it ached.

She spared him a brief glance. "Will it not?"

Could she really believe he'd changed that much?

"No," he replied. "It will not." It would fulfill his promise to his father, but it wouldn't give him back his youth, or Lilith. In fact, the youth he'd wasted trying to protect his family from scandal and rebuild a fortune—the reason he'd lost Lilith in the first place—would only serve to drive her farther away.

"Who was the man I saw you talking to at the theater?"

Her jaw jutted angrily as she answered, "His name is Samuel Bronson. He owns a club called Hazards."

"What is he to you?" Gabriel didn't sound jealous. He sounded downright possessive.

A soft, scoffing chuckle grated his already frayed temper. "Curious, he asked me the same question about you."

"Well?" Damn it, if she didn't tell him he was going to explode.

"He's just another man who would love to see Mallory's close, and he is *my* concern, Gabriel, not yours."

What could he say to that? He had no claim to her, none at all, no matter how much he might think he did. He couldn't force her to confide in him, especially since he hadn't confided all his secrets to her.

But he'd find out just who this Bronson was and why he frightened Lilith. He'd unearth every last one of her secrets if it was the last thing he did. He could only hope that he unearthed hers before she revealed his.

They spent the rest of the ride in stiff silence, both holding their thoughts close. How badly he wanted to tell her everything. She was one of the few people who would understand, other than maybe Brave and Jules. But he hadn't told them and he couldn't tell her, not until he was certain she wouldn't use the information against him.

Lilith left his side the moment they entered the club. He felt her absence sorely, and for that reason he was glad to see her gone. It wasn't easy to be near her. He had to find out once and for all if she had indeed cheated Frederick Foster and others like him. Only then would he know if she deserved the trust he wanted to give her.

He had to search her upstairs office.

He suspected she would have hidden anything that might make her look guilty or, worse yet, prove her own involvement, but maybe something got overlooked. And if Lilith herself wasn't involved, then the club books might give him some clue to who the guilty party was. Regardless, Gabriel was going to keep as much of his investigation from Lilith as he could. The less she knew, the less she could prepare for. If she was guilty, she would try to misguide him, and if she wasn't, there was the chance that she might try to protect her employees in order to keep Gabriel from taking action.

The foyer was deserted save for two gentlemen having a heated debate over whether or not England's lower classes would rise up in rebellion as France's had. It was relatively easy for Gabriel to slip into the passage leading to Lilith's private apartments. She had disappeared into the club with the man she called Latimer and would, he hoped, spend at least several minutes taking care of club business.

He moved quickly and silently up the stairs to the room she'd shown him the other night. A fast perusal proved that he was indeed alone, and closing the door behind him, he crossed the carpet to the desk.

In the bottom drawer was a pile of ledgers. In one of them he found lists of liquor and food shipments, several of which had "Destroyed" written in the margin. That was no doubt a hazard of importing goods, but he noticed the amount of damaged shipments had increased over the past three months. Lilith should change suppliers.

If it was indeed the supplier's fault.

What was it Lilith had said about that other club owner, Bronson? She had said that he would like to see her out of business, too. Were the destroyed shipments Bronson's way of trying to make that happen?

A frown creased his brow at the thought. He was somewhat familiar with Bronson's club—he made it his business to be familiar with almost every club in London—but he knew little about the man himself. He would have to change that. Business rivalry was one thing, but vandalism and threats were another, and if Bronson threatened Lilith, Gabriel would make certain he paid for it.

He picked up another ledger. A list of employees, their hiring dates, their wages and an account of how much money they brought in during the run of a night. The amounts varied from night to night, as one would expect, but everything appeared to be legitimate. All the numbers added up. No significant discrepancies reported on any one occasion.

Next was an accounting of people who frequented the club: who won and who lost and the dates. Several individuals had suffered large losses, some of which had been collected, others that had not. Some losses had even been written off with Lilith's initials in the column beside the date. Why would she write off debts? Unless, of course, the person paid her with something other than cash. Information, perhaps?

He slid his finger down the pages, stopping when he found what he wanted. Frederick's debt was large, as Blaine had told him, only the actual amount was much larger than Frederick had admitted to his father. It also hadn't been completely paid.

Why would Lilith go to all the trouble of cheating Frederick and then not force him to settle the debt? It didn't make sense. He and Garnet extended credit to many customers, but that was with the understanding that regular payments be made. Frederick's entry didn't indicate whether or not payment arrangements had been established. And certainly Blaine could cover the amount.

Most curious.

Putting the ledgers back into their former order, Gabriel put them away and closed the drawer. He had better get back downstairs before Lilith noticed he was gone.

He made it back downstairs unnoticed. Lilith really should have more security. Anyone could sneak upstairs into her apartments, where she lived alone, if they wanted. This was twice he'd entered her living area undetected. Only Mary and Latimer and a few servants lived at the club. Mary had her own rooms off the ladies' club and Latimer's were located closer to the servants'. So anyone could sneak in and wait for Lilith to retire for the evening.

He'd kill anyone who dared harm her. The idea of it filled him with such rage, such dread, that his fingers curled into fists at his sides. But it wasn't so much the thought of someone hurting her that bothered him. It was the idea of losing her again that set his heart pounding and made his throat tight. The thought of having her gone forever, of having no hope at all for the future, hurt more than he cared to admit.

The club bustled with activity. Faintly, above the dull roar of voices, Gabriel could hear music. Looking up, he saw several vents high along the walls. No doubt there were similar vents in the dining room and in the ladies' club as well. Lilith's musicians could sit in one room and play for the entire club, their music floating into the different rooms through these simple vents. It was a clever touch, and saved Lilith the expense of having to hire an orchestra for each room.

Lilith was nowhere to be seen. Gabriel scanned the room for a familiar face—someone he could actually bring himself to speak to. Most of the gentlemen present were of his class or acquaintance, but he had no desire to make conversation with any of them.

Laughter, interspersed with cries of good-natured encouragement and heartfelt disappointment, rose above the din. There was a kind of excitement to the evening. Just being present had Gabriel's heart beating faster. What must it be like for the men actually playing?

Lilith had told him he must have some gambler in him to take a chance in business as he had. Perhaps she was right, but he had been gambling to preserve his way of life, something he wouldn't have had to do if his father's predilection for play hadn't destroyed it in the first place.

If his father were alive today, he would no doubt be sitting at one of these felt-covered tables, raising his glass in a toast to Lilith and her excellent club.

Of course, if his father were alive, Gabriel would have married Lilith years ago and there wouldn't be a Mallory's.

Drifting deeper into the large interior of the club, Gabriel continued to search the crowd. How hard could it be to find one woman? Especially a woman like Lilith? To be sure, there were a few women at the tables, but none of them had Lilith's presence, or her vibrant red hair, although one or two of them obviously had tried to achieve a similar shade through hennas.

Cyprians. Mistresses. Bits of muslin. It wasn't unusual for men to bring their lady loves with them to a gaming club. Vices were traditionally considered more exciting when indulged in two or more at a time, or so Gabriel had heard. The idea of sticking his wick inside a woman who had lain with countless men—and probably several just hours before him—made his stomach churn. He'd experienced sex for the sake of release before, but only with one of the few mistresses he'd had over the years. He preferred to have some degree of fondness for the women with whom he shared a bed.

And it never felt as good as it had that night he and Lilith made love, but he didn't want to think about that. Not now.

A familiar crop of dark curls appeared in his line of vision. Unease crept up his spine. What the devil was Frederick doing here? It hardly seemed normal behavior for a boy who had been cheated to return to the scene of his misfortune, particularly when he still owed the house money. Perhaps he had simply followed some friends, and if he wasn't gaming, he had nothing to worry about.

Blaine's son was with a group of other young men. They'd obviously been drinking, judging from their boisterous behavior and disheveled appearance. They moved through the club like a small storm, forcing others to get out of the way or be run into. Many older men scowled at the boys and voiced their disapproval. But others laughed and urged the lads on.

Frederick and his friends went through the doors on the far wall of the club that led to the private rooms in the back. Giving them enough of a lead so they wouldn't notice him behind them, Gabriel followed them down the large and blessedly empty corridor. The last thing he needed was for someone to call out in greeting and alert Frederick.

The group stumbled to the last door on the right, not far from where Lord Somerville had met Lady Wyndham. Opening the door, they all tried to squeeze through at once, laughing and cursing each other good-naturedly. Gabriel couldn't help but smile at their youthful silliness. He'd been like that once himself.

After the door closed behind them, Gabriel crept toward it. He could hear their muffled voices through the oak. The distant clamor of the club kept him from making out the words. Kneeling on the floral-patterned carpet, he put his eye to the keyhole and peered inside.

What he saw made his jaw tighten.

Frederick most certainly was not a young man who had learned his lesson about the dangers of gambling. In fact, he appeared to be just the opposite.

The boys had set up a game of dice on the floor of their

parlor, and Frederick was eagerly voicing his preference to be the first to throw.

Promise to Blaine or not, Gabriel was going to have a little chat with the viscount's son, but not before he did a little investigation of the dealer who had allegedly fleeced Frederick that night. And if he had to, he'd go to Lilith as well. She wouldn't be impressed that he'd suspected her of being a cheat. She'd be even less impressed to know he'd discovered Frederick and his friends—most of whom were underage—playing illegal dice games in her back rooms.

It was all he needed to shut her down.

Where was he?

Anxiety coiling in her stomach, Lilith wove her way through the crowded club. Talking to Latimer had taken longer than expected, especially since she'd had to stop her loyal friend from personally going after Bronson. She'd told her manservant about her run-in with Bronson at the theater only so he'd be on his guard, and caution the rest of the staff to be careful as well.

And now Gabriel was on the loose in her club. No doubt he'd already searched her office for something to incriminate her with. Let him look; he'd find nothing.

Unless, of course, he went to the back parlors.

Quickening her pace, Lilith headed for the doors in the rear. She had little idea of what most people did in the private rooms, and to be honest, she really didn't care as long as they didn't harm anyone. But she knew that the rooms were often used for sexual trysts and private gaming and other things she was not involved in.

If Gabriel found something illegal or scandalous going on there, it would be all too easy for him to shut Mallory's. He'd have her club closed before she could think of a way to stop him. Even if she threatened to tell the world the Earl of Angelwood had lowered himself to tradesman, she knew Gabriel wouldn't back down.

Panic welled up inside her as she slipped through the doors.

Hiking her skirts well above her ankles, she ran down the corridor, her footfalls muffled by the plush carpet, but nothing could stifle the fear that her labored breathing contained.

She held her breath.

And when she turned the corner and saw Gabriel on his knees at the far end of the hall, all that breath came rushing out in a cry of dismay.

"Lord Angelwood!" she shouted—so loud that whoever was in that room was sure to hear. "*What are you doing?*"

Glaring at her with an intensity Lilith had never seen before, Gabriel slowly rose to his feet. Standing there in his evening attire, the knees of his black trousers slightly dusty and wrinkled, he was the epitome of a most magnificent and intimidating man. If she had any sense, she'd be frightened of him, but she wasn't smart enough to be afraid of Gabriel, even though he was the only man with the power to truly hurt her.

"Get away from that door," she ordered, cursing the slight tremor in her voice.

He did as she bade him. That in itself was worrisome. Silently, his eyes still burning with anger, he moved toward her. He was embarrassed to have been caught snooping, and she hadn't made things any easier by so loudly announcing his presence.

Good. That would teach him to go poking around in her club.

"You have no business back here," she informed him as he came closer. Stubbornly, she held her ground.

Still he said nothing. Annoyance flared within Lilith's breast. "Go ahead and send for Bow Street if you want. By the time the runners get here, the people in that room will be gone, and even if they're not, they won't be doing anything worth Bow Street's attention."

He was standing right in front of her now.

"If you're trying to bully me, it won't work." It was weak bravado, but it would do. "I refuse to curl up and surrender just because you think I should. I—"

"Shut up," he snarled, his fingers curling around her shoulder.

She opened her mouth to respond, but before she could say a word, he opened the door nearest them and thrust her inside. Thankfully, the room wasn't already occupied.

Stumbling, Lilith clutched the back of a brocade sofa for support. Hastily she put it between Gabriel and herself.

"I don't suppose it occurred to you *once* during these last few minutes that perhaps I might have been peering through that keyhole for reasons that have little or nothing to do with you." He folded his arms across his chest. "And that by shouting out my presence, you let the person I was watching know I was there."

Lilith frowned. What was he talking about? "Of course it never occurred to me, Gabe. Why would I think something like that when you've made it known that you intend to close my club?" A sudden thought crossed her mind. Gabriel was friends with Lord Wyndham. Had he seen Lady Wyndham and her lover?

"Who were you watching?"

Gabriel sighed. He didn't look as angry as he had a few moments ago. He moved toward her. "Does Frederick Foster come here often?"

Frederick Foster? Oh, yes, Viscount Underwood's son. What did Gabriel want with Frederick?

"About once or twice a week," she replied. Lately, the young man had been showing up more than that, but Lilith wasn't going to tell Gabriel that until she knew for certain what he was up to.

"He's here tonight." Gabriel took another step forward.

Something about the way he moved made Lilith feel like a mouse cornered by a very wily cat. She edged around a chair, her gaze never leaving his. "I know. Why is that so important?"

There was no anger left in his expression, but he held himself like a man trying very hard to restrain himself. She would not feel bad for interrupting whatever it was he was doing, or for alerting Frederick Foster to his presence. She made the conclusion—a natural one for her—that he was trying to gather information against her. She wouldn't feel guilty for doing the same thing, had their roles been reversed.

"He promised his father he wouldn't gamble anymore."

Lilith couldn't help but laugh. "And his father believed him? Young men will do whatever their friends are doing, not what their fathers want."

Gabriel didn't seem to agree with her, but he didn't take the bait. "Did Frederick settle his debt?"

She shook her head, ready to bolt if he came any closer. She didn't ask how he knew about Frederick's debt. No doubt the boy's father had told him. They were friends after all. "We made a payment schedule. He can settle when he gets his next quarterly."

Gabriel's eyes narrowed. "That's very kind of you."

Licking her dry lips with an almost equally dry tongue, Lilith shrugged. "He's young. Everyone makes mistakes when they're young."

He was at the chair now. "I'm beginning to realize that."

Heart pounding, Lilith made for the safety of a large table, hoping to put it between her and Gabriel. What did he mean? Was he referring to their relationship or how it had ended?

Before she could ask, he grabbed her, spinning her around so that they were face-to-face and pressing her backward. She was caught between the edge of the table and the hardness of his thighs.

"You came here looking for me, Lil," he said in that deceptively low tone of his. "What did you intend to do once you found me?"

Raising her chin, she stared at him defiantly, although she was certain he could see the hammering of the pulse in her throat. What was he doing? Was this perverse seduction meant to intimidate her or punish her?

Or punish himself?

His eyes were bright, like molten silver. Lilith's breath caught at what she saw there. It wasn't anger. It wasn't intimidation. It was desire.

"What *are* you doing?" she demanded, her voice hoarse.

He lifted one hand to her throat. His palm was warm, his fingers strangely soft as they caressed her neck and collarbone. Lilith swallowed hard.

His gaze bore into hers. "I have no idea. A short while ago, I told myself it would be best if I kept my distance from you, but I don't seem to be able to do that. Not for very long."

She tried to ignore the hard ridge pressing into her belly by concentrating on the edge of the table digging into the backs of her thighs. But it was hard, so very, *very* hard. And somewhere deep inside her, her body remembered what it felt like to have him so very deep inside her, to feel him moving there while he held her, his breath hot against her ear as he told her how much he wanted her, needed her, *loved* her.

She wouldn't fall for it this time.

"What were they doing in the room?"

"A dice game," he replied, trailing his fingers along the sensitive flesh just above her breasts. The neckline of her gown was nowhere near as scandalous as some on her other gowns, but Gabriel's touch made this one seem positively indecent.

"Is that all?" It was enough.

His fingers splayed over her breastbone. He nodded, pressing his hips even deeper into hers. So deep she gasped. "Yes. That is all."

Straining back against the table only served to intensify the contact between them. If it became any more intense, Lilith was liable to explode. She gripped the hard oak edge, resisting her body's demands that she raise her hips.

"What are you going to do to me?"

His wide lips curved into a faint smile. "What do I have to do to convince you this goes beyond you and me?"

Just what did he find so bloody amusing? Arching a brow, Lilith replied, "You can tell yourself that if it makes you feel better, Gabe, but I know it's all about you and me. Unless you can prove otherwise, that's what I'll continue to believe."

He cupped her face in both his hands. His gaze was so warm, his touch so gentle, that Lilith's throat tightened.

"Lilith. *Lily.*" He breathed her name like a sigh, pressing his forehead to hers. "If this was just about us, do you think I'd be trying so hard to abolish gaming? Wouldn't it make more sense to just target you?"

It was difficult to look at him when he was this close. Hell, it was impossible to think. "You *have* targeted me."

"But not because I want to hurt you, Lilith." He tilted her chin upward with his thumbs. "If my feelings for you had anything to do with how I feel about gambling, do you think I'd be here right now? Do you think I'd do this?"

And before Lilith could ask what "this" was, Gabriel's lips were on hers, moving with an urgency that would not be denied. She clung to the table as her knees threatened to buckle beneath her.

Why he was doing what he was doing ceased to matter as his tongue met hers. He held her head still, his fingers tangling in her hair so that pins dug into her scalp. It felt as though he wanted to devour her.

She wanted to be devoured.

Tentatively, she released the table and slid her palms along his waist, up the soft wool of his coat to clutch at his lapels. She didn't push as her mind told her to. She didn't pull as her body urged, but simply held on.

His hands left her hair, sending pins clattering to the desk and pulling at her scalp. Down her back to the curve of her hips, his fingers scorched her. He drew her forward as he stepped back, and then his strong arms were around her waist, lifting her as if she weighed no more than a child.

Lilith's eyes flew open as her feet left the ground. Tearing her mouth free of his, she met his smoky gaze. He held her so that they were eye to eye, her breasts flattened against the solid wall of his chest, her hips against his, her toes dangling around his shins.

"Where are you taking me?"

He was already lowering her when she asked the question. Down onto the thickly padded chaise she went, cool silk below her, warm male above.

The weight and size that Gabriel carried should have stolen the breath from her lungs, but they didn't. Pushing her skirts up above her knees, he settled between her legs, the brunt of his weight resting on her pelvis, and on the forearms he braced on either side of her head.

God, but she shouldn't be doing this. She knew she shouldn't, but for the life of her, Lilith couldn't think of a single reason not to. What could possibly be wrong about something she wanted so badly? They were both adults. There weren't reputations or futures at stake here. The worst thing that could happen would be if someone intruded upon them and London's elite found out their Angelic Earl wasn't such an angel after all. It was hardly enough to ruin all of Gabriel's hopes and dreams, although he just might have to forget his ridiculous quest to outlaw gambling.

As for Lilith, it would only prove what society already thought of her. It wasn't as though joining bodies with Gabriel could ruin her a second time. Not socially anyway.

Sweet God, how she burned for him! No other man, and there had been several who tried, had ever made her feel the way Gabriel Warren did. Even as a boy, he'd known just how and where to touch her.

Right now, he was running his lips down her jaw to the heated flesh between her neck and shoulder. His breath was even hotter. Lilith shivered, her nipples tightening in response as her hands slid down his back to his hips.

Flicking the tip of her tongue across the velvety lobe of his ear, she chuckled in satisfaction as his hips jerked against her.

"I remember, too, Gabe," she whispered. He wasn't the only one who knew just where to touch.

He raised his head, the action putting further pressure on the lower halves of their bodies. Lilith gasped. She was throbbing.

"Do you?" he rasped. "I remember you hot and wet and tight around me, Lily. I remember you begging, you wanted me so badly."

Flushing hotly from his words, Lilith rolled her hips. Oh!

"I remember feeling you tremble. I remember you saying you didn't know how long you could last inside me—"

He cut her off with another crushing kiss, grinding her lips with his just as he ground his hips against her. Hooking her ankles over his calves, Lilith grabbed him by the hips, arching up even though his hardness threatened to bruise the soft flesh between her legs.

She lapped his tongue with her own, meeting the same rhythm with their mouths as they did with their bodies. The throbbing grew into a sweet and steady ache. He could bring her over the brink like this. Fully clothed, with only their mouths meeting flesh to flesh. It didn't matter that he would see what kind of power he had over her. All that mattered was that Lilith wanted to shatter.

And she wanted Gabriel to be the one to break the shell she'd erected around herself.

His weight shifted and eased. Lilith felt the loss of him keenly. That damp, burning place between her legs cried out with a thousand wordless cries that echoed throughout her entire body.

His mouth still locked to hers, Gabriel raised himself up on one elbow, even as Lilith tried frantically to pull his hips back to hers.

Cool air whispered against her damp thighs as her skirts were tossed up around her waist. Gasping, Lilith broke the kiss, arching her hips as his fingers brushed the aching wetness of her most sensitive spot. Hard and swollen, slick with need, the tiny protrusion quivered beneath his touch, sending ripple after ripple of mind-numbing pleasure coursing through her.

"Oh, God," Gabriel groaned, his breath hot against her cheek. "You're not wearing any drawers."

"No, I—" Lilith broke off, gasping as he stroked her. "Oh, Gabriel!"

"Is this what you want?" He slipped a finger inside her. "Is this what you want?"

"No," she moaned, moving against his hand. "But it will do."

He chuckled briefly, harshly, against her ear before increasing the tempo of his thrusts. Another finger joined the first. Shamefully, Lilith gave herself up to the pleasure he wrought, lifting her hips to match his rhythm.

"Oh!" she cried as the pressure in her groin built to a feverish pitch. "Oh, yes!"

His fingers plunged faster. His thumb found the center of the tension and rubbed the aching flesh until the coiling inside her wound to a fevered pitch, sending her over that dark, sparkling precipice of pleasure. Shudders racked her body. Spasms rippled through her thighs and belly, convulsing her muscles as she shouted out her release.

She hadn't even caught her breath when she reached for him. She wanted more. She wanted him.

"Lilith," he murmured, peppering her face with kisses. "We have to stop. I don't have a sheath."

Lilith froze, the afterglow vanishing in a wave of cold shock. "What?"

Gabriel raised his head. His eyes were still bright with passion. "I can't make love to you without taking precautions first."

She stroked his back. "It's all right. I'm due to start my menses any day now."

He blinked. "I would still prefer to have protection."

Protection? Raising a brow, Lilith brought her hands up and pushed hard against his shoulders. She didn't lift him very far.

"Protection against what?"

Was it her imagination, or did he flush a bit? "Against pregnancy."

There was an unspoken "and" in there.

Snorting in disgust, Lilith shoved. Hard. This time she moved him, and while he was trying to recover his balance, she swung her shaky legs over the side of the chaise and stood. "And the pox, is that what you meant?"

He didn't have to respond, for the guilty look on his face said it all. Lilith wasn't exactly worldly, but she remembered one night a long time ago, when Gabriel had told her his mother said that French safes helped prevent not only pregnancy but also disease. He'd been dumbfounded at the time that his mother would speak of such things with him. Obviously he'd taken the advice to heart.

"Lilith," Gabriel began, rising to his feet.

She held up a hand. "Don't." Clutching her skirts, she moved backward, every step a shameful, wet reminder of what had just passed between them.

To his credit, he stopped where he stood. He looked embarrassed and uncomfortable. The front of his trousers still bulged with his arousal, although it didn't look nearly as impressive as it had felt a few minutes ago.

"You think that just because I was stupid enough to give myself to you all those years ago, I've been repeating the same mistake with whoever else will have me, is that it?"

Gabriel frowned. "You know it isn't."

"I know nothing!" she shouted, all the hurt and anger she felt inside rushing to the surface. Then, more calmly: "All I know is that ten years ago, you never would have said that to me."

"Ten years ago, I knew I was the only person you'd ever made love to. You knew the same of me." He held her gaze, the bastard.

"Perhaps I should ask you how many women you've f—" Swallowing the obscenity, Lilith took a deep breath. "How many women you made love to as well, then, and whether or not you took *precautions* with them."

He nodded, his face a little paler now. "I always have. You were the only exception."

Perhaps on any other night his confession would have made her feel better, but not tonight. Oh, the thoughts of all those other women—however few or many their number might be—sent a dart right to Lilith's heart. She never expected him to be a saint or a monk, nor to live a chaste life, but it hurt all the same. And she felt sorry for the women, who had been subjected to such an obvious exhibition of distrust. He hadn't trusted them and he didn't trust her. Not anymore.

Lifting her chin, Lilith fought back the tears that burned the backs of her eyes. "Well, what a coincidence," she replied, her tone falsely bright. "Your mother told me to never allow a man inside me unless he 'wrapped his package' first. Such good advice I would have been foolish to ignore. As would you. We whores—and whoresons—have to stick together, you know."

Oh, he was good and pale now. As pale as she had ever seen him. She'd hurt him. Good. If only she had the power to hurt him as deeply as he'd hurt her.

He just stood there and stared at her like a big, stupid dog. Tears threatened again. "I think you'd better leave now."

He took a step forward. "Lilith—"

"Goddamn you, just go!" Throwing her hands up in the air, Lilith stomped to the door and yanked it open.

"You've given me pleasure, Lord Angelwood, and I appreciate it, but I find I've grown tired of your company and I wish you to leave. Now, please."

For the second time she asked him to leave her club, but this time he didn't try to explain. He didn't pause in the doorway and tell her it wasn't over between them. And if he stood out in the corridor after she slammed the door behind him, she didn't know, because as soon as that door closed, Lilith threw herself back onto that damned chaise and sobbed until she hadn't an ounce of strength left in her body.

And then she cried some more.

Chapter 8

He was, without a doubt, the biggest ass in England.

Standing on Lilith's doorstep, a bouquet of lilies in his hand, Gabriel kicked himself one more time for his callousness the night before. He hadn't been thinking—not with his brain anyway.

The real rub was that he hadn't really thought of protection against disease with Lilith. He'd been thinking of preventing pregnancy. It wasn't until she spoke that he realized he should consider the fact that she'd probably had other lovers in the past decade. He'd always been so careful before. His mother's promiscuity had taught him to be.

He'd learned at a very young age—from his mother, of course—that sheaths were believed to help prevent the pox as well as pregnancy, and he made certain he used them. It wasn't the normal behavior of a horny young man and Gabriel hadn't cared. He didn't want to have a doctor give him mercury treatments for the pox, or to be responsible for any children who would grow up with the stigma of "bastard" attached to them.

The truth was, he didn't know whether or not Lilith had been with other men. It nearly drove him insane to think of someone else touching her, but he should know her well enough to trust that she wouldn't have offered herself to him if she had reason not to. She'd trusted him and he'd turned around and slapped her.

When she'd told him that she'd worked out a payment schedule with Frederick, he could have jumped for joy. Frederick very well could have been cheated at Mallory's, but if he had been, Lilith knew nothing of it, of that Gabriel was certain. No one who'd cheated a young man out of a small fortune would allow him to repay it at his leisure.

He'd gone home last night and drunk himself into a stupor, not just to numb the frustration of not having her, but to numb how awful he felt for having treated her like a common doxy. She was *his* Lily, for Christ's sake!

But to make matters even worse, that morning's gossip rags had been filled with speculation about him and Lilith. One writer had dedicated half a column to his visit to Mallory's. It even made mention of his "disheveled appearance" and "rapid departure."

Has the Angelic Earl taken a tumble? the writer asked. *If he has, this author has no doubt of whom he is "tumbling" with . . .*

It needled him. It irked, and would garner him some ribbing at the club, but it was nothing that would prove too damaging—not until someone thought to publicly question his views on gambling. Then his association with Lilith might prove destructive, but he hoped he would have discovered the truth about Frederick's claims before then. He would know what action to take. And then people might consider his relationship with Lilith a harmless fling, or even a ploy on his part to further his goals. He didn't care what they believed as long as in truth neither he nor Lilith was hurt.

Somehow he couldn't see that being possible. He was going to hurt her when he closed her club. He had already hurt her the night before. How much more was he going to make her suffer because he had a personal hostility against gambling, or because his pride drove him to it?

There was a voice inside his head telling him that no amount of pride, no personal grudge, was worth injuring Lilith. It was the same voice that told him he couldn't pursue her and plot against her at the same time, no matter how hard he tried to justify and separate each in his mind.

He could deny it and rationalize it as much as he wanted to, but things had changed between them. He wasn't certain when—perhaps it had been there since that night he first saw her again—but he knew they were more than just former lovers, more than present adversaries. He had no idea what the future held for them, yet he realized that neither of them was going to emerge from this the victor, no matter what the outcome would be. Even if Lilith still had feelings for him, she couldn't have him and her club, and he couldn't have her and abolish gambling—not unless one of them made a change.

What did it say that neither of them was prepared to be that one?

He should stay away from her. He should tell Blaine to find someone else to do his snooping, yet here he was on her doorstep with a fistful of flowers and the foolish need to earn her forgiveness.

Because there would be no forgiveness when he closed her club.

The behemoth Latimer answered the door when Gabriel banged the knocker for the second time.

The man of affairs, or whatever the hell he was, took one look down his broad nose at Gabriel and shook his head. "She doesn't want to see you."

It was only quick reflexes on Gabriel's part that had the door slamming on his foot rather than in his face. Nothing, however, could prevent the sharp grunt that escaped him as pain shot up his leg.

"You might want to move your foot," Latimer suggested dryly.

Gabriel's answering smile was more of a grimace. "There appears to be a door on it."

The larger man actually looked apologetic. "She told me not to let you in, Lord Angelwood."

The man might sound sincere, but that didn't make him lessen the pressure on Gabriel's already throbbing foot. Time for a different approach.

Gabriel held up the flowers. "I've come to beg forgiveness. Surely that's reason enough to disobey your employer."

Latimer shook his head. "Do you think she'll think it was a good enough reason?"

"Good point." The throbbing in his foot had subsided to a dull ache. Still, it was deuced uncomfortable having the foot trapped between the edge of the door and the frame. He could not fight his way past a man of Latimer's stature. Like most men of his class, Gabriel had studied pugilism under Gentleman Jackson, but the man standing between him and Lilith looked as though he'd learned to fight on the street and was half again Gabriel's size.

And he didn't have his foot wedged in a door.

"I will make this easy for you, Mr. Latimer," Gabriel said, waving the bouquet under the man's nose. "You let me in and we'll tell Lady Lilith that I blackmailed you into it. Tell her I threatened to come back tonight with some men from Bow Street to investigate the back rooms."

The huge hulk stiffened. "You wouldn't actually do that, my lord."

By Hades, the man was quicker than he looked!

"No, sir, I would not, but your employer would have no trouble believing me capable of it."

Latimer seemed to ponder that for a moment. With a quick nod of his head, he took a step backward, allowing Gabriel and his throbbing appendage entrance.

Shutting the door, Latimer turned to him. "She's in her office. You know how to find it?"

Gabriel nodded. "I do."

As he limped in the direction of the upstairs stairwell, Gabriel wondered for the fifth time just what the devil he was doing. Why was he apologizing? It would be easier if he didn't.

But he never avoided doing the right thing just because it was easier. He'd behaved badly and Lilith deserved an apology. And an explanation.

And if he were completely honest with himself, he had to admit that after ten years of missing her, it was difficult to go a day without seeing her now that he'd found her again.

"Lord Angelwood."

The bulk of his weight balanced on his good foot, Gabriel pivoted slightly to glance back at Latimer. "Yes?"

The man's broad face was darkly serious. "You make her cry again and you and I are going to have a little talk."

He should be affronted, insulted by such a threat, but all Gabriel could feel was relief for having gotten inside and guilt for having caused Lilith to cry. He hated it when she cried.

The scowling woman waiting for him at the top of the stairs made him reconsider his relief.

She waited until he'd hobbled to the top before demanding, "What are *you* doing here?"

Again he held up the lilies. The poor things were starting to look a little limp. "I've come to offer my head on a silver platter. Is that to your liking?"

The woman scrutinized him from head to throbbing toe and obviously found him wanting.

"It's not the body part *I* would have chosen, but Lilith might find it satisfactory."

Gabriel choked on a bark of laughter.

"How did you get past Latimer?" she demanded as he recovered himself.

"Blackmail." Gabriel had a feeling Latimer wouldn't appreciate her knowing he had defied Lilith's orders out of a sense of romance.

The woman's faunlike eyes narrowed. "I would have expected better from you in your treatment of Lilith and her staff."

Gabriel kept his tone light, despite the tightening in his jaw. "The only expectations I attempt to live up to, madam, are my own. And sometimes those are challenge enough."

Her eyes widened at that. "And what of Lilith's expectations, my lord?"

He shrugged. "I daresay that by now they're so terribly low, I should have no difficulty matching them."

"They're of such a nature, my lord, that I would think you'd rather not meet them at all."

Wincing, Gabriel raked a hand through his hair. "What would you suggest?"

Hands on her narrow hips, the older woman dragged a thoughtful gaze down the entire length of him and back up again, stopping when her eyes locked with his. "I suspect you already know the answer to that, Lord Angelwood, or else you wouldn't have bothered to come here today. The flowers are a nice touch, but only groveling and honesty will earn back that little bit of Lilith's trust you managed to acquire before tossing it away."

Gabriel didn't reply. He didn't have to.

The woman stepped back, allowing him to pass.

Gabriel cocked a brow. "You have more faith in me than your mistress does."

"We have hope, my lord. Hope that you will prove to be the man we think you are."

Now it was Gabriel's turn to gaze speculatively at her. "What kind of man would that be?"

"Worthy of Lilith's heart." She tilted her head to one side. "Are you?"

"I doubt it," he replied honestly.

The woman smiled and nodded. The smile faded as she studied him closely. "Don't hurt her, Lord Angelwood. She's not as strong as she looks."

It was a warning more subtle than Latimer's, but it hit

Gabriel more deeply than the threat of physical violence ever could.

He shouldn't be there. He shouldn't do this to her or to himself, but he couldn't stop himself from wanting her any more than he could bring himself to tell her the truth about what had happened ten years ago.

She deserved to know. But how could he tell her? Then she would learn that the man she looked up to wasn't what she thought he was. And she would hear the scandalous truth. Gabriel didn't know if he could trust her to keep quiet about it, not when something as precious to her as her club was at stake.

The notion that Lilith might use his father against him left a bad taste in his mouth, but he had no more reason to trust her than she had to trust him. Yet Gabriel understood that Lilith was just as drawn to him as he was to her. Her behavior the night before only solidified it.

What a sad pair they were.

When he'd collected his wits, Gabriel found himself alone at the top of the stairs. He looked behind just in time to see the edge of a skirt disappear through the door at the bottom of the staircase.

He and Lilith might not be so trusting, but Lilith's staff certainly was.

He paused for a moment outside Lilith's office to straighten his cravat and roll some of the tension out of his neck and shoulders. He was nervous. More nervous than a man of his age and position was comfortable admitting.

Exhaling a deep breath, he raised his fist and knocked.

"Come in."

With a turn of the knob and a gentle push, Gabriel did as he was bade. The door swung silently open, revealing the interior of the office and the woman at the desk, her head bowed over an open ledger.

"What is it?" she asked, not bothering to look up as Gabriel closed the door.

"We were invited to call on Brave and Rachel this afternoon," he replied. "Or have you forgotten?"

Lilith froze at the sound of his voice. Slowly she raised her head, as though she hoped he would leave during the time it took her to look up.

Or perhaps she had just been reluctant to let him see her face.

Gabriel's heart crawled up into his throat at the sight of her. *Oh, Lil.*

She was pale—too pale. Her eyes were unnaturally dark in her face, as were the circles beneath them. The lids were swollen, the whites of her eyes red, as if she'd spent the better part of the night—and that morning—sobbing.

Forget England. He was the biggest ass in the whole *world.*

"I should have known they'd let you in," she mused with bitter amusement. "Their sense of loyalty is completely misguided."

"Actually, I threatened them." Why he even bothered to continue the charade, he didn't know, but he didn't like being responsible for Lilith's staff's betrayal any more than he liked being responsible for her tears.

"Hmm." She didn't believe him, that much was obvious. "Well, I'm afraid you wasted your time. I haven't the strength to spar with you or anyone else who would love to see Mallory's close its doors. Please leave."

With that, she returned her attention to the ledger, leaving Gabriel to wonder just who the hell "anyone else" was. Bronson, perhaps? He made a mental note to make those inquiries into Bronson and his club.

"Who has tried to persuade you to close Mallory's?" he asked. He had no intention of leaving.

Lilith laughed harshly as she stabbed her quill back into its holder. She raised her gaze to his. The coldness of her eyes chilled him to the very bone.

"I see. It's fine for you to try to put me out of business, but not anyone else, is that it? I thought you said this wasn't about you and me."

"It isn't." *Liar.* From the minute he'd seen her again, it had ceased to be about anything else, whether he chose to admit it or not. She'd made him realize that last night.

Her smile faded, leaving nothing but bitterness behind. "Then my club is none of your damn business."

"Maybe not," he allowed. "But you are."

Obviously that little piece of honesty had been the wrong thing to say. Sparks seemed to ignite within Lilith's eyes, and her cheeks, just seconds ago deathly pale, were suddenly flush with crimson.

"You . . . you arrogant ass!" she cried, leaping up from her chair so quickly it tipped and almost fell over. "How dare you make such a claim after all this time! I most certainly am *not* your business!"

This red-faced and angry Lilith shouting at him was far preferable to the wraith who had just been in her place. This Lilith was more like the one he knew and—once—loved.

Tossing the drooping lilies on the desk, Gabriel folded his arms across his chest and met her flashing glare evenly.

"Last night you wanted me inside you. I felt you shudder beneath me. I think that makes you my concern."

She flushed even darker. "You gave up any right to that when you treated me like a whore."

Gabriel rolled his eyes. "I did not." Not technically. He'd treated her as he'd treated all the other women he'd slept with. That in itself had been a mistake.

"Oh, that's right," Lilith snarled. "Whores get paid."

The thin rein Gabriel had on his temper snapped. "You were the one who jumped to that conclusion. You! I was the one who didn't want you to get pregnant, remember? Or are you so caught up in trying to think the worst of me that you've forgotten that?"

The fight seemed to leak out of her. "You thought it afterward."

"Of course I did!" Sighing, Gabriel raked a hand through his hair. "Lilith, it's been ten years. I've been with other women. Can you tell me you haven't had other lovers as well?"

He waited. Waited for her to tell him there had been no one but him, even though he knew it was selfish of him to want it.

"You made me feel soiled."

The smallness of her voice was his undoing. Even as a part of him went cold with the assumption that she had taken other lovers, another part ached for her.

It was the aching part that won. Reaching out, he wrapped his arms around her shoulders, pulling her against his chest. She didn't even try to fight him, an indication of just how vulnerable she was.

"Lily," he murmured against her hair. "Sometimes I make myself feel soiled. You know how I grew up. You knew my mother."

"I liked your mother." Her voice was muffled by his shoulder.

"I *loved* my mother, but I watched her go through man after man, saw the physicians come to call for one reason or another. I know what people said about her. I don't want them to ever talk about me the same way."

Lilith lifted her head. Bright gray-green eyes met his with a clarity that was startling.

"That's why you became the Angelic Earl. You didn't want to be anything like either of your parents."

Gabriel nodded. "Yes."

Her stare was unnerving. "That's why you hate gambling so much, because of what it did to your father."

His heart flipped over his in chest. What did she know of his father? Oh, yes. The rumors he and Blaine had put out to conceal the truth. She knew what other people thought they knew, that his father had been killed in a duel over gaming debts.

"Yes," he whispered, lying but not lying. "That's why I hate it."

She frowned, as though she was beginning to understand. He wasn't so sure he wanted her to. He certainly didn't want her asking too many questions.

"I'm sorry I called you a whoreson."

He shifted under the weight of her stare, but he couldn't bring himself to look away. She'd know then that he was hiding something.

"I was more upset by you calling yourself a whore." That much at least was true.

"I lied."

"I know."

She gave him one of those long and searching looks that made him feel as if she could see right through to his very soul.

"Forgive me?" he asked before she could gaze any deeper.

Her head tilted thoughtfully. "No."

Christ, what did she want from him? What more could he possibly do or say that would make her realize the problem was with him and not with her?

"But I will."

He raised a brow. "Really?"

Lilith nodded. "Having spent most of my life trying to be what my parents wanted and always being told I wasn't quite good enough, I find it a little difficult to understand why you would try so hard to be nothing like your parents. They seemed like perfect parents to me."

"They weren't." If she only knew just how imperfect they'd been!

Another little nod. "Thank you for telling me."

He knew then that she was already well on her way to forgiving him. To trusting him again. What it meant for their relationship remained to be seen, as did whether or not he deserved it.

There was something he wasn't telling her.

Watching him greet Braven and his wife, Lilith realized she wasn't concerned with Gabriel's secrets. It wasn't as though she hadn't a few of her own, and if his were anything worth discovering, Mr. Francis would find them.

Mary would say they were none of her business, but if they were the reason that Gabriel had never come after her before, Lilith wanted—no, *needed*—to know.

This morning had proved how easily she forgave him. She wanted to forgive him for abandoning her. Would she be so obliging if he succeeded in closing her club and took away everything she held dear a second time?

It was time to stop blaming him for her life. It hadn't turned out so badly after all. And it wasn't as though he'd ruined her all by himself. She'd been as hot for him then as she had been last night in the parlor. The only difference was that then she'd had expectations. Now she had none.

"Lilith! How delightful to see you again." The countess greeted her with such a joyous and cordial tone that Lilith couldn't help but smile.

"It is good to see you again also, Rachel." It was too easy to fall into this trap of overfamiliarity with these people. Lilith would do well to make sure she didn't start to believe they really wanted to be her friends. They were nice to her because of Gabe. They were his friends. Not hers.

"Alexander's not awake yet," Brave said, steering them down the granite-tiled corridor. "I thought perhaps you might indulge me in a game of billiards, Gabe."

Her gaze scanning the portraits of Braven ancestors along the wall, Lilith heard Gabriel chuckle. Deep and rumbling, his laughter washed over her, leaving behind a sensation so bittersweet her stomach twisted with it.

Once upon a time she had been able to make him laugh like that. Now, whenever they were together his laughter always seemed tainted with regret.

"You just want to see me lose," Gabriel accused, humor lacing his tone.

Lilith smiled at that. Glancing over her shoulder, she remarked to Gabriel, "Do not tell me you *still* haven't learned to play billiards properly!"

His gaze was bright and warm as he smiled back. Her stomach tightened at the sight of it. "All right, I won't tell you."

Brave's expression was one of heightened interest. "Do you play, Lilith?"

Gabriel shot his friend an amused glance. "She'll match you."

Laughing, Rachel clapped her hands together. "This I have to see. Shall the four of us play together?"

It was obvious to Lilith that the men would rather see her play against Brave by herself, but she would feel much more comfortable if Rachel played as well. Besides, it would be nice to watch Gabriel attempt something he wouldn't excel at.

"Rachel and I against you and Lilith," Brave told Gabriel. "That should be fair."

Rachel grinned. "I'm not sure how fair it is. Even I am better than Gabriel."

Gabriel made a face at her teasing, but laughed just the same. How lucky he was to have such friends. How she envied his confidence. It didn't seem to matter that he was about to play badly in front of the three of them. He didn't need to prove himself. She had been like that once, but now there seemed to be little point in doing anything if she couldn't win.

The first game went to Brave and Rachel. Rachel was right. She was a better player than Gabriel. For that matter, Brave and Rachel's baby was probably a better player than Gabriel. If possible, the years had diminished rather than improved what little talent he had.

It got so bad that Lilith started giving him instructions when he insisted on another game.

"Relax your hold," she ordered, prying loose his white-knuckle grip on the smooth, polished cue. Her hand tingled where it had touched his. The tingle ran all the way up her arm. It was all she could do not to scowl when her body tightened in response.

"There, that's better. Widen your stance a bit. Bending like that cannot be comfortable." As she nudged his feet apart, her leg brushed against his, sending another frisson of awareness shooting through her.

"Like this?" he inquired after she'd tugged and prodded him into the proper position.

She nodded, not trusting her voice. Only Gabriel could make a billiards lesson feel like lovemaking.

Holding her breath, Lilith watched as Gabriel took the shot.

The cue struck the ball, sending it rolling across the felt tabletop.

The ball loitered on the lip of the pocket for what seemed like an eternity before finally falling in.

"Yes!" Lilith shouted. They'd won the game. And Gabriel had not only finally made a shot, he'd also sunk the winning ball!

Jumping up and down, she caught him around the neck in a brief and altogether far too improper hug. "You did it, Gabe! You did it!"

His arms went around her like a warm iron band, sweeping her off her feet and twirling her around as he laughed out loud with her.

When had she last felt so happy?

"Another game?" Brave asked once Gabriel had set her back on her feet.

Flushing, Lilith turned to face him and Rachel. Lord, what a hoyden they must think her for making such a cake of herself!

But the Earl of Braven and his countess didn't look at all scandalized by her behavior. In fact, they appeared to be amused.

"All right," Gabriel agreed. "One last game."

This time everyone was evenly matched. Even Lilith and Brave fudged a couple of shots, while Rachel and Gabriel improved. It was a close game. And when the time came for Lilith and Gabriel to take their winning shot, it was Gabriel's turn again.

They weren't going to win, of that Lilith was certain. Gabriel had shown vast improvement under her tutelage, but the shots he made were straight-line shots. In order for them to win, he would have to bank the ball off the side of the table and deposit it in the far upper corner.

Lining up his shot, Gabriel pulled back the cue and quickly followed through. The ball ricocheted off the side of the table, bounced against the opposite side and sailed diagonally down the table to plop into the pocket.

Stunned silence followed as the three spectators tried to decipher what had just happened.

Lilith's eyes narrowed as her gaze settled on Gabriel's self-satisfied countenance. Why, the rat! He hadn't needed her coaching at all! He had merely made an excuse to have a little laugh at her expense—at Brave and Rachel's as well. But neither the earl nor his countess looked offended, so Lilith decided not to be, either.

"Looks like we've been duped," she drawled, handing Braven her cue to put away.

The earl flashed her a grin. "Be grateful you were his partner. Rachel and I are the ones who were truly taken in."

Across the table, Gabriel's gaze met hers, so hot and silver she shivered.

"I have been practicing," he replied silkily.

The way he said it made Lilith wonder just what else he'd been practicing for the past decade.

Gabriel smiled. "Want a second match?"

Lilith's stomach fluttered. Was he talking about billiards or about them personally? God, she didn't know which would please her more.

"Wait a moment," Brave intervened. "I'm the one who got beaten. If anyone gets another chance, it should be me."

Shooting his friend an amused glance, Gabriel jabbed his thumb in Lilith's direction. "She may have been my partner, but she wanted to see me lose even worse than you did."

Lilith blushed hotly. Was she that transparent when it came to him?

Laughing, Rachel stepped forward, hooking her arm through her husband's. "Well, I don't care who wants to play again, because it won't happen this afternoon. There's tea waiting for us in the blue drawing room, and I do believe your son is awake, Lord Braven."

The look Brave shot his wife was so full of love and devotion it hurt Lilith to watch them. She didn't want to look at Gabriel, either, for fear he'd see the envy in her eyes. Staring instead at the Grecian Key pattern on the carpet between her feet, Lilith heard the distant cry of an infant. How Rachel had heard it before this was obviously some strange miracle of motherhood.

"Then let us go on to the parlor," Gabriel suggested. "I have waited long enough to meet this child."

As they strode down the corridor behind Rachel and Brave, Gabriel laid the flat of his hand against the small of her back. His touch was light, but the heat of him seemed to scorch her through her gown and shift.

"How about that second match, Lil?" he asked, his breath equally as hot against her ear.

Gooseflesh sprang up along her arms and shoulders. The way she reacted to him was both delicious and humiliating.

Staring straight ahead, she replied coolly, "I would love the opportunity to put you in your place, Lord Angelwood."

He chuckled, sending what must be the one hundredth shiver that day racing down her spine. "I would love for you to put me there, Lady Lilith."

Oh, this was ridiculous! He had her shivering and blushing and feeling all hot. Next he'd have her giggling, and then she'd know she was still the same silly chit she'd been when she'd fallen in love with him the first time.

Lilith froze. The first time. Did that mean she was starting to fall in love with him for a *second* time? Oh, dear God, she hoped not.

Then again, there were days when she wondered if she'd ever fallen *out* of love with him in the first place.

A few steps ahead of her, Gabriel stopped and turned. "What is it?"

The concern in his eyes was genuine—and touching. It was also unwanted. The last thing she wanted to know right now was that he cared about her well-being.

Struggling to regain her composure, she shook her head. "Nothing. I was just thinking."

She was *not* falling in love with him again. It was lust, pure and simple. You didn't have to trust a person to desire him. You didn't have to make yourself vulnerable to a person in order to have him return that desire. More important, no one ever got his heart broken over lust.

He didn't push, and for that Lilith was grateful. He didn't offer his arm or try to touch her again, but she felt his strength and support as clearly as if she'd leaned upon him. It was comforting and vaguely frightening at the same time.

True to Rachel's word, a tray of sandwiches and cakes was waiting for them in the blue drawing room on the first floor. They'd just seated themselves when a maid came in with the tea, followed shortly by the nanny, who had baby Alexander in her arms.

"There's my boy," Brave announced proudly, rising to his feet.

Much to Lilith's surprise, Gabriel asked if he might hold the child. Brave and Rachel exchanged startled glances, but neither objected. With a nod from Rachel, the nanny walked over to where Gabriel sat and deposited the cooing infant into his arms.

The portrait they presented was enough to break even the hardest of hearts, and Lilith's shattered into a million pieces in her chest.

Little Alexander was a healthy baby with apple-pink cheeks and a large, round head lightly dusted with soft brown hair. He had his mother's blue eyes and an expression of curiosity that made Lilith smile.

Gabriel, grinning like an idiot and speaking a language Lilith assumed was understandable only to babies, offered Alexander his finger. The future earl seized it in his fist—a tiny sapling wrapped around a mighty oak—and promptly shoved it in his mouth.

"Careful," Rachel urged. "He's teething."

Gabriel didn't seem to think himself in any danger of being mortally chewed on. Lifting his head, he grinned at his friends. "He is a fine boy."

Rachel beamed. Brave puffed up like a peacock as he took his wife's hand in his. "Yes, he is."

The glance that passed from husband to wife was so intimate, Lilith had to look away. Her attention returned to Gabriel and the baby.

She would have been better off watching Brave and Rachel.

It didn't seem to matter that he had an audience. Gabriel was blissfully impervious to those around him as he watched the child suckle his finger. He rubbed his cheek—the expanse of softer skin above the dark shadow of his beard—against that downy hair.

At that moment Lilith both hated and adored him. How could he have brought her there and shoved her face in the one thing she'd always wanted but had never been allowed to have?

He didn't know. That was how.

Gabriel's expression was one of perfect contentment, of instant and unconditional love. This baby had done nothing to earn such devotion other than be born.

Gabriel had always given love too easily. But once it was lost . . .

He looked up.

Oh, please, God, don't let it be so far gone we can't find it again.

Had she really thought that?

Gabriel grinned at her, so idiotically happy that something inside her snapped. Jumping to her feet, Lilith mumbled something about wanting to see the view and lurched across the carpet to the window.

She should have known he would follow her. She should have known he'd bring the baby with him.

Damn him.

"Is something the matter, Lil?"

Closing her eyes against the gentle prodding of his voice, Lilith shook her head. "I suppose I'm a little envious." There. That hadn't been so hard.

"Would you like to hold him?"

Turning, Lilith dropped her gaze to the bundle in his arms. Alexander still gnawed on Gabriel's finger, but his eyes—deep berry-blue eyes—were fixed firmly on her.

Her arms were up before she could stop them. "Oh, God, yes!"

Gabriel handed him over with a soft laugh.

It was awkward, holding a baby. As a woman, she should feel it was as natural as waking in the morning, but she didn't. She was afraid. Afraid of doing something wrong, of somehow damaging this warm, heavy treasure cradled in her arms.

Oh, but sweet heaven, it felt good to hold him. And for a moment, the most priceless of seconds, she could pretend he was the child she would never have.

A band circled around her throat, pulling tighter until her breathing became strangled. Tears burned the backs of her eyes.

She shoved the baby back at Gabriel. "Take him," she rasped. "Please, take him."

He did. Holding the baby in one arm, Gabriel cupped her cheek with his other hand, wiping away a tear that had fallen there. God, she hoped Brave and Rachel weren't watching all of this. She hadn't the courage to look and see if they were.

"Lilith, why are you crying?"

She shook her head. Her throat was too tight for her to speak.

"Is it because you want a child of your own?"

She nodded. She hadn't thought about it in some time, but seeing Brave and Rachel—seeing Gabriel—had brought those longings back with a vengeance.

"Oh, Lil." His voice was soft, cajoling and altogether too bloody understanding for Lilith's liking. "You'll have a child of your own someday."

She snorted. He was lying, but Lord love him for it.

"I'll never have one of my own."

"Why not?"

She raised her gaze, not caring if he saw the pain or the tears in her eyes. It helped that her vision was too blurry to see his reaction.

"Because," she whispered, "a child deserves better than a mother like me."

And then, with all the courage she could muster, Lilith lifted her chin, mumbled some vague excuse to Brave and Rachel and left the three of them staring after her as she walked out the door.

Chapter 9

Would she see him tonight?

As he slipped his arms into the coat Clifford held, Gabriel silently asked himself the same question he'd been asking ever since Lilith had run out of Brave and Rachel's.

Damn it, she *would* see him tonight even if he had to tear the place apart looking for her. It had been four days since he'd last seen her, and she had been so distraught when she left Brave's that he worried about her.

And he missed her. He missed her so very, very much. So much, in fact, that he found himself hoping that Somerville would stand up in the House and argue against him again, just so he could hear Lilith's words if not her voice.

Meanwhile, his mutterings on the subject of gambling were met with increasing amusement. His association with Lilith was damaging his credibility. There were a few peers who thought perhaps he was setting Lilith up for a fall, but the rest assumed the only falling going on between the two of them was into bed.

He should be bothered by this sort of speculation, but he wasn't. Not really. It wasn't that he had changed his mind about abolishing gaming, it was just that Lilith was foremost in his thoughts. That was why he hadn't shown his face in Parliament or his clubs very often over the past couple of weeks. That was why he didn't feel the same passion for his cause. It was because he was worried about her, not because his priorities were shifting.

He was the Angelic Earl. His priorities never shifted.

"Lord Underwood is waiting for you in the red drawing room, my lord," Robinson informed him as he came downstairs.

Wonderful. Just what he needed, another confrontation with Blaine as to why it was taking him so long to prove that Mallory's had cheated Frederick. And he had no desire to be reminded of his father, or that Lilith was supposed to be the villain in this story.

Sighing, Gabriel strode down the corridor to the red drawing room. He'd make this quick. He'd tell Blaine he was on his way to Mallory's to question some of the workers there, but other than that, his search had turned up no proof that Frederick had been cheated.

In fact—and Gabriel would never say this to his friend—he wondered if Frederick really had been cheated. It was easier to believe Frederick had been mistaken than it was to believe an establishment like Mallory's would risk its reputation by fleecing the son of a peer.

"Blaine," he began with forced joviality as he entered the room, "I was just on my way out. What can I do for you?"

Standing on the crimson, brown and gold Axminster carpet, his hand curved around the oak trim of a velvet sofa, Blaine looked like he'd just stepped out of a portrait. The austere set of his features wore that lord-of-the-manor expression that so many portrait painters seemed to favor these days. All that was missing was the country clothing and a faithful hound or two.

His friend raked him with a shuttered gaze. "On your way to Mallory's, are you?"

Gabriel quirked a brow. He didn't like the older man's tone of voice, but he could understand his disapproval. His relationship with Lilith was something few people would understand. Gabriel himself didn't quite understand it. He could hardly expect anyone else to.

That didn't mean he'd sit back and allow people to comment on it, however.

"Yes."

Apparently Blaine had expected more of an explanation, judging by the tightening of his jaw.

"Might I ask the purpose of tonight's outing?"

Folding his arms across his chest, Gabriel pursed his lips in mock contemplation. "Oh, I thought I'd play a few hands of whist, maybe try my luck at faro and see how much of the fortune I've worked so hard to recover can be squandered in one evening. What do you think the purpose is, Blaine?"

The viscount flushed at Gabriel's sarcasm. "I would hope that you were going there to determine just who cheated my son, but I fear it is the club's owner who draws you there more than any sense of duty."

Gabriel's jaw hardened. "What draws me there is really none of your business, sir."

It had been years since he'd addressed Blaine as "sir." It was a snub against their friendship and Blaine knew it.

The older man's expression was one of amused sorrow, as if he'd expected to be disappointed by Gabriel's answer before he gave it.

"If you were going on Frederick's behalf, you wouldn't have said that."

No, he wouldn't have, but it was badly done of Blaine to point that out. Gabriel didn't bother to tell him that.

"Have you . . . *been* with her?"

His jaw aching from being clenched so tightly, Gabriel jerked his head up to stare at the older man. "*That* most certainly is none of your concern. Any relationship Lilith and I have is no one's business but our own. Now, if you'll excuse me—"

"It most certainly is my business!" Blaine interrupted with more violence than Gabriel had ever heard him use. "It is my business if your 'relationship' with this woman has blinded you to the truth! It is my business because you promised me you would prove her club cheated my son, and so far you've done nothing but get yourself bandied all over the scandal sheets and laughed at behind your back for courting that . . . that *harlot* as though she were a lady!"

Gabriel advanced on Blaine swiftly, his hands balled tightly at his sides. It took all of his strength not to strike him. It would be like striking his father, but he would have done it had he not remembered how good Blaine had been to him after his father's death.

"It is only your friendship with my father that keeps me from demanding satisfaction for that remark," he warned, his voice deep and stiff with anger. "You will not speak of Lilith in such a way."

Blaine stared at him wide-eyed. A chuckle of disbelief broke forth from his lips. "You don't even care what they are saying, do you?"

"Not particularly, no." Not about him anyway. The gossips could say whatever they damn well pleased about him.

That realization in itself should have been alarming.

The older man shook his head and raked a hand through his thick, graying hair. "I cannot believe that, after struggling to live your life with such high standards of right and wrong and justice, you would allow yourself to be taken in by a woman like Lilith Mallory."

"I've heard enough." Gripping Blaine by the upper arm, Gabriel dragged him in the direction of the door. "You have to go now, Blaine." Go willingly or be tossed out.

"A fortnight ago, you believed my son was cheated," Blaine reminded him as he dug his heels into the carpet. "But that was before you knew whom he accused of cheating him. You've found no evidence to the contrary, yet you refuse to act. You can't remain on the fence, Gabriel. Either you believe Frederick or you believe her."

Hot with both anger and exertion, Gabriel dropped Blaine's arm and turned to face the smaller man with an expression that felt like an iron mask on the bones of his face.

"The only thing I believe is that Lilith was not the one who cozened Frederick."

"How do you know?" Blaine challenged. "Have you asked her?"

"Yes."

That obviously wasn't what Blaine had expected to hear. He stared at Gabriel, his mouth working silently for a moment before he snapped it shut and averted his gaze.

"I haven't mentioned Frederick, but she knows about the charges laid against her. I believe her claim that she herself is innocent."

The restrained anger was back in Blaine's gaze. "Do you think my son is a liar?"

Gabriel knew better than to even hint at an affirmative answer. Blaine was one of those fathers who was oddly protective of his son. Gabriel often thought him too strict, too sheltering of Frederick. It wouldn't surprise him at all if Frederick bent the truth to escape his father's disappointment. But such charges as those Frederick had laid upon Mallory's were not the kind of thing an honorable young man made easily, and Gabriel had never known Frederick to be anything but honest and honorable.

The perfect son. A son Blaine tried very hard to mold into a good man, into a mirror image of himself. Hadn't watching Gabriel and his own father taught him that most sons didn't want to be exactly like their fathers?

"No. I do not believe Frederick to be a liar."

Blaine was all too pleased.

"But neither do I think Lilith is one, either," Gabriel added, bizarrely pleased by the souring of Blaine's expression. It was becoming increasingly difficult to remember that the viscount's attitude stemmed from concern for his son.

"And what?" Blaine demanded peevishly. "Is that it?"

Gabriel continued toward the door, alone this time. He didn't care if Blaine followed him or not.

"No, that is not it. Because you were a good friend to my father and because you have always been a good friend to me, I promise you I will discover the truth, but I will not use it to hurt Lilith or her business. If you and Frederick wish to make more of it, you are welcome to try, but you will leave me out of it."

"You still love her, don't you?" Blaine's voice rose over his shoulder. The mocking chill of it flowed over Gabriel, leaving a trail of icy pinpricks in its wake.

There were two things that were guaranteed to come between friends: money and women—or in this case, both.

He left the room in silence, ignoring the question as well as the man, not because the question made him angry, but simply because he had no idea how to answer it.

Latimer nodded to him in greeting as Gabriel entered the club. The burly doorman's silence seemed to mean that Lilith was finally ready to face him. Latimer was loyal enough to stop him from entering if he wasn't wanted.

The idea that Lilith wanted him gave Gabriel more pleasure than he cared to admit. So where was she?

"Lady Lilith is in the ladies' club right now, Lord Angelwood," Latimer told him, obviously taking pity on him. "She had to settle a little dispute."

Gabriel chuckled. "A dispute? What happened, someone step on someone else's hem?"

Smiling, Latimer shook his head. "One of the ladies claimed she was cheated."

All humor vanished as the blood froze in Gabriel's veins. *Dear God, no.*

"Cheated?" His voice rang hollow in his ears.

Blissfully unaware of his companion's change in demeanor, Latimer nodded. "She was playing piquet and accused her opponent of pulling cards out of her sleeve. The other lady took umbrage to the accusation and slapped her. Next thing you know, they're going at it like a couple of she-beasts and Lady Lilith has to go in there and pull them off each other."

Gabriel didn't know whether to laugh or weep. He laughed, a weak chuckle that belied his relief.

He should have known that Lilith and her club weren't to blame. He should have trusted her, but his first thought was that Blaine was right, that his feelings for Lilith had clouded his judgment. He disliked doubting himself.

He disliked doubting Lilith even more.

"I'll wait for her inside, Latimer. Don't bother telling her I'm here. She'll find me when she's ready." It was a lie, of course. He'd find her once he felt he could face her.

Latimer nodded, his dark eyes bright with understanding. "Yes, my lord."

Inside the male half of the club, Gabriel ordered a glass of port and wandered in the direction of the faro table. He watched the play for a few moments, seeing nothing under-handed in the way the dealer handled the cards. Perhaps a different dealer had been working that night, or perhaps he saved his fleecing for green boys and not hardened sharps of the *ton*.

"Angelwood," Lord Pennington announced loudly, look-ing up from the table. "Would you like to join us?"

The man's jest was met with a round of laughter from his companions. Gabriel smiled stiffly. "No, thank you."

After that, Gabriel decided it might be better if he watched the action around him from the sidelines. He wasn't in the mood for more remarks like Pennington's, even if he had no one to blame but himself.

Clusters of men stood and chatted animatedly about horses and politics. Some sat at tables and drank, their conversation slightly more subdued. Others played at cards and billiards.

And some, he noticed, sent amused glances his way and chuckled with their friends.

So it was true. They really were talking about him. It hardly mattered. When all was said and done, a little talk would not damage his reputation, but it was unsettling all the same. How had Lilith borne it? How did she bear it still?

Because those who whispered paid her for the privilege of doing so in her presence. They paid well by paying for her liquor and using her rooms and her tables. And by allowing her to uncover those shameful little secrets they'd rather keep hidden.

No wonder she found owning the club so satisfying. It cast those who would snub her upon her mercy. A little subtle revenge against the society that cast her out.

What about him? Did she have a similar fate in mind for him?

He couldn't believe it, but he would be wise not to completely disregard it, either. Just in case.

He had to get his head straightened out, and fast. He didn't know if he was coming or going anymore. When he was with Lilith—when he was without her, for that matter— nothing and no one else mattered.

Speak of the devil.

Lilith glided into the room, instantly capturing the attention of every man present. Some gazed upon her with indifference, a few even with respect, but it was those who stared at her with hungry eyes who bristled Gabriel's hackles.

She was his. Always had been. Always would be. She would never admit to it, no more than he would if the tables were reversed, but in his heart Lilith belonged to him, and she would until the day he died.

Slipping behind a group of chatting tradesmen, Gabriel studied her as she moved among her customers. She looked lovely, if not a little tired. All that glorious hair was pulled up into a large knot high on the back of her head, little curls lying against her forehead and cheeks. She wore a gown of moss-green silk brocade that brought out the green in her eyes. Matching gloves covered her hands and arms.

And, he noted happily, not a trace of cosmetics tarnished the perfection of her face. A face that was set in an expression of determination as she made her way toward a table at which several young men were playing poker.

What could possibly cause her to descend upon them in such a manner? She looked like a governess about to scold an unruly charge.

Making certain to stay out of her line of vision, Gabriel moved in closer.

Lilith stopped by the table, her attention centered on one unfortunate young man. She spoke, but Gabriel couldn't hear her from this distance. He pressed closer, squeezing between two men with their backs to him.

The young man stood, waving a hand at his friends as he followed Lilith over to a semisecluded corner between a large potted plant and an empty table. Gabriel managed to slip behind the plant, grateful that his behavior hadn't been noticed.

Or if it had been, no one thought it odd enough to comment.

Peering between the leaves of the plant, he could better see and hear Lilith and her companion.

It was Frederick! What the hell was he doing here? For a boy who should by rights despise this club, he certainly seemed to spend a lot of time in it.

"Frederick," he heard Lilith say, "I thought we had an agreement."

Frederick pulled a face. "Oh, but, Lilith, you can't expect—"

Frederick and *Lilith*, was it? Obviously Frederick spent much more time at Mallory's than he'd initially intimated to his father.

More time than Lilith had indicated to him.

"I most certainly can," she interjected in that crisp tone of hers. "Our agreement was that you could pay back the debt you owe this club at your own leisure, but only with the stipulation that you were not to gamble here again until the amount was paid in full."

Gabriel smiled. That certainly wasn't the voice of someone who made a habit of fleecing young men out of their blunt.

"But, Lilith—"

"No. You wanted to pay the debt on your own and those were my terms. Would you rather I went to your father?"

"*No!*"

The vehemence in the young man's voice made Gabriel frown. He wasn't quite certain just what had happened at Mallory's the night Frederick had lost his allowance, but the suspicion that it had been anything but being cheated was growing stronger and stronger.

No, you wouldn't want Lilith to go to your father, you little miscreant.

Lilith smiled—a mother with a wayward child. "Good. Then I suggest you leave the table before you find yourself even further in debt, and to someone not quite as accommodating as I am."

Frederick's expression was petulant. "All right."

Gabriel chose that moment to announce his presence. Backing up a few steps, he tried to make it look as though he'd just happened upon them, rather than having been standing around eavesdropping.

"Good evening."

He didn't know who jumped higher, Lilith or Frederick, but he did know that neither of them believed he'd simply happened upon them. The horror on Frederick's face was proof of that. Without even saying hello, the boy pivoted on his heel and pushed his way through the club as though the building were on fire. He never once looked behind him, not even when he reached the door.

No matter. Gabriel would deal with Mr. Frederick later. Turning his attention to the woman before him, he smiled at her bewildered countenance.

"We need to talk."

She shouldn't be surprised to see him standing so close, but after four days of forcing herself to stay away from him, she found herself unable to determine whether he was real or some cruel trick of her imagination.

"Yes, I suppose we should. Meet me upstairs in my office in ten minutes."

"You don't want to go up together?" His tone was teasing, in direct contrast with the concern she saw in his eyes. "Don't you want them to see us leave together? I thought you wanted to corrupt me in the eyes of the *ton*."

Lilith shook her head. The muscles in her neck and shoulders pulled with the movement. She was so tense her head was beginning to ache.

"Not tonight, Gabe."

His expression was one of such alarm that she couldn't help but smile. "Do not frown so. I'm not ill, I just don't feel like performing for society tonight."

He nodded as though he understood. Perhaps he did. "I'll meet you in ten minutes."

The agreement made, Lilith left him. Her footfalls were silent on the carpet and she spoke to no one, her attention focused on the door across the room, but the crowd parted for her as the Red Sea had parted for Moses. She felt rather than noticed the gazes upon her, the hushing of conversation as she drifted past. She should be used to that by now.

She should have worn something more brash, a little bolder. In her scandalous gowns she felt and acted like a scandalous woman. In this gown, without her mask, she was just plain Lilith Mallory, a woman with no family and few friends. A woman who had more money than she knew what to do with, and yet who yearned for the things that fortune couldn't buy.

No man would marry a woman of her reputation, and she had too much pride to settle for being a mistress. She supposed she could have a child on her own, but she couldn't bear to raise a son or daughter with the stigma of being a bastard. And she wouldn't want the child growing up like herself or Gabriel—she who strove to dishonor her parents' memory by doing everything she could to become the exact antithesis of what they'd been. Moral to the point of righteousness, they'd pushed their daughter in the opposite direction. And Gabriel, born to the parents Lilith should have had, rebelled against his loving yet scandalous parents to become a man who might someday end up resembling Lilith's own father if he weren't careful.

Stepping out in the entrance hall, Lilith closed the door behind her with a sigh of relief. Usually the club was her solace, but not lately. Lately it seemed to be little more than a reminder of just how much of an outsider she really was. She'd never felt this way until Gabriel came back into her life.

What was it about Gabriel and being with him that made her feel everything she did was wrong? Making love to him as a young girl had felt so perfect, so right, but it had ended being so dreadfully, dreadfully wrong. He'd rejected her. Her parents had rejected her. Her friends and society had turned against her. It had taken her years to regain her confidence, to feel even the least bit good about herself, and now . . .

Now she was that girl again, and she hated it.

Down the narrow corridor she walked, and up the stairs, each step heavier than the last.

If she were smart, she'd remove Gabriel from her life—she'd tell him to stay away from her and her club. But telling Gabriel to stay away would be like telling the sun not to shine. You might get one or two cloudy days, but then it would have to rise again. As long as she was in London, she would have no peace from him. And it would only be a matter of time before he consumed her with his light or she extinguished him with her darkness.

It was inevitable. She knew that as surely as she knew her own heart. She could fight it all she wanted to—and she *would* fight it—but someday one of them was going to hurt the other in a way that could never be fixed, and then what?

Then she would leave England and go someplace where no one knew her and try to live a normal life without Gabriel. God knew she wasn't living a normal one with him.

She entered the office and shut the door, enclosing herself in the room that had become her sanctuary these past few days. Within these walls she was in control. In here she could pretend Gabriel and Bronson and her past didn't exist. She could pretend she was still a powerful, mature business-woman instead of a woman closer to thirty than twenty, with more regrets than she cared to admit.

If only Gabriel hadn't shown her baby Alexander. If only she hadn't held him . . .

Oh, for heaven's sake, she was being a maudlin miss! These longings and urges were normal. They were part of being a woman, and no doubt they would pass just as every other re-gret did. All she had to do was put the idea out of her mind. She had to stop imagining what it would be like to have her own child.

Gabriel's child.

"Oh, sweet God!" she cried. "I must be losing my mind!"

"They do say that talking to oneself is the first sign of in-sanity."

With a strangled cry, Lilith jumped and whirled around. She hadn't heard the door open.

"It hasn't been ten minutes." She still had five more min-utes of feeling sorry for herself.

Gabriel shrugged his wide shoulders and smiled. "I could not wait any longer."

Oh, dear, he knew how to twist her heart for all it was worth.

Crossing to the sofa, she seated herself upon the edge of the cushion, her hands locked in her lap.

"What did you want to talk about?"

He moved to sit beside her, flipping out the tails of his coat as he did so. The tiny sofa seemed silly and fragile with his large, startlingly male frame settled on it.

"Relax, Lil. This isn't an inquisition."

"I didn't think it was," she replied, her tone clipped.

"I need that list of your club employees," he said, seem-ingly unfazed by her curtness. "Anyone who has access to your tables and your dealers. I want to know who works on which nights, and I want a detailed accounting of their winnings and losses for the last month."

The throbbing in Lilith's head worsened. "You don't want much, do you?"

His lips curved ever so slightly in a smile of mock innocence. It was too cute and too out of character and it sucked all the fight right out of her.

Bastard.

Smiling despite herself, Lilith nodded. "All right. You'll have to give me a day or two to gather all the information."

Now he frowned. "I would prefer to have it tomorrow."

Chuckling, Lilith shook her head. "Contrary to what you might like to believe, Gabriel, I do not exist solely for you. I have a life and a business and forty other people with problems for me to solve. You will just have to wait your turn. You're fortunate I promised to have the list for you in only two days."

He didn't look as though he thought she had done him a favor. "Fine."

Still smiling, Lilith gave his thigh a gentle pat. "There. That wasn't so hard, was it?"

But his thigh certainly was. The only softness in Gabriel was his heart—and occasionally his head.

Her hand stayed on his leg a little longer than was necessary. They both realized it. Slowly Lilith drew her fingers away from the solid warmth of the thigh beneath those soft black trousers.

Gabriel's gaze was as dark as the smoke off a forest fire. Lilith's heart leapt into her throat at the heat—and unabashed longing—she saw there. He could kiss her now and she wouldn't stop him. He could probably do whatever he wanted and she wouldn't stop him.

He did nothing.

No, that wasn't true. He said the one thing she didn't want to hear. "I'm sorry the visit with Brave and Rachel was so distressing for you."

Lilith jumped to her feet. She couldn't discuss this with him. Not now, not ever. Her hand pressed against her breast to quell the pounding there, she flew toward the cabinet against the far wall.

"I thought you said this wasn't an inquisition. Would you like a drink? I believe I need one."

"A drink would be good. You don't want to discuss this with me, do you?"

Lilith removed the stopper from a crystal decanter with a shaky laugh. "You are very astute, Gabe. You always were a sharp one."

Far across the room, a pasha lounging on her dainty sofa, he was hardly in a position to intimidate her, but he did. He was one of the few people with such power over her. He scared her more than Bronson and his threats ever could.

"Why will you not talk to me, Lily?"

Her eyes fluttered shut at the use of her pet name. Why did he do this to her? Why did he make her want to open up and trust him?

A deep, cleansing breath gave her strength. Her hand barely trembled at all as she poured two liberal glasses of scotch. "It is hardly the kind of thing a woman discusses with a gentleman."

Their gazes locked as she returned with the drinks. What strength she'd gathered now wavered under the scrutiny of those pale eyes.

"But we are not just a woman and a man," he said, his voice feather-soft. And she knew he deliberately hadn't used the word "gentleman." "You are you and I am me."

And that was supposed to say it all.

Sinking down beside him, Lilith handed him his drink and drew her legs up beneath her. He obviously wasn't going to let it go, so she might as well make herself comfortable while he whittled at her defenses.

"You said a child deserved a better mother than you. Why?"

Lilith raised her glass. "Good memory." She took a large swallow, welcoming the burning, the warmth the liquor sent tingling through her limbs.

"I have a habit of remembering foolish things," he replied bluntly. "Your remark was probably one of the most ridiculous statements I have ever heard."

She shot him a sideways glance. "Oh? How did it affect you growing up with a scandalous mother?"

He flushed as her barb struck the target, but somehow she couldn't bring herself to feel any satisfaction at it.

She took another drink. "I would never want my child to grow up thinking he or she had to be better than me, that they had to make up for my mistakes, or worse yet, grow up to be just like me."

"There are worse people to emulate." His tone was gentle as he sipped his drink.

"Like who?" she demanded with a dubious laugh. She was starting to feel the scotch already. No wonder, since she hadn't eaten since luncheon.

"Like *your* mother."

Stunned, Lilith dropped her jaw. Laughter welled up within her, shaking her entire body, making her eyes water and her lungs ache.

When the spasms finally subsided, she wiped her eyes with the back of her hand and looked up to see him grinning at her.

"You are truly awful," she told him with a sniff. "And I thank you for it."

His smile faded a bit, as did the glimmer in his eyes. "You cannot waste time lamenting what you haven't got, Lil."

"That is easy for you to say," she retorted, taking another drink. "You're a man. You can produce children well into your dotage. I only have so many years left."

"You still have plenty of time. You are hardly an old woman."

The scotch was in her head now, loosening her tongue as it slowly numbed her nose. "We could have been married almost ten years now. We could have had several babies." She giggled—it was a mocking, foolish sound. "An heir and plenty to spare."

Gabriel didn't look as though he appreciated her joke. In fact, he looked as though she'd just punched him in the groin. "I know."

Propping her elbow on the back of the sofa, Lilith leaned her head against her palm. It was her turn to unsettle him now. He wanted to talk, then they'd talk, but she was going to force him to be as honest as he would make her be.

"Do you ever wonder how it could have been? If we'd married?"

He drank deeply from his glass and shuddered as he swallowed. "Yes. Yes, I do."

"How do you picture it?"

Smiling self-consciously, he shrugged. He was slowly throwing off his defenses as well.

"Usually we're the age we are now. We're living in the country with our five children—"

"Five!"

Gabriel grinned, flushing a little under her incredulous look. "And one on the way. We've been busy."

Lilith was feeling too mellow to even blush. "I should say so. Are we happy?"

His grin slipped. "Yes." It was little more than a whisper.

The growing languor in her muscles caused by the scotch made the ache in her neck even more acute. Massaging the hardened flesh below her skull, Lilith smiled. "Whenever I think of us being together we're always happy. I always imagine that it is Christmastide and the children are helping us decorate the house. We don't have five, however."

"Is there one on the way?"

He was teasing, but she colored hotly all the same. "Yes."

"I think that's lovely," he told her, his gaze full of something that made her chest tighten and her breath catch.

The room was suddenly charged with tension, hot and thick. Lilith could almost smell it, feel it in the perspiration collecting beneath her breasts. It wound like a band around her chest, raised the hairs on her neck and tingled low in her abdomen. Her fingers tightened around her glass so he couldn't see them tremble.

"You are rubbing your neck," he observed, setting his glass on the low table before them. "Do you have one of your headaches?"

Another hot flush. Years ago, when she was suffering through just such a headache, Gabriel had forced her to confess the cause. For months afterward, right up until their separation, whenever her menses came and they were together, he would rub her neck—away from her parents' watchful eyes, of course.

He shifted to the side, crooking one leg up on the sofa while the other remained draped over the side. He patted the expanse of cushion between his splayed thighs.

"Come here. I'll rub your neck."

She should refuse, but the offer was too good, too delicious, to pass up. In seconds, Lilith had drained her glass and stood up long enough for her wobbly legs to carry her those few steps closer. She plopped herself down into the warm nest of his body, her back pressed against the solid wall of his chest.

"Aah," she moaned as his strong fingers dug into her shoulders. "That feels so good."

"Just lean back and relax. I'll make it go away."

Her head drooped against his shoulder and her heavy eyelids fell closed. "Mmm. I have missed this."

Gabriel didn't respond. She didn't really mind just as long as he kept rubbing.

How much time passed, Lilith had no idea, but as his magic touch eased the tension from her neck and shoulders, lessening the throbbing in her skull, the rest of her relaxed as well. He was putting her to sleep.

Something brushed her temple. Lips, it felt like; soft, warm lips. Also faint brush of stubble. Nice.

In her mind, Lilith allowed herself to pretend that she and Gabriel were those people in her fantasy. They were on the sofa in their home on a winter's evening. The children were asleep and a fire burned in the hearth as snow fell outside.

Her belly was beginning to swell with their fifth child and Gabriel was giving her a massage before bed. He had a special present for her, he whispered. One that he didn't want to wait until morning to give her.

"What is it?" she asked, smiling.

"I still think about what it would be like if we were married," he replied, his breath hot against her temple.

"So do I."

And as sweet, peaceful darkness engulfed her, Lilith didn't even pause to consider that the Gabriel she spoke to wasn't the one inside her head.

Chapter 10

⎯⎯⎯◯◯⎯⎯⎯

Gabriel had never found much to recommend at the Vauxhall Gardens, other than the arrack punch. The food was skimpy and overpriced—whoever heard of charging four shillings for biscuits?—the company sometimes rough and rowdy. But it was all worth it to see the joy on Lilith's face as she drank in the goings-on around them.

"Thank you so much for suggesting we come here," she said, taking another gulp of the rum and benjamin flower punch. "I haven't been to Vauxhall in years."

Under the light of the globe-shaped lanterns, Lilith's eyes were dark and glimmering, her hair like a sleek coil of flame. Never in his life had Gabriel seen such a vibrant creature as she.

Smiling in amusement, he watched as she reached for her glass again. "It hasn't changed much such for the cost of admission rising and a few new sights. Be careful of the punch, Lil. It's heady stuff."

They were alone in the supper booth, observing the

bustling crowd around them in relative privacy. They'd finished their supper of thinly sliced ham and dwarflike chicken and were savoring the tasty cheese cakes Gabriel swore were worth the price if they brought Lilith pleasure.

"I can't eat another bite!" she exclaimed, sliding the plate toward him. "You take the last one."

He held up his hands. "I've already eaten three. That last one belongs to you."

Laughing, Lilith shook her head. "If I eat any more I'll have to get you to loosen the laces on my corset."

Relieving Lilith of her corset was a chore Gabriel would be all too happy to perform, but he wasn't about to tell her. He had already let things between them go further than he meant to. There was an intimacy between them now that hadn't been there a few days ago, and it made him wish they weren't on opposite sides of the gaming issue. A fragile trust was forming between them, and the fact that they shouldn't trust each other made it all the more delicate.

When she fell asleep that night in his arms in the parlor, it had taken all of his willpower not to carry her to her room and coax her into letting him soothe her headache in other ways, but she'd hardly been in any condition—physically or mentally—for that kind of thing. That had been three nights ago, and if Gabriel's calculations were correct, Lilith's menses should be over and done with by now.

Dropping his gaze to the low neckline of her copper-colored satin gown, he could just imagine the pale, heavy globes of her breasts filling his hands, the taut nipples puckering against his palms.

The thought ignited a familiar tightening in his groin. He had no right to entertain such ideas to begin with. It would only make it harder for him to put an end to her club when the time came.

If the time came.

Another thought came to him from some far corner of his mind, the result of the arrack punch and the sweet music wafting through their booth on the warm spring breeze.

"Lilith, if you were given the opportunity to implement gaming laws in England, what would they be?"

She seemed as surprised to hear his question as he was to have asked it.

"Well, I'd have clubs set a limit as to how much money a person can win or lose in a night. I've seen men—and women—lose entire fortunes in one game of cards."

So had Gabriel. His father had done it.

"And I think there needs to be higher penalties for cheating on the clubs *and* the players. I try to ensure that new cards are opened nightly, but even so, I've had them come back with corners bent or little marks on them."

"What about debts?"

She raised a brow. "What about them?"

"I overheard you with Frederick Foster the other night. You were far more understanding and kind than another club owner might have been."

Waving a dismissive hand, Lilith shrugged. "He is a foolish boy. Someday he is going to get himself into serious trouble, but it won't be at my club."

"Doesn't he still owe you an entire disbursement of his quarterly allowance?"

Lilith sucked in her cheeks, her gaze questioning as it locked with his. "You seem to know an awful lot about this."

Damn. He'd said too much. "You know how boys are— they brag to their friends." He didn't want to tell Lilith that Frederick was the one who had accused her of cheating, not that the little bastard didn't deserve to be found out. It was because he'd given Blaine his word, and because he didn't want Lilith to know that the boy she'd been so kind to had stabbed her in the back.

That a young man might brag to his friends seemed easy for her to believe. "They certainly do, although I don't think a gaming debt is anything to brag about."

It was Gabriel's turn to shrug. "Our society views it as a rite of passage. You're not a man until you write your first vowels."

She smiled coyly, teasingly. "I thought you weren't a man until you lost your virginity."

Grinning, Gabriel poured her another glass of punch. He liked it when Lilith drank too much. She seemed happier when having fun rather than fighting about the past—or the future.

"There are different kinds of virginity," he replied, positioning the jug of punch over his own cup, "but the sexual kind is the grandest, I suppose—for a young man, anyway."

Something warm and smoky unfurled in the depths of her eyes. "So you might say I was responsible for making a man out of you."

His heart skipping a beat, Gabriel splashed punch over the side of his glass. "I daresay you were."

Her cheeks were flushed—whether from the punch or the memory of the night they first gave themselves to each other, Gabriel didn't know. Lilith took another swallow of the potent punch.

"I remember feeling so smug, as though making love made me an adult." She laughed. "God, I was so young, so foolish."

"You were never foolish."

"I loved you." Smiling, she shook her head and sighed. "Now I know I'm foxed. I always tell you things I know I shouldn't when I'm too deep in my cups."

"I don't mind," he whispered, afraid to say too much for fear of what he himself might confess.

Her gaze was shrewd. "No, I don't suppose you do. What about you, Gabe? Did you love me even the tiniest little bit?"

How could she even ask? No, he knew. She knew he wasn't telling her everything about what happened to prevent him from marrying her when the scandal broke ten years ago. He was ashamed to tell her. He'd allowed her to be dragged through the mud by the gossips while trying to keep his father's behavior from doing the same to his family. He'd sacrificed Lilith's good name to protect his own. And the fact that he'd been young and ashamed of his father was no excuse for what Lilith had suffered.

"I loved you more than anything else in the world." But it hadn't been enough.

She nodded, a shimmer of wetness in her eyes as though she understood the regret in his voice.

"Would you like to go home?" he asked, knowing their earlier happy mood was not to be regained.

"Yes. Let's go home."

He liked the way that sounded, as though the two of them were going home together, to the same place.

They left the booth in silence. Her hand rested on his arm, yet it felt as though miles separated them, so caught up were they in their own thoughts. Around them, music and laughter carried on the breeze. Drunken bucks and women of dubious virtue trod the same paths as lords and ladies and wealthy cits. Lovers strolled down darkened paths, some with a chaperone in tow, others in search of the perfect trysting spot.

"Remember Hilda?" he asked with fond amusement as they strolled toward the gate.

He and Lilith had come to Vauxhall only once before, and that had been with her maid acting as keeper of Lilith's virtue. Gabriel had done his damnedest to get rid of the girl, but to no avail.

Lilith chuckled. "How could I ever forget?"

"She was like a guard dog," Gabriel observed as they passed through the gardens' exit. "Protecting your innocence with all the vigor of an Amazon."

"Yes, well, she failed miserably, didn't she?"

Thankfully, the remark was made without any trace of bitterness. Still, he didn't look at her as he spoke. "We were too smart for her."

"You know, my mother and father dismissed her after that."

There was no need to say what *that* was.

"I wonder whatever happened to her," Lilith mused.

This time he met her gaze. "The army, I wager."

Lilith's laughter was the sweetest sound he'd ever heard. It twisted his stomach and clutched at his heart, making his

whole body ache with the joy of it. They used to laugh together often when they were younger. They were always
happy. Now he couldn't see her without feeling a bone-deep
sorrow at least once during the visit.

The carriage was waiting for them. One of Gabriel's men
held the door as Gabriel handed Lilith up into the coach.

"May I ask you a question, Gabe?"

Settling against the squabs as the carriage rocked into motion, Gabriel stiffened at her cautious tone.

He kept his own tone carefully bland. "What would you
like to know?"

Meeting his gaze with an earnest one of her own, she
leaned forward, resting her forearms on her knees as she regarded him in the dim lamplight. "Why did you go into
trade?"

It was the kind of question he'd expected—the kind he
didn't want to answer.

"I—" All the lies and excuses he'd thought up to answer
just such a question sprang to mind, rehearsed and sounding
sincere enough to pass for the truth.

Lilith tilted her head at his stuttering silence.

"I needed the money."

That was *not* one of his rehearsed replies!

Lilith appeared as shocked by his reply as he was. Staring
at him, she opened her mouth once, twice, but no sound
came out. Her brow furrowed. Her head tilted to the other
side. She paled. Her eyes widened. Realization dawned.

"Was his gaming that bad?"

There was no one word to describe how Gabriel felt at that
exact moment. He was both relieved and alarmed that she'd
finally put the pieces together. He felt as though one weight
had been lifted only to have another take its place.

He closed his eyes, remembering the young man he'd been.
The shock of finding his father dead, the pain that followed,
trying both to protect his mother from the scandal and to assume the responsibility of the earldom, all that might have
been easier to bear if only he'd had Lilith beside him.

"The day after he died, the creditors started coming. There were so many, Lil. The debts were so immense." He shook his head. "I didn't know how I'd ever pay them. If it hadn't been for Underwood, I don't know what I would have done."

"Which is why you've taken such an interest in the gambling habits of Underwood's son Frederick."

Gabriel nodded. That was one way to put it.

"And it also explains why you didn't come for me."

"I did come for you. I was just too late."

She continued as though she hadn't heard him. "And it also explains why you feel the way you do about gambling—why you want to abolish it."

That was certainly part of it.

Lilith bowed her head, giving it a remorseful shake as she did so. The movement partially obscured her features from him, but he could see a trace of sadness in the set of her mouth.

"Your poor father. How he must have suffered."

"My father!" Gabriel cried, astonishing even himself with the strength of his outburst. "Where the hell did that eulogy come from? He didn't suffer. My mother and I, *we* suffered. I lost my father and the woman I loved. Rest assured, my father didn't suffer."

No. It had been quick, his father's death.

Lilith's smile was one of sympathy and understanding. As if there were any way she could possibly understand. She understood *nothing*. He wanted to tell her that. Wanted to tell her everything just so she could try to understand *that*.

"He lost control, and that's a horrible feeling, Gabe, losing control of oneself."

Gabriel snorted. "He was in perfect control."

Reaching over, she squeezed his clenched fist. Her touch was as firm and gentle as her voice. "He didn't die on purpose, Gabe."

Gabriel said nothing. If only she knew . . .

Even if he wanted to speak, he wouldn't have been able to

say anything. There wasn't time. Lilith had barely withdrawn her hand from his—he was reaching up to keep her from moving away—when the carriage lurched violently to one side.

"What the—?" Banging on the ceiling with his fist, Gabriel yelled, "What's going on up there?"

The only reply was a chorus of raised voices and another lurch. This time the motion was so severe, both Lilith and Gabriel were tossed to one side.

Lilith cried out as she struck the far wall of the carriage. Gabriel grunted as his shoulder also hit.

Flipping up one of the window blinds, he looked outside; he could see nothing but darkness. They were picking up speed, no doubt trying to outrun whatever was assaulting them.

"Are you hurt?" he shouted, above the thunder of the wheels and hooves and voices.

Even though she massaged her arm where it had struck the wall, Lilith shook her head. She was pale, her eyes wide and black in the darkness. "I don't think so!"

The carriage lurched again, extinguishing the lamps. This time the rocking was so severe, Gabriel felt one side of the carriage lift off the road and crash back down again.

"Come over here," he commanded, easing his body closer to the wall.

He didn't have to ask twice. As the vehicle swayed dangerously, Lilith leapt across the space between them and landed on the cushioned bench beside him, diving willingly into his arms.

Gabriel held her tightly, positioning himself so that his back was pressed hard into the corner. If they went over, he would be all there was between Lilith and the street, and he would rather break every bone he had than see her suffer so much as a scratch.

"What's happening?" she cried as the shouting outside grew to a fevered pitch and the swaying of the coach became even more erratic.

Gabriel shook his head, bracing one boot against the opposite bench. "I don't know."

With most women he would at least have tried to think of something to calm them, to make them feel as though they were safe, but Gabriel was too scared to entertain such a deception. Scared not for himself, but for Lilith. Never in his life had he been so scared of losing someone as he was at that moment, not even when she'd disappeared from his life ten years ago.

The carriage tilted, one side lifting and lifting until all of Lilith's weight shoved against him. They seemed to hang there for a moment, clinging to each other with all their strength, Gabriel pushing hard against the other bench, bracing himself for the crash he knew was coming in a matter of seconds.

They hit the street with a scream of men and horses. A loud crack! rang through the air as wood splintered against the cobblestones.

Lilith screamed. Even Gabriel, braced as he was for impact and clenching his jaw, grunted when they hit. The impact on his back sent a ripple of pain coursing through him. His head struck the polished oak, causing brightly colored lights to dance before his eyes.

What felt like an eternity passed in mere seconds. As the lights faded, Gabriel became aware of urgent voices outside the overturned carriage, of the sounds of frightened horses being quieted, of someone climbing the carriage to ask if they were all right, and Lilith's voice answering that she thought they were.

Lilith. Closing his eyes in relief, Gabriel smiled, despite the fact that his entire body felt as if it had been underneath the coach rather than in it. Lilith was safe. And she was warm and heavy against him.

"Gabe," she whispered against his cheek. "Speak to me."

"Hello," he replied inanely, too sore and too relieved to think of anything more intelligent to say.

Above him, Lilith laughed. He could feel her body shake against his. "Oh, thank God you're all right!"

He opened his eyes. "I was just thinking the same thing."

"Can you stand?" she asked.

"Not with you on top of me, I can't."

A few moments later, when Lilith stumbled to her feet beneath the carriage door, Gabriel pulled himself into a standing position. His head and body protested, but he managed to keep himself upright.

The door opened and the tiger stuck his head inside. He was bleeding from a cut above his eye but seemed uninjured otherwise.

"Lord Angelwood, sir. We'll have you and the lady out in just a minute."

They lifted Lilith out first. Gabriel gave her a foot up toward the opening. It took all of his strength and that of the men above to get himself out. He was a little dizzy and sadly lacking in physical strength, but he was able to haul himself outside with a little help.

After he staggered away from the wreck, he surveyed the damage.

The carriage was close to ruin, but it could be replaced. The horses had taken a tumble, but mercifully they appeared to have only minor injuries. The tiger was bruised and the coachman appeared to have broken his arm, but everyone was alive and that was what mattered.

Lilith came to his side and, without thinking, Gabriel gathered her close to him.

"What happened?" he asked over the top of her head.

The coachman, also bleeding from a cut on his face, cradled his wounded arm against his chest.

"We wus run off the road, m'lord." The man's astonishment at the situation echoed in his words. "Ruffians. About a 'alf dozen of 'em—four on horseback, two in a cart. They tormented the horses while the others shoved on the carriage until it finally tipped." Visibly shaken, the coachman shook his head in silence.

The young tiger spat on the street. "Bastards. Beg your pardon, my lady."

Lilith smiled at him.

Gabriel stroked her hair. The heavy mass had fallen free of most of its pins and lay in a tangled mess around her head. She was still a little pale, but he didn't think he'd ever seen anything lovelier.

"Did the men say anything to you?"

The coachman frowned. "Aye, they did. The strangest thing, too. They said 'twas a message from their employer."

Gabriel also scowled. That he knew of, he had no business enemies. "Did they say who that was?"

"No, m'lord. But they did tell that my passenger would know who their master was."

"I certainly intend to find out," Gabriel replied grimly, his jaw set in determination. Such an action would not go without retribution of some kind. Whoever had put him and Lilith in such danger would pay for it.

"Hail a couple of hackneys," he ordered the tiger, handing the young man a coin. "I want the two of you and the horses to return to Mayfair. Have someone come back for the carriage. I'm going to escort Lady Lilith home."

The servant nodded. "Yes, my lord!"

As they waited for a hackney, Gabriel rubbed his hand up and down the length of Lilith's upper arm. Despite the warm evening and the protection of her shawl, he could feel her trembling beneath his hand.

"Well, that was an adventure, wasn't it?" he remarked with forced lightness when she'd been silent for too long.

Jerking her gaze from the destroyed carriage to him and then back again, Lilith shook her head. "Oh, Gabe, I'm so sorry."

He gave her a squeeze. "Don't worry yourself. It's only a carriage. I'll get another."

Even as he said the words, he couldn't shake the sudden feeling of apprehension that shivered through him. Lilith hadn't sounded merely sorry for the state of his conveyance. She'd sounded strange, almost guilty.

If Gabriel didn't know better, he'd swear she sounded almost . . . responsible.

"Lilith, do you have any idea who could be responsible for this?" He voiced the question carefully, keeping his tone neutral lest she thought he was accusing her of something.

She didn't look at him as she shook her head. "I would hope that no one would hate me—or you, for that matter—enough to do such a thing."

Gabriel was silent. Lilith sounded more hopeful than actually convinced. She made it her business to know the secrets of those who entered her club. Perhaps she had uncovered something one of her clients would prefer to remain hidden.

Who would have done such a thing? The only person Lilith could think of was Bronson, but it didn't make sense. He'd been vaguely threatening at the theater, but she'd believed that to be more intimidation than anything else. She couldn't consider him capable of such violence.

Or maybe he didn't *want* her to think him capable.

As they rode to her club in a hired coach, Lilith snuggled against Gabriel's side and knew she should confess her suspicions, but she just couldn't. She knew Gabriel well enough to know how he would react to such news. He'd insist that she close her club, spouting that gaming bred this kind of trouble. Or else he'd go after Bronson himself, and Lilith didn't want or need him to fight her battles for her. It would only make things worse for her if Bronson thought she had the Angelic Earl on her side, and it wouldn't look good for Gabe in Parliament if he took such a stand for her.

Not that it should bother her if his reputation were tarnished, but she didn't want it to happen because of Bronson. He wasn't worth Gabriel's leaving his pedestal.

No, she would first discover whether or not Bronson was responsible, and then she would tell Gabriel, if there was anything to tell.

Dear God, what if the accident had been more serious? What if Gabriel had gotten hurt? She wouldn't be able to live with herself if anything happened to him.

She loved him.

It was more of a disappointment than a shock. She'd loved him so dearly once, it made sense that part of her would still have feelings for him. Whether those feelings were for the boy he once was or the man he'd become was inconsequential. Perhaps he had similar feelings for her; she wasn't certain it even mattered.

One of them was going to have to turn away. Their goals were such that they could not have it both ways.

It would hurt when she lost him again. Possibly it would hurt more than it had before, but that didn't stop her from wanting him. If anything, tonight's incident only made her want him more.

"Come inside," she murmured as the carriage pulled up outside Mallory's.

Something in her expression must have told him how much his acquiescence meant to her. He simply nodded, not saying a word.

"Lady Lilith!" Latimer exclaimed when they walked through the door.

Lilith could only imagine how she and Gabriel must appear. Bruised, dirty and disheveled, they must look as though they'd been to Hell and back.

"Not now, Latimer," she told her wide-eyed servant with a shake of her head. "I'll explain in the morning."

Gabriel followed her down the corridor and up the stairs in silence. Lilith didn't speak, either. They didn't have to. The air between them was charged with things that didn't need to be spoken to be understood.

Tossing her shawl onto a chair as they entered her private apartments, Lilith went straight to the liquor cabinet and poured two stiff drinks of good scotch whiskey. She handed one to Gabriel and downed her own in two swift gulps. He did the same.

Once her stomach stopped burning, Lilith turned to face him, drawing her shoulders back and summoning her courage.

His pale gaze was questioning.

"I haven't had a lover other than myself in years," she confessed softly. "I finished my menses two days ago. I've never had the pox and I don't care what kind of precautions you want to take, but I need you, Gabe. I need you tonight."

He blinked. "You do?"

She nodded. "All I can think about is what could have happened tonight and I don't want to think about it anymore." It wasn't a declaration of unbridled lust, but it was all she was prepared to offer.

Apparently it was the right thing to say, because the next thing Lilith knew, she was in his arms, his lips crushing hers.

"I don't know what I would have done if anything had happened to you," he whispered when they came up for air. "Lilith, I—"

She pressed her fingers against his lips. "Don't. No confessions, no promises. Not tonight, please."

His gaze softened, as though he sensed how vulnerable she truly was at that moment. Tomorrow, perhaps her pride would suffer because of it, but not tonight.

Gabriel smiled, a soft, sweet smile that pulled painfully at her heart. "I haven't had a lover—other than myself—in almost a year. I've never had the pox and I want you so badly I could weep."

Her heart bursting with something very much like joy, Lilith returned the smile. "Come with me."

Holding his hand, she led him from her private parlor into her bedchamber. Someone—Luisa, no doubt—had lit the lamp beside the bed, bathing the entire room in a soft, golden glow.

Lilith pulled the remaining pins from the tangle of her hair as Gabriel removed his coat and waistcoat.

"Unfasten my dress for me?" she asked, sweeping her hair over her shoulder and presenting her back to him.

His fingers were deft and sure with the tiny hooks, flipping them open while his lips brushed the sensitive flesh of her neck and shoulder. The gown sagged around her shoulders and before she could tug her arms free, Gabriel was pushing the fabric down her arms, past her hands and off her hips.

She turned in his arms, her gown twisting around her feet. The linen of his shirt pressed against her corset.

"Why do you wear these things?" he demanded, gazing down the front of her as he began to pop the hooks on it as well.

Lilith sucked in a deep breath when his fingers splayed across her ribs. "Because it makes my waist look smaller."

He popped more hooks. "It squashes your breasts."

And after the last hook let go and the silk-and-whalebone corset fell to the floor, Gabriel's gaze and hands went to the heaviness of her breasts beneath her shift. Lilith's breath caught as he cupped them with his palms, spreading his long fingers underneath them and rubbing the peaks with the pads of his thumbs.

Her nipples hardened instantly, tightening with every caress, sending little ripples of pleasure down between her legs.

Lilith lifted her hands and untied the bows on the front of her shift. Bunching the fabric in his hands, Gabriel tugged the straps off her shoulders, shoving the delicate linen to the floor.

Naked except for her shoes, stockings and diamond earrings, Lilith stood stock-still beneath Gabriel's gaze. Such close, intimate appraisal should make her blush, would normally make her uncomfortable, but whether or not her hips were too big didn't seem to matter when the man staring at her seemed awed by every inch of her.

"You're even more beautiful than you used to be," he whispered, the tips of his fingers skimming the pale roundness of her belly, up to her breasts again.

Lilith shivered at the caress of his voice as well as of his hands. "And you're wearing entirely too many clothes."

Smiling, he held his arms out at his sides. "Then by all means remove them."

It seemed odd, this playfulness, this seeming calm as they undressed each other, but beneath the familiarity something else simmered, waiting to boil over. As she pulled the tails of his shirt free from the waist of his trousers, Lilith trembled with anticipation. She was hot and throbbing between her thighs. Her entire body seemed alive with pinpricks of desire, every inch of her acutely aware of every inch of him.

She pulled his shirt up. He helped when she got to his shoulders and wasn't tall enough to lift it any farther. He pulled it over his head, mussing the thick waves of his hair, and let it drop to the floor.

Her mouth dry at the sight of his strongly muscled chest and broad shoulders, Lilith raised a tentative hand. The skin of his shoulder was warm and smooth. The knobby bone there stood out in sharp relief against the sleek muscle.

Down her fingers slid, to the thickness of his torso and the coarse hair that curled there.

"You have become so big."

"Going into trade can do that to a man."

She traced the indent of his navel with her finger, smiling as he sucked in a quick breath. "All men should be forced to go into trade."

Her gaze slid lower, to the bulge in the front of his trousers. A bolt of longing swept through her. Enough play.

Fingers fumbling, she unfastened the falls of his trousers, sliding them down the lean firmness of his hips and thighs. Kneeling, she removed his shoes and stockings, pulling the trousers off with them.

The hair on his leg brushed her cheek as she turned her attention back to him. The rigid length of his erection jutted proudly before her face. More confident now, knowing that she was responsible for his arousal, she wrapped her fingers around his thickness. His body tensed in response.

She loved this part of him. This part that was capable of

giving her such incredible pleasure, this part that joined them like halves of the same whole. She loved the sensitivity of it, the way that just the right touch could make him gasp and quiver. Neither it nor its reaction to her had changed.

She kissed the tip, ran her tongue along the smooth, silky head. Gabriel gasped, the muscles in his thigh flexing beneath her other hand.

"Perhaps you shouldn't do that," he said, breathless, one hand wrapped firmly around one of the bedposts.

Smiling coyly, Lilith gazed up at him. Another lick. "Do you want me to stop?"

He closed his eyes. "Would you want me to stop?"

God, no.

She bathed him with her tongue, savoring the saltiness of his skin. She took him full into her mouth and out again, pumping him with her hand. His free hand caught in her hair, holding her head as he slowly flexed his hips to match the strokes of her tongue.

This power was intoxicating. Knowing that she could snap his control simply by quickening her movements was a heady thought, but not one she was going to test. Not tonight. She hadn't waited all this time just to have him spend himself in her mouth. When she felt his body start to tense, the pressure against the back of her head increase, that was when she knew to stop.

Releasing him, she rose to her feet. His head resting against his hand on the bedpost, he stared at her beneath heavy lids. His cheeks were flushed, his lips slightly parted with his shallow breathing.

He was absolutely beautiful.

Slowly he straightened, advancing on her like a feline on a mouse. She would have smiled if not for the serious expression on his face. He wanted her. He was going to have her.

He followed her onto the bed, kneeling between her spread knees as she lowered herself onto the mattress. He didn't enter her immediately as she expected him to. She was ready for him; the dampness of her body was apparent even to her.

Braced above her, the blunt head of him pressed against the entrance to her body, he kissed her, sliding his tongue deep within her mouth and tasting her.

She could feel the tension in his arms vibrate the bed as he lowered himself to trail hot, wet kisses along her neck. He nipped gently with his teeth. She gasped.

His mouth went to her breasts, licking and suckling each nipple until they stood tall and distended, red and tingling. They were puckered so tautly they ached, and still she wanted more. Panting and writhing, Lilith pushed her hips upward as his mouth closed around the tip of one breast again. She wanted him inside her. Wanted him to make her feel whole again, like the Lilith she used to be. She didn't want to think about right or wrong or consequences or what the future held. All she wanted was Gabriel.

Digging her heels into the mattress, she raised her hips again. He moved away, just out of reach.

"Gabe," she pleaded.

He lifted his head. His eyes were smoky and dark, his lips moist and shiny. A thick chunk of sable hair fell over his brow. He looked so young, so much like her Gabe, that it brought a lump to her throat.

Now would *not* be a good time to cry.

"Do you want me, Lil?" His voice was hoarse as he slid one hand down the curve of her hip, slipping his fingers into the humid valley of her thighs.

Lilith couldn't help it. Her hips bucked. "You know I do."

He slid a finger inside her. Her lips parted in a soundless moan at the exquisite sensation.

He added another finger, stretching her, curving them inside her and pressing upward until the pleasure became almost too intense to bear.

"Tell me," he demanded. "Tell me how badly you want me."

Thighs tensing, Lilith shoved against his hand. She should be embarrassed, but this was Gabriel and he made her feel so good she'd recite naughty limericks if he asked her.

"I want you so badly I'm going to scream if I don't soon have you."

He stroked his fingers deep inside her. "I'm going to make you scream anyway."

"Oh!" His words shot straight to where his fingers were causing such delicious feelings. She was going to explode soon.

As though sensing just how close she was, he withdrew his fingers. Lilith could feel the heat within herself, feel the wetness as his hand brushed her thigh. Her body felt empty and it oh-so desperately wanted to be filled, filled with Gabe.

He didn't make her ask twice. Bracing himself above her again so that they could watch each other's faces as their bodies joined, he slid himself inside her. A low moan pushed its way out of Lilith's throat at the sweet intrusion. Her body parted and closed around him. Her knees lifted, sliding up past his ribs to take him even deeper as her fingers tightened around the hardness of his biceps.

Lifting one hand, Gabriel reached around and hooked her behind one knee, hauling her leg up even farther, so that her thigh pressed against her chest. His body shook as he supported his weight on one arm, pumping his hips against hers with an urgency that robbed Lilith of all thought other than matching it.

In and out Gabriel plunged. Hot and wet, Lilith thrust against him, every stroke bringing her closer to the edge, making her quake and moan.

Gabriel's movements quickened with his breathing. Digging her fingers into his arms, Lilith pushed upward, pressing her shoulders deep into the mattress and lifting her lower body against his with such force, she lifted them both. She was close . . . oh, so close . . . so . . .

A ragged cry tore from Gabriel's throat as he plunged himself down upon her. He stiffened as his climax rocked him, pounding his hips against hers while crying out above her.

Lilith's own cries mingled with his as her own orgasm exploded. Wave after wave of intense pleasure ripped through her, numbing her to everything else. Her entire body arched as she cried out in release.

They collapsed together, their bodies still joined, their breathing slowly returning to normal.

Gradually, Gabriel withdrew himself from her. Lilith could feel her internal muscles trying to hang on to him, trying to keep him as part of her.

Their arms and legs entwined, they settled against the pillows, Lilith's head cradled against his shoulder. She held him as tightly as he held her.

A long silence stretched between them, but it wasn't uncomfortable, just the opposite. They spent the time caressing each other—the curve of a shoulder, the firmness of a flank—ten years' worth of touching in the span of a few minutes.

Pressing herself flush against him, Lilith frowned. He was shivering.

"Are you cold?" she asked. She was still feeling rather flushed herself.

Gabriel shook his head, the stubble of his beard scratchy against her forehead. "No."

She raised her eyes to his. "But you're trembling."

He smiled. "I always tremble with you."

Chapter 11

"You're whistling."

Brave's tone was a mixture of curiosity and accusation.

Chuckling, Gabriel raised his head. He was poised over the billiards table, cue in hand, preparing to take his final shot that would win him the game.

"Did they make whistling a crime while I was gone?" he asked innocently.

His friend's dark eyes narrowed. "You never whistle."

With a shake of his head, Gabriel took his shot. The ball rolled into the pocket with deceptive ease. He'd won.

"Obviously, I do," he replied, straightening.

Brave took Gabriel's cue and placed it in the rack with the others. "I take it from your bizarre mood that things are good between you and Lilith?"

Gabriel couldn't stop the foolish grin that spread across his face at the mere sound of her name. They'd spent the majority of the past two days in bed, trying their damnedest to make up for lost time. They rarely spoke, and when they did it was about other things—people they once knew, things they once did. The present and the future were purposefully avoided.

"Good is one way to put it."

Brave looked shocked. "My God, you spent the night with her!"

Gabriel shrugged. "A gentleman doesn't speak of such things."

Grimacing, Brave leaned one hip against the billiards table. "The last thing I want is details, my friend. I'm just . . . surprised."

"Why should you be?" Gabriel asked, striding across the carpet to the liquor cabinet. "I thought you'd be pleased. You've been wanting to see me reunited with Lilith for years." He poured them each a liberal measure of brandy.

Brave crossed the room toward him. "I've wanted to see you happy for years," he said. "If that means a reunion with Lilith, then so be it, but are you reunited?"

His friend's words struck a chord. Frowning, Gabriel handed him a snifter. "What do you mean?"

Brave took a drink. His gaze was far too penetrating for Gabriel's comfort.

"What about this silly game you told me about? Doesn't this mean Lilith has won?"

Gabriel shook his head. He didn't believe for a minute that Lilith would use their intimacy against him. "What happened had nothing to do with that. Lilith isn't like that. She's too honest."

No. The past two days were not a trick, of that he was certain. She'd wanted him as much as he'd wanted her. The close call in the carriage had heightened both their emotions, made them think of things they didn't want to face—their feelings for each other. It had nothing to do with that ridiculous promise of hers to ruin him if he tried to ruin her.

"What about you?" Brave countered. "How honest were you?"

Folding his arms across his chest, Gabriel frowned. "What do you mean? Honest about what?"

Brave shrugged. "Have you told her that you still have every intention of closing her club if Foster was telling the truth? I wager you haven't even been honest with yourself on that score."

Gabriel's scowl deepened. He'd tried to put Blaine's request out of his mind, and he'd almost been successful. He didn't want to think about the decision he would have to make if he did indeed discover that someone at Lilith's club was guilty of cheating.

The faro dealer was Jack Mason. He was the one who had been working the table at which Frederick claimed to have been fleeced. Gabriel hadn't investigated the man much beyond that—he'd been too busy with Lilith.

If Mason was guilty, Gabriel was duty-bound to expose him. Once word got out, it wouldn't look good for Mallory's. That was why he was dragging his feet. This kind of scandal would harm Lilith's business. It might very well ruin her, depending on the mood of the *ton*. He didn't like knowing that Lilith would suffer. Before, he'd always had the secret, stupid thought that maybe he could make her see things his way long before his actions could truly affect her.

Abolishing gaming would take a long time. Many things could happen along the way—he could convince Lilith that being with him was more important than the club. It was only now that he was willing to admit he might not succeed in outlawing gambling. The admission didn't bother him as much as it should have. Failing in his quest was one thing, but being responsible for Lilith's losing everything while people like Bronson remained in business was something Gabriel didn't think she would forgive him for. He wasn't sure if he would forgive himself.

Brave sighed into his glass. "You'd better tell her before she finds out from someone else."

Gabriel tensed. "Are you planning to tell her?" He'd known

Braven for years, trusted him with his life, yet it was easy to accuse him. All this anger and anxiety had to go somewhere, and he wasn't quite prepared to direct it where it belonged—at himself.

Laughing, Brave polished off the last of his brandy. "Good God, no! You know me better than that. But women have a way of finding these things out, Gabe. Believe me, you haven't a secret in the world when a woman's around."

And Brave would know all about that. He'd once tried to keep a very personal secret about himself from Rachel, but she'd discovered the truth. In the end, it had helped bring her and Brave closer and had enabled them to have the marriage they enjoyed today. It had been difficult for a while, but they'd made it work.

Somehow Gabriel couldn't see things ending up in the same way for Lilith and himself.

"You're right," Gabriel conceded with a sigh. "I have to tell her." But first, he was going to have to determine whether or not Jack Mason was guilty or if Frederick had caused all this trouble just to avoid his father's wrath.

He shook his head. "I don't think she's going to understand." He didn't really understand himself.

Brave laughed. "Oh, rest assured, my friend, she won't. Not at first. That's when you have to swallow some pride and beg."

Gabriel made a moue of disgust. "I don't think I could do that."

His friend's gaze was earnest. "Oh, you'll do it. For the woman you love, you'll do things you never dreamed of doing."

Apprehension shivered down Gabriel's spine. "I'm not in love with Lilith." Oh, no! He wasn't stupid enough to go down that road again, not when the future was so uncertain—not when Lilith herself was so uncertain.

Brave raised a brow. "You're an idiot, that's what you are. We all are—men, I mean. Fighting our destinies tooth and claw, thinking we can protect ourselves from being hurt, when all we're doing is making it worse."

Gabriel was almost out of patience. He didn't have to listen to this! "You do not know what the hell you are talking about!"

"No? I know you're afraid of giving Lilith your heart again, afraid of what she'll do with it."

Gabriel snorted.

"You don't want to be the one to have to make sacrifices," Brave went on sagely. "You're afraid if you do make changes it'll mean you're weak somehow. It's an affront to your masculine pride. Which would you rather have, Gabe, your pride or Lilith?"

The answer that sprang readily to mind shocked him, robbing him of speech.

Brave nodded, as though he could somehow read Gabriel's thoughts. "Pride makes a poor bedfellow and an even poorer companion. In your heart you know that as well as I. A friend once told me to swallow my pride and go after Rachel when she left me. He said that if he'd had a second chance with the woman he loved, he would not let her get away again. Now, I'm afraid I must take my leave of you. My wife and son are waiting. Good day, Gabe."

Gabriel merely nodded as his friend left him. He remembered that conversation. It had taken place almost two years ago, at a time when he'd believed he would never see Lilith again. Back then—hell, even a month ago—he would have gladly given everything he held dear to have her back in his life.

Fate, it seemed, had a funny way of granting wishes. He could have Lilith again and it wouldn't cost him everything, only his principles. Was it worth it?

Yes, it was.

Lilith told him he would fail if he tried to abolish gaming altogether, and in a distant part of him, he knew she was correct. Vice could not be demolished. It simply burrowed deeper underground, becoming more and more sordid the

deeper it went. The best one could hope for was to have it reasonably contained so it couldn't sink to new lows. Perhaps he
was fighting the wrong battle.

No. It was impossible. He'd be a laughingstock if he
changed his mind now. Everyone would know why he had
done it. He'd be accused of having a ring through his nose.
And what about his father? He had made the old man a
promise and he intended to keep it. Still, a little voice in the
back of his head said he wouldn't be breaking his promise,
just changing the way he kept it.

It was too much to even contemplate right now. He had
too many other things to take care of, such as learning the
truth about Jack Mason and if Samuel Bronson was more of a
threat to Lilith than she thought—or admitted. He would
find out about Mason and then he would go to Lilith with his
findings as he'd promised. Perhaps then she would trust him
enough to tell him the truth about Bronson.

But before he could win Lilith's trust, there was something
he had to do.

He had to betray Blaine's.

Lilith was nowhere to be found when Gabriel entered
Mallory's. It was still too early for her to be downstairs. The
club had just opened for the evening and was virtually empty.

"You didn't see me," he said to Latimer as he passed.

The bulky club manager raised a heavy brow. "Oh?"

Gabriel nodded. "I'll explain to Lilith when I see her tomorrow." For the hundredth time that day, he wished he
hadn't agreed to meet Brave and Rachel at Lady Stanhope's
soiree. As much as he enjoyed the woman's stories, he'd much
rather spend the evening with Lilith.

His wary gaze softening, Latimer bobbed his head in acquiescence. "All right."

"Thank you." Gabriel's tone was a bit more acerbic than
he'd intended, but he didn't care.

Swiftly he turned on his heel and headed for the faro table.
There was only one other man sitting there. It was the perfect

opportunity to watch Jack Mason in action; he was the dealer scheduled to work that night—Lilith had written it on the list she'd given him, exactly when she'd promised she would.

His heart thumped against his ribs as he approached the table. What was he doing? If anyone there realized who he was he could kiss his reputation good-bye. He glanced around the room. Most of the men weren't from the upper ranks. They were merchants and tradesmen, and thankfully, he didn't know any of them.

He sat down at the table.

"Would you care to play, sir?" the dealer asked.

Fixing what he hoped was a believable smile on his face, Gabriel nodded. "Mind if I watch for a bit first? It has been a while since I played."

Mason returned the smile. He was a young man with a fresh, open face. He didn't look like the type who would cheat. A trait that would no doubt serve him well if he were crooked.

Gabriel paid close attention to Mason's hands as he dealt and flipped cards for his customer. Years ago, when Gabriel had first come of age and started doing all those foolish things young men did, his father had taken him aside and shown him what to watch for when playing cards—what people could do to conceal and manipulate the cards. The knowledge had served his father well. Unfortunately, the old man hadn't had enough sense to know when to quit, or that his luck would eventually run out. You didn't need to be cheated to lose everything you owned.

Mason appeared to play a clean game. He was fast, but none of his movements could be described as suspicious. Gabriel saw no hint that any of the cards came from the bottom of the deck or out of the dealer's sleeves. More important, he didn't seem to mind Gabriel watching. The young man was either very sure of himself, or very honest.

After losing for a third time, the other gentleman at the table decided to cut his losses and move on to another game.

An annoying shiver of anxiety moistened Gabriel's palms. This was it.

"Would you like to play now, sir?" Mason asked.

Dry-mouthed, Gabriel nodded. "Yes," he said softly. "I would."

Gabriel found Frederick later that evening at White's, drinking with several of his friends.

Schooling his features, Gabriel moved toward them. The adrenaline from the faro table still raced through his veins. He'd left the table fifty pounds richer and completely certain that Jack Mason was an honest man. He'd talked to the dealer as they played, and knew in his gut that Mason was exactly how he portrayed himself. That, coupled with Frederick's continued patronage of Mallory's, was enough evidence for Gabriel to discern the truth.

Playing faro had also made Gabriel realize something else. Unlike his father, he could get up and walk away, even when luck seemed to be on his side. And if he could walk away, others could as well.

"Good evening, gentlemen," he greeted the young men when he came up to them. "Beg pardon for interrupting your revelry, but I wonder if I might have a word with Foster."

It was obvious the young men were already well on their way to being foxed as they teased Frederick, telling him he was in trouble and laughing loudly at their own foolish wit.

It was also obvious that Frederick didn't want to talk to him. Cheeks pale, he rose from the table stiffly, saying not a word while he followed Gabriel to a table well out of earshot.

"I'd ask if you would like a drink," Gabriel said, flipping out his coattails before seating himself, "but I think you've already had enough."

Frederick gave an insolent snort. "You sound like my father."

Gabriel kept his gaze fastened on the boy's face. "Do I? I will take that as a compliment."

"You do that."

Stifling a sigh of exasperation, Gabriel went on. "Your father cares about you very much."

Frederick's mouth set mulishly. "My father is a tyrant."

Gabriel wasn't about to spend all evening verbally fencing with this pup when he had to go home and get ready to meet Brave and Rachel.

"How many gaming debts do you have, Frederick?"

Frederick's dark eyes blazed. "I *knew* that's why you were here—I knew it! My debts are none of your business, Angelwood."

Gabriel nodded. "So Mallory's is not the only club to hold your vowels."

The boy was silent, but the flush creeping up his cheeks was answer enough.

"I hear you and your friends frequent Mallory's quite often."

Frederick shrugged. "It is the best club in town." He raised his defiant gaze to Gabriel's. "And I'm sure you will agree that Lilith's charms make the place even more agreeable."

That this brat even dared to pretend to understand the quality of Lilith's charms made Gabriel want to laugh.

Instead, he produced a bland smile. "High praise for a club you claim cheated you out of your allowance."

Every ounce of color drained from Frederick's face, leaving behind a chalky mask of shock.

"My father . . ." He trailed off, as though he hadn't the least idea of what to say next.

Leaning back in his chair, Gabriel crossed his legs, bracing his elbow on the armrest. He stroked his jaw thoughtfully.

"Your father came to see me, yes."

The boy's shoulders slumped. "He said he wouldn't tell anyone."

"He was very concerned about his child having been fleeced by this awful gaming hell, but you weren't fleeced at all, were you, Frederick?"

Frederick shook his head, closing his eyes in shame. "No," he murmured.

His answer didn't come as a surprise. Gabriel had entertained the notion but hadn't wanted to believe it because Frederick was Blaine's son, and because it was such a serious charge.

He should be angry that Frederick would treat Lilith and her club's reputation so shoddily, especially since she had gone out of her way to accommodate the stupid pup, but Gabriel felt only pity for the boy.

"Why did you lie to your father?"

Frederick's expression told Gabriel just how silly he thought that question was. "You know my father, how he is. He would murder me if he knew the truth."

Gabriel's smile held no sympathy. "He's going to do worse than that when he finds out you lied. A father expects his son to be foolish once in a while, Frederick. What he doesn't expect is to be lied to."

The young man's cheeks flushed. His eyes glittered with betrayal. "Are you going to tell him?"

"Oh, no!" Gabriel exclaimed with a chuckle. "I'm washing my hands of this situation."

The boy sagged in relief.

"But *you* are going to tell him," Gabriel added with a rueful smile.

Eyes wide with horror, Frederick stared at him. Gabriel might feel sorry for him if he didn't think the brat was getting exactly what he deserved.

"You can't be serious. He'll kill me!"

Folding his arms across his chest, Gabriel shrugged. "I doubt he will do anything so extreme, but you have to tell him the truth."

Frederick's face squinched up. "Why?"

The urge to upset the lad's chair and send him toppling to the floor was overwhelming, but somehow Gabriel managed to control himself.

"Because you have tarnished Lady Lilith's reputation to save your own hide, and that is cowardly and wrong. That's why."

Lip jutting in a pout, Frederick frowned. "It's not like she has a reputation to begin with."

Wrong thing to say. Oh, so wrong! Seething, Gabriel snagged one of the legs of Frederick's chair with his foot and dragged it across the few feet that separated them. Frederick jumped in surprise as he was jerked into motion.

Sitting up, Gabriel leaned forward so that his face was just inches from the boy's frightened one.

"Now, you listen to me, you brainless puppy. Lilith has more elegance and poise in her little finger than you can ever hope to claim for your entire person. And when you speak to her or of her, you will treat her with the respect she deserves or you will answer to me. Do I make myself understood?"

Frederick nodded, eyes huge dark pools against his pallor.

"Good." Shifting his foot, Gabriel pushed the boy's chair back again. "I will be calling on your father tomorrow. I expect to hear that you have made a full confession. If you haven't, I will complete the task for you."

"You said you wouldn't tell him!" Frederick cried, aghast.

Gabriel rose to his feet. "That was before you lowered yourself to insulting a lady who has by all accounts shown you nothing but understanding and kindness. If I were you, I would be heartily ashamed of myself."

Drunk and petulant, Frederick allowed himself one last show of defiance. "If you were me, I'd be poking her."

Gabriel wasn't quite sure how it happened, but one minute Frederick was sitting in front of him and the next he was on the floor, his overturned chair beside him.

Frederick glared at Gabriel as his friends laughed drunkenly from their table.

"Perhaps," Gabriel said coolly as he skirted around the young man, "you shouldn't imbibe any more tonight. Liquor appears to make you quite clumsy."

Then, without offering to help Frederick to his feet, Gabriel turned and walked away.

* * *

"Where are you off to?"

Mary froze halfway between the statue of Venus and the door. Her expression was one of such guilt that Lilith couldn't help but wonder just what her friend was doing. It was midmorning and while Mary was often up before dawn, this was the first Lilith had seen of her so far.

It had been a couple of days since Lilith last spoke to her, which was odd in itself, but not as odd as the care Mary had taken with her appearance. Her hair was drawn up into a neat braided bun with little curls floating around her face. There was color in her cheeks and a sparkle in her brown eyes that Lilith had never seen before. And she wore the pale blue morning gown that she normally saved for church or special occasions.

"I'm going for a walk in the park," Mary replied.

Realization dawned. There was a man involved. Leaning her shoulder against Venus's thigh, Lilith grinned teasingly. "With whom?"

The older woman flushed scarlet. "With the Reverend Geoffrey Sweet."

If Mary had told her she was stepping out with the regent himself, Lilith couldn't have been more surprised.

"The clergyman!" Laughter rumbled inside her. Oh, this was just too funny!

Mary turned her unimpressed gaze up to Lilith's. "I am so glad you find this amusing."

"Of course it's amusing!" Lilith replied, still chuckling. "Not too long ago, you thought the man an overbearing, righteous prig!"

Mary glanced away. "That was before I got to know him."

"And now you think he's . . . ?"

"Now I believe him to be the best man I've ever known."

Her friend still didn't look at her, and the full implication of her words settled onto Lilith like a weight.

"Oh, Mary," she whispered. "You've formed an attachment."

That snapped the older woman's head up. "What if I have? Are you the only woman under this roof allowed to fall—to form an attachment?"

"Of course not." But of the two of them, Lilith wasn't the one who already had a husband.

"Have you told him you are married?"

Mary's mouth thinned. "Have you told Lord Angelwood about Bronson?"

Lilith raised both brows. Mary always became defensive when she was afraid. Lilith couldn't blame her in this case. She had finally met a nice man—a man who seemed to deserve her if he was as good as she claimed—and it might all be ruined by the bastard who'd met her first.

"No," Lilith replied. "Not entirely. It is not quite the same thing, is it?"

"It is still a secret. It is something you're deliberately not telling him."

"Not telling him about Bronson is not going to hurt his feelings."

"No," Mary snapped. "It just almost got him killed." As soon as the words were spoken, she clapped a hand over her mouth, staring at Lilith in horror as she did so.

"Oh, Lilith, I'm—"

Seizing the hand her friend offered, Lilith shook her head. She was right. Gabriel had already been the unwitting victim of one of Bronson's attacks. She couldn't live with herself if something even more serious happened to him.

"Do not apologize, Mary. You are quite right. I should tell Gabriel about Bronson, if for no other reason than his own safety."

The older woman dropped her fingers from her mouth. Her lower lip trembled. "I should never have spoken so. I'm just so worried that Geoffrey—I mean Reverend Sweet— won't want to see me anymore once he finds out about my scandalous past."

Lilith squeezed the fingers in hers and smiled. "My dearest friend, you work for one of the most scandalous women in

London. If he can get past that, he can handle almost anything, I suspect."

Mary shook her head. "I don't know."

"I'll tell you what," Lilith said brightly. "I will tell Gabriel about Bronson if you tell the good reverend about your marriage."

"Do you really think he will understand?"

Lilith would never presume to answer for a man. The perplexing creatures were downright vexing in their unpredictability at times.

"If he's as deserving as you seem to believe he is, then yes, I think he will understand. Besides, you are as good as divorced. The woman you once were doesn't exist anymore." At least Lilith hoped he would see it that way, but being a man, and a man of God, no doubt the reverend would see things differently through his pious vision.

Mary obviously hadn't thought of it that way. "You're right. I'll just tell him I was married, and if he reacts badly I'll tell him my husband's dead."

Lilith burst out laughing. So much for complete honesty. Still, perhaps Mary's situation was one where complete honesty wasn't the best route. Lilith was the last person who would ever claim to know what was right for another person. She had a difficult enough time making these decisions for herself.

She walked Mary down the stairs and wished her good luck at the door. She was just about to head back up when Latimer told her she had a visitor waiting for her in one of the parlors.

"Who is it, Latimer?"

"The Countess Braven, Lady Lilith."

Rachel! "You put a countess in one of the club parlors? How could you?" Oh, what Rachel must be thinking!

Latimer's eyes widened at her outburst, but otherwise his expression remained unchanged. "That's where she wanted to wait, my lady. She asked if she could have a tour of the club, which I obliged her—only the ladies' side, mind you—and when I asked if she'd care to await you upstairs, she said down here was fine. Where else was I to put her and the child?"

Lilith's shoulders sagged even further. First, Mary was out batting her eyelashes at the Reverend Mr. Sweet, and now Rachel *and* her baby were waiting for her in a room that had previously been used for either sex or gambling.

Just bloody wonderful. What else could possibly go wrong?

"Which parlor?" she asked, grinding the heel of her hand against her forehead.

"The green one."

After giving her servant a gentle pat on the arm, Lilith went to join her guests. She found them in the green parlor as Latimer had said, looking as serene as Madonna and child.

"Lilith!" Rachel greeted before Lilith could open her mouth. "I hope you don't mind Alexander and me popping by uninvited."

"Of course not," Lilith replied, coming closer. "You are both welcome here at any time." And she meant it. She had very few friends in this world, but she thought Rachel might very well become one of them.

The blond woman's gaze was the same shade of blue as her pelisse. "I hadn't seen you since that afternoon you came to visit with Gabriel. I wanted to ascertain for myself that we hadn't done anything to upset you."

Touched beyond words by Rachel's concern, Lilith could only shake her head, temporarily struck dumb by such kindness.

"Of course you didn't do anything," she said, gesturing for her to sit. "No, it was my own foolishness that caused me to flee. Had I not been so ashamed of my behavior, I would have called on you to better explain."

Seating herself and her son in a pale green armchair, Rachel smiled. "You have nothing to be ashamed of, I assure you."

Heat blossomed in Lilith's cheeks. "You're very kind to say so, but what sort of woman runs away after holding a child?"

"A woman afraid she will never have one of her own," Rachel replied bluntly, her gaze shrewd and all too understanding.

Struggling to catch her breath, Lilith chuckled self-consciously as she sank onto the nearby sofa. "It seems I'm more transparent than I thought."

"Not at all." Rachel shifted her son to her other shoulder. "I might not have come to that conclusion had I not felt the same way at one time."

Lilith didn't bother to hide her disbelief. "Really? But you and Brave haven't been married that long . . ." She trailed off. She was sticking her nose in where it didn't belong.

"Before I met Brave, my circumstances were such that I thought I'd never marry, let alone become a mother." Rachel glanced at the bundle in her arms. "I am so very glad to have been wrong."

Envy stabbed viciously at Lilith's breast. She wanted what this woman had. She wanted a husband and children and respectability. She wanted stability. To hell with the modern women and their views of matrimony and motherhood as a prison for women. Lilith would gladly give up her fortune, her independence, even her club, for the shackles Rachel wore.

"Would you like to try holding him again?"

Her heart pounding, Lilith held up her hands. "Oh, no! I couldn't."

"Of course you can," Rachel replied with that little smile of hers. Lilith couldn't shake the feeling that the other woman knew something she didn't. Surely she must drive her husband mad with those secretive smiles.

But, from what she'd seen, Lord Braven didn't seem to mind his ignorance at all.

It was futile to object, and so Lilith didn't even bother to try when Rachel rose to her feet and crossed the carpet with her son. The truth was, she wanted to hold the baby.

"Hold out your arms."

Lilith did as she was told.

"There you go. Now, you don't need to hold him so stiffly. He won't break, I assure you. Go ahead, cradle him against you. Relax. There."

Struck by such profound wonder it was almost painful, Lilith stared at the tiny person nestled against the peach silk of her bodice. Alexander had his father's dark brown eyes, and his open gaze made him seem as amazed by Lilith as she was by him.

"He's so quiet," she remarked, lifting her head long enough to glance at Rachel and then back at the child. How could she have ever thought this was difficult? Holding a baby seemed incredibly natural now that she wasn't so nervous.

The countess chuckled. "Not always. I'm afraid he inherited my talkativeness. He and his father have some very long-winded debates."

Lilith smiled at the baby, giving him her finger to curl his tiny fist around. "Are you a talker, little man?"

The most incredible thing happened then. Alexander *smiled*. Little bow lips parted, revealing pink gums and a tiny tongue. A gurgle followed.

"He's smiling!" Lilith exclaimed with a broad grin for Rachel. "He's smiling at *me*!"

Rachel nodded, obviously amused by her enthusiasm. "I think he must like you."

Returning her gaze to the child, Lilith stroked the soft fingers curled around her much larger one. "Well, I know I like you, little Alex. You're the most beautiful, precious thing I've ever seen. Yes, you are."

For a few moments nothing else existed. All of her attention, all the wonder Lilith thought she'd lost with her innocence, were centered solely on the child in her arms. How incredible to give life to such a being. How her heart ached with the sweetness of just gazing upon such a gift, and it wasn't even her own.

"You will make a wonderful mother someday," Rachel remarked, breaking the silence.

Somehow Lilith managed to tear her eyes away from the infant long enough to address his mother. A sharp pain throbbed in her very soul.

"I doubt very much I'll ever have a little miracle like this of my own."

Another one of those knowing smiles. "Oh, I shouldn't want to wager on that."

There was no need to ask for an explanation; the meaning was quite clear. Rachel believed Lilith and Gabriel were going to marry and have children of their own.

Lilith studied the delicate round face close to hers. What would it be like to create such an angel with Gabe? It was a fantasy she'd indulged in many times in the past, but until now it had lacked a sense of realness, a hint of possibility.

And now, with this warm weight pressed against her breast, soft cooing noises singing in her ears, the desire to have a child—Gabriel's child—came crashing down upon her like a stack of bricks.

She didn't realize she was crying until Rachel laid a hand on her shaking shoulder.

"Lilith, my dear, are you all right?"

Her throat was so tight, all she could do was shake her head.

Kneeling on the carpet, Rachel took Alexander from her. Lilith didn't want to let him go, but her vision was blurry and she didn't want to risk harming him in any way. Rachel placed him beside her on the sofa, then wrapped her arms around Lilith's shoulders.

"You poor thing," Rachel murmured against her hair.

When was the last time she'd been comforted by another woman? Mary wasn't a physically affectionate person, save for the odd hand squeeze. Certainly her own mother had never held her this way. Aunt Imogen might have patted her head every once in a while, letting her know the embrace was there if she wanted it, but Lilith had always been too afraid to accept it.

She did so now.

"I feel like such a fool," she muttered when she could breathe again.

Sitting back on her heels, Rachel shook her head. "Don't. We all need to have a good cry now and again."

Lilith choked on a laugh. A good cry? Lord, she'd opened the floodgates!

"Yes, well, thanks to me, you now have a big wet spot on your shoulder."

The blond woman waved a dismissive hand. "I'm used to it. You wouldn't believe how many ways a baby can make you change your clothes during the course of a day."

This time Lilith really did laugh. "Thank you."

Rachel's smile was soft. "What else are friends for?"

At the mention of the word "friends", Lilith thought she actually might start bawling again, but she managed to control herself.

Scooping up her sleeping son, Rachel rose to her feet. "And now I'm afraid we must go. Had I known my visit would cause you such distress, I would have planned to stay longer so that I might make it up to you. As it is, Brave is expecting me home at any minute."

Lilith nodded, also rising. "Perhaps we might get together again sometime soon. I promise not to cry." Lord, did she sound as pathetically hopeful as she thought? Rachel must think her desperate for companionship.

Perhaps she was.

Grinning, Rachel reached out and gave her hand a squeeze. "My friend Belinda—Mrs. Mayhew—and I are going out shopping the day after tomorrow. Would you care to come?"

Speechless, Lilith could only stare. Rachel wanted to go shopping with her and a friend? She wanted to be seen in public with her? Never mind what such a thing could do for Lilith's reputation; the invitation had a far greater effect on her heart. Unfortunately, it could also do great damage to Rachel and her friend.

She shook her head. "I don't think it's a good idea for you and your friend to be seen with someone like me—"

"I'll be seen with whomever I want," Rachel interrupted with such determination in her voice that Lilith was shocked.

"W-well," she conceded, "if it is all right with your friend, I would love to join you."

Instantly, Rachel transformed back into the lively, smiling woman Lilith had first met. "Wonderful! We'll be round for you at two."

A frisson of excitement rippled through Lilith as she agreed. When had she last gone shopping with a friend? It seemed a lifetime ago. Usually Luisa or Mary went with her, but Luisa was her maid and Mary couldn't afford to shop in the same stores Lilith liked—and she rarely allowed Lilith to buy her gifts. It would be lovely to visit the more expensive stores with other women who appreciated them.

She walked Rachel and Alexander to the front door and said good-bye with another hug that left her thinking that she could get used to having friends again.

Yes, it had certainly been a strange day. It couldn't possibly get any stranger.

"Lady Lilith."

She'd just been about to close the door when she heard her name. Glancing down the steps, she saw Frederick Foster standing in a puddle of sunlight, twisting the brim of his hat in his hands. He looked scared and decidedly hung-over.

Apparently the day could—and indeed was about to—get stranger. She would never be ready for the club on time.

"Mr. Foster," she said with some surprise. "To what do I owe this pleasure?"

The young man was silent as he climbed the steps toward her. She hadn't seen a young man so nervous since the first time Gabriel had asked her to dance. She'd been so anxious to impress him, she'd almost tripped over the hem of her skirts.

"Lady Lilith," Frederick stated determinedly when there was but a foot of space between them. "I owe you an apology."

Chapter 12

⟡

The atmosphere at Mallory's was different when Gabriel entered its doors that night. The air seemed thicker, crackling with tension.

Even Latimer was out of sorts. Instead of his usual friendly but gruff posturing, he was strangely subdued, giving Gabriel a look that was a mixture of censure and sympathy.

Apprehension swirled low in Gabriel's stomach. "Good evening, Latimer."

The burly man shook his head. "I'm afraid not, Lord Angelwood."

Schooling his features into a mask of cool composure, Gabriel nodded. "That's unfortunate. Where is Lady Lilith?"

Latimer sighed. "In the gentlemen's club, my lord."

"Thank you." His nerves thrumming, Gabriel strode past the doorman toward the entrance to the male side of the club.

Perhaps he was only being fearful. Things had been going so well for him and Lilith that the cynic in him was just waiting for something awful to happen. But really, what could? Unless she had found out the truth about his father . . .

No. She couldn't have. There was no way. Still, Latimer seemed so odd, as though he pitied him.

The gentlemen's section was its usual self—loud and boisterous with a touch of cigar smoke in the air. The mood was high, but it was still early. No one had lost any large amounts yet, but the winning had begun in earnest. Everyone was feeling lucky.

Everyone except him.

A few heads turned when he made his entrance. Gazes that didn't meet his fastened upon him while voices spoke in hushed whispers. Glances darted to the center of the room and back again. Two men smiled knowingly in his direction as they headed for the betting book in the corner.

Gabriel's sense of unease grew as he continued across the carpet. The music wafting through the vents seemed ominous somehow, even though it sounded the same as on any other night. Conversations halted when he walked by. Hardened players looked up from their cards to spare him a brief glance.

Oh, yes, there was definitely something going on, and if Gabriel's suspicions were correct, it concerned not only him, but also the person in the middle of the room who had almost two dozen men clamoring for her attention.

The pack moved back from their prey as he approached, clearing a path right into the center. Expression neutral, Gabriel walked in. This must be how poor Daniel had felt in the lion's den.

What he saw was more impressive than any pride of lions, however.

It was Lilith, of course. Standing with her profile to him. Some of her glorious, fiery hair was nestled on top of her head, secured there by sparkling diamond combs. The rest fell down her back, almost to her hips, in thick, satiny waves. She wore a black velvet gown with very little bodice. The ivory swells of her breasts were dangerously close to spilling over the daring neckline. Black gloves encased her soft, round arms, and diamonds dripped from her ears and throat.

Someone must have alerted her to his presence, because she hesitated for a second before turning to face him. When she did, his heart twisted in his chest.

She'd painted her face. Pale and matte, her skin lacked its natural luster. Her lips and cheeks were crimson, her eyes smudged with kohl. She managed to look both whorish and exotic, and Gabriel didn't doubt for a moment that her appearance was for his benefit—and his alone.

She was wearing her battle armor. Why? What could have happened since he'd last seen her to warrant this defensive move?

"Hello, Gabe," she purred.

It took all of his strength not to flinch. The low, throaty pitch of her voice revealed the nature of their relationship better than any public display could have. Using his Christian name screamed intimacy, and looking as she did, no one would believe otherwise.

"Lilith," he replied, as though oblivious to what she was doing. "You look stunning this evening."

There it was—a flicker of something in the tempest of her gaze. She wasn't as hard as she tried to appear.

This wasn't just a chance to poke holes in his reputation— he could survive people thinking they were sleeping together. Hell, most men would slap him on the back and congratulate him! No, Lilith was hurt and angry and it was all directed toward him.

Lord, what had he done *this* time?

"I believe we had an appointment this evening, madam," he said, attempting to ignore the snorts and snickers behind him. "Shall we?"

Distaste skipped across her features as she stared at his offered arm, but it was quickly replaced with an expression so seductive, several of her admirers murmured at it.

"With *pleasure*, my lord."

Gabriel suppressed a resigned sigh and steered her

through the curious crowd. Somehow his Lily had gotten swallowed up again by this bold, caricature of a woman wearing the same face.

And he knew without a doubt that when Lilith explained how it happened, the reason was going to be entirely his fault.

Not wanting to add more fuel to the gossip, he guided Lilith toward the private parlors rather than to her upstairs apartments. It didn't really matter. People were going to think they were having sex no matter where he took her.

They walked the corridor in silence. Lilith dropped his arm and paid more attention to the Chinese wallpaper than she did to him. The loss of the past few days' familiarity pained him.

"All right," he said, following her into a parlor and shutting the door behind him. "What the devil is the matter?"

She turned to face him, and for a moment he thought she meant to make him suffer a little longer, but then she seemed to sag a little, as though some of the fight had gone out of her.

"The Honorable Frederick Foster paid me a visit today."

Oh, no. It didn't take much for Gabriel to fill in the rest. Frederick had suffered an attack of conscience—perhaps as a result of confessing all to his father—and had come to Lilith to apologize. So now Lilith knew just who had made the charge against her. And she also knew why Gabriel had been so interested in her relationship with Frederick.

"I can explain."

She swept across the carpet to a gilt-edged chair with cream brocade upholstery and perched upon the seat with all the serenity of a queen.

"By all means, then," she replied, her voice deceptively soft. "Explain why you didn't trust me enough to tell me the truth."

"It wasn't that I didn't trust you—" At her sharp look, he decided not to make things worse. "I didn't want you to know who made the charge in case you decided to take matters into your own hands, either by concealing the truth or by confronting the boy on your own. I hoped to uncover the truth first and then proceed from there."

Her gaze was uncomfortably shrewd. "And if my club had cheated the son of a peer, it would make it easier for you to close me down, wouldn't it?"

It sounded so underhanded when she said it.

"When Blaine approached me, I didn't know the club he spoke of was yours. I didn't even know you were back in town."

Her stormy eyes narrowed. "I find that hard to believe."

Gabriel laughed harshly. "So do I, but it's true."

"But after that night I found you in the office, you certainly knew who owned this club."

"Yes," he admitted. "I did."

Folding her hands in her lap, she stared at him. It didn't matter that she was the one who was sitting. It was Gabriel who felt small.

A harsh bark of laughter burst from her lips. "And here I thought that our lovemaking had changed things."

"What did it change for you?" he asked softly, not certain he wanted to know the answer, but determined to hear it.

Her chin trembled as she lifted it. "It made me think that maybe we had more than just the past holding us together."

Her words wrapped around his heart like a vise, squeezing until every beat was agony.

"You truly believed me capable of cheating that young man, didn't you?"

That penetrating stare of hers was making him itch, but he refused to look away. He had to be completely honest with her. He owed her that much.

"At first I was so angry I wanted to believe you were capable of it, yes. It would have given me something to use in my petition to abolish gaming." He folded his arms across his chest. It made him feel less vulnerable. "But then I wanted to prove that you couldn't have done it—that if it had happened, you had no knowledge of it."

Her full lips quirked at one corner. "So you trusted me not to cheat someone, but you couldn't trust me enough to tell me who had accused me? What did you think I would do? Ruin the stupid boy?"

Gabriel raked a hand through his hair. She was so upset that she was all too ready to believe he'd thought the worst of her. Surely the past few days had taught her differently.

But perhaps it was Lilith who had trouble trusting, not him.

"Of course not. I made a promise to Blaine—"

She leapt to her feet. "A promise!"

Gabriel could only stare. The way those two words set her off told him exactly why she was so angry. She didn't trust him and she didn't trust her feelings for him. Ten years of hurt and betrayal still churned inside her. He'd made a promise to Blaine when he hadn't been able to keep his promise to her. And she didn't know why he hadn't.

He knew her side of the story, but he hadn't told her everything, and she knew it—maybe not consciously, but a part of her knew it was more than his father's death that had kept him from finding her.

He was going to have to tell her.

"Yes," he replied. "I promised Blaine I wouldn't tell anyone about his suspicions."

"And I suppose all the promises you once made to me meant absolutely nothing?"

He stared at her—her color high, even brighter than the rouge on her cheeks—and all he could feel was exhaustion. This had to stop. He didn't want to fight her anymore. He'd rather lose her forever than go through this cycle again.

"Why do you always have to return to this, Lily? I told you why I didn't come after you right away. I told you I looked for you."

She walked toward him, her movements stilted by rage. It was almost as though she wanted him to tell her he hadn't tried to find her, for then she would be able to go back to hating him instead of—

Instead of what? Loving him?

"You told me that you had to recover your father's debts. But what about after? You told me you looked, that you never received my letters, but I find it very hard to accept that my aunt could do such a thing."

There it was. She didn't trust him. She didn't want to trust him. It was easier to believe he had lied, because that wouldn't hurt as much as thinking her beloved aunt had.

Shaking his head, Gabriel ran a hand over his face. Christ, he was tired. "I wrote to your aunt. She told me she didn't know where you were."

Much of the color drained out of her face, leaving behind two ghoulish patches of red on her white cheeks.

"Aunt Imogen would never do such a thing. She knew how much I loved you. She knew how I suffered—" Her voice broke off on a sob. "It's not true!"

He closed the distance between them, cupping both her shoulders with his hands. She tried to shrug him off, but he refused to let go.

"Think about it, Lilith. Did she offer to mail your letters to me? Did she console you when no replies came? Did she tell you that you'd eventually get over your disappointment, that you'd meet someone better when you were older?"

He could tell from the anguish in her eyes that the old witch had done everything he listed.

"Lilith," he murmured. "She was what kept us apart. I searched everywhere for you. I looked for years. I even hired Bow Street."

Her jaw tight, she continued her denial. "No, I don't believe it. I won't believe it."

One look at her face told Gabriel she *couldn't* believe it, because then not only he would have proved to be a liar, but so would Imogen; and right now, Imogen was the only good thing Lilith had to cling to.

He didn't want to destroy that for her, but he wasn't willing to sacrifice their relationship to make someone else look good. Not again.

"Lilith, you were the most important thing in my life. You know that."

She met his gaze. He was struck by the emptiness of hers. "No, Gabe, I do not. I know how important your promise to Blaine was and how important protecting your family after your father's death was. But I have absolutely no idea how important I am or ever was to you."

"Everything," he replied, his voice raw. "You were everything."

Her head tilted to one side. She didn't believe him. "And now what am I?"

Everything. But the word froze in his throat. She wouldn't believe him without the whole story, and he couldn't trust her with it.

She laughed again. "Nothing. Well, that's exactly what you are to me, Gabriel. Nothing."

It hurt, even as his heart denied it. How had they gone from arguing over Frederick's charge to this? Obviously it was something that had been bothering her for a long time.

"You don't mean that. I don't believe it."

Her cold gaze locked with his. "I don't care if you believe it or not. But I shall tell you something you can believe, Lord Angelwood. You can go find some other stupid heart to break. You'll not get a second chance at mine."

And then she was gone, slamming the door behind her.

Half an hour later, standing at the French doors that led into the garden behind the club, Lilith was still feeling shaky from her confrontation with Gabriel, and hating herself for it.

She was *such* an idiot where he was concerned. Even as he stood there, spouting his nonsense about how much she'd meant to him, how he'd looked for her—he'd tried to blame a dead woman, for heaven's sake!—she'd wanted to believe him. She wanted to trust in him even though he had yet to give her any reason to.

Or had he? Only once had he betrayed her trust. Before that, she would have trusted him with anything. It hurt knowing that he didn't trust her, either. *She* wasn't the one who had done anything wrong. She had never betrayed him as he'd betrayed her. And yet he acted as if she should understand.

It hurt. Somewhere deep down inside her, there was a

wound that wouldn't heal. Open and vulnerable, it bled whenever she thought of him. These past few weeks—his attention, his lovemaking—had all been a lie. Just a ruse to distract her while he tried to prove she and her club were dishonest.

It didn't matter that he'd confided the charges made against her. He'd asked her questions about Frederick and never once hinted at his true interest. He'd let her believe he was starting to trust her, that maybe he'd changed his mind about abolishing gambling. He'd convinced her that he was on her side.

But he'd planned to use her as an example. Well, he'd certainly succeeded. Someone should hang a sign around her neck: ATTENTION WOMEN. THIS IS WHAT HAPPENS WHEN YOU FALL IN LOVE WITH THE WRONG MAN.

Gabriel Warren had made a fool of her for the last time. She would *not* allow him to do so again.

But even as she told herself that, a little voice inside her head rushed to his defense by raising a tiny sliver of doubt.

How could all his caresses, the things he said, the way he trembled in her arms, been a lie? Men might be able to have sex without the benefit of love or affection of any kind, but just how much of it could they pretend?

And how hurt he'd looked when she told him to find another heart to break. As if she had broken his in return.

Well, he wouldn't be the first person to realize just what a bitch she could be. Better that he believed it, that he dealt with the fact that she wasn't—that she didn't *want* to be—the girl she used to be. She'd almost forgotten herself. It was a mistake she wouldn't make again. Softness, trust and vulnerability only served to get a heart broken. From now on she would do well to remember that.

She hadn't meant for it to get so out of hand. Yes, she'd been angry that he hadn't told her the truth about Frederick, and yes, she'd purposefully dressed in a manner he wouldn't approve of, but how had everything spun so out of control? Other fears and doubts had risen to the surface unnoticed, making it all too easy to jump to conclusions, to make the fight about so much more than intended.

This example of his distrust, however small, brought her own distrust of him roaring back—because she'd actually started to trust him. To think she'd entertained the notion of telling him her suspicions about Bronson! And that she had Mr. Francis investigating Bronson's involvement in the attack on their carriage. Wouldn't that have given him something good to use against her; gaming-club owners were dangerous criminals, not above using force to get what they want.

Sighing, Lilith held her hand against her forehead. She needed some air. She also needed a good, swift kick in the backside, but thankfully, there was no one nearby to perform the task.

Stepping out into the cool, damp night air, she breathed the scent of jasmine deep into her lungs.

The secluded garden ran the length of the rear of the club, with the entrance closer to the ladies' side than the gentlemen's. Mallory's patrons rarely visited the spot unless they wanted a breath of air or the chance to tryst with a lover in the bushes.

That the garden was so seldom used didn't bother Lilith at all. In fact, she preferred it that way. It often gave her a quiet place in which she could think without having to worry about being interrupted.

Tonight, however, was to be an exception.

"You look good enough to eat."

Oh! Lilith managed not to cry out, but she couldn't stop herself from jumping at the sound of Bronson's voice.

Straightening her spine as he chuckled at her alarm, Lilith turned to face her adversary with more bravado than she felt. After that night at the theater, the mere thought of Bronson and how he'd looked at her was enough to send chills through her. And the "accident" with the carriage made it even worse. The man was ruthless, more than Lilith ever thought of being.

"What are you doing here, Mr. Bronson?"

The club owner shrugged his wide shoulders. "Can't a man pay a visit to a fellow business . . . *person*?"

This certainly was a radical departure from his behavior outside the theater.

"Not when that club owner recently tried to harm that same person, no."

Holding out his hands in a gesture of supplication, Bronson smiled ruefully and stepped toward her. As the light from the garden torches touched his face, Lilith saw that the smile didn't reach his eyes.

"My dear madam, I'm afraid I have no idea what you're talking about."

Lilith's eyes narrowed. "Don't play dumb with me, Bronson. You insult both of us."

Bronson's expression changed to one of mock injury. "You wound me."

Arching a brow, Lilith regarded him warily. "You will recover."

His greatcoat flapping around his legs, Bronson moved closer. It was all Lilith could do to hold her ground. She wanted to run back inside the safety of her club and hide under her desk. Bronson being nice was even more disconcerting than Bronson making threats.

"You still haven't told me what it is you want." If he came any closer, she was going to either run or scream.

As though sensing her skittishness, Bronson stopped a few feet away from her, near a stone bench, where he sat down, placed his forearms on his thighs and observed her with amusement.

"I want a truce," he replied.

Both eyebrows went up this time. "A truce? Without giving me a chance to retaliate for the carriage incident? That's not very chivalrous of you, Mr. Bronson."

Where had this bravado come from? Her tone could have been flirtatious had it not been filled with sarcasm.

Bronson smiled. It was a wolfish baring of teeth, but Lilith saw real humor in it.

"I do like you, Lilith. I really do."

She stiffened. "I haven't given you leave to call me by my Christian name, Mr. Bronson."

"Call me Samuel."

"I'd rather not."

"Lilith." His tone was light, teasing and far too intimate, given their history.

"Don't call me that."

Bronson's expression hardened. "I'll call you whatever I want."

Summoning all the disdain she felt for him, Lilith shook her head. "Not to my face you won't. Good night, Mr. Bronson."

It took all her courage to turn her back on him, but she did just that. Squaring her shoulders, she kept her gaze fixed on the distance door of the club, willing her shaking limbs to keep from turning to jelly until after she was safe.

"Does your lover know about us?" he called to her.

Halting, Lilith turned back to face him. "There is no 'us.'"

Bronson pursed his lips. "Isn't there? I wager I know you better than your Lord Angelwood does."

She laughed at that. She couldn't help it. Bronson didn't seem too impressed by her humor, but what else had he expected? He certainly couldn't have thought she would fall for his nonsense.

"It would be a wager you would lose, Mr. Bronson."

He stood, striding toward her with an arrogance that would have set her teeth on edge five minutes ago, but his ludicrous suggestion had weakened her fear and lowered her guard.

"Really?" He was directly in front of her now, so close that when the breeze picked up, the hem of his coat brushed her legs. He was a large man. Not as tall as Gabriel, but heavier. If the two men were horses, Gabriel would be a thoroughbred, Bronson a workhorse.

She nodded. "Really. Gabriel and I have a lot of history."

Bronson nodded knowingly. "Ah, yes, your ill-fated love affair with him when you were but a girl. He ruined you."

Lilith didn't respond.

Smiling, Bronson reached out and stroked a tendril of her hair that fell over her shoulder. His fingers brushed the flesh of her neck. Lilith shivered in revulsion. Bronson obviously took it for a tremor of desire.

Or perhaps he liked knowing he disturbed her. Whatever the reason, he took a step closer. She could smell him now. Whiskey, soap and clean linen. He smelled better than some gentlemen, but Bronson was no more a gentleman than Lilith was.

"Does *Gabriel* know you keep a loaded pistol in the drawer of your night table?" Bronson inquired silkily, still stroking her hair. "Does he know that you have a delectable habit of sleeping with your legs spread so that a man could mount you before you had time to wake?" He chuckled. "Yes, I suppose he probably does know that."

Shards of ice, followed by a wave of intense heat, rushed from Lilith's head through her body to her hands and feet. The world spun around her, threatening to toss her into complete darkness as she struggled to breathe.

"You've been in my room," she whispered when the buzzing in her head finally stopped. Oh, God, she was going to be ill! The very idea of Bronson watching her while she slept was enough to send her stomach to churning violently. She felt violated and dirty, as though he had somehow marked her.

Smirking, Bronson released her hair. His knuckles touched the swell of her left breast as he dropped his hand. Lilith didn't fool herself for an instant that it had been an accident.

"Yes. It was very easily done as well. You really should lock your windows at night."

Lock them? She *did* lock them. She was going to have bars put on the bloody things first thing in the morning.

Gabriel had told her it was too easy for someone to climb up to her bedroom.

Lilith drew a deep breath through her nostrils. "Spying on me doesn't mean you know me, Bronson. It just means you're a Peeping Tom. Any twelve-year-old boy could know me as well as you do."

Bronson's cheeks darkened in the torchlight. "Would a boy recognize your desire to prove yourself? That your need to show society, your parents, even your precious Gabriel that you don't need any of them is what drives you? You came back to England for revenge, Lilith, and that's something I understand very well indeed."

Shaken by his insight, Lilith couldn't meet his intense gaze. She had started Mallory's to prove to everyone who had turned their backs on her that she wasn't someone to be ignored. She'd wanted to have them all in her power.

Somewhere along the line, her priorities had shifted. She didn't want to have power over people anymore. Her club didn't fill all the empty spaces in her life. She had once believed it could, but now . . .

Now she wanted more than the club could give her.

"You still haven't told me what it is you want," she reminded him, finally gathering the courage to raise her eyes to his.

Bronson smiled. "I want us to stop fighting. I want you to join me."

"Join you!" The very thought was ludicrous.

He ignored her surprise, continuing eagerly. "Help me put a stop to Angelwood and his incessant blathering about outlawing gaming. He won't stand a chance against the two of us. You know his weaknesses and I have no compunction about using them. We could destroy him."

Destroy Gabriel? Whatever gave Bronson the idea that she would wish to destroy Gabriel?

"I know that he set you up," Bronson said. "I know he was trying to pin you with cheating the Foster kid. I can help you make him pay, Lilith. Make all of them pay. I can help you get your revenge."

Lilith's throat went as dry as sand as Bronson's words sank in. At one time, what he offered would have appealed to her, but not now.

"You certainly do seem to know a lot about my life, Mr. Bronson."

He puffed up like a peacock. "You and I are a lot alike, Lilith. People like Angelwood and his friends, they don't understand us. We're both survivors. We get knocked down and we get back up again. We'll fight until the day we die—and we'll win."

I don't want to fight until the day I die. Loving, learning, laughing. These were the things she wanted to spend the rest of her life doing.

"I said you know a lot about my life, Mr. Bronson. Do not confuse that with knowing *me*. You do not know me at all."

Bronson scowled. "I don't understand."

Lilith's lips curved in irony. "Precisely."

His frown deepened. "Are you saying that Angelwood knows you better than I do?"

"Better than you ever could." Only someone who knew her every weakness could hurt her the way Gabriel could. Only someone who knew her every dream could ever make her as happy as when he held her in his arms. She didn't like it, but there was nothing she could do about it. She loved him and that gave him power over her.

"Good night, Mr. Bronson," she said when he didn't respond.

He seized her by the arm as she turned to walk away. Startled, and more than a little fearful, Lilith stared into the paleness of his eyes. Gone was the veneer of civility he'd projected earlier. This was the real Bronson, the man who'd raised the capital to start his club as a prizefighter and a graverobber. There were whispers that many of the corpses he sold for dissection were those of men who had dared to best him in the ring.

He shook her so hard her teeth banged together. "You listen to me, you little—"

"I believe Lady Lilith just asked you to leave, Bronson."

Lilith could have wept in relief. Dear, sweet Latimer had come to her rescue!

Bronson didn't immediately release her. Instead, he gave her servant a challenging glare. "Are you prepared to make me leave?"

Latimer gave a slow nod. "I am."

Glancing between the two men, Lilith realized something she hadn't before. They knew each other. It shouldn't surprise her. Latimer had once made his living as a pugilist as well. Had he and Bronson been rivals even then?

She half expected Bronson to charge, but instead, the club owner laughed. It was a harsh, forced sound. He was afraid. Afraid to fight her quiet, protective man of affairs.

Lilith's respect and regard for Latimer rose.

"You and I will settle our business later, Lilith," Bronson jeered. He pointed a warning finger at Latimer. "And *you*. I'll be seeing you again."

Latimer only nodded.

With a swirl of his coat, Bronson turned on his heel and whipped off into the darkness. Lilith and Latimer waited a few moments before walking back to the club.

"Thank you," Lilith murmured, gripping the big man by the wrist. "I don't know what would have happened if you hadn't come along."

"I do," Latimer replied bluntly, his gaze holding hers. Lilith didn't like the resignation she saw there.

"And don't go thanking me yet, Lady Lilith. Bronson wasn't lying. He'll settle with both of us."

Chapter 13

A s had become his habit over the past week, Gabriel returned home from the Seraph offices tired and sweaty—and very late. It had been months since he'd thrown himself into any physical labor, and he felt acutely the effects of having done so now. As he climbed out of the carriage, every muscle in his body groaned at the effort. His hands were red and raw. The puffy shine of a newly formed blister stood out on his right palm. Still, he felt good. Better than he had in days.

Normally he conducted his business through either his solicitor or the manager of the London office, but lately he'd felt the need to do more than sit around White's twiddling his thumbs.

He needed to take his mind off Lilith. So far it had proved to be a most difficult quest. Most activity succeeded in relieving his torment for mere minutes—sometimes for an hour—but then thoughts of her came rushing back.

He'd challenged her edict that he not come near her only

once. Four days ago, when he had thought for certain that she'd had enough time to calm down, he'd paid a visit to the club, only to be told in no uncertain terms that Lilith didn't want to see him. A red-faced Latimer ascertained that his employer "meant what she said about handing the *ton* his precious secrets."

Secrets. Hmpf. She didn't know all his secrets. She didn't know the most shameful one of all. And Gabriel had no intention of telling her. He was certain he and Blaine had hidden it well enough so no one would ever find out. The doctor who had tended to his father had been paid well enough for his silence. Gabriel would never tell and she would never find out, but not just because he couldn't trust her not to reveal it.

Gabriel had no intention of confiding the whole truth, because he was ashamed of it. And there was always the chance that someone else might find out and then it would spread throughout the *ton*. He couldn't let that happen. Once he'd fooled himself into thinking he kept his silence out of respect for his father, but that wasn't it. It was the scandal. It was loathing for the man who had raised him. He loved his father, but there was very little of him that didn't make his son cringe with embarrassment.

Robinson met Gabriel in the cool marble foyer. "I believe Clifford is preparing your bath at this very moment, my lord."

A bath. Yes, that was what he needed. Good and hot water to soak the aches out of his muscles. Maybe it could take some of the ache out of his heart as well.

"Also, a lady is waiting for you in your study, my lord."

Gabriel's heart lurched to a halt. A lady? Lilith?

The thick-necked butler must have seen the flash of hope in his eyes. With a barely perceivable arch of his brow, he added, "A Mrs. Smith, my lord."

Not Lilith. Despite the disappointment low and heavy in his gut, he should have known she wouldn't come. It would take nothing short of a miracle to get Lilith to relent.

"Have her wait until I've finished my bath."

Robinson cut him off as he tried to leave. Stepping in front of him, the boxy butler cleared his throat. "Begging your pardon, my lord, but she was quite inflexible about seeing you as soon as you returned."

Annoyance furrowed Gabriel's brow. "And I'm quite determined about having my bath. Which one of us pays your salary, Robinson?"

The shorter man didn't even flush. If anything, his expression tightened a bit. Between his butler and Lilith, Gabriel was beginning to feel highly ineffective.

"She said to tell you that she brings news of her employer, my lord. She also said, and I quote, 'Not that your master deserves it.'"

Mary. The woman who worked for Lilith. Hope trembled in Gabriel's stomach.

Hang his dirty clothes and gritty skin. Brushing past Robinson, Gabriel walked briskly in the direction of his study. The walk quickly escalated into a jog.

Mary—Mrs. Smith—sat in one of the high-backed leather chairs in front of his desk. Perched on the edge of the seat in a drab brown gown, with her knees and ankles locked together as tightly as her lips, she looked more like a school matron than a woman who lived in a gaming club.

"Mrs. Smith," he said, closing the door behind him. "How lovely to see you again."

If she thought he was being sarcastic, she didn't show it. Instead, she raised her thin brows and allowed her gaze to drift over him in a lazy and, quite frankly, disrespectful manner.

"Good day, my lord."

Stiffening under her perusal, Gabriel summoned as much arrogance as he could while looking and smelling like a laborer, and met her amused expression with a cool one of his own.

"As you can see, madam, I am in need of a bath. Why don't you tell me what you are doing here before my water cools?"

She blushed a bit but didn't ask forgiveness for her rudeness.

"I have come to discuss Lilith with you, my lord. But perhaps attending to your toilette is more important than the woman whose heart you've broken."

Gabriel regarded Mary coolly. "You have no idea what is important to me, madam. And do not think for a moment that your association with Lilith gives you the right to such speculation. Please state your business or leave."

Suddenly, all the hauteur seemed to drain out of her. Her shoulders sagged and her expression changed from insolence to concern.

"I am worried about Lilith," she said, her voice weak. "I don't know if you even care, but you're the only person I could imagine being able to help her in anyway."

Trying to ignore the frisson of fear that squirmed in his chest, Gabriel nodded. Crossing the thick, dark carpet, he seated himself in the chair next to hers.

"What is it?" He couldn't keep a trace of panic from his voice.

Mary drew a deep breath. "First, I need to know if I'm correct in my assumption of you."

Gabriel couldn't help but snort. "What assumption? That I'm an evil fiend out to destroy your friend?"

The woman's gaze was earnest, almost pitying. He didn't like it.

"That you're the man who loves her enough to put up with her."

Laughter ripped forth from Gabriel's chest. He couldn't control it—didn't want to. A mixture of genuine mirth and bleak despair, it tore at his insides, shook him until tears sprang to his eyes.

"Putting up with" Lilith didn't seem like much of a chore to him and the idea that this might mean he loved her still both saddened and overjoyed him. Saddened him because he might never have her and overjoyed him because he hadn't yet given up all hope.

Surprisingly strong fingers gripped his arm. "Are you all right, Lord Angelwood?"

Gabriel took one look into her concerned face and shook his head. "No, Mrs. Smith, I am not. Please continue."

She withdrew slowly, almost as if she were afraid to make any quick moves. Surely she thought him a little loose in the head.

"Lilith hasn't told me much about what happened between the two of you, but I know that whatever it was hurt her very badly," she revealed, skewering him with her gaze as she spoke.

Gabriel glanced away.

"However, it doesn't take a genius to see that it hurt you as well."

He didn't know how to respond to this, so he didn't. "Go on."

Mary sighed. "I'm concerned about my friend, Lord Angelwood. Since arguing with you, Lilith has lost her appetite, her sparkle and her wit. Before you walked into her life, I worried that she would never be happy. Then you came along and gave us hope, and now . . ."

"Now your hope is lost again?" Gabriel didn't like having people hanging their hopes on him. It made him feel as though he was expected to fix things, and he'd spent most of his life trying to fix things. Hadn't they realized how dismal he was at it?

Shaking her head, Mary reached out and clutched his arm again, as though by touch she could make him understand her.

"We're still hopeful, my lord, because you're the only person I've ever seen move Lilith to any kind of emotion other than anger." She smiled. "Although you do a good job provoking her wrath as well."

Gabriel returned the smile. "You didn't come here just to tell me that you've got high hopes for me, Mrs. Smith."

Again Mary shook her head, the humor fading from her face. The change in her demeanor pinched Gabriel's heart, catching the breath in his throat.

"I'm worried for her safety, Lord Angelwood."

The soft resignation of her tone shivered down Gabriel's spine. "What do you mean?" He kept his voice low and calm.

She removed her hand from his coat and placed it in her lap. "Shortly after Mallory's opened for business, the club drew the attention of a man named Bronson."

Gabriel raised a brow. "The man who owns Hazards?"

Mary nodded.

Gabriel expelled a deep breath, trying to keep a tight rein on the pounding of his heart. Despite Lilith's assurances that Bronson wasn't a threat, Gabriel had begun to suspect otherwise. He'd asked some questions about the club owner and had gleaned information that didn't exactly paint Bronson in a flattering light. Although no one could offer any proof of Bronson's criminal activities, people had warned Gabriel to be careful. Bronson used to be a prizefighter and apparently wasn't above fighting dirty.

"Bronson's club is very popular," he remarked. How casual he sounded! "He must see Mallory's as a threat if he's paying it or Lilith any attention."

Or maybe it's just Mallory's owner he's interested in. Gabriel's jaw clenched.

"He does," Mary replied. "He's been trying to put Lilith out of business ever since."

Gabriel's chin jerked up. "What do you mean?"

Spreading her hands, Mary shrugged. "Oh, my, there's been so many little things . . . He's had countless shipments of club supplies destroyed."

Gabriel thought of the ledgers he'd found in Lilith's office—the items that had been marked "Destroyed" were because of Bronson, not simply an accident.

"There have been illegal entries at the club as well."

Just as he'd feared. He'd discovered for himself how easy it was to sneak in and out of Lilith's club and apartments. Damn it, why hadn't she told him? Surely she knew not to be so foolish as to underestimate such a man?

She hadn't trusted him, just as he hadn't trusted her. The thought jabbed sharply at the back of his brain. Perhaps if he had been more open with her, confided in her about Frederick, she would have told him about Bronson.

And perhaps if she'd told him about Bronson, he would have confided about Frederick.

Christ, what a pair they were.

Mary drew a deep breath. "And recently he's taken to showing up in person."

Gabriel nodded. "He was at the theater when we went."

"Lilith thinks he might be responsible for your carriage accident," Mary explained, and added before he could respond, "And then the night you and Lilith argued, Bronson came to the club."

If it were possible for a person to be both hot and cold, Gabriel was it. Hot rage flooded his veins while icy pinpricks of fear danced along his skin. She'd told him she didn't think Bronson could be responsible. She'd lied. Or perhaps she'd believed it at the time. Perhaps it hadn't become clear until Bronson confronted her.

The realization of just how much danger Lilith could be in curdled like sour milk in his stomach. "Did he touch her?"

Mary blinked at the coldness of his tone. "I . . . I don't know. She wouldn't tell me."

Which meant he probably had, the bastard.

"I'm worried about what he might do next," Mary blurted. "If he would come to the club—"

She didn't need to continue. If Bronson was brazen enough to come to the club, then he certainly wouldn't think twice about allowing himself into Lilith's apartments—if he hadn't already.

Clenching his jaw hard, Gabriel clung to the anger inside him, promising himself that he would make Bronson pay for daring even to look at his woman.

His woman. His Lily.

It was about time Lilith accepted it.

Slowly, his limbs trembling, Gabriel rose out of his chair, his hands balled into fists. Mary followed suit, watching him warily, as one watched a wild animal.

"I must talk to her," he said, thinking out loud. "I have to talk some sense into her before she gets herself hurt. I have to make her trust me. I have to make her understand—" He stopped abruptly, remembering that he wasn't alone.

"Why you did what you did?" Mary queried. "I think she'd like to hear that very much, my lord, regardless of whether or not she seems inclined to listen."

Gabriel met the woman's gaze with a determined one of his own. "I will *make* her listen. I won't leave until she does."

Mary actually smiled at him then. "I think I might have been right about you after all, Lord Angelwood. You are the man for her."

Her words barely registered. "I'll go now," he said, turning toward the door.

"My lord?" Her voice stopped him, made him face her.

"What?" he demanded, his impatience apparent in his voice and in the scowl on his face.

Wrinkling her nose in disgust, Mary waved a hand in front of her face. "Perhaps you should take that bath first."

She was beginning to fear for her sanity.

This is madness. Pacing the length of her bedroom, clad in her nightgown and wrapper, Lilith tried yet again to sort out her feelings where Gabriel was concerned.

If she could just concentrate on the fact that he lied to her, that he'd used her and planned to turn on her, she would be fine. But she kept thinking about how he'd held her, made love to her—and the way he'd trembled in her arms.

Grown men did not tremble, not with women they didn't care about, of that she was certain.

She was also certain that grown men didn't try to blame their mistakes on dead aunts in a cowardly attempt to explain their actions.

The Gabriel she had loved was far too proud to hide behind anyone, let alone a woman. So either he had changed drastically over the past ten years or Lilith was wrong about him.

She *wanted* to be wrong about him. What she didn't want was to be proved wrong about her aunt Imogen.

"You're going to wear a hole in that carpet."

Yelping at the sound of his voice, Lilith whirled around.

She pressed a palm against the pounding of her heart. "Gabe! What are you doing here?"

He hauled himself through the window—the same window he'd climbed through before—to stand before her, tall and gorgeous and looking entirely too sincere for Lilith's liking.

She really was going to have bars installed.

His dark hair was damp and combed back from the broad expanse of his forehead. The black coat he wore over his white shirt and tan breeches was unfastened. He'd forgotten a waistcoat altogether. Obviously Gabriel had dressed himself after his bath. His cravat was tied in a haphazard knot, as though he'd been in too much of a hurry to tie it properly.

"I had to see you," he replied, taking a step closer. "You would not see me, so I decided to let myself in."

Something in his voice started a slow burn low in her abdomen. Despite the warning bells clanging in her head, Lilith stood her ground as he came ever closer. Her breath came faster when she saw the heat in his gaze.

"I stayed away as long as I could, Lil. I tried to do what I thought you wanted, but I can't do it anymore. I had to see you."

He knew just what to say to her. Her throat tightened at his softly spoken words, at the thickness in the deep timbre of his voice.

"Why?" she demanded.

He stopped, leaving only scant inches between them. He didn't touch her, and yet a jolt of arousal, so strong it made her dizzy, struck the very core of her.

"Why what?"

Shaking her head to clear the fog he induced, Lilith gazed at him. "Why did you have to see me?"

He didn't miss a beat. Either he had this rehearsed, or he didn't need to think about it. Raising a hand, he brushed his fingers against her cheek. The warm, rough contact made her jump.

"Because it hurts when I don't see you," he replied.

Blinking back tears, Lilith cursed him for knowing her so well, but she didn't pull away from his touch. "It hurts me when you do see me, Gabe."

He smiled ruefully, his thumb brushing her temple. "I'm sorry."

His thumb brushed her cheek and she felt a slight scratchiness where he touched it.

"Why are your hands so rough?" she demanded, grabbing his fingers and pulling them away from her face.

He didn't reply. He didn't have to. What Lilith saw when she looked at his hand was answer enough.

Impulsively she reached out and grabbed his other hand, holding both palms up for her inspection. He didn't try to stop her. He didn't try to explain.

His hands—his beautiful hands—were pink and callused, torn in some spots. One particularly big blister made her wince.

She wanted to kiss them, to somehow make them better and take the hurt away. They *had* to hurt. And another, awful part of her hoped they did. She hoped he hurt as badly and as deeply as she.

"What have you done?" she whispered hoarsely, raising her gaze to his.

His pale eyes were clear, blindingly honest as they looked at her. "I went to work at the docks—at my company."

"Why?" As if she didn't know the answer. Well, she thought she knew the answer, but she wanted him to tell her.

"Because I needed to do something to get you out of my head."

"Did it help?"

"No. You were still in my heart."

Oh, God. Lilith's ribs seemed to contract, making it difficult for her to breathe, for her heart to beat. She opened her mouth to speak, but he cut her off.

"I want you to tell me about Bronson."

It was like a bucket of ice water in the face. He told her *that* and then he wanted to talk about Bronson?

She dropped his hands, thrusting them away from her as though they burned.

"Why? So I can help you put him out of business before you try to do the same to me?"

"No," he replied softly, his gaze boring into hers. "So I can kill him if he ever comes near you again."

Not fair. Not fair at all.

"I don't need your protection." The protest sounded childish and unconvincing.

He laughed. "My God, Lily, I've never met a woman who needed something from me more than you do."

Flushing hotly, she resisted the urge to stomp on his foot. "And just what do you think I need that you can offer?"

He'd stopped laughing, but he was still smiling. "I think you need me, my wonderful, maddening Lily. You need me. And I need you."

"You mean you need me in your bed," she jeered.

"Yes," he agreed, "But I also need you in my life, Lil."

"Why would I need a man who lies to me and wants to ruin me? At least I know where I stand with Bronson. I can take care of Bronson on my own."

It was the wrong thing to say.

Gabriel's hands whipped out, grabbing her by the shoulders and pulling her toward him so quickly she stumbled into his chest. The impact knocked the air from her lungs but didn't seem to faze him in the least.

"You will *not* go near him alone, do you hear me? You are not to be alone with him."

"All right!" she cried. It was easier than fighting him.

He released her, a slightly dazed expression on his face as he did so. He hadn't meant to lose control, Lilith was certain.

He was worried about her. It was in the tautness of his jaw, the wildness of his eyes, and it warmed her heart and other body parts in a most infuriating manner.

"You can't tell me what to do, Gabe," she murmured. "You haven't the right."

The muscle in his jaw ticked. "I do."

"No, you don't. I can take care of myself."

Folding his arms across his chest, Gabriel dropped his weight to one foot. "Oh, can you? What if you're alone in the carriage next time, Lilith? Or what if Latimer doesn't get there in time? What then?"

These were questions she'd already asked herself—several times, in fact. And now she knew that someone had indeed told Gabriel about Bronson's visit the other night. It was either Latimer or Mary. Lilith would put her money on Mary.

She lifted her chin in defiance. She would not cower from Bronson. "I will not hide behind a man who only wants to use me."

"Use you?"

"Yes, use me!" She jabbed him in the arm. "You were going to set me up as an example in your quest to rid England of the evil gambling, remember?"

"Oh, and I suppose you weren't playing any games with me?"

"Of course I was," she retorted. "I was *honest* about my intentions, remember?"

He stared at her, his jaw ticking, his gaze silver-bright. He looked hurt and angry and confused. Lilith knew the feeling. They both wanted to trust, they both still had feelings for one another and they both knew how unwise it was to give in to either. If only she could trust him; if only he could show that he trusted her.

"You need to go," she announced. "Now."

He stood there for a moment, a stiff figure with a tight mouth and bleak eyes. His head jerked in a brief nod as he dropped his arms to his sides.

"If you wish."

"I do. It wasn't an idle threat I made, to spread your secrets all over town, Gabe. Remember that next time you decide to climb up to my window." Oh, yes, as though she would actually humiliate him in such a way. She couldn't. Not even if he took her club away.

He turned on her, his expression so wild she cringed from it.

"Do you think I care?" he demanded. "Do you honestly believe I would hold my pride, my business, above you again?"

"Again?" Hadn't he said something similar in Vauxhall? He'd put the family fortune above finding her. She didn't blame him then and she still didn't, but she needed to stop him before he tore down all her defenses and broke her heart again.

"It doesn't really matter what I think, does it? What matters is if you really believe I'd do it."

And there it was. A softly spoken truth, cleaving the air between them like a blade.

"I think you should go now," she added when he remained silent.

"How can you do this?" he asked, his voice raw. Lilith didn't even want to guess which emotion made it so. "How can you just turn your back on this . . . this *thing* between us?"

Sighing, Lilith met his gaze with her own weary one. "The only thing between us, Gabe, is us. We're not those children anymore. We're two different people. We have no future. All we have is the past and it's time to let go of that."

It was like slicing herself open, saying those words, but they had to be said. It was the truth. If not for their past, they would have only their rivalry in common, and they certainly wouldn't be drawn to each other as they were now. Lilith wouldn't entertain the idea of giving up her club—everything—for the chance to have the life she should have had.

As Gabriel's wife.

Gabriel shook his head. "No, I won't accept that. You feel it as much as I do, Lilith—I know it."

She dug her nails into her palms to keep from crying. "I don't feel anything."

"That's a lie!"

He grabbed her again, hauling her flush against him. Only this time he didn't stop there. This time he lowered his head to hers and bruised her mouth with his own, moving his lips with a forceful insistence she couldn't have resisted even if she'd wanted to.

Of course she didn't want to. She *never* wanted to resist him. It was her fatal flaw, her weakness where he was concerned. She knew it. She accepted it.

She gave in to it.

Her hands came up to his waist, sliding around the sides of his coat to press against his back. Her breasts flattened against his chest as her mouth opened beneath his, their tongues entwining in a hot, wet, sensual dance.

He kissed her like she mattered to him, like he was a drowning man and she was all he had left to hold on to. And when he held her, everything was right with the world. So why couldn't they just stop playing this game? Why couldn't they find some way to be together?

Because one of them would have to give up something that mattered in order for that to happen, and because neither of them wanted to be the one to do that.

Oh, if she thought there truly was a chance for them to be happy, she would close the club if it meant that much to him, but what about later? Would she resent him for it when all the world looked at her as an example? A victory in Gabe's war against gambling?

A solid push at his shoulders broke the kiss.

"Stop," she commanded when he tried to pull her closer again. "I can't keep doing this. I can't keep distrusting you and wanting you at the same time, Gabe. I just can't."

His mouth opened. She waited for him to talk her into giving in, into doing what they both wanted.

"I didn't come for you because I didn't want you to know about my father," he blurted.

Lilith blinked. Not what she'd expected. "What?"

Releasing her, Gabriel stepped back, as though he needed to distance himself from her in order to speak.

He stared at the carpet. "I was ashamed of how he died. Ashamed that he left my mother and me with nothing and that I had to clean up his mess." He looked up. "That was why your father wouldn't tell me where you were. He said that, even ruined, you were going to marry better than someone with a mountain of debts and blood as tainted with vice as mine."

She could almost hear her father say those exact words, although his voice was little more than a dim memory.

Gabriel continued. "I wanted to make myself worthy of you. It was bad enough that my father . . . died the way he did, but the creditors were at the door before he was in the ground. Blaine and I did what we could to keep the particulars of his death quiet, but it didn't take long for the rumors to start. I was the earl and my father's debts were now mine. So I took a chance on a new shipping company and invested what money I could by selling off some of my father's possessions and a bit of land. I kept the creditors at bay the same way, and eventually it paid off."

Lilith smiled slightly. "So you are a bit of a gambler after all."

It was meant to be a compliment of sorts, a gentle, teasing remark, but Gabriel looked as though she'd slapped him.

"Only because I had to be," he replied hoarsely. "By the time it looked as if the family coffers would recover, you were long gone. I tried to find you. I searched for years, but no one would give me any information. When I never received word from you, I assumed you wanted nothing to do with me."

She still didn't believe that all of her letters could have gone astray, but what else was she to think? He looked so sincere, as though it pained him to admit all of this to her. That in itself meant more to her than she could ever express.

"I'm sorry," he whispered, his eyes hollow. "I'm sorry I didn't come for you right away, but I was young and stupid and everyone was telling me what I should do. All I wanted was to be with you."

Lilith went to him then. It didn't matter whether or not it was the right thing to do; it was what she wanted. He'd offered her more trust than she deserved by admitting his fears and what had happened ten years ago.

"You're with me now," she told him, winding her arms around his neck. Raising up on her toes, she pressed her lips against his, melting against him as he closed his arms around her.

She didn't know what this meant for them, if it would change anything, but at that moment nothing, not even Mallory's, mattered more than Gabe.

He bent down, sweeping her up into his arms without breaking the seal of their kiss. And when he put her down again, it was onto the bed, the soft mattress yielding under their combined weight.

Bracing himself above her on one arm, he slid his other hand down the curve of her breast. Anticipation unfurled in Lilith's belly as the warm roughness of his thumb inched ever so slowly toward the thrust of her nipple. When finally he did touch her there, even through the linen of her wrapper and night rail, it sent a shock of desire straight between her legs.

She slid her legs against his, the hem of her gown riding up as she did so. The fabric of his breeches was soft against the inner flesh of her thighs and tickled the indent of her knees. Her fingers fumbled with the buttons on his coat, pushing the fabric aside so they could do the same to his waistcoat as well.

He struggled out of the clothing without breaking the kiss, as though he thought she might actually tell him to stop if he released her mouth from his. She had no intention of doing anything so silly.

The fingers that had teased her breast were now creeping beneath the bunched cloth of her nightgown, sliding along her upper thigh with a gentleness that made Lilith writhe with impatience. She didn't want gentle. Didn't want slow. She wanted his hands on her, inside her. *Now.*

She got her wish. He moved his lower body to the side, so that the heaviness of his erection dug into her hip and his fingers could move into the greedy dampness between her thighs.

Sighing into his mouth, Lilith slid her palms up his chest to clutch at the billowy softness of his shirt as he slid the callused tip of one finger along the swollen furrow of her sex. She arched her hips, spreading her legs beneath his hand, her body begging for more intimate contact.

She loved how he touched her, how he made her feel. Nothing else mattered, not their differences, not Bronson, not even the future. None of it meant anything when Gabriel made love to her.

His finger slid between the slick folds of her flesh, searching for and ultimately finding the tightened, hooded spot that ached for release. The roughness of his skin was deliciously arousing, making the muscles in her legs jump as he rubbed her into a squirming mass of damp heat.

Lilith's hips undulated with every stroke, bringing herself closer and closer to that precipice of pleasure that lurked just in the distance. She needed this, needed him to give her the one thing he was able to give, the one thing she could demand without either of them having to compromise for it.

His mouth tore free of hers, sliding down her jaw and throat, leaving a warm, moist trail on her flushed skin. Fastening his lips around one nipple, he sucked the hardened peak through the thin layers of linen with an intensity that made her cry out in pain and pleasure.

And then there was only coolness where the heated assault of his mouth had been and he was sliding lower, his fingers working her into a state of mindless arousal as his lips brushed the curve of her stomach.

He went lower still, his shoulders spreading her legs wide as he nestled between them. His fingers left the aching hardness within her to slide downward, filling her, stretching her with slow, languid thrusts.

Arching her back, Lilith moaned, panted, begged for the rapture he promised. And when his mouth replaced his fingers, she cried out in delight.

Firm and wet, his tongue stroked her, plunging into her, licking upward until it brushed that most sensitive spot.

"Oh!" she cried, lifting her hips as he used his fingers to spread her even wider, lapping her essence with his tongue, teasing her hardness until the room spun around her and lights danced behind her tightly clenched eyelids. The stubble of his beard rubbed against her, scratching but not hurting.

Rapidly, the pleasure grew, swirling into a dizzying tempest that threatened to toss her into an abyss of darkness. Tangling her fingers in the soft thickness of Gabriel's hair, Lilith thrust against his mouth, throwing herself over the edge . . .

She screamed wordlessly all the way down. Wave after wave of incredible pleasure rippled through her, tightening her muscles, awakening her nerves.

Gasping for breath, she opened her eyes as she felt him lift his head. She watched as he rose above her, his mouth and chin shiny with her juices, his eyes bright with unspent desire.

One hand lifted her right leg, draping it over his arm as the other tore at the opening of his trousers. The hard length of him sprang free, the blunt head glistening in the lamplight.

Lilith cried out as he plunged into her. Flesh that was still sensitive parted at his intrusion, wrapping around him, drawing him deeper and deeper until his hips pressed hard against the apex of her thighs.

She had a cramp in her thigh and her gown had bunched into a hard ball at the base of her spine, but Lilith didn't care. Keeping her eyes fastened on Gabriel's face, she watched the ecstasy play across his features as he thrust deep within her. Knowing—*seeing*—the effect she had on him was terribly arousing and as her strength returned, she lifted her hips to meet his thrusts, lifting her other leg high in the air to deepen his penetration.

He made her climax a second time. The spasms hit just as he shuddered and cried out above her. Releasing her leg, he fell upon her, replacing the pain in her hip with the sweaty, heaviness of his body.

They stayed that way for the longest time, with him still inside her and his face buried in the curve of her neck and shoulder. When he finally did lift his head, the expression on his face was one of tenderness—and disbelief.

Lilith didn't want his tenderness. It would make her cry.

"I never meant to lose you," he whispered. "I would have given anything to find you. If I'd known you were in Venice I would have come for you. I would have brought you home."

"I know," she replied. And she did.

He rolled off her, onto his side, where he propped his head in his hand and regarded her with a possessive yet loving expression.

"I want you to close the club."

The words sliced through her like shards of ice. So much for the aftermath. *"What?"*

"Just for a few days, until I can get some evidence against Bronson."

Lilith struggled into a sitting position. Gabriel stayed where he was. "I am not closing my club."

Now he pushed himself up. "Lilith, Bronson is dangerous."

"Which is precisely why I'm not going to give him the satisfaction of putting me out of business, even for a few days." She pulled her nightgown down over her knees.

His expression was pleading. "Lilith, you have to trust me on this."

"Trust you?" Something clicked inside Lilith's head, sending a sickening jolt right down to her stomach. "Is that what this was all about? You came here hoping to soften me up with some well-timed soul-baring and a little seduction, hoping I'd just cave in and agree to close my club because you've asked me to?"

Gabriel's jaw tightened as he shook his head. "That wasn't it!"

But Lilith could see the lie in his eyes. Maybe he hadn't planned it this way, but yes, he was hoping that his opening up to her and the passion they'd just shared would convince her to go along with his plan. Why? Was he really worried about Bronson? Did he simply want her to close the club with the hope of making it impossible to reopen it, or was he afraid for her and harboring some secret hope that love would conquer all and she would become the kind of proper, non-club-owning woman he wanted her to be?

"And what are you going to do for me?" she asked in a mockingly sweet tone. "If I agree to close Mallory's for a few days, will you agree to change your views on gambling? Open your mind to a better solution than outright abolition?"

The expression on his face was all the answer she needed. Still, he insisted on speaking. "It's not that easy. I can't just do that."

So he wanted her to compromise, but he was not willing to do the same for her. That hurt. It hurt a lot.

"Then I'm afraid I can't oblige you by closing the club." She slipped off the bed. The evidence of their lovemaking was slick against her thighs and again that awful feeling of dread washed over her. He hadn't used protection. And neither had she. She hadn't taken any efforts to protect herself from him at all. When would she learn?

Gabriel also rose. There was only the bed between them, but the distance felt infinitely larger. "Lilith, don't be foolish!"

"I already was," she replied, cursing herself as she choked on a sob. "And I'm getting increasingly tired of it. It seems you want me to be the one to do all the bending, Gabe, but you have no intention of doing the same. Trusting me with your secrets is only part of it. If you want to be with me, there has to be compromise."

A sneer curved his lips. "You want me to become a laughingstock and publicly change my mind about gaming, do you? It would be a lie, Lilith. I still despise it and I would despise myself for it. Gambling would win."

Sadness came with an overwhelming clarity. "Yet you think nothing of asking me to give up everything I've worked for to suit you. This isn't about winning or losing, Gabriel."

"Isn't it?" he challenged. "Weren't you the one who suggested we play this like a game?"

Lilith held his gaze. "Yes. But I was wrong. The way we're going, we're both going to lose."

"Well, it won't be me." Righting his clothes, Gabriel glared at her with a suppressed rage that seemed directed more at himself than at her. "Ten years ago, I held my father's dead body and I made a promise that I would do everything I could to make certain that never happened to anyone else. If you think I'm going to go back on that promise just because I'm obsessed with you, you're wrong."

Lilith stared at him, a hot, hollow feeling in her chest. He'd been there for his father's death? And was that what he called his feelings for her—obsession? Unhealthy, uncontrollable. Bad. That didn't sound much like love. It didn't sound like much at all.

"Then you'd better leave," she whispered, clenching her jaw to keep her chin from trembling.

His only reply was a stiff nod as he stomped toward the window.

One of these days the fool was going to slip and break his neck. And as much as she tried to tell herself she didn't care, she did. What would she do then? In some twisted sense, she'd rather have him alive and despising her than lose him forever. The tree was old, the bark slippery . . .

"I want you to leave by the front door."

He halted just as he was about to shove his leg out the window. "Excuse me?"

"I want you to leave by the door," she repeated, crossing the carpet and closing the window.

The club was not yet closed for the evening. There was no

telling how many people might see him leave. It would be embarrassing and give the gossips something to titter over, but at least she wouldn't have to worry about him getting hurt. And at least then she wouldn't feel like just one more thing he was ashamed of.

"I'm not leaving through the front door."

Lilith's chin jutted defiantly. "Afraid your reputation might get sullied?"

"No," he replied softly.

He didn't have to continue. She knew without a doubt that it wasn't his own reputation he was concerned about. Damn him. Tears burned the backs of her eyes and blurred her vision.

Oh, God, please don't let him see.

"Lilith—"

"Dammit, how many times do I have to tell you to go?" she cried, anger keeping the tears at bay. "How many times before you get it through your thick skull that I don't want to hear anymore? I just want you to leave!"

He stared at her, obviously stunned by her outburst. Gabriel didn't speak. He simply nodded, and then, just to make Lilith feel even worse, he stomped across the room and left.

The door hung open behind him.

Chapter 14

What the hell had he been thinking?

Better yet, what the hell had he been thinking *with*?

Sitting astride a black gelding named Clive, Gabriel watched but didn't really see the goings-on around him. Hyde Park was crowded at this time of day as the haut monde put itself on display to be adequately oohed and aahed over.

A gentleman tipped his hat to him. Gabriel tipped back. He had no idea who the man was, however. He hadn't been paying that much attention.

Making love to Lilith without a sheath when she could so easily get pregnant—it was a mistake he'd never made before, but making mistakes with Lilith was becoming a habit with him.

He'd been so eager to be inside her, to be part of her, that all common sense had disappeared. And now he might very well have got her with child. He who was always so careful never to let such a thing happen.

Christ, what a mess he'd made! He'd gone to her club last

night to talk to her, to make her trust him, and then he'd done the one thing guaranteed to lose her trust. He'd asked her to close down her club.

She was such a stubborn, bullheaded woman. Couldn't she see that what he asked was for her own good? Better to close down for a few days and let Bronson think he'd won than to remain a target. But Lilith didn't see it that way. She saw it as Gabriel trying to tell her what to do, and his refusal to do what she wanted in return—as if her request had been reasonable!—was all she needed to conclude that he couldn't actually be trusted.

Oh, she'd postured and threatened and tried to make herself sound so cold and removed, but Gabriel knew better. Lilith had always hidden her vulnerability behind a mask of defiance.

He'd even told her the truth about his father—well, enough of it that mattered. And still she accused him of being unbending. Perhaps he was, but she wasn't being exactly flexible herself. How could she expect him to just change his principles, his beliefs, for her?

How can you not?

The voice came from deep within him, startling him and causing Clive to shift uneasily beneath him. What was he thinking? He'd look absolutely ridiculous in the eyes of the *ton* if he suddenly changed his views on gambling. Besides, it would be a lie. He still believed something had to be done. And as much as he wanted Lilith, he couldn't lie. Not even for her.

"Angelwood!"

His attention snagged, Gabriel looked up to see who had called his name. Two men on horseback came toward him. One of them was Brave. The other was . . .

"Julian!" A wide grin spread across Gabriel's face as he urged his horse forward.

His two friends returned his smile as he approached them. Julian Rexley, Earl of Wolfram, looked much the same as he had before Gabriel left for Nova Scotia. He was perhaps a little more tanned, his reddish-brown hair a little longer, but other than that he was exactly the same Julian and the sight of him warmed Gabriel's heart.

They clasped hands in greeting.

"Damn my eyes, it's good to see you!" Gabriel laughed as he shook his friend's hand. "When did you arrive?"

"Only just this morning," Julian replied, his light brown eyes twinkling. "I went to the bookstore to see how the latest volume is selling and met up with Brave and his lovely wife on my way out."

"And how is your latest offering doing? Flying off the shelves, I'll wager. Did any ladies swoon when you walked past?"

Julian was a poet whose popularity had grown in leaps and bounds since Byron left England. Gabriel never missed an opportunity to tease his friend about the way women flocked around him since he'd first been published.

"Only two," Julian replied with equal humor. "I managed to catch both of them before they hit the ground."

"How fortunate that we happened upon you," Brave remarked, laying a calming hand on the head of his restless mount. "We were going to descend upon you before dinner."

Still grinning, Gabriel waved a hand. "Well, now you can join me instead. All of you. Letitia, too, if she wants."

Julian shook his head. "My baby sister is still in Paris, but I will gladly accept."

"Paris!" Gabriel shared knowing glances with Brave before turning his attention back to Julian. "How did she ever convince you to come home without her?"

Rolling his eyes, Julian replied, "She asked if she could stay on with some friends and I said she could. She is a grown woman, you know."

Letitia Rexley was the only family Julian had left. Their parents had been killed in a carriage accident when Julian was but eighteen, leaving him not only an earl, but the sole guardian of two young girls. His sister Miranda had died tragically a few years earlier, leaving only Letitia. Julian was extremely protective of his sister.

"How hard was it for you to leave her behind?" Gabriel asked with a smile.

His expression one of self-mockery, Julian winced. "Harder than I'll ever admit. But enough about me. Tell me about this dinner. Will Lady Lilith be joining us?"

Gabriel's betrayed gaze shot to Brave. "You told him?"

His friend nodded. "It was the first thing out of my mouth."

"No," Gabriel told them, "Lilith will not be joining us. Not unless there's the chance she might get to watch me choke to death on a chicken bone."

Julian chuckled. Brave grimaced. "Your attempt to talk to her did not go well?"

"Like a lead ball," Gabriel replied. "I don't know what to do."

Julian, unused to hearing such words from his friend, frowned. "Is there anything we can do to help?"

Looking at both of them, Gabriel saw the friendship and concern on their faces. They'd been through a lot, the three of them: Julian's tragedies, Brave's brief descent into melancholia and despair. They'd shared it all—except for the death of Gabriel's own father. Oh, his friends had been there to help him through the grief, but they never knew the whole story. It was about time they did.

"Ride with me," he said gruffly, urging the gelding forward. "There is something I need to tell the two of you."

"About what?" Julian asked as they followed.

"About my father."

It would have been comical were it not for the fact that he was desperate.

Dinner had long since ended and the four of them— Gabriel, Brave, Rachel and Julian—were seated in Gabriel's study, having a glass of port and discussing just how Gabriel ought to go about wooing Lilith. It was humiliating, having his love life tossed about by his friends—not that they hadn't been doing exactly that behind his back—but if it got him Lilith, Gabriel would stand on his head in the middle of St. James's Street and sing "The Navy Captain's Daughter" at the top of his lungs.

After he'd told his friends the truth about his father's death, both Brave and Julian had been shocked—but only because he'd kept such a thing from them, and not that it had actually happened. Their lack of censure warmed Gabriel's heart. He should have told them sooner, but he'd been too proud, and too ashamed to share his secret with anyone, even his closest friends.

"I think you should simply talk to her," Brave remarked. His gaze said just what Gabriel had to say as well—the truth.

Rachel smiled innocently at her husband. At Gabriel's request, he'd promised not to tell Rachel the truth immediately, but he'd been adamant about not lying to his wife if she happened to figure it out on her own. She was apparently very good at that sort of thing.

"You mean the way you always talk to me whenever something is bothering you?"

Brave grinned at her teasing. "Yes, only better."

Gabriel listened to their banter and watched their eyes say more, much more, than their words. How he envied them! Their marriage might have gotten off to a shaky start, but Brave and Rachel were the happiest couple he knew. He wanted that for himself. He wanted to have it with Lilith.

"I've tried talking," he informed them. "It doesn't work." Not when Lilith took everything he said and twisted it around until it didn't even resemble what he'd been trying to say.

"What about a letter?" Julian suggested. "That way you can tell her everything you want without being interrupted."

Gabriel shook his head. "Even if I had your talent for words, I doubt Lilith would even read it. She'd probably burn it."

"Well, how are you going to tell her anything if she doesn't want to hear it?" Julian demanded. "It seems to me she's got her mind made up, and what you have to do is change it somehow."

Brave gave his head a rueful shake. "Changing a woman's mind. There's a Herculean task."

His wife shot him a decidedly unamused glance before turning her attention back to Gabriel.

"You can say or write whatever you want," she said. "It won't do you any good unless Lilith believes you mean it. A woman wants action from a man, not words."

Now, this was interesting. This sounded as though it might have potential.

Gabriel stroked his jaw. "What would you suggest?"

Rachel thought for a moment. "Well, it seems that the root of your problem is your petition to abolish gaming. Lilith believes you've tried to use her for your own means and she continues to believe this despite your efforts to tell her otherwise, because she's basically lost what little trust she had for you."

Wincing at her matter-of-fact tone, Gabriel nodded.

"And," Rachel continued, "because she believes you're still keeping secrets from her—which you are." She gazed at their startled faces. "What? The three of you didn't honestly think I would notice how strange you've been acting? Lilith's not going to trust you until you can prove to her that she means more to you than anything else."

"What would you suggest?"

"It's quite simple, really," she informed him with a gentle smile. "You have to change your stance on gambling."

Gabriel almost laughed. Did women have no concept of male honor? Of dignity, or of the importance of keeping a promise?

As though she sensed his hesitation, Rachel turned sympathetic. "Gabriel, you don't really believe you can succeed in ridding the country of gambling, do you?"

His first impulse was to insist that yes, he could, but he stifled the thought. He had to be honest with himself. If he weren't, how could he ever be honest with Lilith?

Lowering his gaze, Gabriel looked away. For so long, his quest to outlaw gaming had seemed like the right thing to do—the only thing that could atone for his father's death and somehow make it seem as though the old man hadn't died in vain. But now . . . now it seemed pointless, ridiculous and downright meaningless when all it did was stand between him and the woman he loved.

"No," he replied finally. "I don't think I can rid the country of it."

A giant weight seemed to lift off his shoulders. The admission was hard for him to make, but already his mind was spinning with new ideas. Perhaps there was some way for him to keep his promise and honor his father and still have Lilith.

After all, not every club owner was like Bronson. Lilith was proof of that. And not every gambler ended up like his father. He knew plenty of people who gambled responsibly. Perhaps he could try to make better laws and protect those people like his father who didn't seem to know when to get up from the card table and walk away. And he could make it harder for people like Bronson to stay in business.

He had some business of his own to take care of where Mr. Bronson was concerned.

"Brave, Julian," he said, looking at each of his friends. "Would the two of you do me a favor?"

"Certainly." There was no hesitation in Julian's voice. "What is it?"

"I wonder if you might investigate a club for me called Hazards. I've been trying to learn all I can about it and its owner, a man named Bronson. Since my appearance there would arouse suspicion, I'd appreciate it if the two of you would do some snooping for me."

With a decisive nod, Brave replied, "Anything in particular that you would like to know?"

Gabriel sipped his port. "Anything that might put him out of business."

Frowning, Rachel leaned forward on the sofa. "What are you up to, Gabriel?"

Gabriel flashed her a charming smile. "Why, I'm taking your advice, Rachel. I'm going to show Lilith how much she means to me."

Lilith despised herself for what she was about to do.

Standing at the foot of the attic stairs, she stared into the musty dimness above her. She had to go up. Aunt Imogen's trunks were there.

Surely if Gabriel was telling the truth, the answer would be there, too.

The past few days had been maddening. She wanted to believe him. She didn't want to believe him. She didn't want to believe her aunt could have deceived her in such a way, and yet that was preferable to believing that Gabriel had been using her.

"Do you mind if I ask just what you hope to find up there?"

Glancing over her shoulder, Lilith saw Mary strolling down the corridor toward her.

"The truth," she replied, turning her attention back to the stairs. At least that was what she hoped to find. What if she found nothing? Whom was she to believe then?

It was a choice she didn't want to make on her own. Either way, she couldn't win.

Mary came up on her left. Out of the corner of her eye Lilith saw that her friend wore a serviceable old gown very much like her own.

"I thought perhaps you might like some help," Mary informed her with a brief glance.

By "help" she no doubt meant "support."

Lilith smiled. "I would, yes."

It was as though she was marching to her execution—only

more melodramatic. Mentally shaking her head at herself, Lilith forced one foot in front of the other, slowly climbing the stairs until she reached the stuffy, dusty confines of the attic.

"Good Lord!" Mary exclaimed from behind her. "Where do we start?"

The attic was crammed full of things Lilith couldn't bear to look at or part with. Trunks of old clothes, paintings, furniture, all piled upon one another or propped up against other dusty pieces draped in Holland covers.

"I like to keep things," she explained.

Mary nodded. "So you will never forget."

She had never thought of it that way before. "I suppose so."

Her gaze still drifting over the endless clutter, Mary responded softly, "There are things I would dearly love to forget."

Lilith shot a concerned glance at her friend. "You told Mr. Sweet about your marriage, didn't you?"

"I did." Eyes downcast, Mary moved toward the center of the attic. "He . . . he did not take it very well."

No, Lilith thought. A pious man wouldn't.

"When did you tell him?" she asked. It must have been recently, as this was the first Lilith had heard of it.

"Last week," came the low reply.

Last week! How much time had they spent together in the past few days? They'd seen each other every day for at least the past seven. And Mary had uttered not a word of her estrangement from her reverend, while Lilith had whined over Gabriel every time Mary asked.

What a selfish dolt she was.

Walking up behind her friend, she placed her hand on the woman's shoulder and squeezed. "I'm sorry."

Mary shrugged off her hand as she turned, but Lilith didn't take offense. There were times when a woman didn't want anyone to see her cry, not even her closest companion.

Mary dabbed the back of one hand to her eyes before

squaring her shoulders with a determined sniff. "Where do we start looking?"

"Over there," Lilith replied, pointing to the right side of the attic. "My aunt's trunks are against the wall."

Single file they maneuvered through the narrow path to where Imogen's belongings were stored. Every so many steps, Lilith stopped to look at a particular piece—a wardrobe that belonged to her grandmother, a marble bust of her great-great-grandfather.

Another item caught her eye. It was the family portrait painted when she was still a child and not yet a huge disappointment to her parents. Idly, she stroked the gentle apples of her brother's cheeks. How she'd adored him back then! Had he ever forgiven her for disgracing him and the rest of the family by allowing Gabe to seduce her? Had he thought of her at all before he died?

"Is that your family?" Mary asked, more certain than curious.

Lilith nodded. "This is the only portrait I have of all of us together." It was for the best, perhaps. Her mother looked happy on this canvas. She'd lost that happiness in later years.

"You look like your mother."

Staring at the face in the portrait, Lilith let her smile slip a bit. "The resemblance ends there, I'm happy to say." *She* would never turn her back on her own child for the sake of what people might say. *She* would be a better mother.

"What are you thinking about?" Mary asked, her wise gaze seeing more than Lilith wanted her to.

"Things it does me no good to contemplate," she replied. "Now, shall we find those trunks? At this rate we'll be up here for a week."

They wove their way through the rest of the clutter to the far wall, where Imogen's belongings sat. There were several trunks containing personal items, but only one with personal correspondence and journals. That was where Lilith hoped she'd find the answers to her questions—if there were any answers to be found.

Several attempts were made to locate the correct trunk, which, of course, was underneath the rest of them. It took all of Lilith's and Mary's combined strength to unearth it and drag it out into a small clearing where they would have enough room to rummage through it.

The hinges groaned as Lilith opened the battered and dusty lid. Choking on a cloud of dust, she coughed as her dismayed gaze fell upon the piles of paper and journals packed within the trunk's blue satin lining.

"Your aunt didn't like to throw anything away, did she?" Mary remarked wryly.

Chuckling, Lilith shook her head. "Aunt Imogen liked to keep all the letters she received. She used to say they often proved useful whenever she had to ask for a favor."

Mary smiled. "So that's where you got it."

Lilith's expression saddened. "I suppose so. Although I don't record all my private thoughts in a journal for someone to read long after I'm gone."

Mary was watching her carefully. "Those private thoughts can't hurt her now."

"No," Lilith replied, her gaze fastened on the mess before her. There were things she didn't want to know in here. Of that she was certain. "But they can hurt other people."

She didn't have to tell Mary who those "other people" were.

"I'll take the letters," Mary announced, plunking herself down on the lid of another trunk. "I'll leave her personal thoughts to you."

Perching herself on a small but sturdy table of Elizabethan design, Lilith dug out the top journal. It was small, bound in black leather, its pages swollen from ink and humidity.

The date on the first yellowed page was July 8, 1802. Years before Lilith went to live with her. It was also the day Lilith's uncle Bertram died.

The entry had nothing to do with her, was none of her business, but Lilith couldn't help but read what her grieving aunt had written on the day her husband died.

*My dearest Bertram is dead, and though I know him to fi-
nally be at peace in Heaven with the other angels, I find it
small consolation when I must pass the rest of my days
without his sweet countenance to gaze upon. I pray for
the day when we will be together again. It cannot come
quickly enough.*

Her throat tight, Lilith closed the journal. Her aunt had
waited almost fourteen years to be reunited with the man she
loved.

"He's in my heart," she'd say every time Lilith's uncle came
up in conversation. "With every beat I am as sure of him as I
was the day we wed."

Casting a glance in Mary's direction, and certain that her
friend wasn't watching, Lilith pressed a hand to her own
heart and felt the steady rhythm there. Were she but able to
put as much faith in her own heart. In her own feelings. In
Gabriel.

With a stifled sigh, she set the journal aside and reached
for another. This one ran from 1803 to 1805. The next, from
1806 to 1807. She was getting close. The one after that should
include 1808, the year Lilith went to live in Italy.

"I have something I think you should hear," Mary said softly,
lifting her head from the creased and faded letter in her lap.

Holding the blue journal to her breast, Lilith tried to quiet
the pounding of her heart. "What is it?"

"It's a letter from your mother. It's dated April 1808."

The month they sent her away.

"Read it." God, did she really want to waste time on this?
She already knew what her mother thought of her. What kind
of self-punishment was it to hear it read out loud?

Lifting the page, Mary began to read. " 'I'm sending Lilith
to you, dear sister. She's a good girl but far, far too wild for her
father and me to handle. What she needs is your patience and
gentle guidance, and to be as far away as possible from that
boy who persuades her to toss propriety to the wind with astounding ease.' "

Lilith's jaw dropped. A good girl? A *good girl*? But too wild for her mother and father to handle.

. . . as far away as possible from that boy who persuades her to toss propriety to the wind . . .

Had Aunt Imogen taken her mother's words to heart?

"I never knew she thought there was any goodness in me," she drawled, her tone one of false indifference, but inside she was a stunned and stammering mess. Her mother had called her many things after finding her with Gabriel. *Good* hadn't been one of them.

"Do you want me to set it aside for you?" Mary asked, her brown eyes dark with concern.

Lilith shook her head. "I'll go through them myself some other time." Whenever she could summon the courage.

Turning her attention back to the journal in her hands, Lilith opened the cover with trembling fingers. Seven-and-twenty years of age, and her mother still had the power to make her feel like a little girl. Damn it.

In April, her aunt mentioned the letter from Lilith's mother. In early May, she announced Lilith's arrival. There were many references to the "poor dear" and the "scoundrel" who'd so callously taken advantage of her innocence. Imogen prayed her niece would recover quickly from her broken heart. Lilith skimmed over these, her love for her aunt growing more and more with every entry, just as Imogen had written of her own love for Lilith growing on each page as well. Her aunt had been so good. So understanding.

An entry dated June 20 slammed Lilith's heart to a stop.

"Lilith," Mary said, her tone ominous.

Lilith held up her hand. "One moment, Mary. I think I found something."

"So do I," came the disbelieving reply, but Lilith ignored her. She was too busy dragging her gaze down the tiny black lines of writing in front of her. Her heart climbed up into her throat as she read; a strange roaring echoed in her ears.

*. . . a letter today from that . . . that man who so used my
dear niece. He says he's trying to find her and did I know
where he might look. I should have told him to go straight
to Hell, but I'm too much of a lady. I don't know what
kind of game he's trying to play to let things go on this
long before looking for Lilith, but I'll not allow him to
hurt her again, not when he's already hurt her so
much . . .*

Squeezing her eyes shut against the stabbing pain in her
chest, Lilith held on to the journal tightly. Waves of hot and
cold lapped at her hands and feet while her head swam with
nauseating shock.

As much as she'd wanted to believe Gabriel, she'd never expected to discover that he had indeed been telling the truth.

"Lilith!" Mary's worried voice cut through the fog in her
brain. Strong fingers clutched her arm. She opened her eyes.

"He was telling the truth," she whispered when her
friend's frowning face swam into focus.

"I know." Mary held up several sheets of aged paper. "I
found his letter."

Dumbly, Lilith stared at it, recognizing the handwriting if
not the words it formed. He had looked for her. He actually
had. He'd wanted her back. Her prayers had been answered,
and her aunt—her loving but so very wrong and misguided
aunt—had sent him away.

Oh, it would be so easy to blame a dead woman for all of
her misfortune, for all of her regrets and stupidity, but Imogen could be held only so accountable before Lilith had to accept some responsibility.

"I have to go to him," she muttered. "I have to . . ." Well,
she didn't know what she had to do. It didn't change things
between them, not really. But at least she could apologize for
not believing him. She owed him that.

Leaving Mary to clean up after them, Lilith rose to her
feet, both the journal and Gabriel's letter in her hands. What

would she say? What would he say? She wasn't naive enough to think he'd change his mind just because she admitted to misjudging him. And this certainly didn't absolve him of wanting to see her out of business, but it changed things. It changed things for her.

Awkwardly, as though her mind and her feet were going in different directions, Lilith shuffled toward the attic door. She was almost to it when the pounding of boots sounded on the stairs below.

"Lady Lilith!" a man's voice cried in panic. "Lady Lilith!"

A curtain lifted in Lilith's mind, tossing everything, even thoughts of Gabriel, aside. Trading worried glances with Mary, she went to the top of the stairs. "What is it?"

Mary hurried up beside her as Harold, one of the footmen, huffed and puffed into sight. The young man's eyes were wide and black with shock, his face white and shiny with sweat.

"Oh, Lady Lilith!" he cried. "You must come quickly. It's Mr. Latimer. He's hurt very badly!"

"Latimer!" Lilith repeated. What could possibly hurt Latimer? He'd always seemed so strong, so indestructible. Why, she'd never known him even to suffer from the sniffles.

"We took him to one of your guest rooms," Harold explained, already halfway back down the flight of stairs. "Malcolm went to fetch a doctor. Please, come quickly!"

He didn't have to ask twice. Hand in hand for strength, Lilith and Mary hiked the front of their skirts high and raced down the stairs behind the leggy young footman. He reached the room where Latimer had been taken long before they did.

A group of servants waited in the corridor outside the bedroom. They comforted each other, wrung their hands and wiped their eyes. And they all looked at her as though they expected her to make it better somehow. As though she would fix everything.

That responsibility weighed heavily on Lilith's chest, as heavy as the fear that she was to blame for whatever had happened to her bodyguard—her friend.

Timidly, she entered the room, Mary right behind her. Two footmen stood at the foot of the bed where Latimer's large form lay. One of the maids fussed with his pillows. Lilith could hear the girl weeping.

"What happened?" she asked when she found her voice. The maid jumped.

" 'Twere Bronson's men," Latimer answered weakly.

Lilith looked at the man on the bed and instantly regretted it. Latimer's clothes were stained with blood, his face swollen and cut. His hair was matted with stuff Lilith didn't even try to identify, and his knuckles were battered and torn to the bone.

He'd fought back. They might not have hurt him so badly if he hadn't fought back.

"Are you in a lot of pain?" she asked.

"Nothing I haven't felt before," he replied with startling humor.

Bronson. He was behind this. This was Latimer's punishment for trying to protect her. He'd warned her that Bronson would come back for them, but the stinking coward had gone through Latimer rather than coming straight for her. And Latimer had taken the men's violence because he knew she couldn't fight Bronson on her own. He'd realized what would happen when he stood up to Bronson, yet he'd still put himself in danger.

What the hell had she ever done to deserve such loyalty?

Whatever it was, she would not allow Latimer's suffering to be in vain. The doctor would be here soon. She would make certain Latimer had the best care possible. There would be someone with him night and day until he recovered.

And he *would* recover. He had to. Lilith wanted him to be there when she finally made Bronson pay for all the trouble he'd caused.

She couldn't do it on her own. She knew that. There were places she couldn't go as a woman, things she couldn't do without attracting far too much attention. But even if it cost her pride, her club, her hopes for the future, she was going to seek retribution.

Holding the journal and the letter in one hand, she wrapped her free arm around Alice's shaking shoulders and glanced back at the footmen standing silent and angry at their friend's bedside.

"I want one of you to go to Mayfair," she instructed, her voice flat and emotionless. "Tell Lord Angelwood that we—that *I* need him."

Chapter 15

O nce the message to Gabriel had been sent, Lilith returned to Latimer's bedside. He was conscious and in surprisingly good humor, given the amount of pain he must be in. Lilith asked the others to leave them for a few minutes.

From her seat on the side of the bed, Lilith gazed at her friend and faithful employee. His eyes were blackened and swollen, his face discolored with bruises that promised to get even uglier. He smiled at her, and despite the mess he was in, it was a beautiful sight.

"Are you certain it was Bronson's men?" she asked after a lengthy silence.

Latimer's smile faded. "He had men with him to hold me, but Bronson did most of this himself."

Lilith fought to keep her horror from showing. How could one man inflict so much damage upon another? It didn't seem possible.

She took Latimer's bandaged hand in her own. Anger and

indignation stirred her blood. "I will make him pay for this, Latimer, I promise you."

The big man shook his head and winced. "No, my lady, you can't do that. You're no match for him alone. I mean you no disrespect, but Bronson hasn't a shred of honor in him. I hate to think what he might do."

Lilith shushed him gently. "I have no intention of fighting him on my own. I've sent for Lord Angelwood." She didn't add that she had no idea if Gabriel would even come, after her behavior the other night.

Latimer seemed pleased by this announcement. "He's a good man. You can depend on him, I think. I knew he was the man for you after I saw how much it meant to him to clear you of that cheating charge."

Frowning, Lilith stared at her employee. What did he mean, he saw how much it meant to Gabriel to clear her name? "What did you see, Latimer?"

His lips curving as much the cuts on them would allow, Latimer looked decidedly rueful. "I promised not to tell, so you have to give me your word that you won't let on I broke mine."

"Of course," Lilith replied impatiently. "Now tell me what you know."

"I put it together afterward, when you told me he thought someone in the club had cheated a customer. Lord Angelwood came to the club one night. I thought he was there to see you, but he wasn't, and he told me he didn't want you knowing about his visit."

At one time, the fact that Gabriel had requested such secrecy would have made Lilith angry and nervous, but now it just made her anxious.

"What did he do?" she prodded.

"It was still early—hardly anyone in the club, so I left the door for a bit to watch him. He went up to Mason's table and sat down. I figured he suspected Mason. He watched another swell play for awhile and then, once he got up, Lord Angelwood played himself. I thought that said a lot, considering how he feels about gaming."

Shock froze Lilith's blood. Latimer must have been mistaken . . . but no, he had seen it with his own two eyes. Gabriel had played faro at Mason's table in order to prove that Mason—and Mallory's—provided honest games.

She'd once told him that the only way to see what kind of establishment she ran was to play at her tables. She never expected him to take her up on it. She never expected him to compromise his principles in such a way for her.

What if someone had seen him? He would have been ruined. He might still be if word got out. *She* could ruin him.

"He's a good man, Lady Lilith," Latimer told her, his tone raspy. "You can trust him. He must care for you very much to do what he did for you."

Yes, Lilith thought numbly. He must. The realization didn't give her as much joy as she had thought it would. In fact, it had quite the opposite effect. She didn't like it. She didn't like it at all. The whole thing made her stomach churn.

It was laughable, really. Both of them, betrayed by their hearts. He'd compromised himself by helping her and she was going to compromise her best interests by keeping his secret. She loved him and she could never betray him in such a way.

"Thank you for telling me this," she murmured as she rose to her feet. Her knees trembled beneath her skirts. "I'll leave you now. You need your rest."

"I am a little tired," he admitted.

"I'm very sorry this happened to you, Latimer."

He waved aside her guilt with his bandaged hand. "None of that, now. I knew what I was getting into when I challenged Bronson. I'd do it again if it came to that. Although I think Lord Angelwood will prove a better ally than I ever could."

Bending at the waist, Lilith brushed her lips across Latimer's forehead—the only part of his face reasonably free of cuts and bruises. "I'll be by to check on you later," she promised.

Shutting the door behind her, Lilith strode down the hall to the stairs, her head and heart full of thoughts of Gabriel and what she was going to do and say when she saw him.

One thing she could not do was let on that Latimer had betrayed his confidence, no matter how much she wanted to. Gabriel was too proud. He would not appreciate her knowing, even if she did give her word to never reveal the truth.

Down the stairs she went, her feet finding each step, taking her in the right direction even though she scarcely paid attention. She went to the billiards room and absently shot balls around the table as she waited.

And she knew with astonishing clarity that the reason for his coming would simply be because she'd asked him to.

When the footman from Mallory's arrived telling Gabriel that Lilith "needed" him, Gabriel didn't even bother to finish what he was doing before shouting for his horse. He left what little information he'd uncovered about Samuel Bronson and his club scattered over the top of his desk, unread and, at the moment, unimportant.

The fog from the morning was lifting, leaving wisps of cloudy mist in its wake. Clive's hooves echoed on the damp cobblestones as he and Gabriel raced through the warm, moist afternoon.

Gabriel hadn't bothered with a hat. He'd only lose it to the wind once Clive reached his top speed. Droplets of mist kissed his forehead and cheeks. The humidity seeped through his clothing, leaving a cool, sticky sensation on his skin as he and his gelding pounded down the street, weaving in and out of the busy traffic and ignoring the outraged cries of those they cut off.

By evening it would be all over the city that the Earl of Angelwood had rode hell-bent through the streets like a madman. Someone would mention seeing him dash into Mallory's long before the club was open for business, and the gossips would speculate as to what was so special about Lilith Mallory that a peer of the realm would behave so recklessly to get to her. No doubt a few gentlemen would offer up a few suggestions. Before the clubs closed that night, fresh wagers would appear in all the betting books and he and Lilith would be at the heart of most of them.

Scandal. What he'd fought so hard to avoid this past decade. He'd loathed it, feared it. Now he spat in the face of it. Let them talk. The only thing that mattered to him was Lilith.

Bending low over Clive's broad neck, Gabriel spurred the gelding onward. The city passed by them in a blur. The tails of Gabriel's coat soared behind him like a pair of slick gray wings. If only he could indeed fly. He'd be with Lilith by now.

By the time he reached the club, his skin was wet beneath his clothes and his hair was plastered to his skull. He was hot and sticky and breathless with worry.

A groom was waiting to take care of Clive. Gabriel swung one leg over the gelding's head and vaulted to the ground, shoving the reins at the man as he did so. He barely remembered to mutter a word of thanks before racing toward the club's entrance.

Right away he knew the situation was serious when it wasn't Latimer who opened the door for him. For the quiet giant to abandon his post, he had to be at Lilith's side, and if he was at Lilith's side, then Lilith was indeed in trouble.

"Where is she?" he demanded as he stepped inside.

"The billiards room, my lord."

With a quick nod at the man, Gabriel ran across the hall and veered left, to the billiards room.

He hesitated outside the door. What now? Did he go charging in like a maniac or should he knock?

Lady Lilith needs you, the footman had told him.

Lilith would send such a blatant plea only if she truly did need him.

Gripping the glass knob, Gabriel twisted his wrist. The door opened . . .

No questioning stares met him. There was nothing at all. No one, that is, save for the lone figure hunched over the billiards table, idly rolling a red ball back and forth across the smooth felt surface.

She looked up as he closed the door. Her eyes were bright with tears that had yet to spill over onto those too pale cheeks. She looked young, like a child who'd just had some of her innocence taken from her.

Neither of them moved.

"You came," she said, her voice little more than a surprised whisper.

He nodded. "You asked."

That was when the tears spilled over. Pressing a palm to her lips, Lilith felt her face crumple. Bowing her head, she rested one hand against the tabletop as sobs shook her entire body.

Something inside Gabriel—something very near the region of his heart—snapped at the sight of her distress. Shucking off his coat and his gloves, he crossed the carpet in a few long, quick strides.

She fell into his arms without hesitation, burying her face against his breast, heedless of his mist-damp clothes.

He didn't shush her. He let her cry until she was ready to stop.

He didn't have to wait very long. Lilith wasn't the kind of person to allow her emotions to rule her for very long, not when there were other matters that needed tending.

As her sobs subsided, Gabriel dug into his pocket for his handkerchief and handed it to her, smiling as she blew her nose with all the grace and elegance of a honking goose.

"What happened?" he asked when she was done.

She lifted her gaze to his, the stormy color of her eyes brightened by her tears.

"Latimer," she whispered, her chin quivering. "And Aunt Imogen."

She must have found out he'd been telling the truth about her aunt. Certainly he could understand her being disappointed with Imogen—he could understand that maybe she felt a little guilty, too—but that was hardly reason for these wretched tears.

"What happened to Latimer?"

"Bronson," came her shaky reply. "He had him beaten. Oh, Gabe! He hurt Latimer so very badly, and it's all my fault!"

Now he shushed her, scared that she'd work herself into a maelstrom of tears again before he could get the entire story out of her.

"How is it your fault, Lily?" he asked, rubbing his hands along her back in a way that seemed to calm her.

"Latimer stood up to him, and now Bronson has taken his revenge! Latimer wouldn't have gotten involved if I'd been able to handle Bronson on my own!"

Gabriel didn't know whether to laugh or to shake her. Only she could take the blame for another person's actions.

"Lilith, it's Latimer's job to protect you. You cannot blame yourself. From what I've heard, he and Bronson have a history. They were bound to butt heads sooner or later. Is Latimer going to be all right?"

She nodded, dabbing at her nose with his handkerchief. "The doctor says he needs to stay abed for some time for his ribs to heal, but he should make a complete recovery."

"There," he said in an overly bright tone. "He's going to be fine."

Pushing against his shoulders, she looked up at him. Not a tear or a quiver to be seen.

"He could have been killed."

"But he wasn't," he reminded her sternly. "And you should concentrate on that rather than on what might have happened."

Staring at his chest, she nodded. "You're right."

Gabriel slid his hands up to her shoulders. He was thankful Bronson had decided to take his rage out on Latimer and not on Lilith herself. But Bronson wasn't stupid. He knew that an attack on Lilith would bring Gabriel after him. A club doorman was much less bothersome than a peer of the realm.

"What is Bow Street going to do about Bronson?"

As soon as he asked the question, even before he felt her

stiffen under his hands, he knew he should have asked *if* Bow Street had even been consulted, let alone what the runners planned to do.

"You did notify Bow Street, didn't you, Lil?"

"Of course not!" She tore free of his embrace, edging around the table as though she needed to put some distance between them.

He followed her. "Why?"

"Because telling Bow Street will only make Bronson all the more vengeful!"

"If you don't tell them, you're letting Bronson get away with it!"

She faced him, hands on her hips and eyes blazing. "He could very well kill Latimer next time."

"It's not Latimer I'm worried about," Gabriel ground out. "It's you!"

"I know," she replied softly.

Gabriel's ears rang. She *knew*? Where were the accusations, the recriminations?

"I found your letter."

She found his what? What letter?

"The one you wrote to Aunt Imogen," she explained when he remained bewildered and silent. "The one she replied to and told you she did not know where I was."

So she had discovered the truth. He should be happy that she believed him, but he wasn't. Not when he knew how much her aunt's betrayal must hurt. Everyone in Lilith's life whom she should have been able to count on had let her down. Her parents. Her aunt. Him.

Her gaze flitted between him and the floor. "Aunt Imogen kept it. She also recorded it in her journal. I'm not sure why she did either, but I'm glad she did. I doubted your honesty and . . . I'm sorry for it."

Her words thrilled him, filled him with a foolishly buoyant happiness, but there was little satisfaction in hearing her admit to being wrong.

"Of course you wanted to believe your aunt," he said

softly. "She loved you. She only did what she thought was best for you."

Lilith nodded wearily. She didn't look convinced.

There was no need to discuss it further. Right now, the actions of a dead woman seemed insignificant compared to their other problems. Regardless of the fact that Lilith now knew the truth, it changed very little—at least until Gabriel put his new plan into motion. And even that paled in the shadow of the threat of Bronson. Gabriel's first, and only, priority was to keep Lilith safe.

"I want you to tell me the whole story about Bronson," he told her as they sat down on the sofa, Lilith tucked into the crook of his arm. "Leave nothing out."

There was a moment of silence as Lilith collected her thoughts. He hoped those thoughts didn't include leaving anything out.

"I first encountered him shortly after the club opened and word leaked out that I was the owner. He paid me what he called a 'friendly' visit. He warned me of what a hard business this could be and that it was no place for a lady such as myself. At the time, I took him for a condescending flirt—nothing serious. That was my first mistake." She glanced up at Gabriel, as though waiting for him to agree. He said nothing. He simply smiled.

"When business began to thrive, I heard from him again. This time his threats were a bit more transparent, but still I didn't believe him to be that much of a menace. I didn't believe for an instant that things would come to . . . this."

"Of course you didn't." Gabriel gave her a quick squeeze. It was hard to remain relaxed and not let his anger take over. But Lilith needed his support, not his ranting and raving. "Bronson is the villain here, not you. When did you first realize he was serious?"

"The first time he destroyed one of my brandy shipments," she replied. "It must have been about six or seven months ago. Since then, there have been other shipments destroyed and the club office was broken into. That's what I thought was happening that night I found you snooping around. I thought Bronson's thieves had returned."

Gabriel stiffened. He'd had no way of knowing about Bronson then, but he couldn't help the stab of guilt that pierced his heart.

And he couldn't help but wonder what Bronson would try next. Each time he threatened Lilith, he seemed to go a little bit further.

Gabriel tried not to think about it. "But he didn't make contact with you again himself until that night at the theater?"

Lilith shook her head, as though her thoughts had slipped away just as his had. "No. And then he came to the club. I haven't seen him since. He's never threatened me in such a physical manner before."

"And he's not going to again if I have anything to do with it," Gabriel announced as he rose to his feet. "I know you do not want to, but I'm sending word to Bow Street."

"No!" Lilith leapt off the sofa after him. "You cannot! It will only make Bronson more vengeful."

Gabriel turned to her with an expression as unyielding as granite. "Then you're closing the club."

Her jaw dropped. "I am *not* giving Bronson that sort of satisfaction!"

"Then we're calling Bow Street in," he replied matter-of-factly. He would not be swayed.

"Gabriel, this is not your concern."

"It became my concern the minute Bronson first threatened you," he informed her in a quiet, unyielding tone. "It became even more of my concern when you sent for me earlier today. It is my concern because it is your concern, and if you cannot see what needs to be done, then *I* will take the necessary measures."

Hands on her hips, Lilith glared at him. "And just what do you think Bronson will do when he discovers we've set the runners after him?"

He arched a brow and folded his arms across his chest.

"What do you think he'll do when you refuse to heed this warning and keep your club open?"

She stared at him. He could almost feel the ice of her gaze, but he held it.

"Fine," she agreed finally, petulantly. "Send for Bow Street."

He moved over her, resting his hands on the warm curve of her shoulders. It was a minor victory, he knew, but it lifted a huge burden off his shoulders.

"I'll send for a runner immediately," he said, his voice low. He paused. He needed to tell her how he felt but couldn't seem to find the words. "I don't know what I'd do if I lost you."

Her storm-blue eyes widened as she regarded him.

"I lost you once," he murmured, unable to stop the confession now that he had started it. "I'm not going to let you out of my sight after this."

"You have to once in a while," she reminded him. "You must go to your office, your clubs. To Parliament."

He hadn't been to the House in quite some time. He'd return as soon as he had made his decision, as soon as he gathered his courage and his convictions.

Reaching up, she stroked the pads of her fingers along the breadth of his jaw. His heart tripped at the soft warmth of her touch. "Thank you for coming when I needed you."

He caught her fingers in his own. "I always will."

And he would.

The simple vow formed a hard, bitter lump in Lilith's throat. They were doomed, the two of them. Each so devoted to the other, yet so utterly opposed. Yes, she would give up her club for him, but someday she would resent him for it. She knew that, just as she knew that he would resent her for forcing him to compromise his principles.

As if he hadn't compromised them enough already.

Raising herself up on her toes, she kissed him. Pressing her lips to his, she caught at his other hand and steered him back toward the sofa. Without breaking the contact between them, she pushed against him, forcing him down onto the plush cushions, guiding his movements until he lay along the brocade length and she could lower herself on top of him.

Need, hot and anxious, rose up within her. It was physical, mental and so acutely emotional that it actually hurt. It was almost frantic, this urge to feel him inside her, as though by taking his body into hers, she might take something else of him as well—something she could hold on to long after he was gone.

And even more than that, she had to show him how much what he had done meant to her. She couldn't tell him and not betray Latimer, so she would have to show him her gratitude in the only way she knew how.

And despite the brave front she put on, she needed him. She needed to take something of him. She needed his strength.

His hands were on her breasts, kneading them, squeezing her nipples through the thin fabric of her gown and shift. The pressure of his fingers was hard, drawing little whimpers from her that were an exquisite mixture of pleasure and pain.

Her own hand slid between them, finding the hard ridge beginning to strain against his trousers. Unfastening the falls, she withdrew the satiny heat of him from the confining fabric, stroking his hardness with the curve of her palm.

"You're hard for me already," she murmured against his lips.

Gabriel groaned as her fingers tightened around him. "I'd be hard for you all the time if it were possible."

Lifting her lower body so she could hike up her skirts, Lilith settled her groin over his. She was already moist and ready for him. He didn't have to massage her breasts for that spot between her legs to throb and ache with wanting. He simply had to be.

She sat down slowly, shuddering as her body parted for the thickness of his flesh. A sweet stretching, the sensation of being deliciously filled, washed over her. The deeper she took his shaft, the more she felt him seeping into her soul and her heart. It was as though their bodies weren't just joining but were actually merging, assimilating themselves into a single life, rather than two separate beings.

Little tingles ran down her thighs as that swollen part of her met the warm friction of impaling herself upon him. He stared up at her through heavy lids, still fondling her breasts as the curve of her buttocks came to rest upon his thighs and her knees brushed his ribs.

"Bend down," he ordered, his voice low and hoarse.

Trembling with need to the point that every nerve in her body danced with anticipation, Lilith did as he bade. The movement pressed her mound against the firm flesh of his pelvis, heightening the yearning between her legs. She pressed down, grinding her hips to his, gasping as the entire length of him filled her and shocks of pleasure shot through her loins.

"Closer," he growled, tugging on the neckline of her gown.

She bent down farther, supporting her upper body with her hands on the arm of the sofa. She locked her elbows in place, but the muscles in her arms and shoulders trembled as she held herself above him, her breasts just inches above his mouth.

Gabriel yanked on the neckline. A sharp, short rip rang out as he forced the fabric down, baring her right breast. Gabriel fastened his mouth around the exposed, puckered nipple.

Lilith cried out at the sharp tugging of his lips, the desperate laving of his tongue against her sensitive flesh. He drew her nipple between his lips as she had taken his erection between the lips of her sex—slowly, deliberately. And as she ground her pelvis against his, his tongue matched the rhythm of her hips.

She rode him, spreading her legs as far as the sofa would allow, taking his body into her as he took her into his, and with every plunge, every hot, wet stroke, she drew closer and closer to climax.

"Oh, Gabe," she moaned. There were so many things she wanted to tell him, so many things she wanted to share—like how it felt to have him inside her—but there weren't words to say such things, even if she were capable of speech. How could she possibly tell him that this act that was as old and natural as the earth itself meant more to her than he could ever know? That being joined with him made her feel whole and complete, and that even though her body pushed and strained toward orgasm, she never wanted this to end?

And how could she tell him that even though he was buried within her as far as he could go, it wasn't good enough? That she wanted not only his body but his heart and his soul, just as he had hers? How could she tell him that she wanted to consume him without frightening him with the depth of her need?

She couldn't. And so she shoved, lifted, churned and ground against him with a ferocity that made her dizzy, arching her back to deepen each thrust. And when the spasms hit, rolling her like a tempest rolls the sea, she plunged her shivering, shuddering body up and down on his until she felt him buck beneath her. Pulling up, she wrenched her breast from his mouth, and as the last of the pleasure danced through her, Lilith watched as Gabriel threw back his head and groaned with his release.

She held him inside her until he was still and both of their breathing had returned to normal.

"Why did you do that?" he asked, out of breath.

Lilith smiled. She didn't know how to answer. Instead, she pressed a kiss to his damp forehead and lifted herself off him. The kink in her hip receded. Her thighs quaked in protest.

I love you, she said with her heart as she gazed upon him.

I need you, she said with her soul as he smiled.

"I want you to send for Bow Street now," she said aloud. It was the only declaration she could give.

Chapter 16

Lilith's one condition for allowing Gabriel to consult Bow Street was that they go to the office rather than bring a runner to Mallory's. This was supposed to be a precaution in case Bronson had men watching the club. Gabriel almost told her that if Bronson had someone watching them, he probably would have them followed as well. But he decided against it. He didn't want to frighten her any more than she already was.

They made the short journey to the environs of Covent Garden in relative silence. Occasionally Lilith asked what he thought Duncan Reed, one of Bow Street's top magistrates, would suggest as to handling the situation with Bronson. Any other conversation was brief, both of them caught up in their own thoughts.

The carriage rolled to a stop in front of the Bow Street offices. At one time only number four Bow Street had been used to house the runners, but several years ago, number three had been added to the lease to allow for more space.

Number three was a larger structure with a building a few yards behind it that had been dubbed "Felons Rooms," as detention facilities were always a problem.

There was nothing special about the building, its smooth front marred by soot and the passing years. It stood tall, narrow and plain beside Johnson's Oyster Warehouse and across from the Brown Bear, a tavern that also served as extra holding space when more room for prisoners was needed. No, Bow Street didn't look like anything special at all.

Of course, it wasn't the house that made Bow Street what it was. No, it was the men in the red coats, trained by the zealous, meticulous Duncan Reed, who gave the runners their reputation as dedicated and determined to always uphold the law.

They were shown to Reed's office with a promptness that pleased Gabriel. He didn't fool himself for a minute that it was his title that had captured the magistrate's attention. No, it was the note he'd sent ahead, informing Reed of just how much danger he feared Lilith was in.

Reed sat with his back to the door—something Gabriel himself would never be able to do were he in the same job. It seemed as though Reed dared anyone to try to sneak up on him.

When the magistrate rose to his feet and turned to greet them, Gabriel was struck by how young the magistrate was. Reed didn't appear to be much older than Gabriel. His hair and eyes were brown. His features were narrow, lending him a lupine air that might make criminals wary but which filled Gabriel with a sense of comfort. This man would see to it that Bronson was put behind bars.

"Thank you for seeing us," Gabriel said once introductions were made and they were seated on the opposite side of the magistrate's oak desk.

Reed waved aside Gabriel's thanks, telling him absolutely, yet without offense, that such sentiments were not in order. It was his job.

"You said in your note that Lady Lilith was in danger," the

magistrate prompted in a quiet tone, fixing his wintry gaze on Lilith. "Why don't you tell me what kind of trouble you're in?"

Gabriel sat and listened while Lilith repeated the tale she'd told him earlier. She left nothing out, giving the magistrate details about everything Bronson had ever done against her or her club. She ended with the attack on Latimer the day before.

Reed looked up from the notes he'd scribbled while Lilith talked.

"I've heard of Bronson before," he said in that quiet voice of his. "I fear he's a very dangerous man, my lady."

Lilith nodded, a humorless curve to her lips. "So I'm beginning to discover, Mr. Reed."

"What would you suggest we do?" Gabriel demanded, frustration finally putting an end to his stoic silence.

The magistrate's dark gaze met his. Most people of lower rank wouldn't risk giving a peer such a frank, blatantly assessing stare, but Duncan Reed hadn't earned his reputation by being like most other people.

"I assume, since you accompanied Miss Mallory, that the two of you are close friends." There was no mockery or innuendo in his tone, but Gabriel's cheeks warmed anyway.

It made no difference that they were lovers. That was no one's business but their own. But, of course, society wouldn't see it that way. People were already saying Gabriel must be a bit like his father, after all, for getting involved with Lilith and her club. It was a comparison he could live with.

"We are," Gabriel replied coolly.

"Then I would suggest that you stay as close to her as you can if you want to keep her safe. Bronson is unlikely to make a move with an earl present."

"He already had my coach run off the road."

"I believe that was designed more to frighten you and Lady Lilith than to injure either of you. Bronson wouldn't want to risk losing his titled customers because he harmed one of their own."

What Reed said made sense, but Gabriel wasn't ready to put all his faith in it. Bronson was street scum—the kind of man who would stoop to anything to get what he wanted. If he decided he wanted Gabriel out of the way, he would no doubt find some method to make it happen—a method that couldn't be traced back to himself. Gabriel would have to be doubly on guard if he were to keep Lilith safe.

"I'm hiring guards for the club," he announced as they left the Bow Street office sometime later.

"Bronson will know," she countered, waiting for the coachman to open the carriage door.

"Then you will have to close the club."

She didn't even look at him. "We've discussed that already. I am not closing the club."

Sighing in frustration, Gabriel leaned over her shoulder and whispered so his coachman couldn't hear. "Then I'm going to start spending more time at your club."

Lilith shrugged. "Agreed."

"Such as my nights," he added. "*All* night."

The glance she sent him over her shoulder as she climbed into the carriage was incredulous. "You most certainly are not!"

He climbed in behind her. "Then you will have to stay with me."

She was still gaping at him when he tapped on the ceiling to signal the driver to depart.

"I am not staying with you and you are not staying with me."

He smiled. She could argue all she wanted, not that it would do her any good. "Yes, I am."

"*No*," she informed him through clenched teeth. "You're not. People will talk."

She was adorable when she was annoyed. Gabriel folded his arms across his chest. "They are already talking. We may as well give them something to talk about."

Scowling, she nudged his shin with the toe of her slipper. "Don't be glib. You know very well we cannot live under the same roof. Think of what your political cronies will say."

So it was his reputation she was concerned with, not her own.

"I don't give a damn what they say," he replied with an indolent shrug.

"Well, you should, if you want their support to abolish gambling."

His smile faded. She was right. He should care. "Perhaps I've changed my mind about that."

She laughed. She didn't believe him. He couldn't really blame her, but it still rankled. "Now I know you're being flippant," she said. "You've never changed your mind about anything."

"I have changed my mind about many things." *Like what is more important, my pride or you.*

"Then change it about this. You are not living in my house." Her tone brooked no refusal, just in case the stubborn set of her jaw didn't get the point across.

He chuckled, determined to win but enjoying the battle. "Oh, but I'm afraid I am."

"Gabriel, my reputation is bad enough as it is. What do you think will happen to it if I allow you to live with me?"

Oh, that was low. Using that pleading tone in combination with a pout and a subtle widening of her eyes, she almost had him. Of course he didn't want to do anything to hurt her, and she knew that. The little brat.

Two could play that game.

He leaned forward, slipping his hand under her skirts. Slowly his fingers slid up the delicate silk of a stocking, past an embroidered garter to the soft, bare flesh of a supple thigh, and higher. Her breath caught.

"Which sounds better to you, Lil?" he asked, parting the downy lips of her sex with his fingers and stroking the moisture there. "Maintaining your present social status or having me in your bed every night?"

The look she shot him was pure heat, melting him right down to the bone.

"Well, when you put it that way . . ."

* * *

"You realize you're committing political suicide?"

The sharpness—the disappointment—in Blaine's voice didn't surprise Gabriel. He didn't have to tell the older man his decision to move in with Lilith, but he'd done it anyway. Of course Blaine would see it in a negative light, instead of as Gabriel doing what was right. After all, it had been he who had urged Gabriel to become active in politics. In fact, it had been Blaine who had decided that the best way to honor his father's memory was by striving to outlaw gaming.

"I'm considering giving up politics," he replied nonchalantly as he sifted through the stack of letters on the desk before him.

"You can't be serious!"

Gabriel lifted his head, smiling at his friend's astonishment. "No, I'm not. I have no plans to vacate my seat in the House just yet, but I have changed my mind on a few topics."

Shaking his head, Blaine sank into a nearby chair and pinched the bridge of his nose with his thumb and forefinger.

"Dare I ask *what* topics?"

Marriage, for one, but that was none of the older man's business. Gabriel's mother's betrothal ring was in his valise, ready to go to Lilith's with him—ready to be slipped on her finger the minute she accepted his proposal.

Her refusal was not something he thought about. Surely she wouldn't refuse him? Not when she heard that he was changing his stance on gambling—not when he made her confess to loving him as much as he loved her.

And he did love her. More than life itself. He had never stopped.

"Gaming," he replied after a lengthy silence. "Instead of trying to abolish it, I want Parliament to form better laws concerning it and the clubs that promote it."

Blaine's expression was painful to see. He looked so . . . betrayed.

"What about your promise to your father?" he demanded,

his voice quivering with anger and frustration. "Does that mean nothing to you now that you have found Lilith again?"

Bristling, Gabriel fought to keep a tight rein on his temper. It would be so easy to tell Blaine it was none of his goddamn business, but that wasn't the right thing to do. Blaine had been a good friend to him, and an even better one to his father. Such loyalty and friendship should not be tossed away over a difference of opinion.

"I promised my father that I would do all I could to prevent what happened to him from happening to someone else," Gabriel reminded Blaine in a low tone. "Trying to snuff gambling out will never work."

Rising to his feet, he crossed the carpet to the liquor cabinet. "In the last ten years as I have built my political influence, have we made any difference? No. We will never be able to stop people from gambling, Blaine."

He poured a glass of port for each of them. Blaine took his without speaking. Reseating himself at the desk, Gabriel continued. "People like my father will always find a game of dice or cards if they want one. All I can do is try to ensure that clubs cannot rob people of their fortunes and that those who play won't risk their entire lives on a game."

Blaine met his gaze. "Or prevent foolish young men from losing their entire quarterly allowance?"

Gabriel grinned. "Precisely. We come down harder on hells and install regulations that protect both the patrons and the clubs."

And the club owners.

The viscount looked decidedly interested now. "Such as limits to how much a person can win or lose in the course of an evening?"

Sipping his port, Gabriel nodded. "Or in one game. Perhaps witnessed vowels to prevent forgery or cheating. An impartial party to watch the tables to make sure the dealer and the players are behaving honorably. Cutting a gentleman out of a game when he's too deep in his cups to play sensibly."

There were so many things that could be done, and while Gabriel knew it wouldn't be easy to get such laws in place, it would be a hell of a lot easier to improve the system than to eliminate it.

Blaine looked at him as though truly seeing him for the first time. Even though he was a grown man, Gabriel warmed at his friend's expression.

"What can I do to help you?" he asked

Gabriel smiled. "I could use your support."

"You have it."

All the breath Gabriel hadn't been aware of holding rushed out in a sigh of relief. "Thank you."

The older man's gaze drifted to the painting above the mantel. Gabriel turned his attention in the same direction. Phillip Warren stared back at them.

"I think he would be very happy with your decision," Blaine announced sagely.

Gabriel studied the portrait. For so many years the smile on his father's face had served as nothing more than a painful reminder of his tragic, senseless death. Now the expression seemed happy, almost hopeful, as if he were telling his son that everything was going to work out just fine.

And at that moment Gabriel believed it would.

I think I'm going to get it right this time, Papa. Not just for you and Lilith, but for me as well.

And from above the fireplace, the late Earl of Angelwood smiled peacefully.

"How is he?"

Mary turned from her vigil beside Latimer's bed as Lilith entered the quiet chamber. Her face showed the strain of the day, but she managed a smile.

"Fine. I've given him some laudanum so he'll rest like he's supposed to."

Lilith nodded. "Good. I was worried he was going to hurt himself further by trying to go back to work."

Motioning with her head for Mary to join her, she stepped

back into the corridor. If Latimer was sleeping, she didn't want to wake him. If he was awake, she didn't want him to overhear their conversation. Mary was the only one who knew that she and Gabriel had gone to see Duncan Reed.

Closing the door behind her, Mary looked up and down the hall before whispering, "How did it go at Bow Street?"

"Fine," Lilith replied in a similar tone. "Mr. Reed is going to have runners watch both Mallory's and Hazards in case Bronson tries anything."

A small smile crossed Mary's wide lips. "And what did your Angelic Earl think of that?"

Lilith shook her head. "He wants to spend more time here. More time as in spending nights."

Mary gaped at her. "Are you going to let him?"

"I didn't have much of a choice." A warm flush crept up Lilith's neck and cheeks as she remembered just how Gabriel had persuaded her to let him stay with her.

It wasn't a good idea and she knew that. She didn't want to do any more damage to his reputation, no matter how appealing the idea had once been. She didn't want people to whisper about him and speculate about his integrity. Gabriel had more integrity than most of the Upper Ten Thousand put together. Having him living with her was just going to complicate things further. It would change things, to what extent she couldn't fathom, but she knew it would be harder for the two of them to walk away in the end.

What she knew and what she wanted were two entirely different things. And keeping them separated wasn't always easy.

Mary's expression was far too knowing. "Does he believe he can keep you any safer than Bow Street can?"

Sighing, Lilith rubbed her hand over the back of her neck. "Gabriel doesn't think anyone can do anything better than he can."

It was almost as though her friend was actually trying to peer inside Lilith's head through her eyes. "What do you think?"

Lilith chuckled dryly. "Most of the time I have to agree with him. However, that doesn't mean I always like it."

"*I'll* like it if he can keep you safe from Bronson," Mary replied. "Personally, I'm glad he bullied you into giving him his way."

Another sigh. "It will certainly set tongues wagging, but I suppose that's nothing when compared to our safety." At Mary's surprised look, she added, "We're all in danger, Mary. I want you to promise me you'll be careful."

Some of the color left her cheeks, but Mary nodded in acquiescence. "I will."

"What about your reverend? Do you think he'll have something to say about Gabriel staying with us?"

Mary shrugged, turning away. "I haven't heard from him since I told him the truth about my marriage. I saw him at the Magdalene shelter earlier this week when I dropped off those blankets you donated. He looked awful, but he carried on as though I wasn't even there."

Poor Mary. Lilith's heart went out to her friend. She knew what it was like to love someone and not be able to be with him, but at least she and Gabriel had a little time together. It was more than Mary and the reverend could have, given his strict moral code.

"Why don't you check with some of your former friends?" Lilith suggested. "Perhaps you will be lucky enough to have been made a widow in the last year."

A bitter laugh shook the other woman's shoulders. "That's doubtful. I wouldn't want to risk him finding me."

"Would you like me to have Mr. Francis look into it? The worst thing that could happen is that your husband is still alive. He won't be able to find you."

Turning, Mary faced her, sagging ever so slightly, as though a weight had settled upon her shoulders. "He threw me away, yet I'm the one who cannot seem to be rid of him."

Lilith wrapped her arms around her friend, drawing her into a swift embrace. "You give me the information and I will give it to Mr. Francis when next I see him."

"Oh!" Mary cried, stepping out of the hug. "I almost forgot. He sent word around earlier, while you were at Bow Street."

"Who?" Lilith asked. "Mr. Francis?"

Mary nodded. "He said he had some information for you and would be by around three o'clock."

Lilith's gaze flew to the small ornate clock sitting on a shelf just above Mary's head. It was a quarter to three.

"He should be here soon, then. Did he not say why he wished to see me?"

Mary shook her head. "As always, his message was very brief. It simply said that he would be here this afternoon at that time."

What news could Mr. Francis possibly have for her? Could it involve Bronson? Perhaps he'd found some information that could lead to Bow Street actually arresting the bastard.

"I must tell George to send him up to my office when he arrives." She paused, concern for her friend returning and overshadowing everything else. "Will you be all right?"

Mary's smile was shaky, but there nevertheless. "I've survived worse than a broken heart. You do what you have to. I'll bring you the information for Mr. Francis shortly."

She was really going to do it. Lilith couldn't quite believe her ears. This Mr. Sweet must mean a great deal to Mary if she was prepared to take a chance on the unlikely hope that she might be a widow now.

Lilith hoped the good reverend deserved her.

She reached out and gave her friend's hand a gentle squeeze. "It'll all work out. You just see if it doesn't."

Mary didn't look very convinced, but she humored Lilith by not disagreeing.

After running downstairs to tell George—the footman who was taking Latimer's place until he recovered—to show Mr. Francis to her office upon his arrival, Lilith went there to enter the previous night's receipts into the books.

Despite the attack on Latimer, Mallory's had been open for business the night before. Lilith had wanted to close it out of respect for her loyal friend and servant, but Gabriel believed that was exactly what Bronson wanted her to do. Once she stopped thinking with her heart and started using her head, Lilith realized he was right. She knew Latimer would never want her to close the club on his account, so she remained open. Gabriel helped her keep an eye on things, as did the rest of her staff, and she was able to look in on Latimer whenever she wanted.

As she tallied up the receipts, she discovered that the club had made a tidy profit the night before, despite her lack of attention. And there were hardly any IOUs, something she was pleased to see. Unfortunately, of the two that were there, both exceeded the house limit.

Lilith tried to enforce the house limit, preventing anyone in the club from gambling more than five thousand pounds at a time. However, there was only so much she could do. She couldn't be everywhere at once, and most of her staff were from the lower classes. If a snotty aristocrat put up a fuss or demanded to be allowed to make as large a bet as he or she wanted, Lilith's staff almost always gave in, being too intimidated by rank to adhere to the rules.

Lilith didn't blame her staff, but she hated seeing it happen. It wasn't so much of a problem if the person could afford to lose a large sum, but if he—or she—couldn't, Lilith ended up with his vowels as he struggled to come up with the blunt. Her greatest fear was that someday someone would suffer a large loss at her club and kill himself rather than face the debt.

Sighing, she withdrew several sheets of vellum from the bottom drawer of her desk. Hastily, she penned a brief note to each gentleman, giving him a time period in which to either settle the debt or discuss a payment schedule. She'd just finished addressing and sealing the two missives when George poked his head in the door to announce Mr. Francis.

The investigator entered the room, looking every inch the wealthy city merchant. Lilith didn't know how anyone could so drastically alter his appearance with as little effort as Mr.

Francis did. It seemed that all it took was a change of clothes and he became an entirely different person.

"Good day, Mr. Francis," she said, gesturing to the chair in front of her desk. "Will you sit?"

He did as she bade him. "Thank you for seeing me, Lady Lilith. I know you've had a spot of trouble recently and I appreciate your giving me the time."

By "spot of trouble," she assumed he meant the whole foul business with Bronson.

"I was intrigued by your note, Mr. Francis. I can't imagine what it is you have to tell me."

Mr. Francis frowned, drawing his silvery brows together in a tight V. "Can you not? You asked me to find out as much about Lord Angelwood and his past as I could. I've managed to uncover something that might be of interest."

Cold heat blossomed in Lilith's chest. She'd forgotten all about asking the investigator to delve further into Gabriel's life.

"There's been a change in my relationship with Lord Angelwood," she replied, trying hard not to blush like a pathetic schoolgirl. "I'm not certain I want, or need, the information you're offering."

Mr. Francis nodded in understanding. "Lady Lilith, I've heard that you were quite close to the current earl's father. Is that correct?"

Lilith didn't bother to ask how he'd discovered this. Mr. Francis would never tell her. He never revealed any of his sources of information—which was probably why he was able to learn so much.

"I had the upmost respect for the old earl, yes."

Slipping one broad hand inside his jacket, Mr. Francis withdrew a thick fold of papers. He handed it to her without hesitation.

"Then whatever your relationship with the current earl, I think you will want to read this."

Something in his tone sent a shiver down Lilith's spine. He sounded so grave, so . . . sympathetic. Why he should feel sorry for her, Lilith had no idea, but it disturbed her all the same. She took the papers from him. Usually he made his reports to her orally, so there was little chance of anyone else getting hold of the contents. The fact that he'd written his findings down was strange enough. That he'd sealed the papers they were written on was downright bizarre.

As Lilith reached for the silver handle of her letter opener to break the seal, Mr. Francis rose from the chair.

Surprised, Lilith glanced up. "Don't you want to wait for me to read it?" Usually they discussed whatever information he brought her.

Mr. Francis shook his silvery head. "No. I think it for the best that you have some privacy when you read this. And if I might be so bold, I suggest you burn those papers when you are finished. I think it for the best if no one else ever sees what they contain."

Now he had her absolutely dreading reading the report. Good Lord, what had he uncovered.

"Thank you," she said, rising to her feet.

He shook his head. "Don't thank me. Sometimes there are secrets better left buried, Lady Lilith. I don't have much pride in being the one to unearth them." Setting his hat on top of his thick hair, he tipped the brim at her and left as quietly as he'd arrived.

Slowly, Lilith sank back into her chair, staring at the sealed papers on the desk. Did she want to know the secrets they contained? What could possibly make a man like Mr. Francis feel bad about it? She wasn't sure she wanted to know, but there was no way she could not look, not when it concerned Gabe or his father.

Gripping the letter opener with determination, she broke the thick wax seal and unfolded the pages.

There were several aged and worn pages of IOUs, each for a sum more staggering than the last and each signed by the Earl of Angelwood—Gabriel's father. These, while surprising in their amounts, weren't that shocking. She had always known that Gabriel's father liked to gamble, and Gabriel had told her of how his father had managed to waste most of the family fortune.

What she found next was a bit more worrisome. They were pages from a journal. They'd been forcibly ripped from their bindings. How Mr. Francis had come upon them, she was glad not to know.

The handwriting was small and cramped, as though written by someone elderly. The date at the top was only a few days after the death of Gabriel's father.

Halfway down the first page, she spotted a reference to Gabriel.

I received a bank draft from the new Lord Angelwood today in the amount of one thousand pounds. Seems too large an amount to waste on an old man like myself. Still, I took it, forever setting a price on my word of honor as a gentleman. He asks that I never tell anyone what I saw that day. I could not bring myself to tell him I would never dream of repeating such a tale. It is hardly the kind of thing one brings up in polite conversation—unless one is the worst sort of gossip. Though I gave my vow the minute I accepted his money, I cannot help but wish he had asked someone else to come that day . . .

Lilith shook her head. This made no sense. The writing went on, saying how he regretted being the one Gabriel had summoned, and then he started talking about the price of potatoes at the market.

There was one more page in the pile. She hoped it would finally provide the answer to this riddle, because now she was very anxious to learn the truth. She had so many suspicions and awful thoughts running through her head, she didn't even want to acknowledge them all. She just wanted to read that whatever had happened, Gabriel had nothing to do with it.

This page was dated earlier than the one she'd just read. It was the day of Gabriel's father's death. Mr. Francis hadn't put them in the correct order.

Found myself summoned to Mayfair today for the first time in decades. Had I known what they wanted me for, I would have told them to ask someone else. I haven't the stomach for these sorts of things anymore. But not knowing the circumstances, only understanding that a family of great lineage and social standing was in need of my assistance, I went. What I saw chilled and saddened me to the very bone. A young man—a very distraught young man—comforted by another, older man, sobbing over the corpse of his father. A man whom I understand to have been a fine if somewhat weak character and a loving father. A man who, in a fit of despair, put a pistol to his head and pulled the trigger, ending his life with a single bullet to the temple and leaving his son to clean up the mess and the scandal. They asked me to say the death was an accident, and the young man so obviously wanted to protect his father's reputation that I would have been heartless to refuse . . .

The papers dropped from Lilith's lifeless fingers to the surface of the desk. Horrified, she could only stare in numbed silence as they fell.

Gabriel's father had killed himself over his gambling debts.

Dear Lord, it was no wonder Gabriel felt the way he did about gambling. No wonder he wanted to abolish the practice altogether.

What must he think of her for running such an establishment as Mallory's? How could he make love to her when to him she must be just like the people who ruined his father and drove him to commit suicide?

No wonder he'd made it his mission to protect England from her and those who were like her.

And he wanted to live with her. To protect her from someone who was even lower than she was. He'd already compromised himself so much by gambling at Mallory's, and now he was going to go even further to protect her. How it must be costing him!

Oh, she was going to be sick. To find out that the old earl had died over debts was one thing, but to learn that he had taken his own life was too much to bear.

Of course Gabriel hadn't been able to come after her. He'd been trying to protect his family from scandal. Dear God, how he must have suffered! To be so young and to find . . . He'd told her he'd held his father as he died. He must have happened upon him just at that moment.

Her stomach lurched again.

Oh, how she wished she could have been there for him! Instead, she'd been feeling sorry for herself, wondering why he didn't rescue her, when all the while he'd had to deal with his father's death. He hadn't even been allowed to truly mourn— he'd spent all his energy trying to keep the truth hidden and rebuild the family fortune. No wonder he'd become a paragon. He was struggling to avoid scandal at all cost.

The scandal of their relationship was relatively small in comparison. She'd thought only of herself at the time. How selfish she'd been!

How could she face him after this? How could she look him in the eye now that she knew the truth? And to think that he'd actually told her he was reconsidering his stance on the gaming issue! As if she'd ever let him compromise his principles now!

If nothing else, this only proved just how utterly wrong they were for each other. There was no way Lilith would allow Gabriel to make any more sacrifices—especially not for her. He deserved better than having people whispering behind his back and judging him because of her. And he certainly didn't deserve a woman who advocated the very thing that had ruined his father.

There was only one thing to do. It was as clear and as painful as a knife in the breast, but in her heart Lilith knew it had to be done.

She had to put as much distance between them as possible. She had to remove him from her life quickly, before the stench of her life, and her involvement with Bronson, could touch him any more than it already had. She would not be the ruin of him.

At that moment Lilith made the most painful decision of her life.

She was going to close her club.

And then she was going to leave England—and Gabriel—for good.

Chapter 17

Gabriel exited his carriage in front of Mallory's and bounded up the front steps with all the exuberance of a young boy home from school.

He shouldn't be so happy, not when Latimer was injured and Lilith's own safety was endangered, but he couldn't help it. His political life was about to make a change that thrilled him with the possibility of actually having some measure of success. The ring he hoped Lilith would consent to wear was in his bag. He was going to ask the woman he loved to marry him, and he was going to spend the next few days making love to her whenever he wished. Surely life didn't get any better than that.

No, wait. It could get better. Someday Lilith would bear him a child—children. Then his life would be complete.

It was early yet; the sun was setting slowly, bathing the front of Mallory's in a golden-pink glow. Lilith would just be starting to ready herself for the evening ahead. Perhaps if he were lucky, she would not have bathed yet and he could join her in the tub.

With the image of Lilith's wet, soapy breasts in his mind, Gabriel pounded his fist on the door.

A footman whose name he didn't remember allowed him in. Once he'd asked the fellow's name, Gabriel quickly made his way through the corridor and up the stairs to Lilith's apartments.

He found her in her bedroom, but instead of up to her chin in hot, slippery water, she was fully clothed and looking decidedly morose.

"Lil," he said, dropping his valise on the floor and hastening to her with open arms. "What is it? What's happened?"

She stopped him with her hand before he could embrace her. "Don't," was all she said before she moved out of arm's reach.

Gabriel lowered his arms. Something was wrong. Dreadfully wrong. What could have happened in so short a time that she would go from willingly giving him her body to refusing his merest touch?

"Lilith," he said, his gaze following her as she put half the cream-and-sage carpet between them. "Tell me what has happened."

Hugging her arms around herself, Lilith nodded toward the mantel. "I want you to take those papers. They're yours to do with whatever you wish."

Papers? Turning his head, Gabriel saw the vellum she referred to folded neatly just inches away. Hesitantly, he reached for them, wary of what he would find written within.

What he read froze the breath in his lungs.

How he kept his fingers tightened on the pages, he didn't know, for he'd lost all feeling in his arms and legs. Raising his head, he expected to see anger in her eyes, but only pain and compassion were evident.

"I was going to tell you," he murmured, even though it was too late for such lame excuses.

She looked amused—and sad. "I know."

That was it? "You're not angry?"

She smiled a little. It didn't reach her eyes. "Is that what you expected? That I'd rant and rave and pout? I think I've done enough of that, don't you?"

"But I put you through scandal to save myself. And I kept the truth about my father from you." He didn't understand. She *should* be angry at him. Lord knew he was. He should have told her before she found out. How she found out didn't really matter. It hadn't been he who told her, and that was something he was going to have to live with.

"You were protecting your family." Then almost as an afterthought, as though she'd been stupid not to figure it out, she said, "No wonder you didn't come."

No. He wouldn't let her make this about her. "I made the wrong choice."

"No, you didn't. You didn't think so then; why should you think so now?"

"*Because*." He raked a hand through his hair in frustration. "I know what I lost by making that decision."

Her smile was sympathetic. "What did you lose? A petulant brat who expected you to live and breathe for her."

"An expectation I would have liked to fulfill," he replied, an odd choking sensation in his throat. A sense of foreboding washed over him. He didn't like her tone. Didn't like the resignation in her eyes.

She took a step toward him before she caught herself. It was as though she didn't trust herself to get too close. "Oh, Gabe. It's too late. We both know that."

Fear, hot and numbing, exploded inside him, along with the tremulous hold on his control. "I won't let you go, not when I've waited so long to find you again."

"You don't have a choice," she informed him with a sad shake of her head. "This time I'm the one making the decision to protect someone I care about.'

His hand was in his hair again. It was all he could do not to pull it out by the roots. How could she do this? After flaunting herself in front of society, how could she suddenly develop a sense of propriety now?

"Dammit, Lilith, I love you." There. Let her argue against that.

Her eyes filled with tears and his heart twisted at the sight of it. "I love you, too. That is why I'm letting you go."

Letting him go? He wasn't some possession she could just toss away, some pet she could give to a new owner. He was a man, dammit! The man who loved her. Who had always loved her. How could she just turn her back on that?

"Why?" he demanded, anger eclipsing all other emotion. She would not simply walk away from him. Not this time. "Give me one good reason why we can't be together. Is it your reputation? I don't give a goddamn what you've done."

She wiped her eyes with the heels of her hands. The pleading in her gaze almost succeeded in penetrating the frustration and hurt surrounding his heart.

"It's not just me, Gabe. It's *you*. Think of your own reputation. Do you really believe we can have a future?" She held her hands palms up, imploring him to understand what she was saying. As if she could ever make him understand that she was throwing away the second chance they'd been given.

When he remained stubbornly silent, she continued. "Society will never accept me. They will laugh at you for being taken in by such a woman as I. All you've worked so hard for in the House will go up in smoke."

His jaw twitched.

"I don't care about that."

She didn't look convinced. "Why? You've cared about it for years. Can you really toss it away for me?"

"Yes." That and anything else he had just to have her.

How could he make her see that without her there was nothing? He wanted to embrace the gifts his wayward parents had given him. He wanted to lose himself in all of life's passions. He wanted to take chances. And he wanted to do it all with Lilith.

Lilith blinked, as though his response frightened her. Perhaps it did. It frightened him. "You are lying."

"You know I'm not," he replied, coming toward her. He stopped when she took a step back, putting one of the oak posts of her bed between them like some kind of shield. "What about you? Would you give up your club for me?"

Her knuckles whitened on the post. "That's not fair."

"Maybe not, but it's simple. I would choose you over everything else, Lil. What would you choose?" He held his breath, waiting for her reply.

She scowled, that awful expression of sadness giving way to anger. Good. He'd rather have her vexed than looking as though she was about to stick her head in a noose for him.

"I'd choose you—you know that, you big oaf. But that doesn't mean that one of us might not regret it later."

Any regrets he might have about loving her were small in comparison to what he would experience if he let her get away again—stubborn, infuriating woman! "What could either of us possibly regret by choosing love?"

"I like my club, Gabe. I like the independence it gives me. I like the excitement and the bustle."

And? What was her point? Those were hardly the kinds of things that made a difference to him where their relationship was concerned.

"Keep your club, I don't care."

Lilith glanced away. She was starting to look harried. Running out of reservations, was she?

"What happens if one day someone kills himself because he took a loss at my tables? Could you still love me then?" Her chin rose defiantly.

So that was it. It had never occurred to Gabe that he wasn't the only one who had spent the past decade becoming a person he didn't particularly like. Lilith might love her club, but she didn't think much of the life she'd led in order to have it.

"I'd love you even if you were the devil incarnate," he answered. It wasn't intended as flattery. He meant it. It didn't matter what she did, he was going to love her. They both might as well accept it.

Arched brows furrowing, she shook her head with great determination. "I cannot let you take that chance."

"It's not your decision."

Her head snapped up, eyes blazing with indignation. Was there anything the two of them *couldn't* argue about?

"Yes, it is! I couldn't bear to have your love—to believe in the future and then lose you again! I'd rather leave you now."

"Why are you doing this?" Gabriel demanded, closing the distance between them so quickly she didn't even have time to react.

"You can have your club, have your back rooms—just let me have you!"

She choked on something that sounded very much like a sob. "You can't give up your principles for me, Gabe. Someday you'll hate me for it."

He reached for her, but she cringed from the contact. If he touched her he could seduce her into his arms, but he knew he couldn't change her mind.

He dropped his hand and once again tried words to appeal to her, "Then help me petition for better gaming laws. Work with me, not against me."

She shook her head. "That's not what you wanted a few weeks ago. How can you have changed your mind so quickly?"

"Because I have finally realized what's important." This time he did touch her. He couldn't help it. He wiped away a tear that trickled down her cheek. "Haven't you?"

She raised her gaze to his. He saw the love in her eyes. What made her punish them both this way?

She caught his hand in her own, pulling it away from her cheek, but she didn't drop it as he thought she would. Instead, she clung to it, her fingers so tight they threatened to cut off the flow of blood to his own. "I cannot let you sacrifice your beliefs for me."

"I haven't sacrificed anything," he insisted. "I've merely changed my approach."

Her grip tightened. He couldn't feel his fingers. "I can't do it. As much as I love you, I can't let you do this for me."

"I'm not doing it for you. I'm doing it for us."

She made a moue of disbelief. "And you give up everything while I give up nothing?"

"If that's the way it has to be."

Her expression darkened, turning her eyes to stone. "No."

He stepped closer, so close that he could feel the heat of her through their clothing. She dropped his hand and tried to move away, but he slipped his other hand around her neck, preventing her escape with no more pressure than a gentle caress.

"You once asked me if I was a gambling man," he reminded her, staring deep into the resolution in her eyes. He wanted to shake her. "I think I must be more like my father than I thought, because I would gladly risk everything for you, Lilith. Don't you understand that? I am not going to let you walk away from me again!"

Her hands came up to his chest and shoved hard. He stumbled backward a few steps, more out of surprise than from the strength of her push.

"You don't have a choice!" she cried. "I'm leaving England at the end of the week."

Time stopped. A heartbeat. Then another.

"You're what?" he rasped when he finally recovered his voice.

Her throat worked as she swallowed. Her hands were pressed against her generous bosom. Her face was white, as though she couldn't believe what she'd said, either.

"I'm leaving," she whispered. "I've already booked passage."

No. No, he wouldn't let her do this.

He ground his teeth in an effort to keep from screaming. "To where?"

Lilith shook her head. If she did it again he was going to grab her hair so she couldn't move from the neck up.

"I can't tell you."

"You won't tell me."

"No."

Gabriel had never been a violent man. In fact, he despised physical aggression, but at that moment he truly wanted to throttle Lilith. The realization of just how angry and afraid he was astonished him.

Fisting his hands at his sides, he took a step backward. "I need to get away from you for a little while," he explained through clenched teeth. "But I'm coming back, and when I do, we are going to finish this discussion. This is *not* over."

She looked at him like a mother trying to quiet an unruly child. "Gabriel, my love—"

His control suddenly snapped. "Do not call me your love!" he shouted.

Lilith flinched.

Sucking in a deep breath, Gabriel grasped desperately at some semblance of reason. "You do not get to love me and leave me, Lilith. Either you stay with me or we say good-bye, but I will not spend the rest of my life pining for a woman I cannot have." It was a desperate ploy, this ultimatum, but Gabriel was a desperate man.

Her lower lip quivered, but she said nothing. She merely jerked her head in a parody of a nod.

An aching, hollow feeling in his gut, Gabriel backed up slowly, inching his way toward the door that he knew was directly behind him. With every breath he felt himself beginning to calm somewhat, even though his entire body trembled with emotion.

She had called his bluff. But he wasn't done. Not yet.

"I expect you to come to your senses before I return," he informed her, a measure of warning in his voice.

Her chin came up a notch, her nostrils flaring in annoyance. "And if I don't?"

He pulled open the bedroom door, almost yanking it clean off its hinges.

"I'm not letting you walk away from my love just because you think you don't deserve it," he informed her. "I'll tear every boat in that harbor apart with my bare hands before I let you leave on one. You can decide which way it's going to be."

And then, before she could drive him completely over the edge by continuing to fight him, Gabriel very quietly closed the door and walked away.

When the door shut, Lilith gave in to the weakness in her limbs and sank onto her bed in a boneless heap, but the tears she'd tried so hard to hold at bay while Gabriel was there wouldn't come now that she was alone. She was numb, completely empty.

She'd resisted him this time, but how could she find the strength to fight him when he returned? She didn't want to fight him.

They were both willing to sacrifice everything to be together, and while it was a terribly romantic notion, it wasn't very sensible. Those kinds of decisions led only to heartbreak, but Gabriel refused to see the disaster that loomed in their future.

It was very tempting to throw caution to the wind and enjoy what time they had, but she couldn't face the idea of one day having Gabriel hate her. She wouldn't have their children hear whispers about their mother as Gabriel had heard about his. She didn't want her children to resent her as both she and Gabriel had resented their parents. Gabriel's children deserved happier lives.

Instinctively, her hand went to the curve of her stomach. The thought of carrying Gabriel's child both overjoyed and terrified her. If by some small chance she was pregnant, she could never let him know. He truly wouldn't let her go if she were going to have his baby.

But she was getting ahead of herself. There was no baby and Gabriel wasn't going to stop her from leaving. It was for the best. Someday he'd see that. Maybe someday Lilith herself would see it as well.

Absently, her gaze went to the small leather bag Gabriel

had left behind. He'd dropped it on the floor when he first walked in, like the man of the house returning home to his devoted wife after a long trip.

It seemed forever ago that he'd seduced her into allowing him to live with her. It felt more like days than hours since his fingers had worked her into a frenzy.

So much had changed in just a few hours.

Pushing herself up into a sitting position, she got off the bed and forced her tired legs to carry her across the carpet to where the bag sat.

The leather was soft and pliable under her hands and she easily slid the strap from the heavy gold buckle. She opened the bag and reached inside.

Shaving gear, two shirts and a pair of trousers. Stockings, cravats and small clothes. Obviously he'd planned to have more things sent over in a day or two.

At the bottom of the bag she noticed a tiny velvet pouch at the bottom. She wouldn't have noticed it at all were it not for the gold cord holding it together. Curious, she reached in and pulled the pouch out.

The minute her hand closed around it, she knew what was in it, but some perverse part of her made her open it just to make sure, even though her pounding heart told her not to look.

She untied the cord with trembling fingers and tipped the pouch into her palm. The ring fell out, cool and heavy in her hand.

It was his mother's ring, and it had been his grand-mother's before that. In fact, it had been in the Warren family for generations. Lilith knew this because Gabriel had shown it to her before—after his mother stopped wearing it because she found it "vulgar."

Someday this will be yours, he'd said, slipping the heavy emerald on her finger. *It will mean something to you.* In other words, she would appreciate it more than his mother had.

"*It will mean the world*," she'd answered, not wanting to take it off again.

He'd planned to propose to her.

Her fingers visibly shaking, Lilith dropped the ring back into the pouch and stuffed it deep inside Gabriel's valise. Frantically, she tossed his belongings in on top of it, as though she could somehow make it disappear if she buried it deep enough.

Somehow she managed to buckle the strap again and left the bag where she'd found it. He was bound to know she'd gone through it.

Oh, God. He wanted to marry her.

Well, what else would she have expected from him? He loved her. Gabriel wasn't the type of man to treat love lightly. She should have seen it coming, but she'd been too busy thinking about why they couldn't be together to realize that he would have viewed marriage as the next logical step.

No wonder he'd been so upset by her announcement.

Burying her face in her hands, Lilith wondered how much more of a mess she could make of her life before she finally got it right.

Lifting her head, she sniffed. She smelled smoke.

Then she saw it. A tiny puff coming from under her dressing room door. Alarmed, she ran toward it. Tentatively, she touched the doorknob. It was still cool.

She wrenched the door open and gazed in terror at the scene before her.

Her entire dressing room was in flames.

As soon as she saw the blaze, felt the heat of it on her face, Lilith knew this was no accident. The fire wasn't confined to one area but encompassed the whole of the room, though it had yet to entirely consume anything—not even the dresses hanging on the far wall, or the lace curtains in the window.

The fire had been set, and she'd bet her life Bronson was responsible. Somehow he had managed to sneak in—the same way he'd sneaked in before. Hadn't Gabriel expressed concern over her lack of security? But how had he gotten past the runner watching the house?

A chill settled over Lilith. Perhaps he hadn't gotten past the runner. Perhaps Bronson had killed him.

She certainly couldn't put the fire out by herself, but it had to be stopped before it spread to the rest of the building. As it was, it was already licking the carpet before her.

She turned and ran. She burst into the corridor yelling, "Fire!" at the top of her lungs.

Without thinking, she made for the room where Latimer was resting. There was no reason for anyone else to be up here with them. All the rest of the staff would be downstairs preparing for that night's business. The only other person on the top floor would be the person who had set the fire.

Who might very well prove to be one of the men who'd hurt Latimer in the first place.

Lilith burst into the room, her heart racing.

Latimer sat on the edge of the bed, weaving groggily.

"I smell smoke," he mumbled.

Dear Lord, he was still half asleep! The effects of the laudanum the physician had ordered, no doubt.

Lilith hurried to him, her heart threatening to burst right out of her chest. She was afraid. If the fire didn't get them, there was a very good chance whoever set it was nearby, waiting for them.

"The building is on fire," she told him, lifting one of his massive arms over her shoulders. "We have to get out of here. Can you walk?"

Some of the fog in his head seemed to clear. "If the alternative is staying here and burning to death, then yes, I can."

Muscles straining, back protesting, Lilith helped her large manservant to his very unsteady feet. She could feel the bandages around his ribs beneath the fabric of his nightshirt—fabric that would burn like paper if the fire caught them. It wouldn't take long to eat through her gown, either.

Every step seemed to take an eternity. The smell of smoke grew stronger and Lilith thought she could hear the crackling of flames as they chewed through the walls of her house.

As they struggled down the stairs, most of Latimer's

weight pressing down hard on her left shoulder, she cast a glance toward her bedchamber. Flames danced along the carpet, devouring the soft velvet of her drapes until there was nothing but blackened ash left behind.

Even if they could put out the fire before it spread any further, her room would be ruined.

More smoke met them as they staggered through the doors that led into the main hall of the club. Lilith wasn't quite sure where it was coming from, but she thought it might be the gentleman's side.

The footman George was ordering the panicked servants about. Some he instructed to fetch water. Others he ordered outside to instruct the men who would come to fight the blaze.

"Lady Lilith!" he cried when he saw her. "Someone's set fire to the club!"

Lilith nodded, sagging in relief as he took the brunt of Latimer's weight from her. "They started one upstairs as well."

George's broad, open face clouded. "And in the back rooms also."

A sharp stabbing pain struck Lilith in the chest. Three fires. There was no way they could battle them all. Her club—all of her possessions—were going to be lost.

"We have to get everyone out of the building, George. I want you to take care of the club staff. Where's Mary?"

"I'm here!"

The smoke was beginning to thicken now, but Lilith could still see her friend as she came toward her.

"I was just checking the ladies' side of the club to make certain no one was in there."

"Help George evacuate the club staff," Lilith instructed with a cough. "I'll check the kitchen. I want everyone outside as quickly as possible. If you have to get something, do it quickly. Whoever set these fires knew what they were doing. They're spreading fast."

With that said, they went their separate ways. Lilith raced across the hall and through the door that led down into the kitchen. The kitchen staff was in an uproar, with people running back and forth yelling at one another. Somehow she managed to make them listen. Some ran from the building immediately. Others ran to collect personal belongings. Others glanced around as though they were lost. These were the ones Lilith personally herded up the stairs and out into the back courtyard.

Fortunately, most of the house staff had been in the kitchen or close by, so Lilith didn't have to run all over the house trying to track people down. Instead, she went out into the courtyard and counted heads. All the servants were accounted for. She went around to the front of the building and did the same with the club staff. Everyone was present.

It was at that moment, when she knew that all of her people were safe, that she realized she'd left Gabriel's valise—the one containing his family ring—in her bedroom.

She couldn't just leave it there, not when she knew how much it meant to him. Not when it meant so much to her.

She gazed up at her club. Flames now leapt out of the windows on the gentleman's side. Farther up, she could see the fire destroying the curtains in the room Latimer had been in.

In the distance she could hear the fire bell. Help was on its way, but it would be too late to save her club. Some things might be salvaged, but the best anyone could hope for was to stop the fire before it spread to the neighboring buildings. The club itself was made of stone and therefore the outside wouldn't burn so easily, but one of the buildings beside it was made of wood and would go up like a pile of dry tinder.

It was foolish to go back inside. Madness, even. But she had to.

"What are you doing?" Mary demanded as she started to walk away from where the group was huddled on the side of the street.

"I have to go back in," Lilith told her, focusing on the door rather than on the smoke billowing out the windows. "I forgot something."

Her friend caught her arm in a tight grip. "You cannot! It's too dangerous!"

"The fire hasn't spread that much," Lilith replied, hoping to God she wasn't lying. "I have to go now while I can. I promise to be careful."

She yanked her arm free and ran toward the building, her skirts hiked up around her calves. If she was quick she might still be able to save Gabriel's ring.

The front hall was filled with smoke. Her eyes watering, Lilith pulled her skirts up so that the hem covered her nose and mouth. There was no one in the building to see her shift, and even if there was, she wouldn't care if it meant the difference between being able to breathe and not.

The smoke made it difficult to see, but Lilith knew the layout of the club by heart. She found the door leading upstairs with no problem. The smoke wasn't quite so bad in this corridor and she could see clearly as she raced up the steps.

At the top of the stairs the smoke thickened again and the temperature rocketed several degrees. The fire was spreading fast.

Her bedroom was almost entirely in flames, but luckily, most of it was confined to the outer perimeter, where there were more things to burn. Still, the flames reached for her as she went inside, her eyes watering from the smoke. A spark landed on her right sleeve, instantly eating through the thin fabric and burning her arm. Lilith cried out, swatting at the spot with her free hand.

Smoke filled the room from her waist up, so she had a good view of the floor. Dropping to her knees, she found Gabriel's valise exactly where she'd left it. She wasted no time in digging out the velvet pouch that contained the ring. At least she would be able to return it to him. It never occurred to her to take the whole bag. The ring was all that mattered.

Wrapping the gold cord of the pouch around her wrist and clinging to it as if it were some kind of lifeline, Lilith fled from the room, shaking the flames from her skirts and slapping at the sparks that singed her hair. Her eyes and lungs burned. Her vision was blurry, and because of this she did not see the man coming up the stairs toward her until she was almost directly on top of him.

The breath rushed from her tortured lungs and her heart froze solid in her chest.

It was Bronson.

He smiled. "I almost thought I'd have to make my escape without seeing you," he shouted above the roar of the fire.

Before Lilith could even think of a reply, Bronson drew back his thick-knuckled fist and let it fly.

Pain exploded in her jaw, snapping her head back onto her shoulders and knocking her skirts from her hand. Her knees buckled beneath her as she fell forward.

Bronson didn't even try to help her. He stepped neatly out of the way, leaving nothing in front of her but the great smoky void of the stairs.

She hit them with a bone-jarring crash that made her scream into the hot, acrid haze.

Then there was nothing.

Chapter 18

Gabriel went only as far as White's on St. James's Street. Two glasses of bourbon, sipped at a leisurely pace, helped to calm his nerves and put things in perspective.

Lilith had shocked him with her announcement that she was leaving him, and he'd reacted badly. He'd gotten angry, rather than trying to explain why he had changed his mind about gaming clubs. She thought it was all for her, and although that was a big part of it, it wasn't the whole truth. Once he told her that, he was certain he could talk her out of leaving at the end of the week.

And if that didn't work, he wasn't above abduction. He was not losing her again.

He'd just polished off the second bourbon when a young dandy burst into the club, his cheeks flush with excitement.

"Mallory's is on fire!" he cried.

Gabriel felt his words like a knife in the gut. Mallory's on fire?

All eyes turned toward him and he knew he hadn't been

mistaken in his hearing. His chair fell behind him as he leapt to his feet. He ran to the door, not caring that people were watching. He didn't care that some even rose to follow. All he cared about was getting to Lilith and making certain she was all right.

He didn't bother with a carriage once he was outside. At this time of night, traffic would be thickening and King Street wasn't that far away.

He ran faster than he'd ever run in his life, arms and legs pumping furiously. His lungs filled to bursting. His heart drummed in his throat. He shouldn't have left her.

It never occurred to him that the fire might have been an accident. It was too coincidental that not even two days after her servant was attacked, Lilith's club would burn, especially since they'd made their trip to Bow Street earlier. Obviously Bronson had had them followed, and this was his way of re-taliating.

If Lilith was hurt, Bronson was going to hang for it. Gabriel would see to that personally.

He smelled the smoke just as he reached the King Street entrance. His heart lurched as the scent filled his nostrils and he pushed his legs to move faster.

A crowd had gathered outside the club. He recognized many of the faces. Some were club staff. Some were cus-tomers. Some were just there to watch the flames shoot out the upstairs windows.

Gabriel stopped dead, and watched in horror while fire scorched the stone surrounding several of the club's win-dows. An ache that had nothing to do with the exertion he'd put himself through pushed heavily at his chest.

Everything Lilith held dear was being reduced to ash.

Strong fingers closed around his arm. He whipped around, hoping to find Lilith beside him. His heart fell a little when he saw it was only Mary.

A very distressed Mary.

"Where is Lilith?" he demanded before the woman even had time to speak.

Her eyes wide with fear, Mary pointed at the club. "She went back inside. She said she had to find something."

Sweet Jesus. All the blood in his body rushed to his knees, causing his head to bristle with hot dizziness. What in the name of all that was holy could Lilith have thought so important to go back in after?

Absently, he realized that he'd left his valise there. The family betrothal ring was in it. While it was something he hated to lose, it wasn't something he'd risk his life for.

Lilith was a different story.

"How long has she been inside?"

Mary shook her head, so obviously distressed she couldn't think straight. "I'm not certain. It seems an awfully long time."

Gabriel's blood turned to ice. "Was she going to her room?"

Mary nodded. "I believe so."

Casting a brief glance at the inferno before him, Gabriel set his jaw in determination.

He would not lose her again. He couldn't bear it.

Taking his handkerchief from his pocket, Gabriel wet it in one of the buckets being used to fight the blaze. Around him, men formed lines to pass the buckets to those closest to the building. Sweat ran down their foreheads from heat and exertion.

Gabriel kept his gaze focused directly ahead. The wet linen over his mouth and nose would help him breathe and keep the smoke from scorching his lungs, but not for long. He had to find Lilith and find her quickly. He had no idea how long she'd been in there or how much smoke she'd inhaled. She could be—

No. He refused to think of that. Lilith was going to live long enough for him to strangle her for being foolish enough to run back into a burning building!

He brushed past the men near the entrance. One tried to stop him, but he shrugged him off without missing a stride.

The entrance hall was little more than a cloud of smoke. Dimly he could make out the faint outline of the statue of

Venus in the middle. He veered left, groping the wall for the door when he reached the back wall.

He found the knob and turned it, pushing the door open.

Blinking against the stinging in his eyes, he tried to peer through the hot haze as he stumbled down the corridor.

He dropped to his hands and knees when he reached the stairs. There was less smoke near the floor, making visibility and breathing easier.

He hadn't even crawled halfway up the stairwell when he found her. Sprawled facedown, her head pointed toward the bottom step, she was unconscious.

"Lilith!" he cried, gingerly scooping her up into his arms. His heart slammed against his ribs and his throat burned, not from the smoke, but from barely restrained tears.

There was blood on her mouth and a huge welt on her cheek and jaw, but she was breathing, and for that Gabriel thanked God.

He removed the handkerchief from around his face and placed it over her mouth and nose, tying a quick knot to keep it in place. Carefully, he maneuvered down the few stairs below him and, with Lilith cradled high against his chest, plowed through the smoke-filled corridor as quickly as he could.

His lungs felt as though they were on fire by the time he made it out into the cool night air. His arms ached under Lilith's limp form and his eyes watered so badly he couldn't see. He could feel himself sagging, but he struggled to remain upright.

Someone tried to take Lilith from him.

"No!" he shouted, clinging to her even as he blinked furiously in an attempt to clear his vision.

And then Mary was beside him. He could just make out the outline of her through the water in his eyes.

"It is all right, Lord Angelwood," she told him. "George just wants to help you carry her."

Gabriel wasn't giving Lilith to anyone. "Get a carriage," he instructed the fuzzy George. "I'm taking her home. And send for a doctor."

The shadowy figure bowed. "Yes, my lord."

Gabriel's knees slowly folded beneath him, as though the clearing of his vision was sapping the strength from the rest of his body. No one came forth to try to assist him. After his outburst at George, they all knew better. So most of them just stood and stared as the Earl of Angelwood slowly sank to his knees on the cobblestones, holding Lilith tight against his chest while Mallory's burned as brightly as the last vestiges of the summer sun sinking in the west.

As he regained his sight, Gabriel's smarting gaze traveled the length of the woman he loved, searching for further injuries. He saw none. Her hair and gown were scorched in places, but he saw no blood, no cause for alarm other than the traces of moist crimson around her mouth, which he could see was from a split in her lower lip.

And then he saw what it was she had gone into the fire to save. Wrapped around her wrist was the velvet pouch containing his family ring. Somehow she had known he'd brought it and she had risked her life to go in after it.

Heedless of his audience, Gabriel buried his face in the warm curve of Lilith's neck. She smelled of smoke and oranges. Faintly, he felt the rise and fall of her chest against his, felt the soft thud of her pulse against his lips. He could have lost her that night. It could have happened so easily—would have happened if he hadn't returned. And all because she had to rescue a ring that had been in his family for generations. A ring he'd been waiting ten years to put on her finger.

Shoulders heaving, Gabriel gave in to the tumult of emotions raging inside him. And with his arms wrapped tightly around the woman he loved, the woman he was never again letting go, the Earl of Angelwood wept openly for all of London to see.

Gabriel sat by Lilith's bedside, reeking of smoke, stroking her brow with a damp cloth and holding her limp hand until the physician arrived. He had sent for Randall Croft, his own physician. Croft was one of the best in the city.

"What happened?" the physician asked once Gabriel had greeted him.

"A fire at her club," Gabriel explained, his heart heavy. "She went back inside."

Croft shot him a surprised glance. A small man with blond hair and shrewd green eyes, Croft was blunt, precise and didn't suffer fools.

"I hope she had a good reason to do something so asinine."

Gabriel swallowed hard against the lump in his throat. "She seemed to think she had."

Again the physician shot him a curious glance. "Where did you find her?"

"On the stairs. I think she must have stumbled in the smoke."

Croft raked his gaze over Lilith's bruised face. "Or perhaps not. Who hit her?"

Gabriel stilled. "I beg your pardon?"

Opening his black leather satchel, Croft jerked his head in Lilith's direction. "Unless I'm mistaken, that mark on her face is the result of having been punched. Judging from the size of it, I'd say a fairly large man was the culprit."

The physician's tone was bland, without a hint of accusation, yet Gabriel couldn't help but feel as though he expected him to know the answer.

The only person he could think of was Bronson. Had he actually set the fire at Mallory's? Was he responsible for Lilith's fall?

Forget letting the bastard hang. Gabriel was going to kill him himself.

"I don't know," he replied tightly. It wasn't a complete lie. "I wasn't there. If I had been, she would not have been hurt."

Croft gazed at him with an expression Gabriel couldn't read. "What is the nature of your relationship with Miss Mallory?"

"Lady Lilith." Gabriel corrected him without a thought. "She's a lady. Why do you ask?"

Crossing to the washbasin on a stand near the door, Croft washed his hands and dried them on a small towel that he left draped across the top of the stand. "I need to know if there's any chance that she might be with child. If she is, the fall down the stairs might have injured it."

Gabriel opened his mouth, but nothing came out right away. It was as if he were lost, tossed from his own world into a strange one where nothing was as it should be.

He stared at Lilith's still form. "She could be."

"I will do an examination just to be safe." Coming up beside him, Croft spared him a brief glance. "I have to ask you to leave, my lord."

No. He couldn't leave her. Last time he'd left her, she could have died. He wasn't leaving her again.

"I can't," he replied. "I can't leave her."

Croft's expression turned sympathetic, something that surprised Gabriel. "I know you don't want to, my lord. But I don't think you would be comfortable watching. I understand how you feel, but it's necessary. It is my job to make a complete evaluation of Lady Lilith's health. It's your job to wait out in the corridor and pace."

Gabriel stared at the doctor, searching for any sign of falsehood in his look or demeanor. He found none.

Reluctantly, Gabriel nodded. "I'll be just outside," he conceded gruffly.

Croft smiled. "Of course you will. I will let you know when I am finished."

And with that, Gabriel found himself expelled from his own chamber. Where else would he have put Lilith? He wanted her close so he could watch over her. He'd let Bronson get to her once. He wasn't going to make the same mistake again.

As the door closed behind him, Gabriel was alone in the empty corridor. Mary was obviously still downstairs with her reverend friend, who'd come to call as soon as he "heard the news."

He took Croft's advice and started to pace. It made him

feel as if he were actually doing something instead of waiting helplessly.

It was his fault that Lilith was hurt. His fault that her club was destroyed. From what he knew, the fire brigade was still battling the blaze. It was under control, but much of Lilith's private apartments and the gentlemen's side of the club had been completely gutted.

But possessions were trivial when compared with what could have been lost.

He shouldn't have made her talk to Bow Street. Or he should have arranged for a plainclothes officer to come to them. He'd known there was a chance Bronson might have them followed, but he'd underestimated the man—his first big mistake.

His second had been leaving her alone. Regardless of how hurt and angry he'd been, he should have realized she would be in danger. He hadn't thought of it. He'd been thinking only of himself.

How could he ever earn her forgiveness? First he'd tossed her aside to keep word of his father's suicide from leaking out, too ashamed to let the world know how weak his father had truly been. Then he'd tried to use her as an example in his senseless quest to abolish gaming. And then he had left her alone so that a madman could make an attempt on her life and destroy her most precious possession.

She didn't think she deserved him. He choked on a bitter laugh. Good God, it was he who didn't deserve her.

He swore, right then and there, that if she could even bear to look at him when she woke up, he would spend the rest of his life making it up to her. If she'd let him.

Duncan Reed would be by once Lilith regained consciousness—of that Gabriel was certain. He would want to know if she actually saw Bronson in the club. If Croft was right and Lilith had been hit, then she most likely had seen the bastard who did it. Even if it wasn't Bronson himself, it was certainly one of his men. Gabriel was going to see that Bronson paid for it, one way or another.

"Gabe."

At the sound of his name, he turned. Coming up the stairs were Julian, Brave and Rachel, each wearing almost identical expressions of concern.

The joy and warmth he felt at the sight of his friends could not be measured. It filled him to the very brim. Immediately he felt strengthened by their presence.

"We came as soon as we heard," Rachel said. Being a woman, she walked right over to him, taking both of his hands in hers and offering him the physical comfort his male friends wouldn't have known he needed.

He didn't bother to ask how they'd heard. No doubt the news had spread through the city as quickly as the fire had spread through Mallory's.

"Thank you," Gabriel told her, squeezing her fingers as he gazed from Brave to Julian. "Thank you all for coming."

"As if we could possibly leave you alone at a time like this," Brave murmured.

Gabriel smiled, releasing Rachel's hands. These were his friends, his family. While no blood bound them, he loved them as dearly as if Brave and Julian were his brothers, and Rachel was becoming more like a sister the better he came to know her.

Julian spoke, asking the question the other two were afraid to ask. "How is she?"

"I'm not sure," Gabriel replied. "Her physician is with her now. I don't think there were any serious injuries."

Except that my child might have taken hold inside her and now it might be lost to us.

Rachel breathed a sigh of relief and pressed a hand against her breast. "Thank God."

The four of them stood together, the three friends forming a tight semicircle around Gabriel. They asked about the fire, and Gabriel told them. Against his better judgment, he left nothing out. He told them everything, even that he'd stormed out after Lilith said she was leaving, and that she went back inside for the ring.

Frowning in concern, Rachel touched his arm. "Are you all right? Do you want me to talk to her, Gabriel?"

Despite the heaviness in his chest, Gabriel smiled. "I am fine, thank you, Rachel. I'm not sure if I will need your services. It depends on whether she's even speaking to me."

Rachel's frown deepened into a bewildered scowl. "Why wouldn't she speak to you?"

Brave cast a quick glance at his wife before returning his gaze to Gabriel. "He feels responsible, Rach. He thinks Lilith's going to blame him as well."

He shouldn't have been so surprised that Brave saw right through him. After all, his friend had put himself through his own share of self-blame.

Rachel swatted Gabriel on the arm. "Now, that's just silly."

He opened his mouth to explain why he felt as he did, but just then the door to his bedroom opened and out walked Croft.

"How is she?" Gabriel demanded, stepping forward with his friends following behind.

Croft smiled. "She is fine. She breathed in a little too much smoke, so she'll have a cough and a raspy voice for a few days—nothing a little honey won't cure. Her jaw will be sore from her injury and she'll ache from the fall down the stairs, but she suffered no serious injuries."

"And the other?" Gabriel asked hesitantly, hoping the physician caught his meaning.

Croft's expression softened. "There was nothing to be concerned about."

Relief that Lilith hadn't lost their child poured through Gabriel, followed by the keenest disappointment he'd ever felt in his life. Lilith wasn't pregnant at all.

Rachel wrapped her arms around him, as though by some kind of woman's intuition she knew exactly what Gabriel and Croft were talking about. Gabriel hugged her back, wondering why it was possible to mourn something that was never there to begin with.

* * *

Lilith's throat felt as though a chimney sweep had stuck one of his stiff-bristled brushes down it—several times.

Where was she? She doubted very much that she was in Heaven. She didn't think people got sore throats in Heaven. Perhaps she was in Hell.

Did Hell smell like sun-dried linen and Gabriel? If so, she'd gladly spend the rest of eternity among the other damned.

She opened her eyes. They hurt a bit—no doubt from the fire—but as she blinked several times to moisten them, she realized that she wasn't in Hell. She was in a bedroom, a man's bedroom—Gabriel's.

She gazed around her, taking in the dark oak furniture and the heavy, dark blue velvet hangings. The room was quietly masculine and strangely calming. Much like Gabe himself.

She turned her head to her right. There was an angel sitting in a chair beside the bed, watching her.

"Hello," she croaked. God, she sounded awful!

Gabriel didn't smile, but he still managed to look very happy to see her. The relief on his face made Lilith wonder just how close to death she'd been.

She tried to smile, but the effort sent a stabbing pain through her jaw and stung her lip. Gingerly, she raised her hand to her face. Her cheek was swollen.

"What happened after you went back inside for the ring?"

Oh, dear. He knew.

"I stumbled upon Bronson," she replied, trying to move her jaw as little as possible. "And his fist."

In the blink of an eye, Gabriel's expression changed from calm relief to murderous darkness.

"I knew he was to blame for this." Just as suddenly, his expression softened once again when his gaze fell upon her.

"I'm so sorry, Lil," he whispered.

Lilith frowned. Either she had suffered minor memory loss or he wasn't making sense.

"Sorry for what?"

"For leaving the way I did. I should have stayed. This never would have happened had I stayed."

She would have laughed—or perhaps cried—if her face didn't hurt so badly. "Gabriel, you could never have known Bronson was going to set fire to the club."

His jaw tightened. "Perhaps not, but if I hadn't stormed out, there wouldn't have been any reason for you to go back for that foolish ring. I would have gotten it myself."

"It is not a foolish ring!" Oh, that hurt. "It has been in your family forever," she rasped, taking pity on her poor throat.

Gabriel took a jar from the bedside table and removed the lid. Inside was a thick golden goo, which he dipped a spoon into before offering it to her.

Lilith sniffed. It was honey.

"It is for your throat," he explained.

Opening her mouth, Lilith allowed him to slip the spoon inside. She licked it clean and swallowed. The sweet, thick honey was cool and soothing on her ravaged throat.

"Thank you," she whispered, the pain eased somewhat.

"Thank Mr. Croft. He's the one who prescribed it."

"You were right, you know," she said instead, changing the subject.

He frowned. "About what?"

"Gambling. It's no good." Reaching out, she took one of his hands in hers. He was warm and strong. "I am done with it. It has brought me nothing but trouble."

From the expression on his face, one would think she'd just informed him she'd decided to enter a convent.

"But you loved your club."

His use of the past tense was a band around Lilith's heart. Her club was gone. "Yes, I did, but I am tired of the whispers, Gabe. I'm tired of the threats from men like Bronson. I'm tired of having to pretend I am something I'm not. I loved Mallory's, but it ended up being no better for me than I am for you."

His fingers tightened around hers. "So you haven't changed your mind about us?"

"No," she whispered, removing her hand from his. "I haven't changed my mind. I'm still planning to leave."

A multitude of emotions played across his face and she made herself watch, because she deserved to know how badly she was hurting him. It hurt her, too, but she loved him too much to drag him down to her level.

And she loved him too much to allow him to be a target for Bronson. Surely this latest attack was in retaliation for their visit to Bow Street. If he'd overturn Gabriel's carriage and set fire to Lilith's club, the man would almost certainly risk revenge against a peer of the realm. He'd be extra careful that no action could be traced back to him.

No, it was time for her to stop fighting and just let Bronson succeed. It was safer that way.

"I am not letting you go."

Lilith sighed. How many times was Gabriel going to say that before he finally stopped? Part of her hoped it was soon, because it tore her apart every time he made his fierce declaration.

"Please, Gabe. I don't want to argue about this now. I'm so tired."

His expression turned to one of concern. "Do you want me to get you anything? A glass of water? More honey?"

She shook her head. "No. I'm fine. Would you . . . that is, do you think you might read to me for a little while?"

She hadn't been read to since she had a nanny, and she felt childish for asking him to do so now, but she wanted something other than the image of her club burning or Bronson drawing back his fist to send her off to sleep. She wanted Gabriel to be there with her when the darkness came. He'd protect her from the demons.

If he was surprised by her request, he didn't show it. In fact, he looked oddly pleased. He picked up a book that was already on the table beside the bed.

"It is *Tom Jones*. Will that do?"

Smiling, Lilith tugged the coverlet up under her chin, even though she wasn't cold. "That is one of my favorites."

Love shone clear and bright in the pale gray of his eyes. "I know."

He opened the book to Chapter 1 and began to read, the low, rich timbre of his voice filling the room.

Closing her eyes, Lilith allowed his voice to carry her away, to a time when women wore skirts almost as wide as they were tall. She lost herself in Tom and his troubles, and when she was too tired to picture the scenes in her head, she settled for just listening to the gentle cadence of Gabriel's voice.

As sleep washed softly over her, the world seemed a peaceful place, where no one would ever want to hurt her and where she and Gabriel were the only people who existed.

Lord, how she wished it were true.

Chapter 19

"Is it true?"

Seated at the breakfast table, Gabriel tried to ignore the pounding in his chest at the sound of her voice—even if she did sound angry and raspy—and raised his head.

Lilith stood in the doorway, clad in a nightgown and wrapper that Gabriel had purchased from a local dressmaker. Her hair—a fiery river of silk—cascaded over her shoulders and down her back. Her feet were bare and pink beneath the white ruffled hem.

"Is what true?" he asked innocently as he lowered his fork. He had a pretty good idea of what had her so riled up, but he wasn't going to admit to anything unless he absolutely had to.

"Mary told me that you are planning to talk to Bronson."

Actually, talking was the last thing Gabriel had in mind. A few threats, warnings and perhaps some well-placed kicks, but not much chatter. So far, Bow Street had yet to take action. Gabriel didn't know what they were waiting for, but he was tired of waiting.

"Mary had no business telling you any such thing," he responded sourly. And just how the hell had she found out, anyway? Was the woman listening at keyholes now? Reading his correspondence? She'd been at the house for only two days, and already Lilith's companion was making his business her own.

Lilith folded her arms across her magnificent chest. "So it *is* true."

Gabriel mimicked her movements, leaning back in his chair in an almost defiant manner. "What if it is?"

She frowned. "I do not want you to go."

His poached eggs forgotten, Gabriel kept his expression carefully bland. "Why not?"

Lilith paused, as though she wasn't sure how to respond. Her hands went to her hips. "Because it's a damned fool thing to do. People will talk."

She was lying. He had no doubt those things concerned her, but that wasn't the real reason she didn't want him to go, and they both knew it.

Gabriel shook his head. "Not good enough. You coming down here in your nightgown was a damned fool thing to do. If the servants see you, it'll be all over town by this afternoon. You might have well spread yourself out on the table and let me ravish you."

First of all, telling Lilith that something she did was foolish was not a terribly good idea if one wanted to get into her good graces—Gabriel could see that from the flash of anger in her eyes.

Second, planting the image of him taking her on the dining room table in either of their minds was not conducive to physical comfort. Lilith's gaze went to the smooth, polished oak surface of the long, sturdy table. A faint blush brightened her cheeks, quickening Gabriel's pulse and his breathing. Yes, he could just imagine the kind of buffet that delicious body would make.

What if he did make love to her there on the table when anyone could walk in? The scandal would be incredible. She'd have to marry him then.

No. Lilith didn't *have* to do anything except leave him. She'd made that perfectly clear.

"As much as I'd love to sit here all morning, admiring the thrust of your nipples through that wonderfully flimsy fabric," he began, growing hard as he spoke, "I do have business to attend to this morning, the least of which is a visit to Mr. Bronson's establishment. Perhaps you should just be honest as to why you don't want me to go, Lilith."

She flushed the hot pink of a flustered redhead. "You *know* why I don't want you to go."

His gaze locked with hers. "Tell me."

"Because he will hurt you and I could not bear it."

Could she see his heart in his eyes? The pulse pounding in his throat? "You've hurt me more than Bronson ever could. You seem to bear that rather well."

She went white—as white as her gown. "That's not fair."

Gabriel smiled. It was brittle. "But true. However noble you may think your actions, I find them cowardly."

She darted toward him, hair streaming out behind her, gown clinging to her curves.

"I'm leaving because I love you!"

Gabriel's chair scraped the floor as he leapt out of it. "Horse shit!" he cried, slamming both palms down onto the table. "You are leaving because you are afraid to love me."

She glared at him, but there was a flicker of uncertainty in her eyes. "Do not be absurd."

"Oh?" He arched a brow. "Letting people say the worst about you is a lot easier than trying to prove them wrong, isn't it, Lilith? You don't have to prove yourself when people have no expectations."

Eyes wide, she took a step back. "You do not know what you're talking about."

Gabriel straightened. "I know that the girl I fell in love with would not back down from such a task. She'd show all those who doubted her just what she was made of, and hang anyone who didn't like it. She wouldn't run away from me just because she was scared of what people might say."

Her chin came up as her fingers curled around the back of a chair. "I was naive and foolish. I'm not that girl anymore."

He didn't bother to try to hide his disappointment. "So I'm finding out."

She cringed as though he'd raised his hand to her. "Better you find out now than after a wedding."

Avoiding her gaze, Gabriel pushed his chair into the table. His guts knotted. "Then we have nothing left to discuss. Please excuse me. I'm late for an appointment."

She called out as he walked away, but he didn't turn around. No matter what he did, she countered it. Why? Why did she fight him when they both wanted to be together? Why was she so afraid to be with him? Did she think he couldn't handle a little gossip? She couldn't possibly see herself as *that* much of a pariah, could she?

And all this nonsense about him sacrificing his principles and beliefs. What fustian!

One thing was for certain. It was going to take more than words to convince her. Rachel had been right about that. Well, if it was action she needed, action she would get. As soon as Gabriel finished with Bronson, he was going to call upon Rachel and solicit her help in showing Lilith just how far he would go to keep her with him.

Robinson met him in the front hall with his cane, hat and gloves.

"Might I offer you some advice, my lord?"

Against his better judgment, Gabriel consented. "What is it?" He yanked on his gloves.

"If Bronson starts to fight dirty, grab him by the twig and berries and *twist*." The stocky butler illustrated with elaborate hand gestures. "Once he's on his knees, a swift kick to the head will put him out like a little baby."

Gabriel stared at Robinson, not quite sure if the man was serious or not. "I shall keep that in mind, thank you."

Marching out into the warm, bright morning, Gabriel wondered if perhaps *he* wasn't the one who needed the swift kick to the head. He was, after all, the one who was marching off alone to confront a notorious, dangerous criminal.

His carriage was waiting as he sauntered down the steps. He left the crest on the door so everyone who saw it would know that Lord Angelwood had paid a visit on Mr. Samuel Bronson. He wanted to set tongues wagging. He wanted them all to know what lengths he would go to in order to protect Lilith.

Gravel crunched beneath his feet, a sharp grating punctuating the distant din of London traffic. Mayfair rose late during the Season, but the sounds of London never ceased.

He nodded to the footman, who bade him good morning and opened the carriage door for him.

Gabriel stepped up into the carriage. A bark of laughter escaped him when he saw what, or rather *who*, waited for him there.

"We are not letting you do this on your own."

Settling into his usual spot as the footman closed the door, Gabriel gazed at Brave and Julian with an expression that was a mixture of amusement and annoyance.

"I've no wish to involve either of you in this." He rapped on the roof with his cane for the driver to leave. Despite the fact that he wanted to pitch them both out into the street, he knew it was a much safer trip with his friends accompanying him.

Sprawled on the opposite seat, Brave snorted. "We are your friends," he stated matter-of-factly. "We are already involved."

"And we are not going to allow you to face a conscience-lacking former pugilist by yourself," Julian added. "Think about what you are doing, man!"

Gabriel shrugged. "I did think. The fact that Bronson is dangerous is exactly why I did not ask the two of you to come with me. But now that you are here, I am thankful for it."

Brave and Julian exchanged startled glances. Apparently they had expected Gabriel to offer more resistance.

"There's no telling how many of his ruffians Bronson will

have with him," Gabriel said, offering an explanation for his capitulation. "I feel much better having both of you—especially you, Jules—with me."

Of the three of them, Julian was the better at fisticuffs. Rarely had either Brave or Gabriel bested him at sparring. Tall, leaner and with longer limbs, the mild-mannered Julian moved with catlike speed and efficiency. When they had been at school, more than one lad had tried to prove himself by putting Julian in the dirt. No one had ever succeeded. These days, however, Julian despised fighting for any reason other than sport, but Gabriel knew he would come to his aid if necessary.

While Julian was good with his fists, Brave was the better with pistols and Gabriel with swords. It was for that reason— and because he knew he could not hold his own against a man like Bronson, who would probably have thugs backing him up—that Gabriel had planned to take a blade concealed in a cane with him to Hazards.

"Does Lilith know you are doing this?" Brave asked, straightening.

Gabriel's heart thumped hard against his ribs. "Yes."

Almost identical expressions of sympathy faced him.

"She was against the idea?" Julian asked.

Gabriel grimaced. "You could say that. I would prefer not to talk about it at this moment if you don't mind."

His friends nodded. "Of course," Brave said.

They pulled up in front of Hazards not long after. Someone finally answered the door after much pounding and kicking. It was a middle-aged man, fairly nondescript, with light brown hair and equally plain eyes.

"Here, now!" the man cried. "What do you think you're about?"

Gabriel brushed past him, followed by Brave and Julian. The servant gasped and moved to stop them.

"I am Angelwood," Gabriel told him in his most imperious voice. "These are Braven and Wolfram. We wish to see your master immediately."

At the sound of Gabriel's title, the man lost a little color.

Either he was involved in Bronson's nefarious activities or he had overheard some of them.

"Where is he?" Gabriel's query came out low, like a growl. Hot, animalistic rage simmered low in his belly.

The man seemed to shrink under the weight of Gabriel's stare. "H-he's in the cl-club."

Turning in the direction the trembling finger pointed, Gabriel and his friends walked down a long, oak-paneled corridor to a set of double doors at the end. They were open.

Gabriel had never set foot inside Hazards before. It was opulent, darkly masculine and lacking in the refinement of Mallory's. Part of that could be attributed to the fact that Lilith was a woman of impeccable taste. The rest of it could be attributed to birth. Lilith had been born into the aristocracy and therefore had had refinement taught to her at an early age. Bronson was new money—and by nature vulgar.

They met a gentleman on his way out. Judging from the scowl on his face, he did not look happy.

"Can I help you gents?" he asked, his tone a tad friendlier than his expression.

"We are looking for Mr. Bronson," Gabriel replied.

The man nodded toward the far end of the large gaming room. "Bastard's in his office. Take the last door on the left and follow it all the way down to the end. Door's on the right."

With that, he brushed past them and stomped down the corridor.

"Mr. Bronson doesn't seem to be terribly well liked," Julian observed dryly as they continued onward.

They found Bronson's office where the frowning man had said they would. Gabriel opened the door without knocking.

A large, rugged man raised his head at the intrusion. He was not what Gabriel had expected. He'd expected a thick-necked, big-nosed, low-browed kind of fellow who looked as though he'd taken one too many blows to the face. Bronson's nose had the slight lean of one that had been broken, but other than that, he looked more like a gentleman than a fighter.

If at all possible, Gabriel's hatred for him grew.

Bronson didn't looked surprised to see him. In fact, he appeared amused. "Lord Angelwood, I presume?"

Gabriel nodded. "Since you know who I am, I trust we can skip the pleasantries."

Bronson chuckled and slumped back in his chair. "Straight to the point. I like that. I assume you've come to accuse me of having something to do with that awful accident at Mallory's?"

Grinding his teeth, Gabriel gripped his cane tighter. *Awful accident?* Bloody bastard knew perfectly well it hadn't been accidental at all.

"I haven't come to accuse you of anything," he replied. "I'll leave that to Bow Street. I have come to advise you that it would be in your best interest to leave town."

Bronson actually laughed, his pale eyes twinkling. If Gabriel didn't know just what a monster he was, he might consider him charming.

"Bow Street has nothing on me, Lord Angelwood, and I am willing to wager no one saw me at Mallory's."

Gabriel held his gaze. "Lady Lilith did."

Bronson didn't even blink. "And who do you think will take her word over mine? I'm a respectable businessman. I have a lot of friends in high places. She's just a notch or two above a common whore."

Somehow Gabriel managed to keep from yanking the sword from his cane and ramming it through Bronson's finely muscled neck.

"I believe her," was his low reply.

More laughter. It was a rough sound. Bronson's veneer was slipping. He was showing his roots as he became more and more confident in himself.

"No offense, Angelwood, but everyone knows how far up her skirts you are. You're buried so far in her cream pot you stink of twat. You'd believe anything she tells you so long as you got a whiff of that salty goodness."

Practically shaking with rage, Gabriel stared deep into

Bronson's mocking gaze. "Listen to me, you two-bit knuckle-biter. You may think you are better than Lilith Mallory, but she was born a lady. You were born in the dirt, and it doesn't matter how much money you make—you'll always be in the dirt because you haven't what it takes to be a gentleman."

He had the satisfaction of watching Bronson's face darken.

"Now, I am telling you that it will go much better for you if you leave town."

Bronson's mouth curved into a sneer. "And I'm telling you that you have nothing on me."

This time it was Gabriel who chuckled. "I don't need to have anything 'on you,' as you put it. I am a peer of the realm." He walked around Bronson's desk until he stood beside his adversary's chair. Pushing some papers away, he leaned his hip against the edge of the desk.

"How do you think my friends and acquaintances will re-act when they learn of what you have done to the future Countess Angelwood?" At Bronson's stunned glance, he con-tinued. "You never thought of that, did you? The aristocracy won't take well to you having tried to kill one of their own, Bronson. Especially a woman. I know these people. I have in-fluence over them. You may have some of them in your debt, but they cannot go out into society without facing me sooner or later. Who do you think they will stand beside then?"

A muscle ticked in Bronson's broad jaw. "You can't do this to me. You don't have that kind of power."

Gabriel smiled. They both knew that he did. "Care to find out? Remember, I was in that carriage you had your men run off the road. I believe attempted murder on a peer of the realm is a hanging offense. Is it not, my friends?" He cast a glance over his shoulder.

Brave and Julian agreed.

"What do you say, Bronson? Do you leave willingly and start over somewhere new? Or do you take your chances in London and risk ruin—or worse?"

Bronson's expression was as hard as granite. "You've made your point, Angelwood. Now get the hell out of my club."

Gabriel turned and looked at Brave. He nodded at the door. Brave crossed the carpet and flipped the lock into place.

Turning back to Bronson, Gabriel tossed his cane onto a nearby sofa and smiled. He heard his friends' footsteps as they came up to stand behind him.

"I don't think so, Mr. Bronson. There is still a matter of that nasty bruise you left on Lady Lilith's cheek."

For the first time since their arrival, Bronson lost some of his bravado. "I don't know what you're talking about."

Gabriel drew back his fist. "Then allow me to illustrate."

Gabriel did not come to see her immediately after his "visit" with Bronson. Nor did he appear that evening, or the following morning, or that evening, either. He left Lilith alone, which she thought she wanted.

As the pain in her face receded to a dull ache and her throat healed, it seemed Lilith's soul began to suffer all the more. The dreams about Bronson and the fire continued, only now Gabriel didn't arrive to save her. He let her burn, and Lilith knew she had no one but herself to blame.

She sat in his bed—the bed that no longer smelled like him—propped up against enough pillows to support a pasha and his harem, and debated whether or not it was worthwhile to even get up and wash.

There seemed to be very little point when no one but Mary came to see her.

What was she doing? This was not like her at all. Why, normally she would be up, dressed and working on the day's business for the club. And even if there no longer was a club, she still had plenty of things she could be taking care of.

Such as her plans to leave London. She would have to go through her belongings salvaged from the fire and determine what could be kept and what should be tossed away. When she thought of how many memories, how many cherished possessions, had been lost, tears burned the backs of her eyes.

But she was alive, and that was what she had to focus on. Furniture and clothing could be replaced, and although paintings and journals and keepsakes could not be, neither could her life, and she was infinitely more glad to have it. Besides, Mary told her that most of the things stored in the attic remained untouched, and that was where all of Aunt Imogen's belongings were. At least she would still have those.

But she would need to buy a whole new wardrobe. Gabriel had purchased a few gowns and underclothes for her, but not enough to do, and they certainly hadn't been made expressly for her, as the tight fit through the bosom emphasized.

One thing was for certain. With all that she had to do, she would not be ready to leave London by the end of the week or even the end of the month. Lord only knew how long it would take to set her affairs to right. And she couldn't remain at Angelwood while she attended to them. She'd disrupted Gabriel's routine enough as it was, and stolen his bed. And if she had to live under the same roof much longer without touching him, she would go absolutely mad.

She was not a strong woman, not when it came to her heart.

She had just tossed back the covers and was about to swing her legs over the side of the high-tester bed when a knock sounded at the door.

Was it Gabriel?

Hauling the covers back up to her waist, Lilith lay back against the pillows. God only knew how frightening she must look. She hadn't even brushed her hair yet.

"Come in," she called.

The door opened. Lilith's heart fell.

It was only Mary.

"Well," the older woman remarked with mock cheerfulness, "had I known this was the reception I would get, I would have stayed downstairs."

Instantly contrite, Lilith smiled at her friend. "Of course I'm happy to see you." She patted the spot beside her on the bed. "You look very happy regardless of my bad manners. Come and tell me all the news."

Mary did look happy. In fact, she looked miraculously

content for a woman who'd recently had her heart smashed to bits.

Smiling, Mary came and sat beside her, a soft blush in her cheeks that made her look years younger.

"Have you had news from Mr. Francis?" That was the only thing Lilith could think of that could make her friend so joyful. That and a visit from the Reverend Geoffrey Sweet.

The good reverend had been by a few times since the fire—only to see Mary, of course. But he had sent Lilith his regards and good wishes. He also sent her a basket of fruit, most of which were apples. The biblical reference was not lost on Lilith. The clergyman was not without a sense of humor, so it seemed.

Mary's smile grew as she nodded. Goodness, but she looked as giddy as a young girl!

"Mr. Francis was here last night."

Lilith stared at her in shock. "And you waited until this morning to tell me? Shame on you!"

Mary's blush deepened. "I would have come to see you after he left, but I wanted to tell Geoffrey the news."

Hope blossomed, warm and tremulous, in Lilith's breast. "Do not say that your husband really is dead?" They had joked about it, but to have it be a reality . . . well, that would be a miracle.

Laughing, the older woman shook her head. "Better."

Lilith frowned. What could possibly be better than dead?

"Don't just sit there grinning at me like a ninny," she chastised. "Tell me what happened!"

Mary shifted on the mattress so that she fully faced Lilith. She leaned in close, as though she was afraid to speak too loudly in the otherwise empty room.

"He was never really my husband," she whispered with a grin so big it eclipsed the sunshine streaming through the window.

"What do you mean, he was never really your husband? There was a ceremony, wasn't there?"

The older woman shushed her with a wave of her hand. "A ceremony, yes, but it wasn't legal."

Her jaw dropping, Lilith gaped at her friend. This was too good to be true. A miracle indeed!

"Not legal in what way?"

Mary grinned. "He was already married to someone else when he married me. Our marriage was never real. He had another wife and a family the entire time. When he told me he was going away to look for work, he was really going to spend time with his other family in Kent."

Any other woman would have been horrified to have been used in such a cruel, heartless manner, but not Mary. Her "husband's" duplicity meant her freedom.

"What does your reverend have to say about this?"

Blushing again, the older woman actually giggled. "He says he wants to court me for a little while before he gives me the wedding I deserve."

So happy she was on the verge of tears, Lilith reached out and snared one of Mary's hands in her own.

"Oh, my dear friend," she gushed, "I am delighted for you!"

Mary's expression sobered somewhat. "I wish I could be this happy for you."

"Society will never accept me as a countess, Mary. They all despise me."

"Do they?"

Something in her tone made Lilith face her again. "You know they do."

Mary lifted her hand. In it was a small stack of letters. "Some of these arrived by messenger yesterday evening. Some arrived this morning. I am of the mind that there will be more in the afternoon post."

Lilith stared at the papers. "What are they?"

Mary shrugged. "I am not certain. But they are for you." She dumped the letters into Lilith's lap. "Why don't you open them?"

For a moment all Lilith could do was sit there dumbly.

Then she reached out and picked up the top note. It was written on pink, rose-scented paper. Even the seal had the imprint of a rose.

The letter was an invitation to tea from the Marchioness of Wynter, a woman who at one time had been thought just as scandalous as Lilith herself until she married the marquess and turned out to be a princess in her own right.

Why would a marchioness invite her to tea?

With hesitant fingers, Lilith set the invitation aside and picked up the next letter. More expensive paper, but unscented. It was an invitation to join Lady Pennington's musical club. Lilith didn't like Lady Pennington. She placed this one in a separate pile from the marchioness's.

As she continued to open invitation after invitation, Lilith was filled with a strange mixture of awe and unease. Why were these women sending her these invitations? Lady Jersey invited her to a garden party, for heaven's sake! One of the patronesses of that bastion of society, Almack's, invited *her* to a garden party!

There were also notes from Mr. Dunlop—along with a bouquet of flowers—and Lady Wyndham, both wishing her a speedy recovery and promising to call when she felt better. Lilith wondered what Lady Wyndham and Lord Somerville would do now that they no longer had Mallory's to meet at.

"What the devil is going on?" she demanded of Mary when she opened the last letter—an invitation to a ball at Carlton House. "This is bloody ridiculous."

Mary smiled, looking as bewildered as Lilith felt, although Mary seemed a bit more relaxed with the situation. Lilith didn't trust it. Was someone blackmailing these people into inviting her? Was Gabriel using his pull to have them pretend to want her at their functions? It sounded far-fetched, but she wouldn't put it past him. And it was the only explanation that made sense.

"Is he here?" Lilith demanded. There was no need to define who "he" was.

"No," Mary replied. "He had to go out."

"I just bet he did." Oh, she didn't know whether to seethe or to cry. Who did he think he was, manipulating people in such a way? Did he expect her to be happy that he had to force society to open its doors for her? It didn't change anything. It wasn't going to make her stay. She would not accept false friendship.

But she loved him for trying all the same.

"Ring for bathwater, will you please, Mary? And I shall need your help getting dressed. I am going downstairs to wait for our host to return. I believe he has some explaining to do."

The warning tone of her voice didn't stop a huge smile from spreading across Mary's face. "Of course."

An hour later, Lilith was downstairs in Gabriel's study, waiting for him to return. She sat on a sofa made of rich, dark oak and covered in a sumptuous midnight-green velvet. Half an hour later, she kicked off her slippers and dug her toes into the plush gold, green and brown patterned carpet. She'd take her stockings off, too, if she didn't think that would be the time Gabriel would choose to return.

This whole room reflected him. It was quiet and sturdy. Masculine yet elegant. Subdued but with a hint of boldness. Warm and inviting.

As she waited, she imagined him behind the desk, working on something to do with his shipping business. In her mind's eye she could see him bent over a stack of papers—oh, wait! He looks up. He sees her on the sofa! He stands up and comes toward her, each step like the deliberate stalking of a hunter who knows his prey cannot possibly escape. Her heart begins to pound as he removes his coat, then his waistcoat. His cravat flutters to the ground. His shirt lifts, revealing the hairy, muscular contours of his stomach and chest. He pulls the linen over his head and tosses it behind him. Lilith's mouth goes dry as his hands go to the front of his trousers . . .

"Beg your pardon, Lady Lilith, but you have a caller."

Heart hammering, lungs straining, cheeks flaming, Lilith stared at the thickly built man who had to have the worst timing in the world.

"Who is it, Mr. . . ." Who was this fellow anyway?

"Robinson, my lady. And your caller is Lady Braven."

Rachel! Oh, now *that* was worth the disruption of her fantasy!

"Show her in, please, Mr. Robinson."

The butler bowed and backed out of the room. A few minutes later, he announced Rachel, who bounced into the room like a ray of sunshine dressed in rose muslin.

"Lilith!" she cried. "How good to see you again!"

Lilith stood just in time to be engulfed in a sweetly scented embrace. She was happy to see Rachel. The only thing that would have made her happier would have been if Rachel had brought little Alexander with her.

"I am so pleased to see you," she said as they sat. "It seems an age since we last met."

Rachel leaned over in her chair and patted Lilith gently on the leg. "I wanted to make certain you were recovered enough for visitors before I came. How are you, my dear?"

Her concern was touching. Lilith wasn't used to any woman other than Mary showing such anxiety over her health.

"I am well, thank you, Rachel. My throat is almost back to normal, and as you can tell, the bruise on my face is healing."

Rachel's lovely face darkened as her gaze fell on Lilith's cheek. "I despise men who use violence as a means to an end."

Lilith's brow puckered. Had Rachel known such a man? It certainly sounded as if she had.

The blond woman's usual good cheer returned as quickly as it had faded. "Whatever are you doing here in Gabriel's study? The blue parlor is so much cozier."

Now it was Lilith's turn to lose her humor. "I am waiting for him to return so that I might have a word with him."

"Oh, dear. What has he done now?"

Reaching under her leg, Lilith withdrew the invitations she'd received earlier. "Look." She thrust them at Rachel.

Her friend took the notes and sifted through them. She looked at Lilith with an expression of amused confusion. "What is wrong with them? I received several myself."

"They are awful," Lilith informed her brusquely. "They were issued to me only because Gabriel somehow black-mailed or pressured the senders. None of these people would willingly acknowledge a woman like me."

Rachel arched a brow. "I willingly acknowledge you."

Lilith scowled impatiently and waved her hand. She didn't want to go down this road. "Yes, but you are different. If not for Brave and Gabriel's friendship, we would not have met, but we did and we have become friends. These people do not even know me. They do not *want* to know me. They never have, not since the scandal. So why are they being so friendly now? I will tell you why—because Gabriel thinks I will stay with him if society accepts me. Well, I'm *not* staying just be-cause he's talked a few people into pretending to receive me. I do not want that kind of charity."

Folding her arms across her chest, Lilith bobbed her head determinedly.

Rachel burst out laughing.

"What are you laughing for?" Lilith demanded. "I'm seri-ous!"

Anger turned to hurt as Rachel continued to laugh. Of course she could find this amusing. She didn't know what it was like to have people whisper behind her back. She was a countess.

"Oh, Lilith!" she cried, wiping her eyes. "That is not what happened at all!"

Lilith stilled. How did Rachel know what was the truth and what wasn't? Was she involved?

"What do you know?" she asked carefully. The spoiled child within her wanted to stomp her foot and demand to be told the truth, but that wasn't the way to get what she wanted.

Sniffing, Rachel raised her gaze to hers. "I know that Gabriel has not forced anyone to do anything. He simply planted a few rumors with the right people and let them run. I know because I helped plant those rumors."

Lilith's eyes narrowed. She hated rumors. They'd followed her mercilessly for the past ten years.

"What kind of rumors?"

Rachel didn't even look uncomfortable. If she noticed Lilith's growing ire, she happily ignored it. The thought should have made Lilith madder, but instead, it gave her an odd sense of calm.

"Oh, we told a few people how you and Gabriel were so horribly torn apart when you were younger. We told others how he planned to marry you, but then his father's tragic suicide forced him to cover up the scandal and take over the title."

Ice formed over Lilith's heart. Gabriel had revealed the truth about his father?

"Some people we told how your parents sent you away and hid your whereabouts from him. How he searched for years to find you, only to be deceived at every turn." Rachel smiled. "It didn't take long for those people to talk to each other and compare notes. The entire story was all over London by that night. Everyone thinks of the two of you as ill-fated lovers, finally reunited."

Lilith stared at the other woman as she giggled. She could scarcely breathe. What had Gabriel done? He'd revealed everything, even his father's death.

"And now that he has changed his position on gaming in the House, everyone believes you to be the reason for it," Rachel continued. "He's saying that 'someone' has shown him the error of his ways."

Oh, Lord. She was going to be sick. This was worse than she thought.

"He's not actually for gambling now, is he?" she asked hoarsely, her stomach churning.

Rachel's smile was sympathetic. "No. He's actively seeking better gaming laws. To protect not only the players, but the club owners as well. He loves you, Lilith. He doesn't care who knows it. He wants to be with you." She held up the invitations. "Expect a deluge of these later today. Everyone else wants him to be with you as well."

Numb with shock, Lilith stared at her stocking-clad toes.

They were dug so hard into the carpet, her feet were beginning to cramp.

Rachel wrapped a hand around her clenched fist. Lifting her chin, Lilith looked into her friend's earnest lavender-blue gaze.

"Lilith, the decision is yours. He has done everything he can to convince you of how much he loves you. Can you overcome your fear and allow yourself to return that love? Or should I help you pack?"

The question shocked Lilith. Was Rachel saying she'd still be her friend even if she turned Gabriel down? When was the last time she'd had a friend her own age who promised to stand beside her no matter what?

"What I would like you to do," Lilith said, rising to her feet and making for Gabriel's desk, "is help me answer these invitations. I have a feeling I'm going to need all the help I can get once the afternoon post arrives."

Chapter 20

I t was late afternoon when Gabriel returned home. He'd spent the morning making certain the stories about him and Lilith were spread all over town, fielding sometimes indelicate questions about his father and helping Duncan Reed and Bow Street ensure that Bronson boarded his ship to Nova Scotia. It was one of Seraph's own ships and he'd sent word to Garnet to keep an eye on the former club owner.

Now all that was left was to face Lilith and hope that all his plotting, planning and airing of skeletons had done what he wanted. Such as show Lilith just how much he truly loved her and was willing to do to keep her.

And if that wasn't enough to convince her, then he was going to have to go through with plan B, which was to lock her in the wine cellar until she came to her senses.

Robinson met him at the door.

"Lady Lilith requires your presence in her—in *your*—bedchamber, my lord," the butler informed him without expression as he took Gabriel's hat and gloves.

"Thank you, Robinson." Anticipation clenched hard at Gabriel's stomach. *Please*, he prayed silently. *Please*.

He could feel his butler's cool gaze upon him and so he forced himself to walk up the stairs in his normal fashion, even though what he wanted to do was race up them like a madman.

By the time he arrived at the door to his bedroom, his stomach was nothing more than one big knot.

His knuckles rapped against the solid oak. He waited.

"Come in," came Lilith's muffled voice.

Gabriel turned the knob. The door drifted open. He stepped inside.

Lilith stood beside the bed in one of the gowns he'd bought her. It was one the dressmaker had made for someone else and then never sold. It was a little short and too small in the bosom, but it was a good color and style. The golden hue brought out the warmth of Lilith's skin and the fire in her hair.

"Took you long enough," she said, her tone crisp.

Gabriel smiled. "If I had known you were waiting, I would have come home sooner."

She chuckled at that. "If I were in your place, I would have let me wait a little bit longer. It would have served me right for being such an idiot."

Gabriel's heart lurched. Did that mean she had changed her mind about leaving him?

"I've heard some disturbing rumors, Gabriel."

Oh, no. "Such as?"

She moved toward him, each step slow and deliberate. "Such as your putting Bronson on a boat for Nova Scotia this morning."

He shrugged. She was standing right in front of him now. He could smell the clean scent of her. No perfume, just soap and skin.

"I did."

She moved closer. Her thighs brushed against his legs. Her breasts pressed against his chest. A familiar tingling unfurled in his groin.

"I also heard you told everyone the truth about your father."

The low timbre of her voice sent a shiver down his spine. "Yes."

"You told people I thought I wasn't good enough for you."

Was she angry? He couldn't tell. "Yes."

Her gaze lowered to his mouth, then lifted again. "You told all of London that you loved me. That you have always loved me."

Gabriel swallowed. The tightening between his legs was growing increasingly uncomfortable, as was the dryness in his throat. "Yes."

Lilith sighed. "Do you have any idea how much I love you for that?"

"Tell me." It was a hoarse whisper.

Standing on her tiptoes, Lilith wrapped soft, round arms around his neck and pressed her groin up and against his. His erection throbbed at the contact.

"I love you so much it hurts," she whispered, her eyes still locked with his. "So much that I think I'm going to need at least the next fifty years to show you how deeply and completely I love and adore you."

His chest constricted. His heart soared. Clamping his arms around her waist just in case this was a dream and she tried to escape, Gabriel asked, "Enough to become my countess?"

She didn't answer. She simply leaned forward, flattening the soft warmth of her breasts against the wall of his chest and touching that sweet bow of a mouth to his.

Every nerve in Gabriel's body jumped at the contact. It was just the joining of lips, yet he felt it so profoundly, so intensely, that the hard, pulsating flesh between his legs ached to bury itself inside her. Only with Lilith had he ever known a sensual need so consuming, so insatiable.

Was this her way of saying yes? She didn't speak, but the touch of her hands, the taste of her, said more than any words ever could. Joy, unfettered exultation, soared in his chest. She was giving herself to him. Not only her body, but her heart and soul as well. He would damn well take her response as a yes.

He slid his hands up the soft muslin that covered her back, up to where the row of tiny buttons began, just below the nape of her neck. One by one, his fingers popped them loose, until the neckline was nothing more than a large fold of material gaping around her shoulders.

He broke the kiss. "Take it off," he whispered.

She smiled at him, her eyes dark and heavy with desire. "Do it yourself."

He did. He slipped the dress off her like the peel of some exotic fruit, pulling it down her arms, pushing it down over the generous curve of her hips. It pooled around her feet in a soft golden whisper.

Lilith stood before him in her shift and corset—an ivory satin confection of lace and bows. It emphasized the swell of her breasts and cinched her waist. He ran the flat of his palm up the front of the shiny fabric, stopping when he could feel the pounding of her heart beneath his hand.

His fingers closed over her breast. She'd had to lower her arms when he removed her gown, and now she brought her own hand up and placed it against his chest, right above his heart.

"Take my coat off," he commanded softly.

Her fingers went to the shiny gold buttons down his front, quickly unfastening each of them.

She removed his waistcoat as well, and his cravat, but when her hands went to the fastenings on his shirt, he stopped her.

"My turn." Slowly he brought both hands to the curve of her breasts, pushing them together as his thumbs popped the tiny hooks that held her corset together. He felt her breath hitch beneath his palms and he slid them lower, over the rapid rise and fall of her ribs as he forced the rest of the hooks open. At last his hands were at the indent of her waist and the stays fell to the floor with her gown.

His gaze left hers, roaming over her face and down to the swell of her breasts. Through the thin, wrinkled lawn he could make out the shadowy thrust of her nipples and the dark circles of her aureolas.

She was perfection in every sense of the word and he trembled at the magnificence of her.

"Now you can remove my shirt," he told her.

Greedy fingers yanked his shirt free of his trousers and pulled upward. Lifting his arms, Gabriel grabbed the linen and pulled when it became apparent that she couldn't push it up any farther. He tossed the shirt across the room and dropped his arms to his sides as his gaze returned to Lilith.

She ran her soft little hands through the dark hair on his chest, down along the ticklish flesh of his ribs, past the waist of his trousers to cup his erection through the soft wool.

It felt good. Damn good. His hips flexed, pushing against her palm.

Abruptly she dropped her hand and looked up at him with a coy smile. "Your turn."

Her shift was all that remained between him and the pale splendor of her body. Gabriel's mouth went dry.

"Lift your arms."

She did as he instructed. Slowly, almost hesitantly, Gabriel bunched the gossamer-thin garment in his hands and pulled it upward, his hungry gaze devouring every inch of creamy flesh that came into view.

The soft length of her calves, followed by the generous curve of her thighs, to the enticing auburn nest between them. His palms itched to caress the abundance of her hips and belly, the warm hollow of her waist and finally the heavy fullness of her coral-tipped breasts.

The shift flew in the same direction as his shirt.

Bare before him, Lilith was a Venus emerged from her shell. Gabriel couldn't take his eyes off her. Could scarcely breathe for wanting her.

"You have me at a disadvantage," she purred, her fingers curving around the waist of his trousers.

"I don't think so," he replied dumbly as she slid the soft wool down his legs. He toed off his boots and shoved his small clothes and stockings down as well.

Lilith chuckled. "You were supposed to let me do that."

"Some other time," he growled as her hand found the throbbing heat of his erection. "Oh, Christ, don't do that."

Her grip tightened, sending a shudder of sensual pleasure snaking up Gabriel's spine.

She released him and backed toward the bed, a smile of carnal promise on her full lips as she raised her hands to her hair. The movement thrust her breasts upward, the puckered nipples standing at attention.

She plucked the pins from her hair, sending the rich, dark red mass tumbling over her shoulders.

Venus would weep in envy.

"Come here," she commanded in little more than a whisper.

Like the slave he was, Gabriel did as he was bidden, almost tripping over his boots in his hurry to do so.

Lilith climbed up onto the bed, treating him to a glimpse of her delectable backside. She patted the mattress. "Come lie down."

She didn't need to tell him twice. Without a word, he stretched himself out on his back on the coverlet, his mouth dry and his body throbbing as he waited to see what she had in store for him.

She feathered his face with kisses. Nibbled on his neck and ears, and burned a trail down his chest with her mouth. A warm, moist tongue flicked at his navel. He gasped.

And then she slid even lower, slipping the soft velvet of her lips over the head of his cock, until the entire length of him was at the mercy of her mouth and tongue. She stroked him, laved him and licked him until he thought he was going to explode in the back of her throat.

Cool air hit his aching flesh as she released him. She drew her body up his, dragging her nipples along his heated skin, pressing the damp V of her legs against his thigh.

"Your turn," she whispered against his ear.

Gabriel shivered. Every inch of him was pulled taut, so taut that his skin didn't seem to fit him anymore. As Lilith rolled onto her back, he rolled with her, immediately lowering his head to her breasts when he finally raised himself above her.

He licked the pale globes, took each puckered nipple into his mouth and sucked it until she whimpered and writhed against him. And when she began grinding her hips against his, arching that damp heat against the pleading hardness between his legs, he pulled back and kissed his way down between her thighs the same way she had teased and tortured him.

The scent of her filled his senses. Sweet, salty musk tantalized him. Slowly he lowered his mouth to that glistening pink flesh, burying his tongue between the slick folds and drawing it upward until he found the hooded hardness he sought.

Lilith's thighs tightened as he licked her. He pushed them apart and held them spread wide with his hands. She was completely open to the assault of his mouth and he attacked her mercilessly, probing and lapping at her until her whimpers turned to long-drawn-out moans. She stiffened, her thighs pushing hard against his hands as her hips arched against his mouth. She cried out, her muscles trembling beneath him, and fell back upon the mattress, panting.

Still holding her legs spread, Gabriel rose up onto his knees between those trembling splayed thighs. He was covered in the scent and taste of her essence and the flush of orgasm on her pale flesh snapped what was left of his fragile control. With one hard thrust, he buried his cock inside her.

Lilith gasped as he filled her. Her sensitive flesh accepted him eagerly, stretching to accommodate the hot length of him.

Opening her eyes, she gazed up at him, at this man who made her feel things she'd never felt before.

His mouth was damp from pleasuring her, his eyes a dark, smoky pewter as his fingers bit into the backs of her legs. Her buttocks brushed his thighs, her knees raised up toward her shoulders. He was so deep, so very deep inside her. Every thrust of his hips seemed to drive him deeper still, sent a tremor of pleasure through her loins, took her closer to yet another mind-numbing climax.

This was what the rest of her life would be like. Until one of them died, she and Gabriel would be part of each other—physically and emotionally. There would always be this giving and taking, this sharing of themselves. The thought of such intimacy should scare her, would normally make her doubt herself; but right now, all she could do was give herself up to it—to *him*—and let it take her where it would.

The movements of his hips quickened. His breathing became more shallow. As the pressure mounted deep within her, Lilith watched as Gabriel's eyes closed, as his forehead furrowed in concentration. The cords of his neck and shoulders bunched as he tightened his grip on her legs.

Lilith felt as though something inside her was being lifted. Higher and higher it took her, and then it dropped into a void where nothing existed but her and Gabriel and the sweet, pulsating friction between their bodies. It shook her, rippled through her, and she let it have her as a wordless scream tore from her throat.

Seconds later, she heard Gabriel cry out, felt him stiffen above her, and then felt the bed shake as the fullness of his weight came down onto forearms on either side of her head. He buried his face in the crook of her neck and was still.

They stayed like that until Lilith's hip kinked and she began to lose feeling in her legs.

"Gabe," she murmured. "You need to get off me."

He did, slowly disengaging their bodies and rolling to the side. Lilith stretched the kink out of her hip as he drew her into his arms.

"You have to marry me now," he told her.

Raising her head at his teasing tone, Lilith smiled lazily. He looked so pleased with himself. He should be. She was.

"Oh, I have to, do I? Why is that?"

His smug expression faded as he reached up and stroked her hair back from her face. "Because you've ruined me."

Was he serious? What did he mean? Was he referring to that stupid wager they made? Or did he mean that no one else would have him now that she had? That was what ruin meant in their world.

He must have seen the alarm on her face, because he lifted his other hand and cupped his fingers around her head.

"You have ruined me for anyone else," he told her, gazing intently into her eyes. "I could never love another the way I love you."

Lilith released the breath she'd been holding. "Oh."

"Say yes, Lily."

Tears pricked the backs of Lilith's eyes. Hot, stinging wetness that threatened to spill over onto her cheeks. "Yes."

Gabriel grinned. He pulled her head down to his and kissed her so soundly, so thoroughly, that Lilith forgot where she was—who she was.

"I have something for you," he whispered against her lips. Then he rolled toward the far side of the bed and reached into the drawer of the bedside table. He withdrew the black velvet pouch.

The delicate emerald ring tumbled into his palm as he turned to face her. "Give me your hand."

Lilith did. Her fingers shook.

"Now who is trembling?" Gabriel joked as he took her unsteady hand in his much larger one. He held her still as he slipped the ring on her finger. It was a perfect fit—just as it had been ten years ago.

"I want to marry by special license," he told her, gathering her close once more. "I don't want to give you the chance to change your mind."

Smiling, Lilith snuggled against his chest. "Oh, I do believe you are stuck with me now, Lord Angelwood."

"Good."

They kissed. They talked. Lilith admired the way the ring

on her finger sparkled in the bright afternoon sun streaming through the windows.

Gabriel drew a blanket over them and wrapped his arms around her, holding her tightly as he closed his eyes and muttered about how it was "about bloody time" they got this "whole marriage thing" sorted out.

Lilith only smiled and listened to his breathing as it slowly evened out and became more shallow. He was asleep.

She yawned. She was tired, too. Exhausted, actually. She lay awake for a little while longer, half expecting her mother—even though she knew it was impossible—or someone else to burst in and scream that the wedding couldn't take place, or try to send her away again.

But that didn't happen, and Lilith finally drifted off to sleep, her head on Gabriel's chest, his heart beneath her hand.

All of society wanted them to have a big wedding so everyone could watch Gabriel Warren, Eighth Earl of Angelwood, finally take Lady Lilith Mallory as his lawfully wedded wife. But Gabriel hadn't the patience to plan such an affair. Nor had he the patience to allow Lilith to plan such an affair. He did have the patience, however, to allow Rachel to plan a ball to be held in their honor the night of the wedding. It wasn't a terribly fancy affair, as Rachel had only a few days to make arrangements, but if anyone was upset with the simple decorations and delicious but modest fare, he or she never said. It seemed the only reason anyone attended was to lay eyes on the happy couple, who had waited ten years to finally be together.

Reverend Sweet, who had performed the ceremony, danced once with the bride, during which he apologized profusely for all the nasty things he'd said about her in his column. Lilith merely laughed and told him to make it up to her by making an honest woman out of Mary.

While his wife danced, Gabriel approached Julian, who was standing in a corner, watching the merriment around him but not partaking of it.

"Who are you looking for?" Gabriel asked as his friend's gaze once again swept across the sea of dancers.

Julian shook his head. "Someone I don't want to see."

Gabriel frowned. That was an odd reply.

"Come talk to Brave and Rachel," Gabriel suggested. "You can see the door better from over there."

Not long after that, just after supper, Julian made his apologies and took his leave. Gabriel watched him go with a sympathetic heart.

"What is wrong with Julian?" Lilith asked from beside him. She also was watching Julian's departure.

Gabriel shook his head, turning to face her. "I have no idea. I think he's feeling a little lonely now that Brave and I are both married."

His wife—his *wife*—curved her lips into a patient smile. "I am certain he will meet his match some day."

He gazed at her intently. They were in public and he couldn't kiss her, couldn't hold her and touch her the way he wanted, so he let his eyes tell her what he wanted to do to her, how much he loved her.

"Take me home," she whispered, her cheeks flushed with color and her eyes bright with need.

Gabriel did. They said good-bye to their guests with a quick announcement. They thanked Brave and Rachel for everything they had done to prepare for the ball—as well as for being such good friends—and then they made their escape.

When they arrived at Angelwood, Gabriel carried his wife upstairs, despite her protests of being too heavy and that he'd hurt himself, and made love to her as slowly and thoroughly as he could. And then, because she'd wanted to be proper and had stayed at Brave and Rachel's after she recovered from the fire, he made love to her again, since he had several days to make up for.

"Again?" Lilith giggled as his hardness nudged her hip.

"Yes, again," he replied with mock gruffness. "We're going to do this at least twice—perhaps three times—a day until the last decade has been accounted for."

His wife did not offer any objection.

* * *

It was the next evening, while they were en route to a ball—one that Lilith had been invited to before the wedding—that Gabriel finally told Lilith she could have her wedding present.

"I'd begun to despair of ever receiving one," she joked while her heart secretly swelled with love. God bless Gabriel. He knew she was nervous about making her first appearance in public, other than their wedding celebration, as Lady Angelwood. No one would dare insult her at their wedding, but now . . . well, she would be open game. Gabriel's present was the perfect thing to take her mind off her fears.

"Brat," he murmured with a smile that curled her toes, it was so blatantly sensual and loving.

It was dark in the carriage, and they were alone . . . Blushing furiously, Lilith pushed the idea aside. It was too scandalous, even for her. Still, it wasn't nearly as naughty as what she and Gabriel had done the night before. She hadn't known it was possible to make love that way! But now that she did, she wondered how many other positions they might try. Or how many new locations.

"Where are we?" she asked sometime later as the carriage rolled to a stop. Glancing out the window, she saw that they weren't in Mayfair at all.

"Gabriel, the ball is in Grosvenor Square. Why are we on King Street?"

"I told you," he replied with a secretive smile. "I'm giving you your wedding gift."

Unless he'd managed to salvage something from the fire that she hadn't, Lilith had no idea what this "gift" might be. She sincerely hoped that he hadn't taken it upon himself to begin repairs on Mallory's. She'd already decided to sell what was left of it and the property. She was through being a club owner. *Countess* was more than enough excitement for her.

He opened the carriage door and hopped out, holding out his hand to assist her. Hesitantly, Lilith placed her hand in his and stepped down.

It wasn't Mallory's burned shell she stared up at, but it was almost as bad. The building had obviously been vacant for some time. Its stone front was chipped in several places and the windows were covered with grime. Still, it had a picturesque quality that Lilith found appealing. With a little—no, with a *lot* of work—the place might actually be quite lovely.

Gabriel took a key from his pocket. "Want to see inside?"

Lilith's head whipped around to face him. "Gabriel? What is this place?"

Grinning, he grabbed her by the hand and hauled her toward the door. "Mind your skirts," he warned, slipping the key in the lock. "I had the floors swept earlier, but that does not mean the rest of the place isn't still filthy."

If the windows were any indication, Lilith would guess that was a safe bet.

The double doors opened into a front hall that took Lilith's breath away, despite the dirt and cobwebs. Even in the dark she could see that a huge staircase swept up one wall from a floor tiled in blue, gold and rose. Fluted columns rose toward an equally stunning ceiling. Robert Adam had to have designed it himself.

"Welcome to *Eden*," Gabriel told her with a theatrical flourish.

Tearing her gaze away from the gorgeous ceiling, Lilith turned to him. "Eden?"

He nodded. "Would you prefer a different name?"

Looking around in wonder, Lilith shook her head. Eden was certainly suitable. The promise in the building was incredible.

"Gabriel," she said, turning to him once again, "where are we?"

"It is your wedding gift," he replied, his smile becoming hopeful. "Do you like it?"

"I love it!" She laughed in astonishment. It was hers? It was certainly more grand than the playing-card cravat pin she had given him. Even if it did have the Queen of Hearts on it.

"A new club," he told her. "A new beginning."

Lilith's heart fell. A new club? But she didn't want a new club.

The happiness in her husband's handsome face made her heart fall even lower. How could she tell him she didn't want another club when he was so obviously pleased with himself?

"Come in here."

She glanced up. He was across the hall, standing in an open doorway.

Slowly, dragging her feet, Lilith joined him. She felt awful. She *was* awful. There was no way she could turn down such a gift.

Gabriel drew her into the room. It smelled musty, but in the silvery moonlight Lilith could see it was even more of a mess than the hall. It had just as much promise, however. Oh, she could make such a club out of this mess! And for a split second she considered it.

"Here is where we'll put the billiards table," Gabriel said, gesturing to the center of the room.

Lilith glanced at him, noting the wicked gleam in his eyes. Yes, she remembered what happened the last time they'd encountered a billiards table.

"Looking for another game, Lord Angelwood?" She hadn't forgotten that game they'd played with Brave and Rachel, either.

He grinned wolfishly. "Only if it includes making love to you."

A sensual shiver raced down Lilith's spine. Oh, yes, that sounded good!

But back to the matter at hand. "What do you mean, this is where 'we' will put the billiards table?"

Gabriel's smile slipped, revealing a vulnerability Lilith hadn't seen there before. "I want us to run Eden together. As partners."

Lilith's mouth fell open. Partners? He wanted to be her partner?

He drew her to him, his hands warm on her bare shoulders. "Lil, I want this to be our club. I want Eden to be the cumulation of both our dreams. We'll set an example with it. We'll make it the kind of club people like my father can frequent without the possibility of losing their entire fortune. When Parliament sees how beneficial stricter gaming laws are, they'll have no choice but to implement them."

Lilith stared at him and saw the hope and determination in his eyes. Yes. They could do this together. They could have limits on the amount wagered and limits on how much the house could lose. They'd protect both the gambler and the club.

And she could make this place even more spectacular than Mallory's. It would be incredible. A place where people could come to gamble, to eat and dance and socialize. It could be the kind of club of which London had never seen the like before.

"Oh, Gabriel!" she cried, throwing her arms around his neck and showering him with kisses. "I love it! I love it! I love it! Thank you so much!"

He actually lifted her off her feet and swung her around, laughing with her as he did so. "Then you like it?" he asked when he finally set her down.

"Like it?" She was incredulous. "I love it! And I love you." She kissed him again, long and slow this time, stroking her tongue against his, showing him just how much she truly did love him and his gift.

The hard ridge of his arousal pressed against her hip.

"I wish I could make love to you," he whispered, his breath hot against her mouth.

Lilith's entire body awakened at the mere suggestion. "Quick!" she cried, grabbing his hand. "The carriage!"

Laughing, Gabriel ran behind her as she hiked up her skirts with her free hand and took off in the direction of the coach. He stopped only long enough to lock the doors behind them.

Inside the carriage, as they lurched into movement once more, he pulled her into his arms. Lilith marveled at just how badly her body craved his.

"I love you," he whispered.

She smiled in the mellow lamplight. Her hands slid between them to the falls of his trousers, caressing his throbbing erection through the fabric. Too damn much fabric, she thought.

"I know." She slid the falls aside, releasing him. He was hot and silky in her hand, but it wasn't her hand she wanted him in. "I love you, too."

"People will talk if you show up at the ball with your gown wrinkled and your hair mussed up." He was only half joking. She could see it in his eyes. He didn't want her to do anything—no matter how pleasureful for both of them—that she might regret.

As if she could ever regret loving him as deeply as she did.

Lifting her skirts as she squirmed around to straddle him, Lilith shrugged. "Let them talk."

He stared at her. She'd surprised him with her answer. "Really?"

Poised above him, the aching heat of her sex just inches from his, Lilith reached for that satiny hardness again.

"Really. I've learned something about people who whisper behind other people's backs, Gabriel."

"Oh?" He groaned as she lowered herself onto him.

Sighing as the entire length of him slid deep, oh-so-deep, inside her, Lilith began to move.

"Yes. Oh! They're . . . ooohhh. . . . just . . . ahhhhh. . . . jealous."

Gabriel laughed at that, but his laughter quickly faded into groans of pleasure as Lilith rode her body up and down on his.

When the Angelwood carriage halted in front of the estate of the Marquess and Marchioness of Wynter, it was several minutes before the earl and the countess stepped out. If anyone commented on this strange behavior, or on how wrinkled the countess's skirt was, or about the ridiculous grins on their faces, Gabriel and Lilith were oblivious to it.

"Look at them," Gabriel heard one lady remark to another as he and Lilith walked past. "It is obviously a love match."

Gabriel winked at the woman as his fingers entwined with his wife's. Lilith was right. They were jealous.

Happier than he'd ever been and so in love his heart ached with it, Gabriel gave Lilith's hand a quick squeeze. She gazed up at him as they entered the ballroom. He grinned at her as the murmuring started. She grinned back.

Let them talk.